MARY HIGGINS CLARK

SIMON & SCHUSTER

I'll Be Seeing You

A NOVEL

NEW YORK • LONDON • TORONTO • SYDNEY • TOKYO • SINGAPORE

SIMON & SCHUSTER
SIMON & SCHUSTER BUILDING
ROCKEFELLER CENTER
1230 AVENUE OF THE AMERICAS
NEW YORK, NEW YORK 10020

SIMON & SCHUSTER AND COLOPHON ARE REGISTERED TRADEMARKS
OF SIMON & SCHUSTER INC.
DESIGNED BY EVE METZ
MANUFACTURED IN THE UNITED STATES OF AMERICA

1   3   5   7   9   10   8   6   4   2

LIBRARY OF CONGRESS CATALOGING-IN-PUBLICATION DATA IS AVAILABLE.

ISBN 0-671-67366-1

FOR MY NEWEST GRANDCHILD
JEROME WARREN DERENZO
"SCOOCHIE"
WITH LOVE AND JOY.

ACKNOWLEDGMENTS

The writing of this book required considerable research. It is with great gratitude I acknowledge those who have been so wonderfully helpful.

B. W. Webster, M.D., Associate Director, Reproductive Resource Center of Greater Kansas City; Robert Shaler, Ph.D., Director of Forensic Biology, New York City Medical Examiner's Office; Finian I. Lennon, Mruk & Partners, Management Consultants—Executive Search; Leigh Ann Winick, Producer Fox/5 TV News; Gina and Bob Scrobogna, Realty Executives, Scottsdale, Arizona; Jay S. Watnick, JD, ChFC, CLU, President of Namco Financial Associates, Inc.; George Taylor, Director—Special Investigation Unit, Reliance National Insurance Company; James F. Finn, Retired Partner, Howard Needles Tammen & Bergendoff, Consulting Engineers; Sergeant Ken Lowman (Ret.), Stamford, Conn., City Police.

Forever thanks to my longtime editor, Michael V. Korda, and his associate, senior editor Chuck Adams, for their terrific and vital guidance. Sine qua non.

As always, my agent Eugene H. Winick and my publicist Lisl Cade have been there every step of the way.

Special thanks to Judith Glassman for being my other eyes and my daughter Carol Higgins Clark for her ideas and for helping to put the final pieces of the puzzle together.

And to my dear family and friends, now that this is over, I'm happy to say I'll Be Seeing You!

His honour rooted in dishonour stood,
And faith unfaithful kept him falsely true.

—Alfred, Lord Tennyson

Part One

1

*M*eghan Collins stood somewhat aside from the cluster of other journalists in Emergency at Manhattan's Roosevelt Hospital. Minutes before, a retired United States senator had been mugged on Central Park West and rushed here. The media were milling around, awaiting word of his condition.

Meghan lowered her heavy tote bag to the floor. The wireless mike, cellular telephone and notebooks were causing the strap to dig into her shoulder blade. She leaned against the wall and closed her eyes for a moment's rest. All the reporters were tired. They'd been in court since early afternoon, awaiting the verdict in a fraud trial. At nine o'clock, just as they were leaving, the call came to cover the mugging. It was now nearly eleven. The crisp October day had turned into an overcast night that was an unwelcome promise of an early winter.

It was a busy night in the hospital. Young parents carrying a bleeding toddler were waved past the registration desk through the door to the examination area. Bruised and shaken passengers of a car accident consoled each other as they awaited medical treatment.

Outside, the persistent wail of arriving and departing ambulances added to the familiar cacophony of New York traffic.

A hand touched Meghan's arm. "How's it going, Counselor?"

It was Jack Murphy from Channel 5. His wife had gone through NYU Law School with Meghan. Unlike Meghan, however, Liz was practicing law. Meghan Collins, Juris Doctor, had worked for a Park Avenue law firm for six months, quit and got a job at WPCD radio as a news reporter. She'd been there three years now and for the past month had been borrowed regularly by PCD Channel 3, the television affiliate.

"It's going okay, I guess," Meghan told him. Her beeper sounded.

"Have dinner with us soon," Jack said "It's been too long." He rejoined his cameraman as she reached to get her cellular phone out of the bag.

The call was from Ken Simon at the WPCD radio news desk. "Meg, the EMS scanner just picked up an ambulance heading for Roosevelt. Stabbing victim found on Fifty-sixth Street and Tenth. Watch for her."

The ominous ee-aww sound of an approaching ambulance coincided with the staccato tapping of hurrying feet. The trauma team was heading for the Emergency entrance. Meg broke the connection, dropped the phone in her bag and followed the empty stretcher as it was wheeled out to the semicircular driveway.

The ambulance screeched to a halt. Experienced hands rushed to assist in transferring the victim to the stretcher. An oxygen mask was clamped on her face. The sheet covering her slender body was bloodstained. Tangled chestnut hair accentuated the blue-tinged pallor of her neck.

Meg rushed to the driver's door. "Any witnesses?" she asked quickly.

"None came forward." The driver's face was lined and weary, his voice matter-of-fact. "There's an alley between two of those old tenements near Tenth. Looks like someone came up from behind, shoved her in it and stabbed her. Probably happened in a split second."

"How bad is she?"

"As bad as you can get."

"Identification?"

"None. She'd been robbed. Probably hit by some druggie who needed a fix."

The stretcher was being wheeled in. Meghan darted back into the emergency room behind it.

One of the reporters snapped, "The senator's doctor is about to give a statement."

The media surged across the room to crowd around the desk. Meghan did not know what instinct kept her near the stretcher. She watched as the doctor about to start an IV removed the oxygen mask and lifted the victim's eyelids.

"She's gone," he said.

Meghan looked over a nurse's shoulder and stared down into the unseeing blue eyes of the dead young woman. She gasped as she took in those eyes, the broad forehead, arched brows, high cheekbones, straight nose, generous lips.

It was as though she was looking into a mirror.

She was looking at her own face.

2

*M*eghan took a cab to her apartment in Battery Park City, at the very tip of Manhattan. It was an expensive fare, but it was late and she was very tired. By the time she arrived home, the numbing shock of seeing the dead woman was deepening rather than wearing off. The victim had been stabbed in the chest, possibly four to five hours before she was found. She'd been wearing jeans, a lined denim jacket, running shoes and socks. Robbery had probably been the motive. Her skin was tanned. Narrow bands of lighter skin on her wrist and several fingers suggested that rings and a watch were missing. Her pockets were empty and no handbag was found.

Meghan switched on the foyer light and looked across the room. From her windows she could see Ellis Island and the Statue of Liberty. She could watch the cruise ships being piloted to their berths on the Hudson River. She loved downtown New York, the narrowness of the streets, the sweeping majesty of the World Trade Center, the bustle of the financial district.

The apartment was a good-sized studio with a sleeping alcove and kitchen unit. Meghan had furnished it with her mother's castoffs, intending eventually to get a larger place and gradually redecorate. In the three years she'd worked for WPCD that had not happened.

She tossed her coat over a chair, went into the bathroom and changed into pajamas and a robe. The apartment was pleasantly warm, but she felt chilled to the point of illness. She realized she was avoiding looking into the vanity mirror. Finally she turned and studied herself as she reached for the cleansing cream.

Her face was chalk white, her eyes staring. Her hands trembled as she released her hair so that it spilled around her neck.

In frozen disbelief she tried to pick out differences between herself and the dead woman. She remembered that the victim's face had been a little fuller, the shape of her eyes round rather than oval, her chin smaller. But the skin tone and the color of the hair and the open, unseeing eyes were so very like her own.

She knew where the victim was now. In the medical exam-

iner's morgue, being photographed and fingerprinted. Dental charts would be made.

And then the autopsy.

Meghan realized she was trembling. She hurried into the kitchenette, opened the refrigerator and removed the carton of milk. Hot chocolate. Maybe that would help.

She settled on the couch and hugged her knees, the steaming cup in front of her. The phone rang. It was probably her mother, so she hoped her voice sounded steady when she answered it.

"Meg, hope you weren't asleep."

"No, just got in. How's it going, Mom?"

"All right, I guess. I heard from the insurance people today. They're coming over tomorrow afternoon again. I hope to God they don't ask any more questions about that loan Dad took out on his policies. They can't seem to fathom that I have no idea what he did with the money."

In late January, Meghan's father had been driving home to Connecticut from Newark Airport. It had been snowing and sleeting all day. At seven-twenty, Edwin Collins made a call from his car phone to a business associate, Victor Orsini, to set up a meeting the next morning. He told Orsini he was on the approach to the Tappan Zee Bridge.

In what may have been only a few seconds later, a fuel tanker spun out of control on the bridge and crashed into a tractor trailer, causing a series of explosions and a fireball that engulfed seven or eight automobiles. The tractor trailer smashed into the side of the bridge and tore open a gaping hole before plunging into the swirling, icy waters of the Hudson River. The fuel tanker followed, dragging with it the other disintegrating vehicles.

A badly injured eyewitness who'd managed to steer out of the direct path of the fuel tanker testified that a dark blue Cadillac sedan spun out in front of him and disappeared through the gaping steel. Edwin Collins had been driving a dark blue Cadillac.

It was the worst disaster in the history of the bridge. Eight

lives were lost. Meg's sixty-year-old father never made it
home that night. He was assumed to have died in the explosion. The New York Thruway authorities were still searching
for scraps of wreckage and bodies, but now, nearly nine
months later, no trace had as yet been found of either him or
his car.

A memorial mass had been offered a week after the accident, but because no death certificate had been issued, Edwin
and Catherine Collins' joint assets were frozen and the large
insurance policies on his life had not been paid.

Bad enough for Mom to be heartbroken without the hassle
these people are giving her, Meg thought. "I'll be up tomorrow afternoon, Mom. If they keep stalling, we may have to
file suit."

She debated, then decided that the last thing her mother
needed was to hear that a woman with a striking resemblance
to Meghan had been stabbed to death. Instead she talked
about the trial she'd covered that day.

FOR A LONG TIME, MEGHAN LAY IN BED, DOZING FITFULLY.
Finally she fell into a deep sleep.

A high-pitched squeal pulled her awake. The fax began to
whine. She looked at the clock: it was quarter-past four.
What on earth? she thought.

She switched on the light, pulled herself up on one elbow
and watched as paper slowly slid from the machine. She
jumped out of bed, ran across the room and reached for the
message.

It read: MISTAKE. ANNIE WAS A MISTAKE.

3

om Weicker, fifty-two-year-old news director of PCD Channel 3, had been borrowing Meghan Collins from the radio affiliate with increasing frequency. He was in the process of handpicking another reporter for the on-air news team and had been rotating the candidates, but now he had made his final decision: Meghan Collins.

He reasoned that she had good delivery, could ad lib at the drop of a hat and always gave a sense of immediacy and excitement to even a minor news item. Her legal training was a real plus at trials. She was damn good looking and had natural warmth. She liked people and could relate to them.

On Friday morning, Weicker sent for Meghan. When she knocked at the open door of his office, he waved her in. Meghan was wearing a fitted jacket in tones of pale blue and rust brown. A skirt in the same fine wool skimmed the top of her boots. Classy, Weicker thought, perfect for the job.

Meghan studied Weicker's expression, trying to read his thoughts. He had a thin, sharp-featured face and wore rimless glasses. That and his thinning hair made him look older than his age and more like a bank teller than a media powerhouse. It was an impression quickly dispelled, however, when he began to speak. Meghan liked Tom but knew that his nickname, "Lethal Weicker," had been earned. When he began borrowing her from the radio station he'd made it clear that it was a tough, lousy break that her father had lost his life in the bridge tragedy, but he needed her reassurance that it wouldn't affect her job performance.

It hadn't, and now Meghan heard herself being offered the job she wanted so badly.

The immediate, reflexive reaction that flooded through her was, I can't wait to tell Dad!

THIRTY FLOORS BELOW, IN THE GARAGE OF THE PCD BUILD-ing, Bernie Heffernan, the parking attendant, was in Tom Weicker's car, going through the glove compartment. By some genetic irony, Bernie's features had been formed to give him the countenance of a merry soul. His cheeks were plump, his chin and mouth small, his eyes wide and guileless, his hair thick and rumpled, his body sturdy, if somewhat rotund. At thirty-five the immediate impression he gave to observers was that he was a guy who, though wearing his best suit, would fix your flat tire.

He still lived with his mother in the shabby house in Jackson Heights, Queens, where he'd been born. The only times he'd been away from it were those dark, nightmarish periods when he was incarcerated. The day after his twelfth birthday he was sent to a juvenile detention center for the first of a dozen times. In his early twenties he'd spent three years in a psychiatric facility. Four years ago he was sentenced to ten months in Riker's Island. That was when the police caught him hiding in a college student's car. He'd been warned a dozen times to stay away from her. Funny, Bernie thought—he couldn't even remember what she looked like now. Not her and not any of them. And they had all been so important to him at the time.

Bernie never wanted to go to jail again. The other inmates frightened him. Twice they beat him up. He had sworn to Mama that he'd never hide in shrubs and look in windows again, or follow a woman and try to kiss her. He was getting very good at controlling his temper too. He'd hated the psychiatrist who kept warning Mama that one day that vicious temper would get Bernie into trouble no one could fix. Bernie knew that nobody had to worry about him anymore.

His father had taken off when he was a baby. His embittered mother no longer ventured outside, and at home Bernie had to endure her incessant reminders of all the inequities life had inflicted on her during her seventy-three years and how much he owed her.

Well, whatever he "owed" her, Bernie managed to spend most of his money on electronic equipment. He had a radio that scanned police calls, another radio powerful enough to receive programs from all over the world, a voice-altering device.

At night he dutifully watched television with his mother. After she went to bed at ten o'clock, however, Bernie snapped off the television, rushed down to the basement, turned on the radios and began to call talk show hosts. He made up names and backgrounds to give them. He'd call a right-wing host and rant liberal values, a liberal host and sing the praises of the extreme right. In his call-in persona, he loved arguments, confrontations, trading insults.

Unknown to his mother he also had a forty-inch television and a VCR in the basement and often watched movies he had brought home from porn shops.

The police scanner inspired other ideas. He began to go through telephone books and circle numbers that were listed in women's names. He would dial one of those numbers in the middle of the night and say he was calling from a cellular phone outside her home and was about to break in. He'd whisper that maybe he'd just pay a visit, or maybe he'd kill her. Then Bernie would sit and chuckle as he listened to the police scanners sending a squad car rushing to the address. It was almost as good as peeking in windows or following women, and he never had to worry about the headlights of a police car suddenly shining on him, or a cop on a loudspeaker yelling, "Freeze."

The car belonging to Tom Weicker was a gold mine of information for Bernie. Weicker had an electronic address book in the glove compartment. In it he kept the names, addresses and numbers of the key staff of the station. The big shots, Bernie thought, as he copied numbers onto his own electronic pad. He'd even reached Weicker's wife at home one night. She had begun to shriek when he told her he was at the back door and on his way in.

Afterwards, recalling her terror, he'd giggled for hours.

What was getting hard for him now was that for the first time since he was released from Riker's Island, he had that scary feeling of not being able to get someone out of his mind. This one was a reporter. She was so pretty that when he opened the car door for her it was a struggle not to touch her.

Her name was Meghan Collins.

4

*S*omehow Meghan was able to accept Weicker's offer calmly. It was a joke among the staff that if you were too gee-whiz-thanks about a promotion, Tom Weicker would ponder whether or not he'd made a good choice. He wanted ambitious, driven people who felt any recognition given them was overdue.

Trying to seem matter-of-fact, she showed him the faxed message. As he read it he raised his eyebrows. "What's this mean?" he asked. "What's the 'mistake'? Who is Annie?"

"I don't know. Tom, I was at Roosevelt Hospital when the stabbing victim was brought in last night. Has she been identified?"

"Not yet. What about her?"

"I suppose you ought to know something," Meghan said reluctantly. "She looks like me."

"She resembles you?"

"She could almost be my double."

Tom's eyes narrowed. "Are you suggesting that this fax is tied into that woman's death?"

"It's probably just coincidence, but I thought I should at least let you see it."

"I'm glad you did. Let me keep it. I'll find out who's handling the investigation on that case and let him take a look at it."

For Meghan, it was a distinct relief to pick up her assignments at the news desk.

IT WAS A RELATIVELY TAME DAY. A PRESS CONFERENCE AT the mayor's office at which he named his choice for the new police commissioner, a suspicious fire that had gutted a tenement in Washington Heights. Late in the afternoon, Meghan spoke to the medical examiner's office. An artist's sketch of the dead girl and her physical description had been issued by the Missing Persons Bureau. Her fingerprints were on the way to Washington to be checked against government and criminal files. She had died of a single deep stab wound in the chest. Internal bleeding had been slow but massive. Both legs and arms had been broken some years ago. If not claimed in thirty days, her body would be buried in potter's field in a numbered grave. Another Jane Doe.

At six o'clock that evening, Meghan was just leaving work. As she'd been doing since her father's disappearance, she was going to spend the weekend in Connecticut with her mother. On Sunday afternoon, she was assigned to cover an event at the Manning Clinic, an assisted reproduction facility located forty minutes from their home in Newtown. The clinic was having its annual reunion of children born as a result of in vitro fertilization carried out there.

The assignment editor collared her at the elevator. "Steve

will handle the camera on Sunday at Manning. I told him to meet you there at three."

"Okay."

During the week, Meghan used a company vehicle. This morning she'd driven her own car uptown. The elevator jolted to a stop at the garage level. She smiled as Bernie spotted her and immediately began trotting to the lower parking level. He brought up her white Mustang and held the door open for her. "Any news about your dad?" he asked solicitously.

"No, but thanks for asking."

He bent over, bringing his face close to hers. "My mother and I are praying."

What a nice guy! Meghan thought, as she steered the car up the ramp to the exit.

5

*C*atherine Collins' hair always looked as though she'd just run a hand through it. It was a short, curly mop, now tinted ash blond, that accentuated the pert prettiness of her heart-shaped face. She occasionally reminded Meghan that it was a good thing she'd inherited her own father's determined jaw. Otherwise, now that she was fifty-three, she'd look like a fading Kewpie doll, an impression enhanced by her diminutive size. Barely five feet tall, she referred to herself as the house midget.

Meghan's grandfather Patrick Kelly had come to the United States from Ireland at age nineteen, "with the clothes on my back and one set of underwear rolled under my arm," as the story went. After working days as a dishwasher in the kitchen of a Fifth Avenue hotel and nights with the cleaning crew of a funeral home, he'd concluded that, while there were a lot of things people could do without, nobody could give up eating or dying. Since it was more cheerful to watch people eat than lie in a casket with carnations scattered over them, Patrick Kelly decided to put all his energies into the food business.

Twenty-five years later, he built the inn of his dreams in Newtown, Connecticut, and named it Drumdoe after the village of his birth. It had ten guest rooms and a fine restaurant that drew people from a radius of fifty miles. Pat completed the dream by renovating a charming farmhouse on the adjoining property as a home. He then chose a bride, fathered Catherine and ran his inn until his death at eighty-eight.

His daughter and granddaughter were virtually raised in that inn. Catherine now ran it with the same dedication to excellence that Patrick had instilled in her, and her work there had helped her cope with her husband's death.

Yet, in the nine months since the bridge tragedy, she had found it impossible not to believe that someday the door would open and Ed would cheerfully call, "Where are my girls?" Sometimes she still found herself listening for the sound of her husband's voice.

Now, in addition to all the shock and grief, her finances had become an urgent problem. Two years earlier, Catherine had closed the inn for six months, mortgaged it and completed a massive renovation and redecoration project.

The timing could not have been worse. The reopening coincided with the downward trend of the economy. The payments on the new mortgage were not being met by present income, and quarterly taxes were coming due. Her personal account had only a few thousand dollars left in it.

For weeks after the accident, Catherine had steeled herself for the call that would inform her that her husband's body had been retrieved from the river. Now she prayed for that call to come and end the uncertainty.

There was such a total sense of incompletion. Catherine

would often think that people who ignored funeral rites didn't understand that they were necessary to the spirit. She wanted to be able to visit Ed's grave. Pat, her father, used to talk about "a decent Christian burial." She and Meg would joke about that. When Pat spotted the name of a friend from the past in the obituary column, she or Meg would tease, "Oh, by God, I hope he had a decent Christian burial."

They didn't joke about that anymore.

ON FRIDAY AFTERNOON, CATHERINE WAS IN THE HOUSE, GET-ting ready to go to the inn for the dinner hour. Talk about TGIF, she thought. Friday meant Meg would soon be home for the weekend.

The insurance people were due momentarily. If they'll even give me a partial payout until the Thruway divers find wreck-age of the car, Catherine thought as she fastened a pin on the lapel of her houndstooth jacket. I need the money. They're just trying to wiggle out of double indemnity, but I'm willing to waive that until they have the proof they keep talking about.

But when the two somber executives arrived it was not to begin the process of payment. "Mrs. Collins," the older of the two said, "I hope you will understand our position. We sympathize with you and understand the predicament you are in. The problem is that we cannot authorize payment on your husband's policies without a death certificate, and that is not going to be issued."

Catherine stared at him. "You mean it's not going to be issued until they have absolute proof of his death? But sup-pose his body was carried downriver clear into the Atlantic?"

Both men looked uneasy. The younger one answered her. "Mrs. Collins, the New York Thruway Authority, as owner and operator of the Tappan Zee Bridge, has conducted ex-haustive operations to retrieve both victims and wreckage from the river. Granted, the explosions meant that the vehi-cles were shattered. Nevertheless, heavy parts like transmissions and engines don't disintegrate. Besides the tractor trailer and fuel tanker, six vehicles went over the side, or seven if we were to include your husband's car. Parts from all the others have been retrieved. All the other bodies have been recovered as well. There isn't so much as a wheel or tire or door or engine part of a Cadillac in the riverbed below the accident site."

"Then you're saying . . ." Catherine was finding it hard to form the words.

"We're saying that the exhaustive report on the accident about to be released by the Thruway Authority categorically states that Edwin Collins could not have perished in the bridge tragedy that night. The experts feel that even though he may have been in the vicinity of the bridge, no one believes Edwin Collins was a victim. We believe he escaped being caught with the cars that were involved in the accident and took advantage of that propitious happening to make the disappearance he was planning. We think he reasoned he could take care of you and your daughter through the insurance and go on to whatever new life he had already planned to begin."

6

*M*ac, as Dr. Jeremy MacIntyre was known, lived with his seven-year-old son, Kyle, around the bend from the Collins family. The summers of his college years at Yale, Mac had worked as a waiter at the Drumdoe Inn. In those summers he'd formed a lasting attachment for the area and decided that someday he'd live there.

Growing up, Mac had observed that he was the guy in the crowd the girls didn't notice. Average height, average weight, average looks. It was a reasonably accurate description, but actually Mac did not do himself justice. After they took a second look, women *did* find a challenge in the quizzical expression in his hazel eyes, an endearing boyishness in the sandy hair that always seemed wind tousled, a comforting steadiness in the authority with which he would lead them on the dance floor or tuck a hand under their elbow on an icy evening.

Mac had always known he would be a doctor someday. By the time he began his studies at NYU medical school he had begun to believe that the future of medicine was in genetics. Now thirty-six, he worked at LifeCode, a genetic research laboratory in Westport, some fifty minutes southeast of Newtown.

It was the job he wanted, and it fit into his life as a divorced, custodial father. At twenty-seven Mac had married. The marriage lasted a year and a half and produced Kyle. Then one day Mac came home from the lab to find a babysitter and a note. It read: "Mac, this isn't for me. I'm a lousy wife and a lousy mother. We both know it can't work. I've got to have a crack at a career. Take good care of Kyle. Goodbye, Ginger."

Ginger had done pretty well for herself since then. She sang in cabarets in Vegas and on cruise ships. She'd cut a few records, and the last one had hit the charts. She sent Kyle expensive presents for his birthday and Christmas. The gifts were invariably too sophisticated or too babyish. She'd seen Kyle only three times in the seven years since she'd taken off.

Despite the fact that it had almost come as a relief, Mac still harbored residual bitterness over Ginger's desertion. Somehow, divorce had never been a part of his imagined future, and he still felt uncomfortable with it. He knew that his son missed having a mother, so he took special care and special pride in being a good, attentive father.

On Friday evenings, Mac and Kyle often had dinner at the Drumdoe Inn. They ate in the small, informal grill, where the special Friday menu included individual pizzas and fish and chips.

Catherine was always at the inn for the dinner hour. Growing up, Meg had been a fixture there too. When she was ten and Mac a nineteen-year-old busboy, she had wistfully told him that it was fun to eat at home. "Daddy and I do sometimes, when he's here."

Since her father's disappearance, Meg spent just about every weekend at home and joined her mother at the inn for dinner. But this Friday night there was no sign of either Catherine or Meg.

Mac acknowledged that he was disappointed, but Kyle, who always looked forward especially to seeing Meg, dismissed her absence. "So she's not here. Fine."

"Fine" was Kyle's new all-purpose word. He used it when he was enthusiastic, disgusted or being cool. Tonight, Mac wasn't quite sure what emotion he was hearing. But hey, he told himself, give the kid space. If something's really bothering him it'll come out sooner or later, and it certainly can't have anything to do with Meghan.

Kyle finished the last of the pizza in silence. He was mad at Meghan. She always acted like she really was interested in the stuff that he did, but Wednesday afternoon, when he was outside and had just taught his dog, Jake, to stand up on his hind legs and beg, Meghan had driven past and ignored him. She'd been going real slow, too, and he'd yelled to her to stop. He knew she'd seen him, because she'd looked right at him. But then she'd speeded up the car, driven off, and hadn't even taken time to see Jake's trick. Fine.

He wouldn't tell his dad about it. Dad would say that Meghan was just upset because Mr. Collins hadn't come home for a long time and might have been one of the people whose car went into the river off the bridge. He'd say that sometimes when people were thinking about something else, they could go right past people and not even see them. But Meg *had* seen Kyle Wednesday and hadn't even bothered to wave to him.

Fine, he thought. Just fine.

7

*W*hen Meghan arrived home she found her mother sitting in the darkened living room, her hands folded in her lap. "Mom, are you okay?" she asked anxiously. "It's nearly seven-thirty. Aren't you going to Drumdoe?" She switched on the light and took in Catherine's blotched, tear-stained face. She sank to her knees and grabbed her mother's hands. "Oh God, did they find him? Is that it?"

"No, Meggie, that's not it." Haltingly Catherine Collins related the visit from the insurers.

Not Dad, Meghan thought. He couldn't, wouldn't do this to Mother. Not to her. There had to be a mistake. "That's the craziest thing I ever heard," she said firmly.

"That's what I told them. But Meg, why would Dad have borrowed so much on the insurance? That haunts me. And even if he did invest it, I don't know where. Without a death certificate, my hands are tied. I can't keep up with expenses. Phillip has been sending Dad's monthly draw from the company, but that's not fair to him. Most of the money due him in commissions has been in for some time. I know I'm conservative by nature, but I certainly wasn't when I reno-

direct questions. A couple of times I've wanted to toss them out bodily. Like everyone else, I expected Ed's car, or wreckage from it, would be recovered. It's possible that a lot of it would have been carried downstream by the tide or become lodged in the riverbed, but it doesn't help that not a trace of the car has been found. So to answer you, yes, it's possible. And no, I can't believe your father capable of a stunt like that."

It was what she expected to hear, but that didn't make it easier. Once when she was very little, Meghan had tried to take a burning piece of bread out of the toaster with a fork. She felt as though she was experiencing again the vivid pain of electrical current shooting through her body.

"And of course it doesn't help that Dad took the cash value out of his policies a few weeks before he disappeared."

"No, it doesn't. I want you to know that I'm doing the audit for your mother's sake. When this becomes public knowledge, and be sure it will, I want to be able to have a certified statement that our books are in perfect order. This sort of thing starts rumors flying, as you can understand."

Meghan looked down. She had dressed in jeans and a matching jacket. It occurred to her that this was the kind of outfit the dead woman was wearing when she was brought to Roosevelt Hospital. She pushed the thought away. "Was my father a gambler? Would that explain his need for a cash loan?"

Carter shook his head. "Your father wasn't a gambler, and I've seen enough of them, Meg." He grimaced. "Meg, I wish I could find an answer, but I can't. Nothing in Ed's business or personal life suggested to me that he would choose to disappear. On the other hand, the lack of physical evidence from the crash is necessarily suspicious, at least to outsiders."

Meghan looked at the desk, the executive swivel chair behind it. She could picture her father sitting there, leaning back, his eyes twinkling, his hands clasped, fingers pointing in what her mother called "Ed's saint-and-martyr pose." She could see herself running into this office as a child.

vated the inn. I really overdid it. Now I may have to sell Drumdoe."

The inn. It was Friday night. Her mother should be there now, in her element, greeting guests, keeping a watchful eye on the waiters and busboys, the table settings, sampling the dishes in the kitchen. Every detail automatically checked and rechecked.

"Dad didn't do this to you," Meg said flatly. "I just know that."

Catherine Collins broke into harsh, dry sobs. "Maybe Dad used the bridge accident as a chance to get away from me. But why, Meg? I loved him so much."

Meghan put her arms around her mother. "Listen," she said firmly, "you were right the first time. Dad would never do this to you, and one way or the other, we're going to prove it."

8

The Collins and Carter Executive Search office was located in Danbury, Connecticut. Edwin Collins had started the firm when he was twenty-eight, after having worked five years for a Fortune 500 company based in New York. By then he'd realized that working within the corporate structure was not for him.

Following his marriage to Catherine Kelly, he'd relocated his office to Danbury. They wanted to live in Connecticut, and the location of Edwin's office was not important since he spent much of his time traveling throughout the country, visiting clients.

Some twelve years before his disappearance, Collins had brought Phillip Carter into the business.

Carter, a Wharton graduate with the added attraction of a law degree, had previously been a client of Edwin's, having been placed by him in jobs several times. The last one before they joined forces was with a multinational firm in Maryland.

When Collins was visiting that client, he and Carter would have lunch or a drink together. Over the years they had developed a business-oriented friendship. In the early eighties, after a difficult midlife divorce, Phillip Carter finally left his job in Maryland to become Collins' partner and associate.

They were opposites in many ways. Collins was tall, classically handsome, an impeccable dresser and quietly witty, while Carter was bluff and hearty, with attractively irregular features and a thick head of graying hair. His clothes were expensive, but never looked quite put together. His tie was often pulled loose from the knot. He was a man's man, whose stories over a drink brought forth bursts of laughter, a man with an eye for the ladies, too.

The partnership had worked. For a long time Phillip Carter lived in Manhattan and did reverse commuting to Danbury, when he was not traveling for the company. His name often appeared in the columns of the New York newspapers as having attended dinner parties and benefits with various women. Eventually he bought a small house in Brookfield, ten minutes from the office, and stayed there with increasing frequency.

Now fifty-three years old, Phillip Carter was a familiar figure in the Danbury area.

He regularly worked at his desk for several hours after everyone else had left for the day because, since a number of clients and candidates were located in the Midwest and on the West Coast, early evening in the East was a good time to contact them. Since the night of the bridge tragedy, Phillip rarely left the office before eight o'clock.

When Meghan called at five of eight this [...] reaching for his coat. "I was afraid it was con[...] said after she'd told him about the visit fr[...] "Can you come in tomorrow around noon?"[...]

After he hung up he sat for a long time a[...] he picked up the phone and called his acco[...] we'd better audit the books right now," he s[...]

9

When Meghan arrived at the Colli[...] utive Search offices at two o'clock on S[...] three men working with calculators at [...] usually held magazines and plants. She [...] Carter's explanation to confirm that the[...] his suggestion, they went into her father'[...]

She had spent a sleepless night, her mi[...] questions, doubts and denial. Phillip [...] indicated one of the two chairs in front [...] the other one, a subtlety she appreciated[...] to see him behind her father's desk.

She knew Phillip would be honest [...] "Phillip, do you think it's remotely poss[...] still alive and chose to disappear?"

The momentary pause before he [...] enough. "You *do* think that?" she pro[...]

"Meg, I've lived long enough to k[...] possible. Frankly, the Thruway investi[...] have been around here for quite a wh[...]

vated the inn. I really overdid it. Now I may have to sell Drumdoe."

The inn. It was Friday night. Her mother should be there now, in her element, greeting guests, keeping a watchful eye on the waiters and busboys, the table settings, sampling the dishes in the kitchen. Every detail automatically checked and rechecked.

"Dad didn't do this to you," Meg said flatly. "I just know that."

Catherine Collins broke into harsh, dry sobs. "Maybe Dad used the bridge accident as a chance to get away from me. But why, Meg? I loved him so much."

Meghan put her arms around her mother. "Listen," she said firmly, "you were right the first time. Dad would never do this to you, and one way or the other, we're going to prove it."

The Collins and Carter Executive Search office was located in Danbury, Connecticut. Edwin Collins had started the firm when he was twenty-eight, after having worked five years for a Fortune 500 company based in New York. By then he'd realized that working within the corporate structure was not for him.

Following his marriage to Catherine Kelly, he'd relocated his office to Danbury. They wanted to live in Connecticut, and the location of Edwin's office was not important since he spent much of his time traveling throughout the country, visiting clients.

Some twelve years before his disappearance, Collins had brought Phillip Carter into the business.

Carter, a Wharton graduate with the added attraction of a law degree, had previously been a client of Edwin's, having been placed by him in jobs several times. The last one before they joined forces was with a multinational firm in Maryland.

When Collins was visiting that client, he and Carter would have lunch or a drink together. Over the years they had developed a business-oriented friendship. In the early eighties, after a difficult midlife divorce, Phillip Carter finally left his job in Maryland to become Collins' partner and associate.

They were opposites in many ways. Collins was tall, classically handsome, an impeccable dresser and quietly witty, while Carter was bluff and hearty, with attractively irregular features and a thick head of graying hair. His clothes were expensive, but never looked quite put together. His tie was often pulled loose from the knot. He was a man's man, whose stories over a drink brought forth bursts of laughter, a man with an eye for the ladies, too.

The partnership had worked. For a long time Phillip Carter lived in Manhattan and did reverse commuting to Danbury, when he was not traveling for the company. His name often appeared in the columns of the New York newspapers as having attended dinner parties and benefits with various women. Eventually he bought a small house in Brookfield, ten minutes from the office, and stayed there with increasing frequency.

Now fifty-three years old, Phillip Carter was a familiar figure in the Danbury area.

He regularly worked at his desk for several hours after everyone else had left for the day because, since a number of clients and candidates were located in the Midwest and on the West Coast, early evening in the East was a good time to contact them. Since the night of the bridge tragedy, Phillip rarely left the office before eight o'clock.

When Meghan called at five of eight this evening, he was reaching for his coat. "I was afraid it was coming to this," he said after she'd told him about the visit from the insurers. "Can you come in tomorrow around noon?"

After he hung up he sat for a long time at his desk. Then he picked up the phone and called his accountant. "I think we'd better audit the books right now," he said quietly.

9

*W*hen Meghan arrived at the Collins and Carter Executive Search offices at two o'clock on Saturday, she found three men working with calculators at the long table that usually held magazines and plants. She did not need Phillip Carter's explanation to confirm that they were auditors. At his suggestion, they went into her father's private office.

She had spent a sleepless night, her mind a battleground of questions, doubts and denial. Phillip closed the door and indicated one of the two chairs in front of the desk. He took the other one, a subtlety she appreciated. It would have hurt to see him behind her father's desk.

She knew Phillip would be honest with her. She asked, "Phillip, do you think it's remotely possible that my father is still alive and chose to disappear?"

The momentary pause before he spoke was answer enough. "You *do* think that?" she prodded.

"Meg, I've lived long enough to know that anything is possible. Frankly, the Thruway investigators and the insurers have been around here for quite a while asking some pretty direct questions. A couple of times I've wanted to toss them out bodily. Like everyone else, I expected Ed's car, or wreckage from it, would be recovered. It's possible that a lot of it would have been carried downstream by the tide or become lodged in the riverbed, but it doesn't help that not a trace of the car has been found. So to answer you, yes, it's possible. And no, I can't believe your father capable of a stunt like that."

It was what she expected to hear, but that didn't make it easier. Once when she was very little, Meghan had tried to take a burning piece of bread out of the toaster with a fork. She felt as though she was experiencing again the vivid pain of electrical current shooting through her body.

"And of course it doesn't help that Dad took the cash value out of his policies a few weeks before he disappeared."

"No, it doesn't. I want you to know that I'm doing the audit for your mother's sake. When this becomes public knowledge, and be sure it will, I want to be able to have a certified statement that our books are in perfect order. This sort of thing starts rumors flying, as you can understand."

Meghan looked down. She had dressed in jeans and a matching jacket. It occurred to her that this was the kind of outfit the dead woman was wearing when she was brought into Roosevelt Hospital. She pushed the thought away. "Was my father a gambler? Would that explain his need for a cash loan?"

Carter shook his head. "Your father wasn't a gambler, and I've seen enough of them, Meg." He grimaced. "Meg, I wish I could find an answer, but I can't. Nothing in Ed's business or personal life suggested to me that he would choose to disappear. On the other hand, the lack of physical evidence from the crash is necessarily suspicious, at least to outsiders."

Meghan looked at the desk, the executive swivel chair behind it. She could picture her father sitting there, leaning back, his eyes twinkling, his hands clasped, fingers pointing up in what her mother called "Ed's saint-and-martyr pose."

She could see herself running into this office as a child.

Her father always had candy for her, gooey chocolate bars, marshmallows, peanut brittle. Her mother had tried to keep that kind of candy from her. "Ed," she'd protest, "don't give her that junk. You'll ruin her teeth."

"Sweets to the sweet, Catherine."

Daddy's girl. Always. He was the fun parent. Mother was the one who made Meghan practice the piano and make her bed. Mother was the one who'd protested when she quit the law firm. "For heaven's sake, Meg," she had pleaded, "give it more than six months; don't waste your education."

Daddy had understood. "Leave her alone, love," he'd said firmly. "Meg has a good head on her shoulders."

Once when she was little Meghan had asked her father why he traveled so much.

"Ah, Meg," he'd sighed. "How I wish it wasn't necessary. Maybe I was born to be a wandering minstrel."

Because he was away so much, when he came home he always tried to make it up. He'd suggest that instead of going to the inn he'd whip up dinner for the two of them at home. "Meghan Anne," he'd tell her, "you're my date."

This office has his aura, Meg thought. The handsome cherrywood desk he'd found in a Salvation Army store and stripped and refinished himself. The table behind it with pictures of her and her mother. The lion's-head bookends holding leather-bound books.

For nine months she had been mourning him as dead. She wondered if at this moment she was mourning him more. If the insurers were right, he had become a stranger. Meghan looked into Phillip Carter's eyes. "They're not right," she said aloud. "I believe my father is dead. I believe that some wreckage of his car will still be found." She looked around. "But in fairness to you, we have no right to tie up this office. I'll come in next week and pack his personal effects."

"We'll take care of that, Meg."

"No. Please. I can sort things out better here. Mother's in rough enough shape without watching me do it at home."

Phillip Carter nodded. "You're right, Meg. I'm worried about Catherine too."

"That's why I don't dare tell her about what happened the other night." She saw the deepening concern on his face as she told him about the stabbing victim who resembled her and the fax that came in the middle of the night.

"Meg, that's bizarre," he said. "I hope your boss follows it up with the police. We can't let anything happen to you."

AS VICTOR ORSINI TURNED HIS KEY IN THE DOOR OF THE Collins and Carter offices, he was surprised to realize it was unlocked. Saturday afternoon usually meant he had the place to himself. He had returned from a series of meetings in Colorado and wanted to go over mail and messages.

Thirty-one years old with a permanent tan, muscular arms and shoulders and a lean disciplined body, he had the look of an outdoorsman. His jet black hair and strong features were indicative of his Italian heritage. His intensely blue eyes were a throwback to his British grandmother.

Orsini had been working for Collins and Carter for nearly seven years. He hadn't expected to stay so long, in fact he'd always planned to use this job as a stepping-stone to a bigger firm.

His eyebrows raised when he pushed open the door and saw the auditors. In a deliberately impersonal tone, the head man told Orsini that Phillip Carter and Meghan Collins were in Edwin Collins' private office. He then hesitantly acquainted Victor with the insurers' theory that Collins had chosen to disappear.

"That's crazy." Victor strode across the reception area and knocked on the closed door.

Carter opened it. "Oh, Victor, good to see you. We didn't expect you today."

Meghan turned to greet him. Orsini realized she was fighting back tears. He groped for something reassuring to say but could come up with nothing. He had been questioned by the investigators about the call Ed Collins made to him just before the accident. "Yes," he'd said at the time, "Edwin said he was getting on the bridge. Yes, I'm sure he didn't say he was getting off it. Do you think I can't hear? Yes, he wanted to see me the next morning. There wasn't anything unusual about that. Ed used his car phone all the time."

Victor suddenly wondered how long it would be before anyone questioned that it was his word alone that placed Ed Collins on the ramp to the Tappan Zee that night. It was not difficult for him to mirror the concern on Meghan's face when he shook the hand she extended to him.

10

*A*t three o'clock on Sunday afternoon, Meg met Steve Boyle, the PCD cameraman, in the parking lot of the Manning Clinic.

The clinic was on a hillside two miles from Route 7 in rural Kent, a forty-minute drive north from her home. It had been built in 1890 as the residence of a shrewd businessman whose wife had had the good sense to restrain her ambitious husband from creating an ostentatious display on his meteoric rise to the status of merchant prince. She convinced him that, instead of the pseudopalazzo he had planned, an English manor house was better suited to the beauty of the countryside.

"Prepared for children's hour?" Meghan asked the cameraman as they trudged up the walk.

"The Giants are on and we're stuck with the Munchkins," Steve groused.

Inside the mansion, the spacious foyer functioned as a reception area. Oak-paneled walls held framed pictures of the children who owed their existence to the genius of modern science. Beyond, the great hall had the ambiance of a comfortable family room, with groupings of furniture that invited intimate conversations or could be angled for informal lectures.

Booklets with testimonials from grateful parents were scattered on tables. "We wanted a child so badly. Our lives were incomplete. And then we made an appointment at the Manning Clinic . . ." "I'd go to a friend's baby shower and try not to cry. Someone suggested I look into in vitro fertilization, and Jamie was born fifteen months later . . ." "My fortieth birthday was coming, and I knew it would soon be too late . . ."

Every year, on the third Sunday in October, the children who had been born as a result of IVF at the Manning Clinic were invited to return with their parents for the annual reunion. Meghan learned that this year three hundred invitations were sent and over two hundred small alumni accepted. It was a large, noisy and festive party.

In one of the smaller sitting rooms, Meghan interviewed Dr. George Manning, the silver-haired seventy-year-old director of the clinic, and asked him to explain in vitro fertilization.

"In the simplest possible terms," he explained, "IVF is a method by which a woman who has great difficulty conceiving is sometimes able to have the baby or babies she wants so desperately. After her menstrual cycle has been monitored, she begins treatment. Fertility drugs are administered so that her ovaries are stimulated to release an abundance of follicles, which are then retrieved.

"The woman's partner is asked to provide a semen sample to inseminate the eggs contained in the follicles in the laboratory. The next day an embryologist checks to see which, if any, eggs have been fertilized. If success was achieved, a physician will transfer one or more of the fertilized eggs, which are now referred to as embryos, to the woman's uterus. If requested, the rest of the embryos will be cryopreserved for later implantation.

"After fifteen days, blood is drawn for the first pregnancy test." The doctor pointed to the great hall. "And as you can see from the crowd we have here today, many of those tests prove positive."

"I certainly can," Meg agreed. "Doctor, what is the ratio of success to failure?"

"Still not as high as we'd prefer, but improving constantly," he said solemnly.

"Thank you, Doctor."

TRAILED BY STEVE, MEGHAN INTERVIEWED SEVERAL OF THE mothers, asking them to share their personal experiences with in vitro fertilization.

One of them, posing with her three handsome offspring, explained, "They fertilized fourteen eggs and implanted three. One of them resulted in a pregnancy, and here he is." She smiled down at her elder son. "Chris is seven now. The other embryos were cryopreserved, or, in simpler terms, frozen. I came back five years ago, and Todd is the result. Then I tried again last year, and Jill is three months old. Some of the embryos didn't survive thawing, but I still have two cryopreserved embryos in the lab. In case I ever find time on my hands for another kid," she said laughing as the four-year-old darted away.

"Have we got enough, Meghan?" Steve asked. "I'd like to catch the last quarter of the Giants game."

"Let me talk to one more staff member. I've been watching that woman. She seems to know everybody's name."

Meg went over to the woman and glanced at her name tag. "May I have a word with you, Dr. Petrovic?"

"Of course." Petrovic's voice was well modulated, with a

hint of an accent. She was of average height, with hazel eyes and refined features. She seemed courteous rather than friendly. Still, Meg noticed that she had a cluster of children around her.

"How long have you been at the clinic, Doctor?"

"It will be seven years in March. I'm the embryologist in charge of the laboratory."

"Would you care to comment on what you feel about these children?"

"I feel that each one of them is a miracle."

"Thank you, Doctor."

"We've got enough footage inside," Meg told Steve when they left Petrovic. "I do want a shot of the group picture, though. They'll be gathering for it in a minute."

The annual photo was taken on the front lawn outside the mansion. There was the usual confusion that attended lining up children from toddler age to nine-year-olds, with mothers holding infants standing in the last row and flanked by staff members.

The Indian summer day was bright, and as Steve focused the camera on the group, Meghan had the fleeting thought that every one of the children looked well dressed and happy. Why not? she thought. They were all desperately wanted.

A three-year-old ran from the front row to his pregnant mother, who was standing near Meghan. Blue eyed and golden haired, with a sweet, shy smile, he threw his arms around his mother's knees.

"Get a shot of that," Meghan told Steve. "He's adorable." Steve held the camera on the little boy as his mother cajoled him to rejoin the other children.

"I'm right here, Jonathan," she assured him as she placed him back in line. "You can see me. I promise I'm not going away." She returned to where she had been standing.

Meghan walked over to the woman. "Would you mind answering a few questions?" she asked, holding out the mike.

"I'd be glad to."

"Will you give us your name and tell us how old your little boy is?"

"I'm Dina Anderson, and Jonathan is almost three."

"Is your expected baby also the result of in vitro fertilization?"

"Yes, as a matter of fact, he's Jonathan's identical twin."

"Identical twin!" Meghan knew she sounded astonished.

"I know it sounds impossible," Dina Anderson said happily, "but that's the way it is. It's extremely rare, but an embryo can split in the laboratory just the way it would in the womb. When we were told that one of the fertilized eggs had divided, my husband and I decided that I would try to give birth to each twin separately. We felt that individually they might each have a better chance for survival in my womb, and actually it's practical. I've got a responsible job, and I'd hate to have left two infants with a nanny."

The photographer for the clinic had been snapping pictures. A moment later he yelled, "Okay kids, thanks." The children scattered, and Jonathan ran to his mother. Dina Anderson scooped up her son in her arms. "I can't imagine life without him," she said. "And in about ten days we'll have Ryan."

What a human interest segment that would make, Meghan thought. "Mrs. Anderson," she said persuasively, "if you're willing, I'd like to talk to my boss about doing a feature story on your twins."

11

*O*n the way back to Newtown, Meghan used the car phone to call her mother. Her alarm at getting the answering machine turned to relief when she dialed the inn and was told

Mrs. Collins was in the dining room. "Tell her I'm on my way," she instructed the receptionist, "and that I'll meet her there."

For the next fifteen minutes Meghan drove as though on automatic pilot. She was excited about the possibility of the feature story she would pitch to Weicker. And she could get some guidance on it from Mac. He was a specialist in genetics. He'd be able to give her expert advice and reading material she could study to know more about the whole spectrum of assisted reproduction, including the statistics on success and failure rates. When the traffic slowed to a halt, she picked up her car phone and dialed his number.

Kyle answered. Meghan raised her eyebrow at the way his tone changed when he realized she was the caller. What's eating him? she wondered, as he pointedly ignored her greeting and passed the phone to his father.

"Hi, Meghan. What can I do for you?" As always the sound of Mac's voice gave Meghan a stab of familiar pain. She'd called him her best friend when she was ten, had a crush on him when she was twelve, and had fallen in love with him by the time she was sixteen. Three years later he married Ginger. She'd been at the wedding, and it was one of the hardest days of her life. Mac had been crazy about Ginger, and Meg suspected that even after seven years, if Ginger had walked in the door and dropped her suitcase, he'd *still* want her. Meg would never let herself admit that no matter how hard she tried, she'd never been able to stop loving Mac.

"I could use some professional help, Mac." As the car passed the blocked lane and picked up speed, she explained the visit to the clinic and the story she was putting together. "And I sort of need the information in a hurry so I can pitch the whole thing to my boss."

"I can give it to you right away. Kyle and I are just heading for the inn. I'll bring it along. Want to join us for dinner?"

"That works out fine. See you." She broke the connection.

It was nearly seven when she reached the outskirts of town. The temperature was dropping, and the afternoon breeze had turned to gusts of wind. The headlights caught the trees, still heavy with leaves that were now restlessly moving, sending shadows over the road. At this moment, they made her think of the dark, choppy water of the Hudson.

Concentrate on how you'll pitch the idea of doing a special on the Manning Clinic to Weicker, she told herself fiercely.

PHILLIP CARTER WAS IN DRUMDOE, AT A WINDOW TABLE SET for three. He waved Meghan over. "Catherine's in the kitchen giving the chef a hard time," he told her. "The people over there"—he nodded to a nearby table—"wanted the beef rare. Your mother said what they got could have passed for a hockey puck. In fact, it was medium rare."

Meghan sank into a chair and smiled. "The best thing that could happen to her would be if the chef quit. Then she'd have to get back in the kitchen. It would keep her mind off things." She reached across the table and touched Carter's hand. "Thanks for coming over."

"I hope you haven't eaten. I've managed to make Catherine promise to join me."

"That's great, but how about if I have coffee with you? Mac and Kyle should be here any minute, and I said I'd join them. The truth is, I need to pick Mac's brain."

At dinner, Kyle continued to be aloof to Meghan. Finally she raised her eyebrows in a questioning look at Mac, who shrugged and murmured, "Don't ask me." Mac cautioned her about the feature story she was planning. "You're right. There are a lot of failures, and it's a very expensive procedure."

Meg looked across the table at Mac and his son. They were so alike. She remembered the way her father had pressed her hand at Mac's wedding. He'd understood. He'd always understood her.

When they were ready to leave, she said, "I'll sit with Mother and Phillip for a few minutes." She put an arm around Kyle. "See you, buddy."

He pulled away.

"Hey, come on," Meghan said. "What's all this about?"

To her surprise she saw tears well in his eyes. "I thought you were my friend." He turned swiftly and ran to the door.

"I'll get it out of him," Mac promised as he rushed to catch up with his son.

AT SEVEN O'CLOCK, IN NEARBY BRIDGEWATER, DINA ANDERSON was holding Jonathan on her lap and sipping the last of her coffee as she told her husband about the party at the Manning Clinic. "We may be famous," she said. "Meghan Collins, that reporter from Channel 3, wants to get the go-ahead from her boss to be in the hospital when the baby is born and get early pictures of Jonathan with his brand-new brother. If her boss agrees, she might want to do updates from time to time on how they interact."

Donald Anderson looked doubtful. "Honey, I'm not sure we need that kind of publicity."

"Oh, come on. It could be fun. And I agree with Meghan that if more people who want babies understood the different kinds of assisted birth, they'd realize IVF really is a viable option. This guy was certainly worth all the expense and effort."

"This guy's head is going in your coffee." Anderson got up, walked around the table and took his son from his wife's arms. "Bedtime for Bonzo," he announced, then added, "If you want to do it, it's okay with me. I guess it would be fun to have some professional tapes of the kids."

Dina watched affectionately as her blue-eyed, blond husband carried her equally fair child to the staircase. She had all Jonathan's baby pictures in readiness. It would be such fun to compare them with Ryan's pictures. She still had one cryopreserved embryo at the clinic. In two years we'll try for another baby, and maybe that one will look like me, she thought, glancing across the room to the mirror over the serving table. She studied her reflection, her olive skin, hazel eyes, coal black hair. "That wouldn't be too bad a deal either," she murmured to herself.

AT THE INN, LINGERING OVER A SECOND CUP OF COFFEE WITH her mother and Phillip, Meghan listened as he soberly discussed her father's disappearance.

"Edwin's borrowing so heavily on his insurance without telling you plays right into the insurers' hands. As they told you, they're taking it as a signal that for his own reasons he was accumulating cash. Just as they won't pay his personal insurance, I've been notified they won't settle the partnership insurance either, which would be paid to you as satisfaction for his senior partnership in Executive Search."

"Which means," Catherine Collins said quietly, "that because I cannot prove my husband is dead I stand to lose everything. Phillip, is Edwin owed any more money for past work?"

His answer was simple. "No."

"How is the headhunter business this year?"

"Not good."

"You've advanced us $45,000 while we've been waiting for Edwin's body to be found."

He suddenly looked stern. "Catherine, I'm glad to do it. I only wish I could increase it. When we have proof of Ed's death, you can repay me out of the business insurance."

She put a hand over his. "I can't let you do that, Phillip. Old Pat would spin in his grave if he thought I was living on borrowed money. The fact is, unless we can find some proof that Edwin did die in that accident, I will lose the place my father spent his life creating, and I'll have to sell my home." She looked at Meghan. "Thank God I have you, Meggie." That was when Meghan decided not to drive back to New York City as she had planned, but to stay the night.

WHEN SHE AND HER MOTHER GOT BACK TO THE HOUSE, BY unspoken consent they did not talk any more about the man who had been husband and father. Instead they watched the ten o'clock news, then prepared for bed. Meghan knocked on the door of her mother's bedroom to say good night. She realized that she no longer thought of it as her parents' room. When she opened the door, she saw with a thrust of pain that her mother had moved her pillows to the center of the bed.

Meghan knew that was a clear message that if Edwin Collins was alive, there was no room for him anymore in this house.

12

*B*ernie Heffernan spent Sunday evening with his mother, watching television in the shabby sitting room of their bungalow-type home in Jackson Heights. He vastly preferred watching from the communications center he had created in the crudely finished basement room, but always stayed upstairs until his mother went to bed at ten. Since her fall ten years earlier, she never went near the rickety basement stairs.

Meghan's segment about the Manning Clinic was aired on the six o'clock news. Bernie stared at the screen, perspiration beading his brow. If he were downstairs now, he could be taping Meghan on his VCR.

"Bernard!" Mama's sharp voice broke into his reverie.

He plastered on a smile. "Sorry, Mama."

Her eyes were enlarged behind the rimless bifocals. "I asked you if they ever found that woman's father."

He'd mentioned Meghan's father to Mama once and always regretted it. He patted his mother's hand. "I told her that we're praying for her, Mama."

He didn't like the way Mama looked at him. "You're not thinking on that woman, are you, Bernard?"

"No, Mama. Of course not, Mama."

After his mother went to bed, Bernie went down to the basement. He felt tired and dispirited. There was only one way to get some relief.

He began his calls immediately. First the religious station in Atlanta. Using the voice-altering device, he shouted insults at the preacher until he was cut off. Then he dialed a talk show in Massachusetts and told the host he'd overheard a murder plot against him.

At eleven he began calling women whose names he had checked off in the phone book. One by one he warned them that he was about to break in. From the sound of their voices he could picture how they looked. Young and pretty. Old. Plain. Slim. Heavy. Mentally he'd create the face, filling in the details of their features with each additional word they said.

Except tonight. Tonight they all had the same face.

Tonight they all looked like Meghan Collins.

13

When Meghan went downstairs Monday morning at six-thirty she found her mother already in the kitchen. The aroma of coffee filled the room, juice had been poured and bread was in the toaster. Meghan's protest that her mother should not have gotten up so early died on her lips. From the deep shadows around Catherine Collins' eyes, it was clear that she had slept little if at all.

Like me, Meghan thought, as she reached for the coffeepot. "Mother, I've done a lot of thinking," she said. Carefully choosing her words, she continued, "I can't understand a single reason why Dad would choose to disappear. Let's say there was another woman. That certainly could happen, but if it did, Dad could have asked you for a divorce. You'd have been devastated, of course, and I'd have been angry for you, but in the end we're both realists, and Dad knew that. The insurance companies are hanging everything on the fact that they haven't found either his body or the car, and that he borrowed against his own policies. But they were *his* policies, and as you said, he may have wanted to make some kind of investment he knew you wouldn't approve of. It *is* possible."

"Anything's possible," Catherine Collins said quietly, "including the fact that I don't know what to do."

"I do. We're going to file suit demanding payment of those policies, including double indemnity for accidental death. We're not going to sit back and let those people tell us that Dad pulled this on you."

AT SEVEN O'CLOCK MAC AND KYLE SAT ACROSS FROM EACH other at their kitchen table. Kyle had gone to bed still refusing to discuss his coolness toward Meg, but this morning his mood had changed. "I was thinking," he began.

Mac smiled. "That's a good start."

"I mean it. Remember last night Meg was talking about the case she was covering in court all day Wednesday?"

"Yes."

"Then she couldn't have been up here Wednesday afternoon."

"No, she wasn't."

"Then I didn't see her drive by the house."

Mac looked into his son's serious eyes. "No, you wouldn't have seen her Wednesday afternoon. I'm sure of that."

"I guess it was just somebody who looked a lot like her." Kyle's relieved smile revealed two missing teeth. He glanced down at Jake, who was stretched out under the table. "Now, by the time Meg gets a chance to see Jake when she comes home next weekend, he'll be *perfect* at begging."

At the sound of his name, Jake jumped up and lifted his front paws.

"I'd say he's perfect at begging now," Mac said dryly.

MEGHAN DROVE DIRECTLY TO THE WEST FIFTY-SIXTH STREET garage entrance of the PCD building. Bernie had the driver's door open at the exact moment she shifted into Park. "Hi, Miss Collins." His beaming smile and warm voice brought a responsive smile to her lips. "My mother and I saw you at that clinic, I mean we saw the news last night with you on. Must have been fun to be with all those kids." His hand came out to assist her from the car.

"They were awfully cute, Bernie," Meghan agreed.

"My mother said it seems kind of weird—you know what I mean—having babies the way those people do. I'm not much for all these crazy scientific fads."

Breakthroughs, not fads, Meghan thought. "I know what you mean," she said. "It does seem a little like something out of *Brave New World.*"

Bernie stared blankly at her.

"See you." She headed for the elevator, her leather folder tucked under her arm.

Bernie watched her go, then got in her car and drove it down to the lower level of the garage. Deliberately he put it in a dark corner at the far wall. During lunch break all the guys chose a car to relax in, where they'd eat and read the paper or doze. The only management rule was to make sure you didn't smear ketchup on the upholstery. Ever since some dope burned the leather armrest of a Mercedes, no one was allowed to smoke, even in cars where the ashtray was filled with butts. The point was, nobody saw anything funny about always taking a break in the same car or the same couple of cars. Bernie felt happy sitting in Meghan's Mustang. It had a hint of the perfume she always wore.

MEGHAN'S DESK WAS IN THE BULL PEN ON THE 30TH FLOOR. Swiftly she read the assignment sheet. At eleven o'clock she was to be at the arraignment of an indicted inside stock trader.

Her phone rang. It was Tom Weicker. "Meg, can you come in right away?"

There were two men in Weicker's private office. Meghan recognized one of them, Jamal Nader, a soft-spoken black detective whom she'd run into a number of times in court. They greeted each other warmly. Weicker introduced the other man as Lt. Story.

"Lt. Story is in charge of the homicide you covered the other night. I gave him the fax you received."

Nader shook his head. "That dead girl really is a look-alike for you, Meghan."

"Has she been identified?" Meghan asked.

"No." Nader hesitated. "But she seems to have known you."

"Known me?" Meghan stared at him. "How do you figure that?"

"When they brought her into the morgue Thursday night they went through her clothing and found nothing. They sent everything to the district attorney's office to be stored as evidence. One of our guys went over it again. The lining of the jacket pocket had a deep fold. He found a sheet of paper torn from a Drumdoe Inn notepad. It had your name and direct phone number at WPCD written on it."

"My name!"

Lt. Story reached into his pocket. The piece of paper was

encased in plastic. He held it up. "Your first name and the number."

Meghan and the two detectives were standing at Tom Weicker's desk. Meghan gripped the desktop as she stared at the bold letters, the slanted printing of the numbers. She felt her lips go dry.

"Miss Collins, do you recognize that handwriting?" Story asked sharply.

She nodded. "Yes."

"Who . . . ?"

She turned her head, not wanting to see that familiar writing anymore. "My father wrote that," she whispered.

14

*O*n Monday morning, Phillip Carter reached the office at eight o'clock. As usual he was the first to arrive. The staff was small, consisting of Jackie, his fifty-year-old secretary, the mother of teenagers; Milly, the grandmotherly part-time bookkeeper; and Victor Orsini.

Carter had his own computer adjacent to his desk. In it he kept files that only he could access, files that listed his personal data. His friends joked about his love for going to land auctions, but they would have been astonished at the amount of rural property he had quietly amassed over the years. Unfortunately for him, much of the land he had acquired cheaply had been lost in his divorce settlement. The property he bought at sky-high prices he acquired after the divorce.

As he inserted the key in the computer he reflected that

when Jackie and Milly learned that Edwin Collins' presumed death was being challenged, they would not lack for noon-hour gossip.

His essential sense of privacy recoiled at the notion that he would ever be the subject of one of the avid discussions Jackie and Milly shared as they lunched on salads that seemed to him to consist mostly of alfalfa sprouts.

The subject of Ed Collins' office worried him. It had seemed the decent thing to leave it as it was until the official pronouncement of his death, but now it was just as well Meghan had said she wanted to pack up her father's personal effects. One way or the other, Edwin Collins would never use it again.

Carter frowned. Victor Orsini. He just couldn't like the man. Orsini had always been closer to Ed, but he did a damn good job, and his expertise in the field of medical technology was absolutely necessary today, and particularly valuable now that Ed was gone. He had handled most of that area of the business.

Carter knew there was no way to avoid giving Orsini Ed's office when Meghan had finished clearing it out. Victor's present office was cramped and had only one small window.

Yes, for the present, he needed the man, like him or not.

Nevertheless, Phillip's intuition warned him that there was an elusive factor about Victor Orsini's makeup that should never be ignored.

LT. STORY ALLOWED A COPY OF THE PLASTIC-ENCLOSED scrap of paper to be made for Meghan. "How long ago were you assigned that phone number at the radio station?" he asked her.

"In mid-January."

"When was the last time you saw your father?"

"On January 14th. He was leaving for California on a business trip."

"What kind of business?"

Meghan's tongue felt thick, her fingers were chilled as she held the photocopy with her name looking incongruously bold against the white background. She told him about Collins and Carter Executive Search. It was obvious that Detective Jamal Nader had already told Story that her father was missing.

"Did your father have this number in his possession when he left?"

"He must have. I never spoke to him or saw him again after the fourteenth. He was due home on the twenty-eighth."

"And he died in the Tappan Zee Bridge accident that night."

"He called his associate Victor Orsini as he was starting onto the bridge. The accident happened less than a minute after their phone conversation. Someone reported seeing a dark Cadillac spin into the fuel tanker and go over the side." It was useless to conceal what this man could learn by one phone call. "I must tell you that the insurance companies have now refused to pay his policies on the basis that at least parts of all the other vehicles have been found, but there's been no trace of my father's car. The Thruway divers claim that if the car went into the river at that point, they should have located it." Meghan's chin went up. "My mother is filing suit to have the insurance paid."

She could see the skepticism in the eyes of all three men. To her own ears—and with this paper in her hand—she sounded like one of those unfortunate witnesses she had seen in court trials, people who stick doggedly to their testimony even in the face of irrefutable proof that they are either mistaken or lying.

Story cleared his throat. "Miss Collins, the young woman who was murdered Thursday night bears a striking resemblance to you and was carrying a slip of paper with your name and phone number written on it in your father's handwriting. Have you any explanation?"

Meghan stiffened her back. "I have no idea why that young

woman was carrying that piece of paper. I have no idea how she got it. She did look a lot like me. For all I know my father might have met her and commented on the similarity and said, 'If you're ever in New York, I'd like you to meet my daughter.' People do resemble each other. We all know that. My father was in the kind of business where he met many people; knowing him, that would be the kind of comment he'd make. There is one thing I am sure of, if my father were alive, he would not have deliberately disappeared and left my mother financially paralyzed."

She turned to Tom. "I'm assigned to cover the Baxter arraignment. I'd better get moving."

"You okay?" Tom asked. There was no hint of pity in his manner.

"I'm absolutely fine," Meghan said quietly. She did not look at Story or Nader.

It was Nader who spoke. "Meghan, we're in touch with the FBI. If there's been any report of a missing woman who fits the description of Thursday night's stabbing victim, we'll have it soon. Maybe a lot of answers are tied up together."

15

$\mathcal{H}$elene Petrovic loved her job as embryologist in charge of the laboratory of the Manning Clinic. Widowed at twenty-seven, she had emigrated to the United States from Rumania, gratefully accepted the largess of a family friend, worked for her as a cosmetician and begun to go to school at night.

Now forty-eight, she was a slender, handsome woman whose eyes never smiled. During the week, Helene lived in New Milford, Connecticut, five miles from the clinic, in the furnished condo she rented. Weekends were spent in Lawrenceville, New Jersey, in the pleasant colonial-style house she owned. The study off her bedroom there was filled with pictures of the children she had helped bring into life.

Helene thought of herself as the chief pediatrician of a nursery for newborns on the maternity ward of a fine hospital. The difference was that the embryos in her care were more vulnerable than the frailest preemie. She took her responsibility with fierce seriousness.

Helene would look at the tiny vials in the laboratory, and, knowing the parents and sometimes the siblings, in her mind's eye she saw the children who might someday be born. She loved them all, but there was one child she loved the best, the beautiful towhead whose sweet smile reminded her of the husband she had lost as a young woman.

THE ARRAIGNMENT OF THE STOCKBROKER BAXTER ON INSIDE trader charges took place in the courthouse on Centre Street. Flanked by his two attorneys, the impeccably dressed defendant pleaded not guilty, his firm voice suggesting the authority of the boardroom. Steve was Meg's cameraman again. "What a con artist. I'd almost rather be back in Connecticut with the Munchkins."

"I wrote up a memo and left it for Tom—about doing a feature on that clinic. This afternoon I'm going to pitch it to him," Meghan said.

Steve winked. "If I ever have kids, I hope I have them the old-fashioned way, if you know what I mean."

She smiled briefly. "I know what you mean."

AT FOUR O'CLOCK, MEGHAN WAS AGAIN IN TOM'S OFFICE. "Meghan, let me get this straight. You mean this woman is about to give birth to the identical twin of her three-year-old?"

"That's exactly what I mean. That kind of divided birth has been done in England, but it's news here. Plus the mother in this case is quite interesting. Dina Anderson is a bank vice president, very attractive and well spoken, and obviously a terrific mother. And the three-year-old is a doll.

"Another point is that so many studies have shown that identical twins, even when separated at birth, grow up with identical tastes. It can be eerie. They may marry people with the same name, call their children by the same names, decorate their houses in the same colors, wear the same hairstyle, choose the same clothes. It would be interesting to know how the relationship would change if one twin is significantly older than the other.

"Think about it," she concluded. "It's only fifteen years since the miracle of the first test tube baby, and now there are thousands of them. There are more new breakthroughs in assisted reproduction methods every day. I think ongoing segments on the new methods—and updates on the Anderson twins—could be terrific."

She spoke eagerly, warming to her argument. Tom Weicker was not an easy sell.

"How sure is Mrs. Anderson that she's having the identical twin?"

"Absolutely positive. The cryopreserved embryos are in individual tubes, marked with the mother's name, Social Security number and date of her birth. And each tube is given its own number. After Jonathan's embryo was transferred, the Andersons had two embryos, his identical twin and one other. The tube with his identical twin was specially labeled."

Tom got up from his desk and stretched. He'd taken off his coat, loosened his tie and opened his collar button. The effect was to soften his usual flinty exterior.

He walked over to the window, stared down at the snarled traffic on West Fifty-sixth Street, then turned abruptly. "I liked what you did with the Manning reunion yesterday. We've gotten good response. Go ahead with it."

He was letting her do it! Meghan nodded, reminding herself that enthusiasm was out of order.

Tom went back to his desk. "Meghan, take a look at this. It's an artist's sketch of the woman who was stabbed Thursday night." He handed it to her.

Even though she had seen the victim, Meghan's mouth went dry when she looked at the sketch. She read the statistics, "Caucasian, dark brown hair, blue-green eyes, 5'6", slender build, 120 pounds, 24–28 years old." Add an inch to the height and they'd describe her.

"If that 'mistake' fax was on the level and meant you were the intended victim, it's pretty clear why this girl is dead," Weicker commented. "She was right in this neighborhood, and the resemblance to you is uncanny."

"I simply don't understand it. Nor do I understand how she got that slip of paper with my father's writing."

"I spoke to Lt. Story again. We both agreed that until the killer is found it would be better to pull you off the news beat, just in case there is some kind of nut gunning for you."

"But, Tom—" she protested. He cut her off.

"Meghan, concentrate on that feature. It could make a darned good human interest story. If it works, we'll do future segments on those kids. But as of now, you are off the news beat. Keep me posted," he snapped as he sat down and pulled out a desk drawer, clearly dismissing her.

16

By Monday afternoon, the Manning Clinic had settled down from the excitement of the weekend reunion. All traces of the festive party were gone, and the reception area was restored to its usual quiet elegance.

A couple in their late thirties was leafing through magazines as they waited for their first appointment. The receptionist, Marge Walters, looked at them sympathetically. She had had no problem having three children in the first three years of her marriage. Across the room an obviously nervous woman in her twenties was holding her husband's hand. Marge knew the young woman had an appointment to have embryos implanted in her womb. Twelve of her eggs had become fertilized in the lab. Three would be implanted in the hope that one might result in a pregnancy. Sometimes more than one embryo developed, leading to a multiple birth.

"That would be a blessing, not a problem," the young woman had assured Marge when she signed in. The other nine embryos would be cryopreserved. If a pregnancy did not result this time, the young woman would come back and be implanted with some of those embryos.

Dr. Manning had called an unexpected lunchtime staff meeting. Unconsciously, Marge riffled her fingers through short blond hair. Dr. Manning had told them that PCD Channel 3 was going to do a television special on the clinic and tie it in with the impending birth of Jonathan Anderson's identical twin. He asked that all cooperation be given to Meghan Collins, respecting of course the privacy of the clients. Only those clients who agreed in writing would be interviewed.

Marge hoped that she'd get to appear in the special. Her boys would get such a kick out of it.

To the right of her desk were the offices for senior staff. The door leading to those offices opened and one of the new secretaries came out, her step brisk. She paused at Marge's desk long enough to whisper, "Something's up. Dr. Petrovic just came out of Manning's office. She's very upset, and when I went in, he looked as though he was about to have a heart attack."

"What do you think is going on?" Marge asked.

"I don't know, but she's cleaning out her desk. I wonder if she quit—or was fired?"

"I can't imagine her choosing to leave this place," Marge said in disbelief. "That lab is her whole life."

ON MONDAY EVENING, WHEN MEGHAN PICKED UP HER CAR, Bernie had said, "See you tomorrow, Meghan."

She had told him that she wouldn't be around the office for a while, that she would be on special assignment in Connecticut. Saying that to Bernie had been easy, but as she drove home, she wrestled with the problem of how to explain to her mother that she'd been switched from the news team after just getting the job.

She'd simply have to say that the station wanted the feature to be completed quickly because of the impending birth of the Anderson baby. Mom's upset enough without having to worry that I might have been an intended murder victim, Meghan thought, and she'd be a wreck if she knew about the slip of paper with Dad's writing.

She exited Interstate 84 onto Route 7. Some trees still had leaves, although the vivid colors of mid-October had faded. Fall had always been her favorite season, she reflected. But not this year.

A part of her brain, the legal part, the portion that separated emotion from evidence, insisted that she begin to consider all the reasons why that paper with her name and phone number could have been in the dead woman's pocket. It's not disloyal to examine all the possibilities, she reminded herself fiercely. A good defense lawyer must always see the case through the prosecutor's eyes as well.

Her mother had gone through all the papers that were in the wall safe at home. But she knew her mother had not examined the contents of the desk in her father's study. It was time to do that.

She hoped she had taken care of everything at the newsroom. Before she left, Meg made a list of her ongoing assignments for Bill Evans, her counterpart from the Chicago affiliate, who would sub for her on the news team while the murder investigation was going on.

Her appointment with Dr. Manning was set for tomorrow at eleven o'clock. She'd asked him if she could go through an initial information and counseling session as though she were a new client. During a sleepless night, something else had occurred to her. It would be a nice touch to get some tape on Jonathan Anderson helping his mother prepare for the baby. She wondered if the Andersons had any home videos of Jonathan as a newborn.

When she reached home, the house was empty. That had to mean her mother was at the inn. Good, Meghan thought. It's the best place for her. She lugged in the fax machine they'd lent her at the office. She'd hook it up to the second line in her father's study. At least I won't be awakened by crazy, middle-of-the-night messages, she thought as she closed and locked the door and began switching on lights against the rapidly approaching darkness.

Meghan sighed unconsciously as she walked around the house. She'd always loved this place. The rooms weren't large. Her mother's favorite complaint was that old farmhouses always looked bigger on the outside than they actually were. "This place is an optical illusion," she would lament. But in Meghan's eyes there was great charm in the intimacy of the rooms. She liked the feel of the slightly uneven floor with its wide boards, the look of the fireplaces and the French doors and the built-in corner cupboards of the dining room. In her eyes they were the perfect setting for the antique maple furniture with its lovely warm patina, the deep comfortable upholstery, the colorful hand-hooked rugs.

Dad was away so much, she thought as she opened the door of his study, a room that she and her mother had avoided since the night of the bridge accident. But you always knew he was coming back, and he was so much fun.

She snapped on the desk lamp and sat in the swivel chair. This room was the smallest on the first floor. The fireplace was flanked by bookshelves. Her father's favorite chair, maroon leather with a matching ottoman, had a standing lamp on one side and a piecrust table on the other.

The table as well as the mantel held clusters of family pictures: her mother and father's wedding portrait; Meghan as a baby; the three of them as she grew up; old Pat, bursting with pride in front of the Drumdoe Inn. The record of a happy family, Meghan thought, looking from one to another of a group of framed snapshots.

She picked up the picture of her father's mother, Aurelia. Taken in the early thirties when she was twenty-four, it showed clearly that she had been a beautiful woman. Thick wavy hair, large expressive eyes, oval face, slender neck, sable skins over her suit. Her expression was the dreamy posed look that photographers of that day preferred. "I had the prettiest mother in Pennsylvania," her father would say, then add, "and now I have the prettiest daughter in Connecticut. You look like her." His mother had died when he was a baby.

Meghan did not remember ever having seen a picture of Richard Collins. "We never got along," her father had told her tersely. "The less I saw of him, the better."

The phone rang. It was Virginia Murphy, her mother's right-hand at the inn. "Catherine wanted me to see if you were home and if you wanted to come over for dinner."

"How is she, Virginia?" Meghan asked.

"She's always good when she's here, and we have a lot of reservations tonight. Mr. Carter is coming at seven. He wants your mother to join him."

Hmm, Meghan thought. She'd always suspected that Phillip Carter was developing a warm spot in his heart for Catherine Collins. "Will you tell Mom that I have an interview in Kent tomorrow and need to do a lot of research for it? I'll fix something here."

When she hung up, she resolutely got out her briefcase and pulled from it all the newspaper and magazine human interest stories on in vitro fertilization a researcher at the station had assembled for her. She frowned when she found several cases where a clinic was sued because tests showed the woman's husband was not the biological father of the child. "That is a pretty serious mistake to make," she said aloud, and decided that it was an angle that should be touched on in one segment of the feature.

At eight o'clock she made a sandwich and a pot of tea and carried them back to the study. She ate while she tried to absorb the technical material Mac had given her. It was, she decided, a crash course in assisted reproductive procedures.

The click of the lock a little after ten meant that her mother was home. She called, "Hi, I'm in here."

Catherine Collins hurried into the room. "Meggie, you're all right?"

"Of course. Why?"

"Just now when I was coming up the driveway I got the queerest feeling about you, that something was wrong—almost like a premonition."

Meghan forced a chuckle, got up swiftly and hugged her mother. "There *was* something wrong," she said. "I've been trying to absorb the mysteries of DNA, and believe me, it's tough. I now know why Sister Elizabeth told me I had no head for science."

She was relieved to see the tension ease from her mother's face.

HELENE PETROVIC SWALLOWED NERVOUSLY AS SHE PACKED the last of her suitcases at midnight. She left out only her toiletries and the clothes she would wear in the morning. She was frantic to be finished with it all. She had become so jumpy lately. The strain had become too much, she decided. It was time to put an end to it.

She lifted the suitcase from the bed and placed it next to the others. From the foyer, the faint click of a turning lock reached her ears. She jammed her hand against her mouth to muffle a scream. He wasn't supposed to come tonight. She turned around to face him.

"Helene?" His voice was polite. "Weren't you planning to say goodbye?"

"I . . . I was going to write you."

"That won't be necessary now."

With his right hand, he reached into his pocket. She saw the glint of metal. Then he picked up one of the bed pillows and held it in front of him. Helene did not have time to try to escape. Searing pain exploded through her head. The future that she had planned so carefully disappeared with her into the blackness.

AT FOUR A.M. THE RINGING OF THE PHONE TORE MEGHAN from sleep. She fumbled for the receiver.

A barely discernible, hoarse voice whispered, "Meg."

"Who is this?" She heard a click and knew her mother was picking up the extension.

"It's Daddy, Meg. I'm in trouble. I did something terrible."

A strangled moan made Meg fling down the receiver and rush into her mother's room. Catherine Collins was slumped on the pillow, her face ashen, her eyes closed. Meg grasped her arms. "Mom, it's some sick, crazy fool," she said urgently. "Mom!"

Her mother was unconscious.

17

At seven-thirty Tuesday morning, Mac watched his lively son leap onto the school bus. Then he got in his car for the drive to Westport. There was a nippy bite in the air, and his glasses were fogging over. He took them off, gave them a quick rub and automatically wished that he were one of the happy contact lens wearers whose smiling faces reproached him from poster-sized ads whenever he went to have his glasses adjusted or replaced.

As he drove around the bend in the road he was astonished to see Meg's white Mustang about to turn into her driveway. He tapped the horn and she braked.

He pulled up beside her. In unison they lowered their windows. His cheerful, "What are you up to?" died on his lips as he got a good look at Meghan. Her face was strained and pale, her hair disheveled, a striped pajama top visible between the lapels of her raincoat. "Meg, what's wrong?" he demanded.

"My mother's in the hospital," she said tonelessly.

A car was coming up behind her. "Go ahead," he said. "I'll follow you."

In the driveway, he hurried to open the car door for Meg. She seemed dazed. How bad is Catherine? he thought, worried. On the porch, he took Meg's house key from her hand. "Here, let me do that."

In the foyer, he put his hands on her shoulders. "Tell me."

"They thought at first she'd had a heart attack. Fortunately they were wrong, but there is a chance that she's building up to one. She's on medication to head it off. She'll be in the hospital for at least a week. They asked—get this—had she been under any stress?" An uncertain laugh became a stifled sob. She swallowed and pulled back. "I'm okay, Mac. The tests showed no heart damage as of now. She's exhausted, heartsick, worried. Rest and some sedatives are what she needs."

"I agree. Wouldn't hurt you either. Come on. You could use a cup of coffee."

She followed him into the kitchen. "I'll make it."

"Sit down. Don't you want to take your coat off?"

"I'm still cold." She attempted a smile. "How can you go out on a day like this without a coat?"

Mac glanced down at his gray tweed jacket. "My topcoat has a loose button. I can't find my sewing kit."

When the coffee was ready, he poured them each a cup and sat opposite her at the table. "I suppose with Catherine in the hospital you'll come here to sleep for a while."

"I was going to anyhow." Quietly she told him all that had been happening: about the victim who resembled her, the note that had been found in the victim's pocket, the middle-of-the-night fax. "And so," she explained, "the station wants me off the firing line for the time being, and my boss gave me the Manning Clinic assignment. And then early this morning the phone rang and . . ." She told him about the call and her mother's collapse.

Mac hoped the shock he was feeling did not show in his face. Granted, Kyle had been with them Sunday night at dinner. She might not have wanted to say anything in front of him. Even so, Meg had not even hinted that less than three days earlier she had seen a murdered woman who might have died in her place. Likewise, she had not chosen to confide in Mac about the decision of the insurers.

From the time she was ten years old and he was a college sophomore working summers at the inn, he'd been the willing confidante of her secrets, everything from how much she missed her father when he was away, to how much she hated practicing the piano.

The year and a half of Mac's marriage was the only time he hadn't seen the Collinses regularly. He'd been living here since the divorce, nearly seven years now, and believed that he and Meg were back on their big brother-little sister basis. Guess again, he thought.

Meghan was silent now, absorbed in her own thoughts, clearly neither looking for nor expecting help or advice from him. He remembered Kyle's remark: *I thought you were my friend.* The woman Kyle had seen driving past the house on Wednesday, the one he'd thought was Meghan. Was it possible that she was the woman who died a day later?

Mac decided instantly not to discuss this with Meghan until he had questioned Kyle tonight and had a chance to think. But he did have to ask her something else. "Meg, forgive me, but is there any chance however remote that it was your father calling this morning?"

"No. No. I'd know his voice. So would my mother. The one we heard was surreal, not as bad as a computer voice, but not right."

"He said he was in trouble."

"Yes."

"And the note in the stabbing victim's pocket was in his writing."

"Yes."

"Did your father ever mention anyone named Annie?"

Meghan stared at Mac.

Annie! She could hear her father teasing as he called, *Meg . . . Meggie . . . Meghan Anne . . . Annie . . .*

She thought in horror, *Annie* was always his pet name for me.

18

On Tuesday morning, from the front windows of her home in Scottsdale, Arizona, Frances Grolier could see the first glimmer of light begin to define the McDowell Mountains, light that she knew would become strong and brilliant, constantly changing the hues and tones and colors reflected on those masses of rock.

She turned and walked across the long room to the back windows. The house bordered on the vast Pima Indian reservation and offered a view of the primordial desert, stark and open, edged by Camelback Mountain; desert and mountain now mysteriously lighted in the shadowy pink glow that preceded the sunrise.

At fifty-six, Frances had somehow managed to retain a fey quality that suited her thin face, thick mass of graying brown hair and wide, compelling eyes. She never bothered to soften the deep lines around her eyes and mouth with makeup. Tall and reedy, she was most comfortable in slacks and a loose smock. She shunned personal publicity, but her work as a sculptor was known in art circles, particularly for her consummate skill in molding faces. The sensitivity with which she captured below-the-surface expressions was the hallmark of her talent.

Long ago she had made a decision and stuck by it without regret. Her lifestyle suited her well. But now . . .

She shouldn't have expected Annie to understand. She should have kept her word and told her nothing. Annie had listened to the painful explanation, her eyes wide and shocked. Then she'd walked across the room and deliberately knocked over the stand holding the bronze bust.

At Frances' horrified cry, Annie had rushed from the house, jumped in her car and driven away. That evening Frances tried to phone her daughter at her apartment in San Diego. The answering machine was on. She'd phoned every day for the last week and always got the machine. It would be just like Annie to disappear indefinitely. Last year, after she'd broken her engagement to Greg, she'd flown to Australia and backpacked for six months.

With fingers that seemed to be unable to obey the signals from her brain, Frances resumed her careful repair of the bust she had sculpted of Annie's father.

FROM THE MOMENT SHE ENTERED HIS OFFICE AT TWO o'clock on Tuesday afternoon, Meghan could sense the difference in Dr. George Manning's attitude. On Sunday, when she'd covered the reunion, he had been expansive, cooperative, proud to display the children and the clinic. On the phone yesterday, when she'd made the appointment, he'd been quietly enthusiastic. Today the doctor looked every day of his seventy years. The healthy pink complexion she had noted earlier had been replaced by a gray pallor. The hand that he extended to her had a slight tremor.

This morning, before he left for Westport, Mac had insisted that she phone the hospital and check on her mother. She was told that Mrs. Collins was sleeping and that her blood pressure had improved satisfactorily and was now in the high-normal range.

Mac. What had she seen in his eyes as he said goodbye? He'd brushed her cheek with his usual light kiss, but his eyes held another message. Pity? She didn't want it.

She'd lain down for a couple of hours, not sleeping but at least dozing, sloughing off some of the heavy-eyed numbness. Then she'd showered, a long, hot shower that took some of the achiness from her shoulders. She'd dressed in a dark green suit with a fitted jacket and calf-length skirt. She wanted to look her best. She had noticed that the adults at the Manning Clinic reunion were well dressed, then reasoned that people who could afford to spend somewhere between ten and twenty thousand dollars in the attempt to have a baby certainly had discretionary income.

At the Park Avenue firm where she'd set out to practice law, it was a rule that no casual dress was permitted. As a radio and now television reporter, Meghan had observed that people being interviewed seemed to be naturally more expansive if they felt a sense of identity with the interviewer.

She wanted Dr. Manning to subconsciously think of her and talk to her as he would to a prospective client. Now, standing in front of him, studying him, she realized that he was looking at her the way a convicted felon looked at the sentencing judge. Fear was the emotion emanating from him. But why should Dr. Manning be afraid of her?

"I'm looking forward to doing this special more than I can tell you," she said as she took the seat across the desk from him. "I—"

He interrupted. "Miss Collins, I'm afraid that we can't cooperate on any television feature. The staff and I had a meeting, and the feeling was that many of our clients would be most uncomfortable if they saw television cameras around here."

"But you were happy to have us on Sunday."

"The people who were here on Sunday have children. The women who are newcomers, or those who have not succeeded in achieving a successful pregnancy, are often anxious and depressed. Assisted reproduction is a very private matter." His voice was firm, but his eyes betrayed his nervousness. About what, she wondered?

"When we spoke on the phone," she said, "we agreed that no one would be interviewed or caught on-camera who wasn't perfectly willing to discuss being a client here."

"Miss Collins, the answer is no, and now I'm afraid I'm due at a meeting." He rose.

Meghan had no choice but to stand up with him. "What happened, Doctor?" she asked quietly. "You must know I'm aware that there's got to be a lot more to this sudden change than belated concern for your clients."

He did not reply. Meghan left the office and walked down the corridor to the reception area. She smiled warmly at the receptionist and glanced at the nameplate on the desk. "Mrs. Walters, I have a friend who'd be very interested in any literature I can give her about the clinic."

Marge Walters looked puzzled. "I guess Dr. Manning forgot to give you all the stuff he had his secretary put together for you. Let me call her. She'll bring it out."

"If you would," Meghan said. "The doctor *was* willing to cooperate with the story I've been planning."

"Of course. The staff loves the idea. It's good publicity for the clinic. Let me call Jane."

Meghan crossed her fingers, hoping Dr. Manning had not told his secretary of his decision to refuse to be involved in the planned special. Then, as she watched, Walters' expression changed from a smile to a puzzled frown. When she replaced the receiver, her open and friendly manner was gone. "Miss Collins, I guess you know that I shouldn't have asked Dr. Manning's secretary for the file."

"I'm only asking for whatever information a new client might request," Meghan said.

"You'd better take that up with Dr. Manning." She hesitated. "I don't mean to be rude, Miss Collins, but I work here. I take orders."

It was clear that there would be no help from her. Meghan turned to go, then paused. "Can you tell me this? Was there very much concern on the part of the staff about doing the feature? I mean, was it everybody or just a few who objected at the meeting?"

She could see the struggle in the other woman. Marge Walters was bursting with curiosity. The curiosity won. "Miss Collins," she whispered, "yesterday at noon we had a staff meeting and everyone applauded the news that you were doing a special. We were joking about who'd get to be on-camera. I can't imagine what changed Dr. Manning's mind."

19

*M*ac found his work in the LifeCode Research Laboratory, where he was a specialist in genetic therapy, to be rewarding, satisfying and all-absorbing.

After he left Meghan, he drove to the lab and got right to work. As the day progressed, however, he admitted to himself that he was having trouble concentrating. A dull sense of apprehension seemed to be paralyzing his brain and permeating his entire body so that his fingers, which could as second nature handle the most delicate equipment, felt heavy and clumsy. He had lunch at his desk and, as he ate, tried to analyze the tangible fear that was overwhelming him.

He called the hospital and was told that Mrs. Collins had been removed from the intensive care unit to the cardiac section. She was sleeping, and no calls were being put through.

All of which is good news, Mac thought. The cardiac section was probably only a precaution. He felt sure Catherine would be all right and the enforced rest would do her good.

It was his worry about Meghan that caused this blinding unease. Who was threatening her? Even if the incredible were true and Ed Collins was still alive, surely the danger was not coming from him.

No, his concern all came back to the victim who looked like Meghan. By the time he'd tossed out the untasted half of his sandwich and downed the last of his cold coffee, Mac knew that he would not rest until he had gone to the morgue in New York to see that woman's body.

STOPPING AT THE HOSPITAL ON HIS WAY HOME THAT EVEning, Mac saw Catherine, who was clearly sedated. Her speech was markedly slower than her usual spirited delivery. "Isn't this nonsense, Mac?" she asked.

He pulled up a chair. "Even stalwart daughters of Erin are allowed time out every now and then, Catherine."

Her smile was acknowledgment. "I guess I've been traveling on nerve for a while. You know everything, I suppose."

"Yes."

"Meggie just left. She's going over to the inn. Mac, that new chef I hired! I swear he must have trained at a takeout joint. I'll have to get rid of him." Her face clouded. "That is, if I can figure a way to hang on to Drumdoe."

"I think you'd better put aside that kind of worry for at least a little while."

She sighed. "I know. It's just that I can *do* something about a bad chef. I can't *do* anything about insurers who won't pay and nuts who call in the middle of the night. Meg said that kind of sick call is just a sign of the times, but it's so rotten, so upsetting. She's shrugging it off, but you can understand why I'm worried."

"Trust Meg." Mac felt like a hypocrite as he tried to sound reassuring.

A few minutes later he stood up to go. He kissed Catherine's forehead. Her smile had a touch of resiliency. "I have a great idea. When I fire the chef, I'll send him over to this place. Compared to what they served me for dinner, he comes through like Escoffier."

MARIE DILEO, THE DAILY HOUSEKEEPER, WAS SETTING THE table when Mac got home, and Kyle was sprawled on the floor doing his homework. Mac pulled Kyle up on the couch beside him. "Hey, fellow, tell me something. The other day, how much of a look did you get at the woman you thought was Meg?"

"A pretty good look," Kyle replied. "Meg came over this afternoon."

"She did?"

"Yes. She wanted to see why I was mad at her."

"And you told her?"

"Uh-huh."

"What'd she say?"

"Oh, just that Wednesday afternoon she was in court and that sometimes when people are on television other people like to see where they live. That stuff. Just like you, she asked how good a look I got at that lady. And I told her that the lady was driving very, very slow. That's why when I saw her, I ran down the driveway and I called to her. And she stopped the car and looked at me and rolled down the window and then she just took off."

"You didn't tell me all that."

"I said that she saw me and then drove away fast."

"You didn't say she stopped and rolled down the window, pal."

"Uh-huh. I *thought* she was Meg. But her hair was longer. I told Meg that too. You know, it was around her shoulders. Like that picture of Mommy."

Ginger had sent Kyle one of her recent publicity pictures, a head shot with her blond hair swirling around her shoulders, her lips parted, revealing perfect teeth, her eyes wide and sensuous. In the corner she'd written, "To my darling little Kyle, Love and kisses, Mommy."

A publicity picture, Mac had thought in disgust. If he'd been home when it arrived, Kyle would never have seen it.

AFTER STOPPING TO SEE KYLE, VISITING HER MOTHER AND checking on the inn, Meghan arrived home at seven-thirty. Virginia had insisted on sending dinner home with her, a chicken potpie, salad and the warm salty rolls Meghan loved. "You're as bad as your mother," Virginia had fussed. "You'll forget to eat."

I probably would have, Meghan thought as she changed quickly into old pajamas and a robe. It was an outfit that dated back to college days and was still her favorite for an early, quiet evening of reading or watching television.

In the kitchen, she sipped a glass of wine and nibbled on the salt roll as the microwave oven zapped the temperature of the potpie to steaming hot.

When it was ready, she carried it on a tray into the study and settled down in her father's swivel chair. Tomorrow she would begin digging into the history of the Manning Clinic. Researchers at the television station could quickly come up with all the background available on it. And on Dr. Manning, she thought. I'd like to know if there are any skeletons in *his* closet, she told herself.

Tonight she had a different project in mind, however. She absolutely had to find any shred of evidence that might link her father to the dead woman who resembled her, the woman whose name might be Annie.

A suspicion had insinuated itself into her mind, a suspicion so incredible that she could not bring herself to consider it yet. She only knew that it was absolutely essential to go through all her father's personal papers immediately.

Not surprisingly the desk drawers were neat. Edwin Collins had been innately tidy. Writing paper, envelopes and stamps were precisely placed in the slotted side drawer. His day-at-a-glance calendar was filled out for January and early February. After that, only standing dates were entered. Her mother's birthday. Her birthday. The spring golf club outing. A cruise her parents had planned to take to celebrate their thirtieth wedding anniversary in June.

Why would anyone who was planning to disappear mark his calendar for important dates months in advance? she wondered. That didn't make sense.

The days he had been away in January or had planned to be away in February simply carried the name of a city. She knew the details of those trips would have been listed in the business appointment book he carried with him.

The deep bottom drawer on the right was locked. Meghan searched in vain for a key, then hesitated. Tomorrow she might be able to get a locksmith, but she did not want to wait. She went into the kitchen, found the toolbox and brought back a steel file. As she hoped, the lock was old and easily forced open.

In this drawer stacks of envelopes were held together by rubber bands. Meghan picked up the top packet and glanced through it. All except the first envelope were written in the same hand.

That one contained only a newspaper clipping from the *Philadelphia Bulletin.* Below the picture of a handsome woman, the obituary notice read:

Aurelia Crowley Collins, 75, a lifelong resident of Philadelphia, died in St. Paul's Hospital on 9 December of heart failure.

Aurelia Crowley Collins! Meghan gasped as she studied the picture. The wide-set eyes, the wavy hair that framed the oval face. It was the same woman, now aged, whose portrait was prominently placed on the table a few feet away. *Her grandmother.*

The date on the clipping was two years old. Her grandmother had been alive until two years ago! Meghan leafed through the other envelopes in the packet she was holding. They all came from Philadelphia. The last one was postmarked two and a half years ago.

She read one, then another, and another. Unbelieving, she went through the other stacks of envelopes. At random, she kept reading. The earliest note went back thirty years. All contained the same plea.

Dear Edwin,
    I had hoped that perhaps this Christmas I might have word from you. I pray that you and your family are well. How I would love to see my granddaughter. Perhaps someday you will allow that to happen.
                                With love,
                                Mother

Dear Edwin,
    We are always supposed to look ahead. But as one grows older, it is much easier to look back and bitterly regret the mistakes of the past. Isn't it possible for us to talk, even on the telephone? It would give me so much happiness.
                                Love,
                                Mother

After a while Meg could not bear to read any more, but it was clear from their worn appearance that her father must have pored over them many times.

Dad, you were so kind, she thought. Why did you tell everyone your mother was dead? What did she do to you that was so unforgivable? Why did you keep these letters if you were never going to make peace with her?

She picked up the envelope that had contained the obituary

notice. There was no name, but the address printed on the flap was a street in Chestnut Hill. She knew that Chestnut Hill was one of Philadelphia's most exclusive residential areas.

Who was the sender? More important, what kind of man had her father really been?

20

*I*n Helene Petrovic's charming colonial home in Lawrenceville, New Jersey, her niece, Stephanie, was cross and worried. The baby was due in a few weeks, and her back hurt. She was always tired. As a surprise, she had gone to the trouble of preparing a hot lunch for Helene, who had said she planned to get home by noon.

At one-thirty, Stephanie had tried to phone her aunt, but there was no answer at the Connecticut apartment. Now, at six o'clock, Helene had still not arrived. Was anything wrong? Perhaps some last-minute errands came up and Helene had lived alone so long she was not used to keeping someone else informed of her movements.

Stephanie had been shocked when on the phone yesterday Helene told her that she had quit her job, effective immediately. "I need a rest and I'm worried about you being alone so much," Helene had told her.

The fact was that Stephanie loved being alone. She had never known the luxury of being able to lie in bed until she decided to make coffee and get the paper that had been delivered in the predawn hours. On really lazy days, still resting in bed, she would eventually watch the morning television programs.

She was twenty but looked older. Growing up, it had been her dream to be like her father's younger sister, Helene, who had left for the United States twenty years ago, after her husband died.

Now that same Helene was her anchor, her future, in a world that no longer existed as she knew it. The bloody, brief revolution in Rumania had cost her parents their lives and destroyed their home. Stephanie had moved in with neighbors whose tiny house had no room for another occupant.

Over the years, Helene had occasionally sent a little money and a gift package at Christmas. In desperation, Stephanie had written to her imploring help.

A few weeks later she was on the plane to the United States.

Helene was so kind. It was just that Stephanie fiercely wanted to live in Manhattan, get a job in a beauty salon and go to cosmetician school at night. Already her English was excellent, though she'd arrived here last year knowing only a few English words.

Her time had almost come. She and Helene had looked at studio apartments in New York. They found one in Greenwich Village that would be available in January, and Helene had promised they would go shopping to decorate it.

This house was on the market. Helene had always said she was not going to give up her job and the place in Connecticut until it sold. What had made her change her mind so abruptly now, Stephanie wondered?

She brushed back the light brown hair from her broad forehead. She was hungry again and might as well eat. She could always warm up dinner for Helene when she arrived.

At eight o'clock, as she was smiling at a rerun of *The Golden Girls,* the front door bell pealed.

Her sigh was both relieved and vexed. Helene probably had an armful of packages and didn't want to search for her

key. She gave a last look at the set. The program was about
to end. After being so late, couldn't Helene have waited one
more minute? she wondered as she hoisted herself up from
the couch.

Her welcoming smile faded and vanished at the sight of a
tall policeman with a boyish face. In disbelief she heard that
Helene Petrovic had been shot to death in Connecticut.

Before grief and shock encompassed her, Stephanie's one
clear thought was to frantically ask herself, *what will become
of me?* Only last week Helene had talked about her intention
of changing her will, which left everything she had to the
Manning Clinic Research Foundation. Now it was too late.

21

*B*y eight o'clock on Tuesday evening, traffic in the garage had slowed down to a trickle. Bernie, who frequently
worked overtime, had put in a twelve hour day and it was
time to go home.

He didn't mind the overtime. The pay was good and so
were the tips. All these years the extra money had paid for
his electronic equipment.

This evening when he went to the office to check out he
was worried. He hadn't realized the big boss was on the
premises when at lunchtime that day he'd sat in Tom
Weicker's car and flipped through the glove compartment
again for possible items of interest. Then he'd looked up to
see the boss staring through the car window. The boss had
just walked away, not saying a word. That was even worse.
If he'd snarled at him it would have cleared the air.

Bernie punched the time clock. The evening manager was sitting in the office and called him over. His face wasn't friendly. "Bernie, clean out your locker." He had an envelope in his hand. "This covers salary, vacation and sick days and two weeks severance."

"But . . . " The protest died on Bernie's lips as the manager raised a hand.

"Listen, Bernie, you know as well as I do that we've had complaints of money and personal items disappearing from cars that were parked in this garage."

"I never took a thing."

"You had no damn business going through Weicker's glove compartment, Bernie. You're through."

When he got home, still angry and upset, Bernie found that his mother had a frozen macaroni and cheese dinner ready to be put in the microwave. "It's been a terrible day," she complained as she took the wrapper off the package. "The kids from down the block were yelling in front of the house. I told them to shut up and they called me an old bat. You know what I did?" She did not wait for an answer. "I called the cops and complained. Then one of them came over, and he was rude to me."

Bernie grasped her arm. "You brought the cops in here, Mama? Did they go downstairs?"

"Why would they go downstairs?"

"Mama, I don't want the cops in here, ever."

"Bernie, I haven't been downstairs in years. You're keeping it clean down there, aren't you? I don't want dust filtering up. My sinuses are terrible."

"It's clean, Mama."

"I hope so. You're not a neat person. Like your father." She slammed the door of the microwave. "You hurt my arm. You grabbed it hard. Don't do that again."

"I won't, Mama. I'm sorry, Mama."

THE NEXT MORNING, BERNIE LEFT FOR WORK AT THE USUAL time. He didn't want his mother to know he got fired. Today, however, he headed for a car wash a few blocks from the house. He paid to have the full treatment on his eight-year-old Chevy. Vacuum, clean out trunk, polish the dashboard, wash, wax. When the car came out, it was still shabby but respectable, the basic dark green color recognizable.

He never cleaned his car except for the few times a year his mother announced she was planning to go to church on the following Sunday. Of course it would be different if he were taking Meghan for a ride. He'd really have it shining for her.

Bernie knew what he was going to do. He had thought about it all night. Maybe there was a reason he'd lost the job at the garage. Maybe it was all part of a greater plan. For weeks it hadn't been enough to see Meghan only in the few minutes when she dropped off or picked up her Mustang or a Channel 3 car.

He wanted to be around her, to take pictures of her that he could play during the night on his VCR.

Today he'd buy a video camera on Forty-seventh Street.

But he had to make money. No one was a better driver, so he could earn it by using his car as a gypsy cab. That would give him a lot of freedom too. Freedom to drive to Connecticut where Meghan Collins lived when she wasn't in New York.

He had to be careful not to be noticed.

"It's called 'obsession,' Bernie," the shrink at Riker's Island had explained when Bernie begged to know what was wrong with him. "I think we've helped you, but if that feeling comes over you again, I want you to talk to me. It will mean that you might need some medication."

Bernie knew he didn't need any help. He just needed to be around Meghan Collins.

22

The body of Helene Petrovic lay all Tuesday in the bedroom where she had died. Never friendly with her neighbors, she'd already said goodbye to the few with whom she exchanged greetings, and her car was hidden from sight in the garage of her rented condo.

It was only when the owner of the condo stopped by late that afternoon that she found the dead woman at the foot of the bed.

The death of a quiet embryologist in New Milford, Connecticut, was briefly mentioned on New York television news programs. It wasn't much of a story. There was no evidence of a break-in, no apparent sexual attack. The victim's purse with two hundred dollars in it was in the room, so robbery was ruled out.

A neighbor across the street volunteered that Helene Petrovic had one visitor she'd observed, a man who always came late at night. She'd never really gotten a good look at him but knew he was tall. She figured he was a boyfriend, because he always pulled his car into the other side of Petrovic's garage. She knew he had to have left during the night, because she'd never seen him in the morning. How often had she seen him? Maybe a half-dozen times. The car? A late model dark sedan.

AFTER THE DISCOVERY OF HER GRANDMOTHER'S OBITUARY notice, Meghan had phoned the hospital and was told that her mother was sleeping and that her condition was satisfactory. Tired to the bone, she'd rummaged through the medicine cabinet for a sleeping pill, then gone to bed and slept straight through until her alarm woke her at 6:30 A.M.

An immediate call to the hospital reassured her that her mother had had a restful night and her vital signs were normal.

Meghan read the *Times* over coffee, and in the Connecticut section was shocked to read of the death of Dr. Helene Petrovic. There was a picture of the woman. In it, the expression in her eyes was both sad and enigmatic. I talked with her at Manning, Meghan thought. She was in charge of the lab with the cryopreserved embryos. Who had murdered that quiet, intelligent woman? Meghan wondered. Another thought struck her. According to the paper, Dr. Petrovic had quit her job and had planned on moving from Connecticut the next morning. Did her decision have anything to do with Dr. Manning's refusal to cooperate on the television special?

It was too early to call Tom Weicker, but it probably wasn't too late to catch Mac before he left for work. Meghan knew there was something else she had to face, and now was as good a time as any.

Mac's hello was hurried.

"Mac, I'm sorry. I know this is a bad time to call but I have to talk to you," Meghan said.

"Hi, Meg. Sure. Just hang on a minute."

He must have put his hand over the phone. She heard his muffled but exasperated call, "Kyle, you left your homework on the dining room table."

When he got back on he explained, "We go through this every morning. I tell him to put his homework in his schoolbag at night. He doesn't. In the morning he's yelling that he lost it."

"Why don't *you* put it in his schoolbag at night?"

"That doesn't build character." His voice changed. "Meg, how's your mother?"

"Good. I really think she's okay. She's a strong lady."

"Like you."

"I'm not that strong."

"Too strong for my taste, not telling me about that stabbing victim. But that's a conversation we'll have another time."

"Mac, could you stop by for three minutes on your way out?"

"Sure. As soon as His Nibs gets on the bus."

MEGHAN KNEW THAT SHE HAD NO MORE THAN TWENTY MINutes to shower and dress before Mac arrived. She was brushing her hair when the bell rang. "Have a quick cup of coffee," she said. "What I'm about to ask isn't easy."

Was it only twenty-four hours ago they had sat across from each other at this table? she wondered. It seemed so much longer. But yesterday she'd been in near-shock. Today, knowing her mother was almost certainly all right, she was able to face and accept whatever stark truth came to light.

"Mac," she began, "you're a DNA specialist."

"Yes."

"The woman who was stabbed Thursday night, the one who resembles me so much?"

"Yes."

"If her DNA was compared to mine, could kinship be established?"

Mac raised his eyebrows and studied the cup in his hand. "Meg, this is the way it works. With DNA testing we can positively know if any two people had the same mother. It's complicated, and I can show you in the lab how we do it. Within the ninety-ninth percentile we can establish if two people had the same father. It's not as absolute as the mother-child scenario, but we can get a very strong indication of whether or not we're dealing with half siblings."

"Can that test be done on me and the dead woman?"

"Yes."

"You don't seem surprised that I'm asking about it, Mac."

He put down the coffee cup and looked at her squarely. "Meg, I already had decided to go to the morgue and see that woman's body this afternoon. They have a DNA lab in the medical examiner's office. I was planning to make sure they were preserving a sample of her blood before she's removed to potter's field."

Meg bit her lip. "Then you're thinking in the same direction I am." She blinked her eyes to blot out the vivid memory of the dead woman's face. "I have to see Phillip this morning and stop in at the hospital," she continued. "I'll meet you at the medical examiner's. What time is good for you?"

They agreed to meet around two o'clock. As Mac drove away he reflected that there was no good time to look down at the dead face of a woman who resembled Meghan Collins.

23

Phillip Carter heard the news report detailing Dr. Helene Petrovic's death on his way to the office. He made a mental note to have Victor Orsini follow up immediately on the vacancy her death had left at Manning Clinic. She had, after all, been hired at Manning through Collins and Carter. Those jobs paid well, and there would be another good fee if Collins and Carter was commissioned to find a replacement.

He arrived at the office at a quarter of nine and spotted Meghan's car parked in one of the stalls near the entrance of the building. She had obviously been waiting for him, because she got out of her car as he parked.

"Meg, what a nice surprise." He put an arm around her.

"But for goodness sake, you have a key. Why didn't you go inside?"

Meg smiled briefly. "I've just been here a minute." Besides, she thought, I'd feel like an intruder walking in.

"Catherine's all right, isn't she?" he asked.

"Doing really well."

"Thank God for that," he said heartily.

The small reception room was pleasant with its brightly slipcovered couch and chair, circular coffee table and paneled walls. Meghan once again had a reaction of intense sadness as she hurried through it. This time they went into Phillip's office. He seemed to sense that she did not want to go into her father's office again.

He helped her off with her coat. "Coffee?"

"No thanks. I've had three cups already."

He settled behind his desk. "And I'm trying to cut down, so I'll wait. Meg, you look pretty troubled."

"I am." Meghan moistened her lips. "Phillip, I'm beginning to think I didn't know my father at all."

"In what way?"

She told him about the letters and the obituary notice she had found in the locked drawer, then watched as Phillip's expression changed from concern to disbelief.

"Meg, I don't know what to tell you," he said when she finished. "I've known your father for years. Ever since I can remember, I've understood that his mother died when he was a kid, his father remarried and he had a lousy childhood, living with the father and stepmother. When my father was dying, your dad said something I never forgot. He said, 'I envy you being able to mourn a parent.' "

"Then you never knew either?"

"No, of course not."

"The point is, why did he have to lie about it?" Meg asked, her voice rising. She clasped her hands together and bit her lip. "I mean, why not tell my mother the truth? What did he have to gain by deceiving her?"

"Think about it, Meg. He met your mother, told her his

family background as he'd told it to everyone else. When they started getting interested in each other it would have been pretty difficult to admit he'd lied to her. And can you imagine your grandfather's reaction if he'd learned that your father was ignoring his own mother for whatever reason?"

"Yes, I can see that. But Pop's been dead for so many years. Why couldn't he . . . ?" Her voice trailed off.

"Meg, when you start living a lie, it gets harder with every passing day to straighten it out."

Meghan heard the sound of voices in the outside office. She stood up. "Can we keep this between us?"

"Of course."

He got up with her. "What are you going to do?"

"As soon as I'm sure Mother is okay I'm going to the address in Chestnut Hill that was on the envelope with the obituary notice. Maybe I'll get some answers there."

"How's the feature story on the Manning Clinic going?"

"It's not. They're stonewalling me. I've got to find a different in vitro facility to use. Wait a minute. You or Dad placed someone at Manning, didn't you?"

"Your dad handled it. As a matter of fact, it's that poor woman who was shot yesterday."

"Dr. Petrovic? I met her last week."

The intercom buzzed. Phillip Carter picked up the phone. "Who? All right, I'll take it."

"A reporter from the *New York Post,*" he explained to Meghan. "God knows what they want of me."

Meghan watched as Phillip Carter's face darkened. "That's absolutely impossible." His voice was husky with outrage. "I . . . I will not comment until I have personally spoken with Dr. Iovino at New York Hospital."

He replaced the receiver and turned to Meghan. "Meg, that reporter has been checking on Helene Petrovic. They never heard of her at New York Hospital. Her credentials were fraudulent, and we're responsible for her getting the job in the laboratory at Manning."

"But didn't you check her references before you submitted her to the clinic?"

Even as she asked the question, Meghan knew the answer, she could see it in Phillip's face. Her father had handled Helene Petrovic's file. It would have been up to him to validate the information on her curriculum vitae.

24

*D*espite the best efforts of the entire staff of the Manning Clinic there was no hiding the tension that permeated the atmosphere. Several new clients watched uneasily as a van with a CBS television logo on the sides pulled into the parking area and a reporter and cameraman hurried up the walkway.

Marge Walters was at her receptionist best, firm with the reporter. "Dr. Manning declines to be interviewed until he has investigated the allegations," she said. She was unable to stop the cameraman, who began to videotape the room and its occupants.

Several clients stood up. Marge rushed over to them. "This is all a misunderstanding," she pleaded, suddenly realizing she was being recorded.

One woman, her hands shielding her face, exploded in anger. "This is an outrage. It's tough enough to have to resort to this kind of procedure to have a baby without being on the eleven o'clock news." She ran from the room.

Another said, "Mrs. Walters, I'm leaving too. You'd better cancel my appointment."

"I understand." Marge forced a sympathetic smile. "When would you like to reschedule?"

"I'll have to check my appointment book. I'll call."

Marge watched the retreating women. No you won't, she thought. Alarmed, she noticed Mrs. Kaplan, a client on her second visit to the clinic, approach the reporter.

"What's this all about?" she demanded.

"What it's all about is that the person in charge of the Manning Clinic lab for the last six years apparently was not a doctor. In fact her only training seems to have been as a cosmetologist."

"My God. My sister had in vitro fertilization here two years ago. Is there any chance she didn't receive her own embryo?" Mrs. Kaplan clenched her hands together.

God help us, Marge thought. That's the end of this place. She'd been shocked and saddened when she heard on the morning news of Dr. Helene Petrovic's death. It was only when she arrived at work an hour ago that she'd heard the rumor of something being wrong with Petrovic's credentials. But hearing the reporter's stark statement and watching Mrs. Kaplan's response made her realize the enormity of the possible consequences.

Helene Petrovic had been in charge of the cryopreserved embryos. Dozens upon dozens of test tubes, no bigger than half an index finger, each one containing a potentially viable human being. Mislabel even one of them and the wrong embryo might be implanted in a woman's womb, making her a host mother, but not the biological mother of a child.

Marge watched the Kaplan woman rush from the room followed by the reporter. She looked out the window. More news vans were pulling in. More reporters were attempting to question the women who had just left the reception area.

She saw the reporter from PCD Channel 3 getting out of a car. Meghan Collins. That was her name. She was the one who'd been planning to do the television special that Dr. Manning called off so abruptly . . .

MEGHAN WAS NOT SURE IF SHE REALLY SHOULD BE HERE, especially since her father's name was certain to come up in

the course of the investigation into Helene Petrovic's credentials. As she left Phillip Carter's office she'd been beeped by
the news desk and told that Steve, her cameraman, would
meet her at the Manning Clinic. "Weicker okayed it," she
was assured.

She'd tried to reach Weicker earlier, but he was not yet in.
She felt she had to speak to him about the possible conflict
of interest. It was easier for the moment, however, to simply
accept the assignment. The odds were that the lawyers for
the clinic would not permit any interviews with Dr. Manning
anyway.

She did not attempt to join the rest of the media in flinging
questions to the departing clients. Instead she spotted Steve
and motioned for him to follow her inside. She opened the
door quietly. As she had hoped, Marge Walters was at her
desk, speaking urgently into the phone. "We've got to cancel
all of today's appointments," she was insisting. "You'd better
tell them in there that they've got to make some kind of
statement. Otherwise the only thing the public is going to see
is women bolting out of here."

As the door closed behind Steve, Walters looked up. "I
can't talk anymore," she said hurriedly and clicked down the
receiver.

Meghan did not speak until she was settled in the chair
across from Walters' desk. The situation required tact and
careful handling. She had learned not to fire questions at a
defensive interviewee. "This is a pretty rough morning for
you, Mrs. Walters," she said soothingly.

She watched as the receptionist brushed a hand over her
forehead. "You bet it is."

The woman's tone was guarded, but Meghan sensed in her
the same conflict she had noticed yesterday. She realized the
need for discretion, but she was dying to talk to someone
about all that had been going on. Marge Walters was a born
gossip.

"I met Dr. Petrovic at the reunion," Meghan said. "She
seemed like a lovely person."

"She was," Walters agreed. "It's hard to believe she wasn't qualified for the job she was doing. But her early medical training was probably in Rumania. With all the changes in government over there, I'll bet anything they find out she had all the degrees she needed. I don't understand about New York Hospital saying she didn't train there. I bet that's a mistake too. But finding that out may come too late. This bad publicity will ruin this place."

"It could," Meghan agreed. "Do you think that her quitting had something to do with Dr. Manning's decision to cancel our session yesterday?"

Walters looked at the camera Steve was holding.

Quickly Meghan added, "If you can tell me anything that will balance all this negative news I'd like to include it."

Marge Walters made up her mind. She trusted Meghan Collins. "Then let me tell you that Helene Petrovic was one of the most wonderful, hardest working people I've ever met. No one was happier than she when an embryo was brought to term in its mother's womb. She loved every single embryo in that lab and used to insist on having the emergency generator tested regularly to be sure that in case of power failure the temperature would stay constant."

Walters' eyes misted. "I remember Dr. Manning telling us at a staff meeting last year how he'd rushed to the clinic during that terrible snowstorm in December, when all the electricity went down, to make sure the emergency generator was working. Guess who arrived a minute behind him? Helene Petrovic. And she hated driving in snow or ice. It was a special fear of hers, yet she drove here in that storm. She was that dedicated."

"You're telling me exactly what I felt when I interviewed her," Meghan commented. "She seemed to be a very caring person. I could see it in the way she was interacting with the children during the picture session on Sunday."

"I missed that. I had to go to a family wedding that day. Can you turn off the camera now?"

"Of course." Meghan nodded to Steve.

Walters shook her head. "I wanted to be here. But my cousin Dodie finally married her boyfriend. They've only been living together for eight years. You should have heard my aunt. You'd think a nineteen-year-old out of convent school was the bride. I swear to God the night before the wedding I bet she told Dodie how babies come to be born."

Walters grimaced as the incongruity of her remark in this clinic occurred to her. "How most of them come to be born, I mean."

"Is there any chance I can see Dr. Manning?" Meghan knew if there was a chance it was through this woman.

Walters shook her head. "Just between us, an assistant state attorney and some investigators are with him now."

That wasn't surprising. Certainly they were looking into Helene Petrovic's abrupt departure from the clinic and asking questions about her personal life. "Did Helene have any particularly close friends here?"

"No. Not really. She was very nice but a little formal— you know what I mean. I thought maybe it was because she was from Rumania. Although when you think about it, the Gabor women came from there, and they've had more than their share of close friends, especially Zsa Zsa."

"I'm quite sure the Gabors are Hungarian, not Rumanian. So Helene Petrovic didn't have any particular friends or an intimate relationship you're aware of?"

"The nearest to it was Dr. Williams. He used to be Dr. Manning's assistant, and I wondered if there wasn't a little something going on between him and Helene. I saw them at dinner one night when my husband and I went to a little out-of-the-way place. They didn't look happy when I stopped by their table to say hello. But that was just one time six years ago, right after she started working here. I have to say I kept my eye on them after that and they never acted at all special to each other."

"Is Dr. Williams still here?"

"No. He was offered a job to open and run a new facility and he took it. It's the Franklin Center in Philadelphia. It has a wonderful reputation. Between us, Dr. Williams was a top-drawer manager. He put together the whole medical team here, and believe me, he did a terrific job."

"Then he was the one who hired Petrovic?"

"Technically, but they always hire the top staff through one of those headhunter outfits that recruits and screens them for us. Even so, Dr. Williams worked here for about six months after Helene came on staff, and believe me, he'd have noticed if she seemed incompetent."

"I'd like to talk with him, Mrs. Walters."

"Please call me Marge. I wish you *would* talk to him. He'd tell you how wonderful Helene was in that lab."

Meghan heard the front door opening. Walters looked up. "More cameras! Meghan, I'd better not say any more."

Meghan stood up. "You've been a great help."

Driving home, Meghan reflected that she would not give Dr. Williams the chance to put her off over the phone. She'd go to the Franklin Center in Philadelphia and try to see him. With luck she could persuade him to tape an interview for the in vitro feature.

What would he have to say about Helene Petrovic? Would he defend her, like Marge Walters? Or would he be outraged that Petrovic had managed to deceive him, as she had deceived all her other colleagues?

And, Meghan wondered, what would she learn at her other stop in the Philadelphia area? The house in Chestnut Hill, from which someone had notified her father of his mother's death.

25

*V*ictor Orsini and Phillip Carter never socialized for lunch. Orsini knew that Carter considered him to be Edwin Collins' protégé. When the job at Collins and Carter had come up nearly seven years ago it had been between Orsini and another candidate. Orsini had been Ed Collins' choice. From the beginning his relationship with Carter was cordial, but never warm.

Today, however, after they had both ordered the baked sole and house salad, Orsini was in full sympathy with Carter's obvious distress. There had been reporters in the office and a dozen phone calls from the media asking how it was possible that Collins and Carter had not detected the lies in Helene Petrovic's curriculum vitae.

"I told them the simple truth," Phillip Carter said as he drummed his fingers nervously on the tablecloth. "Ed always researched prospective candidates meticulously, and it was his case. It only adds fuel to the fire that Ed is missing and the police are openly saying they don't believe he died in the bridge accident."

"Does Jackie remember anything about the Petrovic case?" Orsini asked.

"She'd just started working for us then. Her initials are on the letter, but she has no memory of it. Why should she? It was a usual glowing recommendation attached to the curriculum vitae. After he received it Dr. Manning had a meeting with Petrovic and hired her."

Orsini said, "Of all the fields in which to have been caught verifying fraudulent references, medical research is about the worst."

"Yes, it is," Phillip agreed. "If any mistakes were made by Helene Petrovic and the Manning Clinic is sued, there's a damn good chance the clinic will sue us."

"And win."

Carter nodded glumly. "And win." He paused. "Victor, you worked more directly with Ed than you did with me. When he called you from the car phone that night, he talked about wanting to meet with you in the morning. Was that all he said?"

"Yes, that's all. Why?"

"Damn it, Victor," Phillip Carter snapped, "let's stop playing games! If Ed did manage to get over the bridge safely, do you have any inkling from that conversation whether he might have been in the state of mind to use the accident as his opportunity to disappear?"

"Look, Phillip, he said he wanted to make sure I was in the office in the morning," Orsini replied, his voice taking on an edge. "It was a lousy connection. That's all I can tell you."

"I'm sorry. I keep looking for anything that might start to make sense." Carter sighed. "Victor, I've been meaning to speak to you. Meghan is clearing out Ed's personal things from his office on Saturday. I want you to take that office as of Monday. We haven't had a great year but we can certainly refurbish it within reason."

"Don't worry about that right now."

They had little else to say to each other.

Orsini noticed that Phillip Carter did not hint that after the matter of Ed Collins' legal situation was somehow straightened out, he would offer Orsini a partnership. He knew that offer would never be made. For his part it was only a matter of weeks before the position he'd almost gotten on the Coast last year became available again. The guy they'd hired for the job didn't work out. This time Orsini was being offered a bigger salary, a vice presidency and stock options.

He wished that he could leave today. Pack up and fly out there right now. But under the circumstances that was impossible. There was something he wanted to find, something he wanted to check out at the office, and now that he could move into Ed's old office, the search might be easier.

26

*B*ernie stopped at a diner on Route 7 just outside Danbury. He settled on a stool at the counter and ordered the deluxe hamburger, French fries and coffee. Increasingly content as he munched and swallowed, he reviewed with satisfaction the busy hours he'd spent since he left home this morning.

After the car was cleaned up, he'd purchased a chauffeur's hat and dark jacket at a secondhand store in lower Manhattan. He'd reasoned that outfit would give him a leg up on all the other gypsy cabs in New York. Then he'd headed for La Guardia Airport and stood near the baggage area, with the other chauffeurs waiting to make pickups.

He lucked out right away. Some guy about thirty or so came down the escalator and searched the name cards drivers were holding. There was no one waiting for him. Bernie could read the guy's mind. He'd probably hired a driver from one of the dirt-cheap services and was kicking himself. Most of the drivers from those places were guys who had just arrived in New York and spent their first six months on the job getting lost.

Bernie had approached the man, offered to take him into the city, warned that he didn't have a fancy limo but a nice clean car and bragged he was the best driver anyone could hire. He quoted a price of twenty bucks to drive the fellow to West Forty-eighth Street. He got him there in thirty-five minutes and received a ten-dollar tip. "You are a hell of a driver," the man said as he paid.

Bernie remembered the compliment with pleasure as he reached for a French fry and smiled to himself. If he kept making money this way, adding it to his severance and vacation pay, he could last a long time before Mama knew he wasn't at the old job. She never called him there. She didn't like talking on the phone. She said it gave her one of her headaches.

And here he was, free as a bird, not accountable to anyone and out to see where Meghan Collins lived. He had bought a street map of the Newtown area and studied it. The Collins house was on Bayberry Road, and he knew how to get there.

At exactly two o'clock he was driving slowly past the white-shingled house with the black shutters. His eyes narrowed as he drank in every detail. The large porch. Nice. Kind of elegant. He thought of the people next door to his house in Jackson Heights who had poured concrete over most of their minuscule backyard and now grandly referred to the lumpy surface as their patio.

Bernie studied the grounds. There was a huge rhododendron at the left corner of the macadam driveway, a weeping willow off center in the middle of the lawn. Evergreens made a vivid hedge separating the Collins place from the next property.

Well satisfied, Bernie leaned his foot on the accelerator. In case he was being watched, he certainly wouldn't be dope enough to do a U-turn here. He drove around the bend, then jammed on his brakes. He'd almost hit a stupid dog.

A kid came flying across the lawn. Through the window, Bernie could hear him frantically calling the dog. "Jake! Jake!"

The dog ran to the kid, and Bernie was able to start up the car again. The street was quiet enough that through the closed window, he could hear the kid yell, "Thanks, mister. Thanks a lot."

. . .

MAC ARRIVED AT THE MEDICAL EXAMINER'S OFFICE ON EAST Thirty-first Street at one-thirty. Meghan was not due until two o'clock, but he had phoned and made an appointment with Dr. Kenneth Lyons, the director of the lab. He was escorted to the fifth floor, where in Dr. Lyons' small office, he explained his suspicions.

Lyons was a lean man in his late forties with a ready smile and keen, intelligent eyes. "That woman has been a puzzle. She certainly didn't have the look of someone who would simply disappear and not be missed. We were planning to take a DNA sample from her before the body is taken to potter's field anyway. It will be very simple to take a sample from Miss Collins as well and see if there's the possibility of kinship."

"That's what Meghan wants to do."

The doctor's secretary was seated at a desk near the window. The phone rang and she picked it up. "Miss Collins is downstairs."

It wasn't just the normal apprehension of viewing a dead body in the morgue that Mac saw in Meghan's face as he stepped from the elevator. Something else had added to the pain in her eyes, the drawn, tired lines around her mouth. It seemed to him that there was a sadness in her that was removed from the grief she had lived with since her father's disappearance.

But she smiled when she saw him, a quick, relieved smile. She's so pretty, he thought. Her chestnut hair was tousled around her head, a testament to the sharp afternoon wind. She was wearing a black-and-white tweed suit and black boots. The zippered jacket reached her hips, the narrow skirt was calf length. A black turtleneck sweater accentuated the paleness of her face.

Mac introduced her to Dr. Lyons. "You'll be able to study the victim more closely downstairs than in the viewing room," Lyons said.

The morgue was antiseptically clean. Rows of lockers lined the walls. The murmur of voices could be heard from behind the closed door of a room with an eight-foot window on the corridor. The curtains were drawn over the window. Mac was sure an autopsy was being performed.

An attendant led them down the corridor almost to the end. Dr. Lyons nodded to him and he reached for the handle of a drawer.

Noiselessly, the drawer slid out. Mac stared down at the nude, refrigerated body of the young woman. There was a single deep stab wound in her chest. Slender arms lay at her sides; her fingers were open. He took in the narrow waist, slim hips, long legs, high-arched feet. Finally he studied the face.

The chestnut hair was matted on her shoulders, but he could imagine it with the same wind-tossed life as Meghan's hair. The mouth, generous and with the promise of warmth, the thick eyelashes that arched over the closed eyes, the dark brows that accentuated the high forehead.

Mac felt as though a violent punch had caught him in the stomach. He felt dazed, nauseated, light-headed. This could be Meg, he thought, *this was meant to happen to Meg.*

27

*C*atherine Collins touched the button at her hand, and the hospital bed tilted noiselessly up until she stopped it at a semireclining position. For the last hour, since the lunch tray was taken out, she had tried to sleep, but it was useless. She was irritated at herself for her desire to escape into sleep. It's time to face up to life, my girl, she told herself sternly.

She wished she had a calculator and the account books of the inn. She needed to figure out for herself how long she could hold on before she was forced to sell Drumdoe. The mortgage, she thought—that damn mortgage! Pop would never have put so much money in the place. Do without and make do, that had been his slogan when he was a greenhorn. How often had she heard that?

But once he got his inn and his house he'd been the most generous husband and father. Provided you weren't ridiculously extravagant, of course.

And I was ridiculous giving that decorator so much leeway, Catherine thought. But that's water under the bridge.

The analogy made her shiver. It brought to mind the horrible photographs of wrecked cars being hauled to the surface from under the Tappan Zee Bridge. She and Meghan had studied the photos with magnifying glasses, dreading to find what they were expecting to see: some part of a dark blue Cadillac.

Catherine threw back the covers, got out of bed and reached for her robe. She walked across the room to the tiny bathroom and splashed water on her face, then looked in the mirror and grimaced. Put on a little war paint, dear, she told herself.

Ten minutes later she was back in bed and feeling somewhat better. Her short blond hair was brushed; blusher on her cheeks and lipstick had camouflaged the gaunt pallor she had seen in the mirror; a blue silk bed jacket made her feel presentable to possible visitors. She knew Meghan was in New York for the afternoon, but there was always the chance someone else might drop by.

Someone did. Phillip Carter tapped on the partially open door. "Catherine, may I come in?"

"You bet."

He bent down and kissed her cheek. "You look much better."

"I feel much better. In fact I'm trying to get out of here, but they want me to stay a couple of days more."

"Good idea." He pulled the one comfortable chair close to the bed and sat down.

He was wearing a casual tan jacket, dark brown slacks and a brown-and-beige print tie, Catherine noticed. His strong male presence made her ache for her husband.

Edwin had been strikingly handsome. She had met him thirty-one years ago, at a party after a Harvard-Yale football game. She was dating one of the Yale players. She had noticed Ed on the dance floor. The dark hair, the deep blue eyes, the tall thin body.

The next dance, Edwin had cut in on her, and the next day he was ringing the bell at the farmhouse, a dozen roses in his hand. "I'm courting you, Catherine," he'd announced.

Now Catherine tried to blink back sudden tears.

"Catherine?" Phillip's hand was holding hers.

"I'm fine," she said, withdrawing her hand.

"I don't think you'll feel that way in a few minutes. I wish I could have spoken to Meg before I came."

"She had to go into the city. What is it, Phillip?"

"Catherine, you may have read about the woman who was murdered in New Milford."

"That doctor. Yes. How awful."

"Then you haven't heard that she wasn't a doctor, that her credentials were falsified and that she was placed at the Manning Clinic by our company?"

Catherine bolted up. "What?"

A nurse hurried in. "Mrs. Collins, there are two investigators from the New Milford police in the lobby who need to speak with you. The doctor is on his way. He wants to be here but said I should warn you they'll be up in a few minutes."

Catherine waited until she heard retreating footsteps in the corridor before she asked, "Phillip, you know why those people are here."

"Yes, I do. They were in the office an hour ago."

"Why? Forget about waiting for the doctor. I have no intention of collapsing again. Please, I do need to know what I'm facing."

"Catherine, the woman who was murdered last night in New Milford was Ed's client. Ed had to have known her credentials were falsified." Phillip Carter turned away as though to avoid seeing the pain he knew he was going to inflict. "You know that the police don't think Ed was drowned in the bridge accident. A neighbor who lives across the street from Helene Petrovic's apartment said Petrovic was visited regularly late at night by a tall man who drove a dark sedan." He paused, his expression grim. "She saw him there two weeks ago. Catherine, when Meg called the ambulance the other night a squad car came as well. When you came to, you told the policeman you'd had a call from your husband."

Catherine tried to swallow but could not. Her mouth and lips were parched. She had the incongruous thought that this is what it must be like to experience severe thirst. "I was out of it. I meant to say Meg had a call from someone saying he was her father."

There was a tap on the door. The doctor spoke as he came in. "Catherine, I'm terribly sorry about this. The assistant state attorney insists that the investigators of a murder in New Milford ask you a few questions, and I could not in conscience say you weren't well enough to see them."

"I'm well enough to see them," Catherine said quietly. She looked at Phillip. "Will you stay?"

"I certainly will." He got up as the investigators followed a nurse into the room.

Catherine's first impression was surprise that one of them was a woman, a young woman around Meghan's age. The other was a man she judged to be in his late thirties. It was he who spoke first, apologizing for the intrusion, promising to take only a few moments of her time, introducing himself and his partner. "This is Special Investigator Arlene Weiss. I'm Bob Marron." He got straight to the point. "Mrs. Collins, you were brought here in shock because your daughter received a phone call in the middle of the night from someone who claimed to be your husband?"

"It wasn't my husband. I'd know his voice anywhere, under any circumstances."

"Mrs. Collins, I'm sorry to ask you this, but do you still believe your husband died last January?"

"I absolutely believe he is dead," she said firmly.

"Beautiful roses for you, Mrs. Collins," a voice chirped as the door was pushed open. It was one of the volunteers in pink jackets who delivered flowers to the rooms, brought around the book cart and helped feed the elderly patients.

"Not now," Catherine's doctor snapped.

"No, it's all right. Just put them on the nightstand." Catherine realized she welcomed the intrusion. She needed a moment to get hold of herself. Again stalling for time, she reached for the card the volunteer was detaching from the ribbon on the vase.

She glanced at it, then froze, her eyes filled with horror. As everyone stared at her, she held up the card with trembling fingers, fighting to retain her composure. "I didn't know dead people could send flowers," she whispered.

She read it aloud. " 'My dearest. Have faith in me. I promise this will all work out.' " Catherine bit her lip. "It's signed, 'Your loving husband, Edwin.' "

Part Two

28

On Wednesday afternoon, investigators from Connecticut drove to Lawrenceville, New Jersey, to question Stephanie Petrovic about her murdered aunt.

Trying to ignore the restless stirring in her womb, Stephanie clasped her hands together to keep them from trembling. Having grown up in Rumania under the Ceauşescu regime, she had been trained to fear the police, and even though the men who were sitting in her aunt's living room seemed very kind and were not wearing uniforms, she knew enough not to trust them. People who trusted the police often ended up in prison, or worse.

Her aunt's lawyer, Charles Potters, was there as well, a man who reminded her of an official of the village where she had been born. He too was being kind, but she sensed that his kindness was of the impersonal variety. He would do his duty and he had already informed her that his duty was to carry out the terms of Helene's will, which left her entire estate to the Manning Clinic.

"She intended to change it," Stephanie had told him. "She planned to take care of me, to help me while I went to cosmetology school, to get me an apartment. She promised she would leave money to me. She said I was like a daughter to her."

"I understand. But since she did not change her will, the only thing I can say is that until this house is sold you may live in it. As trustee, I can probably arrange to hire you as a caretaker until a sale is completed. After that, I'm afraid, legally you're on your own."

On her own! Stephanie knew that unless she could get a green card and a job there was no way she could stay in this country.

One of the policemen asked if there were any man who had been her aunt's particular friend.

"No. Not really," she answered. "Sometimes in the evening we go to parties given by other Rumanians. Sometimes Helene would go to concerts. Often on Saturday or Sunday, she would go out for three or four hours. She never told me where." But Stephanie knew of no man at all in her aunt's life. She told again how surprised she had been when Helene abruptly quit her job. "She was planning to give up work as soon as she sold her house. She wanted to move to France for a while." Stephanie knew she was stumbling over the English words. She was so afraid.

"According to Dr. Manning, he had no inkling that she was contemplating leaving the clinic," the investigator named Hugo said in Rumanian.

Stephanie flashed a look of gratitude at him and switched to her native language as well. "She told me that Dr. Manning would be very upset and she dreaded breaking the news to him."

"Did she have another job in mind? It would have meant her credentials being checked again."

"She said she wanted to take some time off to rest."

Hugo turned to the lawyer. "What was Helene Petrovic's financial situation?"

Charles Potters answered, "I can assure you it was quite good. Doctor, or rather Ms. Petrovic lived very carefully and made good investments. This house was paid off, and she had eight hundred thousand dollars in stocks, bonds and cash."

So much money, Stephanie thought, and now she would not have a penny of it. She rubbed her hand across her forehead. Her back hurt. Her feet were swollen. She was so tired. Mr. Potters was helping her arrange the funeral mass. It would be held at St. Dominic's on Friday.

She looked around. This room was so pretty, with its blue brocaded upholstery, polished tables, fringed lamps and pale blue carpet. This whole house was so pretty. She'd liked being in a place like this. Helene had promised that she could take some things from here for her apartment in New York. What would she do now? What was the policeman asking?

"When do you expect your baby, Stephanie?"

Tears gushed down her cheeks as she answered. "In two weeks." She burst out, "He told me it was my problem and he's moved to California. He won't help me. I don't know where to find him. I don't know what to do."

29

The shock that Meghan had felt at once again seeing the dead woman who resembled her had dulled by the time a vial of blood was drawn from her arm.

She did not know quite what reaction she expected from Mac when he viewed the body. The only one she had detected was a tightening of his lips. The only comment he made was that he found the resemblance so startling he felt the DNA comparison was absolutely necessary. Dr. Lyons voiced the same opinion.

Neither she nor Mac had eaten lunch. They left the medical examiner's office in separate cars and drove to one of Meg's favorite spots, Neary's on Fifty-seventh Street. Seated side by side on a banquette in the cozy restaurant, over a club sandwich and coffee, Meghan told Mac about Helene Petrovic's falsified credentials and her father's possible involvement.

Jimmy Neary came over to inquire about Meghan's mother. When he learned Catherine was in the hospital, he brought his portable phone to the table for Meghan to call her.

Phillip answered.

"Hi, Phillip," Meghan said. "Just thought I'd phone and see how Mom is doing. Would you put her on, please?"

"Meg, she's had a pretty nasty shock."

"What kind of shock?" Meghan demanded.

"Somebody sent her a dozen roses. You'll understand when I read the card to you."

Mac had been looking across the room at the framed pictures of the Irish countryside. At Meghan's gasp, he turned to her, then watched as her eyes widened in shock. Something's happened to Catherine, he thought. "Meg, what is it?" He took the phone from her shaking fingers. "Hello . . ."

"Mac, I'm glad you're there."

It was Phillip Carter's voice, even now, sounding confident and in charge.

Mac put his arm around Meghan as Carter tersely related the events of the past hour. "I'm staying with Catherine for a while," he concluded. "She was pretty upset at first, but she's calmer now. She says she wants to speak to Meg."

"Meg, it's your mother," Mac said, holding the receiver out to her. For a moment he wasn't sure Meghan had heard him, but then she reached for the phone. He could see the effort she was making to sound matter-of-fact.

"Mom, you're sure you're okay? . . . What do I think? I think it's some kind of cruel joke too. You're right, Dad would never do anything like that. . . . I know . . . I know how tough it is. . . . Come on, you certainly do have the strength to handle this. You're old Pat's daughter, aren't you?

"I have an appointment with Mr. Weicker at the station in an hour. Then I'll come directly to the hospital. . . . Love you too. Let me talk to Phillip for a minute.

"Phillip, stay with her, won't you? She shouldn't be alone now. . . . Thanks."

When Meg replaced the receiver, she cried, "It's a miracle my mother didn't have a full-blown heart attack, what with investigators asking about Dad and those roses being delivered." Her mouth quivered and she bit her lip.

Oh, Meg, Mac thought. He ached to put his arms around her, to hold her to him, to kiss the pain from her eyes and lips. Instead he tried to reassure her about the primary fear that he knew was paralyzing her.

"Catherine isn't going to have a heart attack," he said firmly. "At least put that worry out of your mind. I mean it, Meg. Now, did I get it right from Phillip that the police are trying to tie your dad to that Petrovic woman's death?"

"Apparently. They kept coming back to the neighbor who said a tall man with a dark late-model sedan visited Petrovic regularly. Dad was tall. He drove a dark sedan."

"So do thousands of other tall men, Meg. That's ridiculous."

"I know it is. Mom knows it too. But the police categorically don't believe Dad was in the bridge accident, which means to them that he's probably still alive. They want to know why he vouched for Petrovic's falsified credentials. They asked Mom if she thought he might have had some kind of personal relationship with Petrovic."

"Do you believe that he's alive, Meg?"

"No, I don't. But if he put Helene Petrovic in that job knowing she was a fraud, something was wrong. Unless she somehow fooled him too."

"Meg, I've known your father since I was a college freshman. If there's one point on which I can reassure you, it's that Edwin Collins is or was a very gentle man. What you told Catherine is absolutely true. That middle-of-the-night phone call and sending those flowers your mother received just aren't things your father would have done. They're the kind of games cruel people play."

"Or demented people." Meghan straightened up as though just aware of Mac's arm around her. Quietly, Mac removed it.

He said, "Meg, flowers have to be paid for, with cash, with a credit card, with a charge account. How was the payment for the roses handled?"

"I gather the investigators are hot onto that scenario."

Jimmy Neary offered an Irish coffee.

Meghan shook her head. "I sure could use one, Jimmy, but we'd better take a rain check. I have to get to the office."

Mac was going back to work. Before they got into their cars, he put his hands on her shoulders. "Meg, one thing. Promise me you'll let me help."

"Oh, Mac," she sighed, "I think you've had your share of the Collins family's problems for a while. How long did Dr. Lyons say it would take to get the results of the DNA comparison?"

"Four to six weeks," Mac said. "I'll call you tonight, Meg."

HALF AN HOUR LATER, MEGHAN WAS SITTING IN TOM Weicker's office. "That was a hell of a good interview with the receptionist at the Manning Clinic," he told her. "No one else has anything like it. But in view of your father's connection to Petrovic, I don't want you to go near that place again."

It was what she expected to hear. She looked squarely at him. "The Franklin Center in Philadelphia has a terrific reputation. I'd like to substitute that in vitro facility for Manning in the feature." She waited, dreading to hear that he was pulling her off that too.

She was relieved when he said, "I want the feature completed as soon as possible. Everybody's buzzing about in vitro fertilization because of Petrovic. The timing is great. When can you go to Philadelphia?"

"Tomorrow."

She felt dishonest not telling Tom that Dr. Henry Williams, who headed the Franklin Center, had worked with Helene Petrovic at Manning. But, she reasoned, if she had any chance of getting in to talk to Williams it would be as a PCD reporter, not as the daughter of the man who had submitted Petrovic's bogus résumé and glowingly recommended her.

BERNIE DROVE TO MANHATTAN FROM CONNECTICUT. SEEING Meghan's house brought back memories of all the other times he'd followed a girl home, then hidden in her car or garage or even in the shrubbery around her house, just so he could watch her. It was like being in a different world where it was just the two of them alive, even though the girl didn't know he was there.

He knew he had to be near Meghan, but he'd have to be careful. Newtown was a ritzy little community, and cops in places like that were always on the lookout for strange cars driving around a neighborhood.

Suppose I'd hit that dog, Bernie thought as he drove through the Bronx toward the Willis Avenue bridge. The kid who owned it probably would have started yelling his head off. People would have rushed out to see what happened. One of them might have started asking questions, like what's a guy in a gypsy cab doing in this neighborhood, on a dead end street? If somebody'd called the cops, they might have checked my record, Bernie thought. He knew what that would mean.

There was only one thing for him to do. When he got to midtown Manhattan, he drove to the discount shop on Forty-seventh Street where he acquired most of his electronic gadgets. For a long time he'd had his eye on a real state-of-

the-art video camera there. Today he bought that and a police scanner radio for the car.

He then went to an art supply store and bought sheets of
pink paper. This year pink was the color of the press passes
the police issued to the media. He had one at home. A reporter had dropped it in the garage. On his computer, he
could copy it and make up a press pass that looked official,
and he'd also make himself a press parking permit to stick in
his windshield.

There were bunches of local cable stations around that no
one paid any attention to. He'd say he was from one of them.
He'd be Bernie Heffernan, news reporter.

Just like Meghan.

The only problem was, he was going through his vacation
and severance pay too fast. He had to keep money coming
in. Fortunately he managed to pick up a fare to Kennedy
Airport and one back into the city before it was time to go
home.

AT DINNER HIS MOTHER WAS SNEEZING. "ARE YOU GETTING
a cold, Mama?" he asked solicitously.

"I don't get colds. I just have allergies," she snapped. "I
think there's dust in this house."

"Mama, you know there's no dust here. You're a good
housekeeper."

"Bernard, are you keeping the basement clean? I'm trust-
ing you. I don't dare attempt those stairs after what happened."

"Mama, it's fine."

They watched the six o'clock news together and saw
Meghan Collins interviewing the receptionist at the Manning
Clinic.

Bernie leaned forward, drinking in Meghan's profile as she
asked questions. His hands and forehead grew damp.

Then the remote selector was yanked from his hand. As
the television clicked off, he felt a stinging slap on his face.

"You're starting again, Bernard," his mother screamed. "You're watching that girl. I can tell. I can just tell! Don't you ever learn?"

WHEN MEGHAN GOT TO THE HOSPITAL, SHE FOUND HER mother fully dressed. "Virginia brought me some clothes. I've got to get out of here," Catherine Collins said firmly. "I can't just lie in this bed and think. It's too unsettling. At least at the inn I'll be busy."

"What did the doctor say?"

"At first he objected, of course, but now he agrees, or at least he's willing to sign me out." Her voice faltered. "Meggie, don't try to change my mind. It really is better if I'm home."

Meghan hugged her fiercely. "Are you packed yet?"

"Down to the toothbrush. Meg, one more thing. Those investigators want to talk to you. When we get home, you have to call and set up an appointment with them."

THE PHONE WAS RINGING WHEN MEGHAN PUSHED OPEN THE front door of the house. She ran to get it. It was Dina Anderson. "Meghan. If you're still interested in being around when the baby is born, start making plans. The doctor is going to put me into Danbury Medical Center on Monday morning and induce labor."

"I'll be there. Is it all right if I come up Sunday afternoon with a cameraman and take some pictures of you and Jonathan getting ready for the baby?"

"That will be fine."

CATHERINE COLLINS WENT FROM ROOM TO ROOM, TURNING on the lights. "It's so good to be home," she murmured.

"Do you want to lie down?"

"That's the last thing in the world I want to do. I'm going

to soak in a tub and get properly dressed and then we're going to have dinner at the inn."

"Are you sure?" Meghan watched as her mother's chin went up and her mouth settled in a firm line.

"I'm very sure. Things are going to get a lot worse before they get better, Meg. You'll see that when you talk to those investigators. But no one is going to think that we're hiding out."

"I think Pop's exact words were, 'Don't let the bastards get you.' I'd better call those people from the state attorney's office."

JOHN DWYER WAS THE ASSISTANT STATE ATTORNEY ASSIGNED to the Danbury courthouse. His jurisdiction included the town of New Milford.

At forty, Dwyer had been in the state attorney's office for fifteen years. During those years, he'd sent some upstanding citizens, pillars of the community, to prison for crimes ranging from fraud to murder. He'd also prosecuted three people who'd faked their deaths in an attempt to collect insurance.

Edwin Collins' supposed death in the Tappan Zee Bridge tragedy had generated much sympathetic coverage in the local media. The family was well known in the area, and the Drumdoe Inn was an institution.

The fact that Collins' car almost certainly had not gone over the side of the bridge and his role in the verification of Helene Petrovic's bogus credentials had changed a shocking suburban murder to a statewide scandal. Dwyer knew that the State Department of Health was sending medical investigators to the Manning Clinic to determine how much damage Petrovic might have done in the lab there.

Late Wednesday afternoon, Dwyer had a meeting in his office with the investigators from the New Milford police, Arlene Weiss and Bob Marron. They had managed to get Petrovic's file from the State Department in Washington.

Weiss reviewed the specifics of it for him. "Petrovic came

to the United States twenty years ago, when she was twenty-seven. Her sponsor ran a beauty salon on Broadway. Her visa application lists her education as high school graduate with some training at a cosmetology school in Bucharest."

"No medical training?" Dwyer asked.

"None that she listed," Weiss confirmed.

Bob Marron looked at his notes. "She went to work at her friend's salon, stayed there eleven years and in the last couple took secretarial courses at night."

Dwyer nodded.

"Then she was offered a job as a secretary at the Dowling Assisted Reproduction Center in Trenton, New Jersey. That's when she bought the Lawrenceville house.

"Three years later, Collins placed her at the Manning Clinic as an embryologist."

"What about Edwin Collins? Does his background check out?" Dwyer asked.

"Yes. He's a Harvard Business graduate. Never been in trouble. Senior partner in the firm. Got a gun permit about ten years ago after he was held up at a red light in Bridgeport."

The intercom buzzed. "Miss Collins returning Mr. Marron's call."

"That's Collins' daughter?" Dwyer asked.

"Yes."

"Get her in here tomorrow."

Marron took the phone and spoke to Meghan, then looked at the assistant state attorney. "Eight o'clock tomorrow morning all right? She's driving to Philadelphia on assignment and needs to come in early."

Dwyer nodded.

After Marron confirmed the appointment with Meghan and replaced the receiver, Dwyer leaned back in his swivel chair. "Let's see what we have. Edwin Collins disappeared and is presumed dead. But now his wife receives flowers from him, which you tell me were charged to his credit card."

"The order was phoned in to the florist. The credit card

has never been canceled. On the other hand, until this afternoon, it hasn't been used since January," Weiss said.

"Wasn't it tagged after his disappearance to see if there was activity on the account?"

"Until the other day, Collins was presumed to have drowned. There was no reason to put an alert on his cards."

Arlene Weiss was looking over her notes. "I want to ask Meghan Collins about something her mother said. That phone call that landed Mrs. Collins in the hospital, the one that she swears didn't sound like her husband . . ."

"What about it?"

"She thought she heard the caller say something like, 'I'm in terrible trouble.' What did that mean?"

"We'll ask the daughter what she thinks when we talk to her tomorrow," Dwyer said. "I know what I think. Is Edwin Collins still listed as missing-presumed-dead?"

Marron and Weiss nodded together. Assistant State Attorney Dwyer got up. "We probably should change that. Here's the way I see it. One, we've established Collins' connection to Petrovic. Two, he almost certainly did not die in the bridge accident. Three, he took all the cash value from his insurance policies a few weeks before he disappeared. Four, no trace of his car has been found, but a tall man in a dark sedan regularly visited the Petrovic woman. Five, the phone call, the use of the credit card, the flowers. I say it's enough. Put out an APB on Edwin Collins. Make it, 'Wanted for questioning in the murder of Helene Petrovic.' "

30

$\mathcal{J}$ust before five o'clock, Victor Orsini received the call he was afraid might come. Larry Downes, president of Downes and Rosen, phoned to tell him that it would be better all around if he held off giving notice at Collins and Carter.

"For how long, Larry?" Victor asked quietly.

"I don't know," Downes said evasively. "This fuss about the Petrovic woman will all die down eventually, but you have too much negative feedback attached to you for you to come here now. And if it turns out that Petrovic mixed up any of those embryos at the clinic, there'll be hell to pay, and you know it. You guys placed her there, and you'll be held responsible."

Victor protested. "I'd just started when Helene Petrovic's application was submitted to the Manning Clinic. Larry, you let me down last winter."

"I'm sorry, Victor. But the fact is, you were there six weeks before Petrovic began working at Manning. That means you were there when the investigation into her credentials should have been taking place. Collins and Carter is a small operation. Who's going to believe you weren't aware of what was going on?"

Orsini swallowed. When he spoke to the reporters he'd said that he'd never heard of Petrovic, that he'd barely been hired when she was okayed for Manning. They hadn't picked up that he'd obviously been in the office when her application was processed. He tried one more argument. "Larry, I've helped you people a lot this year."

"Have you, Victor?"

"You placed candidates with three of our best accounts."

"Perhaps our candidates for the jobs were stronger."

"Who told you those corporations were looking to fill positions?"

"I'm sorry, Victor."

Orsini stared at the receiver as the line went dead. Don't call us. We'll call you, he thought. He knew the job with Downes and Rosen probably would never be given to him now.

Milly poked her head into his office. "I'm on my way. Hasn't it been a terrible day, Mr. Orsini? All those reporters coming in and all those calls." Her eyes were snapping with excitement.

Victor could just see her at her dinner table tonight, repeating with relish every detail of the day. "Is Mr. Carter back?"

"No. He phoned that he was going to stay with Mrs. Collins at the hospital and then go directly home. You know, I think he's getting sweet on her."

Orsini did not answer.

"Well, good night, Mr. Orsini."

"Good night, Milly."

WHILE HER MOTHER WAS DRESSING, MEGHAN SLIPPED INTO the study and took the letters and obituary notice from the drawer in her father's desk. She hid them in her briefcase and prayed her mother would not notice the faint scratches on the desk where the file had slipped when she was breaking into the drawer. Meghan would have to tell her about the letters and the death notice eventually, but not yet. Maybe after she'd been to Philadelphia she might have some sort of explanation.

She went upstairs to her own bathroom to wash her face and hands and freshen her makeup. After hesitating a moment, she decided to call Mac. He had said he'd call her, and she didn't want him to think anything was wrong. More wrong than it already is, she corrected herself.

Kyle answered. "Meg!" It was the Kyle she knew, delighted to hear her voice.

"Hi, pal. How's it going?"

"Great. But today was really bad."

"Why?"

"Jake nearly got killed. I was throwing a ball to him. He's getting real good at catching it, but I threw too hard and it went in the street and he ran out and some guy almost hit him. I mean you should have seen the guy stop his car. Like just *stop.* That car *shook.*"

"I'm glad Jake's okay, Kyle. Next time toss the ball to him in the backyard. You've got more room."

"That's what Dad said. He's grabbing the phone, Meg. See you."

Mac came on. "I was *not* grabbing it. I reached for it. Hi, Meg. You've gotten all the news from this end. How's it going?"

She told him that her mother was home. "I'm driving to Philadelphia tomorrow for the feature I'm trying to put together."

"Will you also check out that address in Chestnut Hill?"

"Yes. Mother doesn't know about that or those letters."

"She won't hear it from me. When will you get back?"

"Probably not before eight o'clock. It's nearly a four-hour drive to Philadelphia."

"Meg." Mac's voice became hesitant. "I know that you don't want me interfering, but I wish you'd let me help. I sense sometimes that you're avoiding me."

"Don't be silly. We've always been good buddies."

"I'm not sure we are anymore. Maybe I've missed something. What happened?"

What happened, Meghan thought, is that I can't think of that letter I wrote you nine years ago, begging you not to marry Ginger, without writhing in humiliation. What happened is that I'll never be anything more than your little buddy and I've managed to separate myself from you. I can't risk going through Jeremy MacIntyre withdrawal again.

"Nothing happened, Mac," she said lightly. "You're still

my buddy. I can't help it if I don't talk about piano lessons anymore. I gave them up years ago."

THAT NIGHT WHEN SHE WENT TO HER MOTHER'S ROOM TO turn down the bed she switched the ringer on the phone to the off position. If there were any more nocturnal calls, they would be heard only by her.

31

D r. Henry Williams, the sixty-five-year-old head of the Franklin Assisted Reproduction Center in the renovated old town section of Philadelphia, was a man who looked vaguely like everyone's favorite uncle. He had a head of thick graying hair, a gentle face that reassured even the most nervous patient. Very tall, he had a slight stoop that suggested he was in the habit of bending down to listen.

Meghan had phoned him after her meeting with Tom Weicker, and he had readily agreed to an appointment. Now Meghan sat in front of his desk in the cheerful office with its framed pictures of babies and young children covering the walls.

"Are these all children born through in vitro fertilization?" Meghan asked.

"Born through assisted reproduction," Williams corrected. "Not all are in vitro births."

"I understand, or at least I believe I do. In vitro is when

the eggs are removed from the ovaries and fertilized with semen in the laboratory."

"Correct. You realize that the woman has been given fertility drugs so that her ovaries will release a number of eggs at the same time?"

"Yes. I understand that."

"There are other procedures we practice, all variations of in vitro fertilization. I suggest I give you some literature that explains them. Basically it amounts to a lot of heavy-duty terms that all boil down to assisting a woman to have the successful pregnancy she craves."

"Would you be willing to be interviewed on-camera, to let us do some footage on the facilities and speak to some of your clients?"

"Yes. Frankly we're proud of our operation, and favorable publicity is welcome. I would have one stipulation. I'll contact several of our clients and ask if they'd be willing to speak to you. I don't want you approaching them. Some people do not choose to let their families know that they have used assisted birth procedures."

"Why would they object? I should think they'd just be happy to have the baby."

"They are. But one woman whose mother-in-law learned about the assisted birth openly said that, because of her son's very low sperm count, she doubted if it was her son's child. Our client actually had DNA testing done on her, the husband and the baby to prove it was the biological offspring of both parents."

"Some people do use donor embryos, of course."

"Yes, those who simply cannot conceive on their own. It's actually a form of adoption."

"I guess it is. Doctor, I know this is a terrible rush, but could I come back late this afternoon with a cameraman? A woman in Connecticut is giving birth very soon to the identical twin of her son who was born three years ago through in vitro fertilization. We'll be doing follow-up stories on the progress of the children."

Williams' expression changed, becoming troubled. "Sometimes I wonder if we don't go too far. The psychological aspects of identical twins being born at separate times concerns me greatly. Incidentally, when the embryo splits in two and one is cryopreserved, we call it the clone, not the identical twin. But to answer your question, yes, I'd be available later today."

"I can't tell you how grateful I am. We'll do some establishing shots outside and in the reception area. I'll lead in with when the Franklin Center started. That's about six years ago, I understand."

"Six years ago this past September."

"Then I'll stick to specific questions about in vitro fertilization and the freezing, I mean cryopreservation, of the clone, as in Mrs. Anderson's case."

Meghan got up to go. "I've got some fast arrangements to make. Would four o'clock be all right for you?"

"It should be fine."

Meghan hesitated. She had been afraid to ask Dr. Williams about Helene Petrovic before she established some rapport with him, but she could not wait any longer. "Dr. Williams, I don't know if the papers here have carried the story, but Helene Petrovic, a woman who worked in the Manning Clinic, was found murdered, and it's come out that her credentials were falsified. You knew her and actually worked with her, didn't you?"

"Yes, I did." Henry Williams shook his head. "I was Dr. Manning's assistant, and I knew everything that went on in that clinic and who was doing the job. Helene Petrovic certainly fooled me. She kept that lab the way labs should be kept. It's terrible that she falsified credentials, but she absolutely seemed to know what she was doing."

Meghan decided to take a chance that this kindly man would understand why she needed to ask probing questions. "Doctor, my father's firm and specifically my father have been accused of verifying Helene Petrovic's lies. Forgive me, but I must try to find out more about her. The receptionist at

Manning Clinic saw you and Helene Petrovic at dinner. How well did you get to know her?"

Henry Williams looked amused. "You mean Marge Walters. Did she also tell you that as a courtesy I always took a new staff member at Manning to dinner? An informal welcome . . ."

"No, she didn't. Did you know Helene Petrovic before she went to Manning?"

"No."

"Have you had any contact with her since you left?"

"None at all."

The intercom buzzed. He picked up the receiver and listened. "Hold it for a moment, please," he said, turning to Meghan.

She took her cue. "Doctor, I won't take any more of your time. Thank you so much." Meghan picked up her shoulder bag and left.

When the door closed behind her, Dr. Henry Williams again put the receiver to his ear. "Put the call through now, please."

He murmured a greeting, listened, then said nervously, "Yes, of course I'm alone. She just left. She'll be back at four with a cameraman. Don't tell me to be careful. What kind of fool do you take me for?"

He replaced the receiver, suddenly infinitely weary. After a moment, he picked it up again and dialed. "Everything under control over there?" he asked.

HER SCOTTISH ANCESTORS CALLED IT SECOND SIGHT. THE gift had turned up in a woman in different generations of Clan Campbell. This time it was Fiona Campbell Black who was granted it. A psychic who was regularly called upon by police departments throughout the country to help solve crimes and by families frantic to find missing loved ones, Fiona treated her extraordinary abilities with profound respect.

Married twenty years, she lived in Litchfield, Connecticut, a lovely old town that was settled in the early seventeenth century.

On Thursday afternoon Fiona's husband, Andrew Black, a lawyer with offices in town, came home for lunch. He found her sitting in the breakfast room, the morning paper spread in front of her, her eyes reflective, her head tilted as though she were expecting to hear a voice or sound she did not want to miss.

Andrew Black knew what that meant. He took off his coat, tossed it on a chair and said, "I'll fix us something."

Ten minutes later when he came back with a plate of sandwiches and a pot of tea, Fiona raised her eyebrows. "It happened when I saw this." She held up the local newspaper with Edwin Collins' picture on the front page. "They want this man for questioning in the Petrovic woman's death."

Black poured the tea. "I read that."

"Andrew, I don't want to get involved, but I think I have to. I'm getting a message about him."

"How clear is it?"

"It isn't. I have to handle something that belongs to him. Should I call the New Milford police or go directly to his family?"

"I think it's better to go through the police."

"I suppose so." Slowly, Fiona ran her fingertips over the grainy reproduction of Edwin Collins' face. "So much evil," she murmured, "so much death and evil surrounding him."

32

*B*ernie's first fare on Thursday morning was from Kennedy Airport. He parked the Chevy and wandered over to where the suburban buses picked up and deposited passengers. Bernie glanced at the schedule. A bus for Westport was due in, and a group of people were waiting for it. One couple in their thirties had two small kids and a lot of luggage. Bernie decided that they'd be good prospects.

"Connecticut?" he asked them, his smile genial.

"We're not taking a cab," the woman snapped impatiently as she grabbed the two-year-old's hand. "Billy, stay with me," she scolded. "You can't run around here."

"Forty bucks plus tolls," Bernie said. "I've got a pickup around Westport, so any fare I get is found money."

The husband was trying to hang onto a squirming three-year-old. "You've got a deal." He did not bother to look to his wife for approval.

Bernie had run his car through the car wash and vacuumed the interior again. He saw the disdain that initially flashed on the woman's face turn to approval at the Chevy's clean interior. He drove carefully, never above the speed limit, no quick changes from lane to lane. The man sat in front with him. The woman was in the back, the kids strapped in beside her. Bernie made a mental note to buy some car seats and keep them in the trunk.

The man directed Bernie to Exit 17 off the Connecticut Turnpike. "It's just a mile and a half from here." When they reached the pleasant brick home on Tuxedo Road, Bernie was rewarded with a ten dollar tip.

He drove back to the Connecticut Turnpike, south to Exit 15 and once again got on Route 7. It was as though he couldn't stop the car from going to where Meghan lived. Be careful, he tried to tell himself. Even with the camera and the press pass it might look suspicious for him to be on her street.

He decided to have a cup of coffee and think about it. He pulled in at the next diner. There was a newspaper vending machine in the vestibule between the outer and inner doors. Through the glass, Bernie saw the headline, all about the Manning Clinic. That was where Meghan had done the interview yesterday, the one he and Mama had watched. He fished in his pocket for change and bought a paper.

Over coffee he read the article. The Manning Clinic was about forty minutes away from Meghan's town. There'd probably be media hanging around there because they were checking out the laboratory where that woman had worked.

Maybe Meghan would be there too. She'd been there yesterday.

Forty minutes later Bernie was on the narrow, winding road that led from the quaint center of Kent to the Manning Clinic. After he left the diner he'd sat in the car and studied the map of this area so carefully that it was easy to figure out the most direct way to get there.

Just as he'd hoped, there were a number of media vans in the parking lot of the clinic. He parked at a distance from them and stuck his parking permit in the windshield. Then he studied the press pass he'd created. It would have taken an expert to spot that it wasn't genuine. It listed him as Bernard Heffernan, Channel 86, Elmira, New York. It was a local community station, he reminded himself. If anyone asked why that community would be interested in this story, he'd say they were thinking of building a facility like the Manning Clinic there.

Satisfied that he had his story straight, Bernie got out of the car and pulled on his windbreaker. Most reporters and cameramen didn't dress up. He decided to wear dark glasses, then got his new video camera from the trunk. State of the art, he told himself proudly. It had cost a bundle. He'd put it on his credit card. He'd rubbed some dust on it from the basement so it didn't look too new, and he'd painted the Channel 86 call letters on the side.

THERE WERE A DOZEN OR SO REPORTERS AND CAMERAMEN IN the clinic's lobby. They were interviewing a man who Bernie could see was stonewalling them. He was saying, "I repeat, the Manning Clinic is proud of its success in assisting women to have the children they so ardently desire. It is our belief that, despite the information on her visa application, Helene Petrovic may have trained as an embryologist in Rumania. None of the professionals who worked with her detected the slightest word or action on her part that suggested she did not thoroughly know her job."

"But if she made mistakes?" one reporter asked. "Suppose she mixed up those frozen embryos and women have given birth to other people's children?"

"We will perform DNA analysis for any parents who wish the clinical test for themselves and their child. The results take four to six weeks to achieve, but they are irrefutable. If parents wish to have that testing done at a different facility, we will pay the expense. Neither Dr. Manning nor any of the senior staff expect a problem in that area."

Bernie looked around. Meghan wasn't here. Should he ask people if they'd seen her? No, that would be a mistake. Just be part of the crowd, he cautioned himself.

But as he'd hoped, no one was paying any attention to him. He pointed his camera at the guy answering questions and turned it on.

When the interview was over, Bernie left with the group, taking care not to get too close to any of the others. He had spotted a PCD cameraman but did not recognize the burly man who was holding the mike. At the foot of the porch steps, a woman stopped her car and got out. She was pregnant and obviously upset. A reporter asked, "Ma'am, are you a client here?"

Stephanie Petrovic tried to shield her face from the cameras as she cried. "No. No. I just came to beg them to share my aunt's money with me. She left everything to the clinic. I am thinking that perhaps somebody from here killed her because they were afraid that after she quit she would change her will. If I could prove that, wouldn't her money be mine?"

FOR LONG MINUTES, MEGHAN SAT IN HER CAR IN FRONT OF the handsome limestone house in Chestnut Hill, twenty miles from downtown Philadelphia. The graceful lines of the three-story residence were accentuated by the mullioned windows, antique oak door and the slate roof that gleamed in shades of deep green in the early afternoon sun.

The walkway that threaded through the broad expanse of lawn was bordered by rows of azaleas that Meghan was sure would bloom with vivid beauty in the spring. A dozen slender white birches were scattered like sentinels throughout the property.

The name on the mailbox was C. J. Graham. Had she ever heard that name from her father? Meghan didn't think so.

She got out of the car and went slowly up the walk. She hesitated a moment, then rang the bell and heard the faint peal of chimes sound inside the house. A moment later the door was opened by a maid in uniform.

"Yes?" Her inquiry was polite but guarded.

Meghan realized she did not know who she should ask to see. "I would like a word with whoever lives in this house who might have been a friend of Aurelia Collins."

"Who is it, Jessie?" a man's voice called.

Behind the maid, Meghan saw a tall man with snow white hair, approaching the door.

"Invite the young woman in, Jessie," he directed. "It's cold out there."

Meghan stepped inside. As the door closed, the man's eyes narrowed. He waved her closer. "Come in, please. Under the light." A smile broke over his face. "It's Annie, isn't it? My dear, I'm glad to see you again."

33

Catherine Collins had an early breakfast with Meghan before Meg left to meet with the investigators at the Danbury courthouse and then to drive to Philadelphia. Catherine carried a second cup of coffee upstairs and turned on the television in her room. On the local news she heard that her husband's official listing with the law was no longer missing-presumed-dead, but had been changed to wanted-for-questioning in the Petrovic death.

When Meg called to say she was finished with the investigators and about to leave for Philadelphia, Catherine asked, "Meg, what did they ask you?"

"The same kind of questions they asked you. You know they're convinced Dad is alive. So far they have him guilty of fraud and murder. God knows what else they'll come up with. You're the one who warned me yesterday that it was going to get worse before it got better. You sure were right."

Something in Meg's voice chilled Catherine. "Meg, there's something you're not telling me."

"Mom, I have to go. We'll talk tonight, I promise."

"I don't want anything held back."

"I swear to God I won't hold anything back."

THE DOCTOR HAD CAUTIONED CATHERINE TO STAY AT HOME and rest for at least a few days. Rest and give myself a real heart attack worrying, she thought as she dressed. She was going to the inn.

She'd been away only a few days, but she could see a

difference. Virginia was good but missed small details. The flower arrangement on the registration desk was drooping. "When did this come?" Catherine asked.

"Just this morning."

"Call the florist and ask him to replace it." The roses she had received in the hospital were dewy fresh, Catherine remembered.

The tables in the dining room were set for lunch. Catherine walked from one to the other, examining them, a busboy behind her. "We're short a napkin here, and on the table by the window. A knife is missing there and that saltcellar looks grimy."

"Yes, ma'am."

She went into the kitchen. The old chef had retired in July after twenty years. His replacement, Clive D'Arcette, had come with impressive experience, despite being only twenty-six years old. After four months, Catherine was coming to the conclusion that he was a good second banana, but couldn't yet do the job on his own.

He was preparing the luncheon specials when Catherine entered the kitchen. She frowned as she noticed the grease spatters on the stove. Clearly they came from the dinner preparation the night before. The garbage bin had not been emptied. She tasted the hollandaise sauce. "Why is it salty?" she asked.

"I wouldn't call it salty, Mrs. Collins," D'Arcette said, his tone just missing politeness.

"But I would, and I suspect anyone who orders it would."

"Mrs. Collins, you hired me to be the chef here. Unless I can be the chef and prepare food my way, this situation won't work."

"You've made it very easy for me," Catherine said. "You're fired."

She was tying an apron around her waist when Virginia Murphy hurried in. "Catherine, where's Clive going? He just stormed past me."

"Back to cooking school, I hope."

"You're supposed to be resting."

Catherine turned to her. "Virginia, my salvation is going to be at this stove for as long as I can hang onto this place. Now what specials did Escoffier line up for today?"

They served forty-three lunches as well as sandwiches in the bar. It was a good seating. As the new orders slowed down, Catherine was able to go into the dining room. In her long white apron, she went from table to table, stopping for a moment at each. She could see the questioning eyes behind the warm smiles of greeting.

I don't blame people for being curious, with all they're hearing, she thought. I would be too. But these are my friends. This is my inn, and no matter what truth comes out, Meg and I have our place in this town.

CATHERINE SPENT THE LATE AFTERNOON IN THE OFFICE going over the books. If the bank will let me refinance and I hock or sell my jewelry, she decided, I might be able to hang on for six months longer at least. By then maybe we'll know something about the insurance. She closed her eyes. If only she hadn't been fool enough to put the house in both her and Edwin's names after Pop died . . .

Why did I do it? she wondered. I know why. I didn't want Edwin to think of himself as living in my house. Even when Pop was alive, Edwin had always insisted on paying for the utilities and repairs. "I have to feel as though I belong here," he'd said. Oh, Edwin! What had he called himself? Oh yes, "a wandering minstrel." She'd always thought of that as a joke. Had he meant it as a joke? Now she wasn't so certain.

She tried to remember verses of the old Gilbert and Sullivan song he used to sing. Only the opening line and one other came back to her. The first line was, "A wandering minstrel, I, a thing of shreds and patches." The other line: "And to your humors changing, I tune my subtle song."

Plaintive words when you analyzed them. Why had Edwin felt they applied to him?

Resolutely, Catherine went back to studying the accounts. The phone rang as she closed the last book. It was Bob Marron, one of the investigators who had come to see her in the hospital. "Mrs. Collins, when you weren't home I took a chance on calling you at the inn. Something has come up. We felt we needed to pass on this information to you, though we certainly don't necessarily recommend that you act on it."

"I don't know what you're talking about," Catherine said flatly.

She listened as Marron told her that Fiona Black, a psychic who had worked with them on cases of missing persons, had called. "She says she is getting very strong vibrations about your husband and would like to be able to handle something of his," Marron concluded.

"You're trying to send me some quack?"

"I know how you feel, but do you remember the Talmadge child who was missing three years ago?"

"Yes."

"It was Mrs. Black who told us to concentrate the search in the construction area near the town hall. She saved that kid's life."

"I see." Catherine moistened her lips with her tongue. Anything is better than not knowing, she told herself. She tightened her grasp on the receiver. "What does Mrs. Black want of Edwin's? Clothing? A ring?"

"She's here now. She'd like to come to your house and select something if that's possible. I'd bring her over in half an hour."

Catherine wondered if she should wait for Meg before she met this woman. Then she heard herself say, "Half an hour will be fine. I'm on my way home now."

MEGHAN FELT FROZEN IN TIME AS SHE STOOD IN THE FOYER with the courtly man who obviously believed they had met before. Through lips almost too numb to utter the words, she managed to say, "My name isn't Annie. It's Meghan. Meghan Collins."

Graham looked closely at her. "You're Edwin's daughter, aren't you?"

"Yes, I am."

"Come with me, please." He took her arm and guided her through the door to the study, on the right of the foyer. "I spend most of my time in here," he told her as he led her to the couch and settled himself in a high-backed wing chair. "Since my wife passed away, this house seems awfully big to me."

Meghan realized that Graham had seen her shock and distress and was trying to defuse it. But she was beyond phrasing her questions diplomatically. She opened her purse and took out the envelope with the obituary notice. "Did you send this to my father?" she asked.

"Yes, I did. He didn't acknowledge it, but then I never expected that he would. I was so sorry when I read about the accident last January."

"How do you know my father?" Meghan asked.

"I'm sorry," he apologized. "I don't think I've introduced myself. I'm Cyrus Graham. Your father's stepbrother."

His stepbrother! I never knew this man existed, Meghan thought.

"You called me 'Annie' just now," she said. "Why?"

He answered her with a question. "Do you have a sister, Meghan?"

"No."

"And you don't remember meeting me with your father and mother about ten years ago in Arizona?"

"I've never been there."

"Then I'm totally confused," Graham told her.

"Exactly when and where in Arizona did you think we met?" Meghan asked urgently.

"Let's see. It was in April, close to eleven years ago. I was in Scottsdale. My wife had spent a week in the Elizabeth Arden Spa, and I was picking her up the next morning. The evening before, I stayed at the Safari Hotel in Scottsdale. I was just leaving the dining room when I spotted Edwin. He was sitting with a woman who might have been in her early forties and a young girl who looked very much like you." Graham looked at Meghan. "Actually, both you and she resemble Edwin's mother."

"My grandmother."

"Yes." Now he looked concerned. "Meghan, I'm afraid this is distressing you."

"It's very important that I know everything I can about the people who were with my father that night."

"Very well. You realize it was a brief meeting, but since it was the first time I'd seen Edwin in years it made an impression on me."

"When had you seen him before that?"

"Not since he graduated from prep school. But even though thirty years had passed, I recognized him instantly. I went over to the table and got a mighty chilly reception. He introduced me to his wife and daughter as someone he'd known growing up in Philadelphia. I took the hint and left immediately. I knew through Aurelia that he and his family lived in Connecticut and simply assumed that they were vacationing in Arizona."

"Did he introduce the woman he was with as his wife?"

"I think so. I can't be sure about that. He may have said something like 'Frances and Annie, this is Cyrus Graham.' "

"You're positive the girl's name was *Annie?*"

"Yes, I am. And I know the woman's name was Frances."

"How old was Annie then?"

"About sixteen, I should think."

Meghan thought, that would make her about twenty-six now. She shivered. And she's lying in the morgue in my place.

She realized Graham was studying her.

"I think we could use a cup of tea," he said. "Have you had lunch?"

"Please don't bother."

"I'd like you to join me. I'll ask Jessie to put something together for us."

When he left the room, Meghan clasped her hands on her knees. Her legs felt weak and wobbly, as though if she stood up they would not support her. *Annie,* she thought. A vivid memory sprang into her mind of discussing names with her father. "How did you pick Meghan Anne for me?"

"My two favorite names in the world are Meghan and Annie. And that's how you became Meghan Anne."

You got to use your two favorite names, after all, Dad, Meghan thought bitterly. When Cyrus Graham returned, followed by the maid carrying a luncheon tray, Meghan accepted a cup of tea and a finger sandwich.

"I can't tell you how shocked I am," she said, and was glad she was able to at least sound calm. "Now tell me about *him.* Suddenly my father has become a total stranger to me."

It was not a pretty story. Richard Collins, her grandfather, had married seventeen-year-old Aurelia Crowley when she became pregnant. "He felt it was the honorable thing," Graham said. "He was much older and divorced her almost immediately, but he did support her and the baby with reasonable generosity. A year later, when I was fourteen, Richard and my mother married. My own father was dead. This was the Graham family home. Richard Collins moved in, and it was a good marriage. He and my mother were both rather rigid, joyless people, and as the old saying goes, God made them and matched them."

"And my father was raised by his mother?"

"Until he was three years old, at which point Aurelia fell madly in love with someone from California who did not want to be saddled with a child. One morning she arrived here and deposited Edwin with his suitcases and toys. My mother was furious. Richard was even more furious, and little Edwin was devastated. He worshiped his mother."

"She abandoned him to a family where he wasn't wanted?" Meghan asked incredulously.

"Yes. Mother and Richard took him in out of duty, but certainly not out of desire. I'm afraid he was a difficult little boy. I can remember him standing every day with his nose pressed to the window, so positive was he that his mother would come back."

"And did she?"

"Yes. A year later. The great love affair went sour, and she came back and collected Edwin. He was overjoyed and so were my parents."

"And then . . ."

"When he was eight, Aurelia met someone else and the scenario was repeated."

"Dear God!" Meghan said.

"This time Edwin was really impossible. He apparently thought that if he behaved very badly they'd find a way to send him back to his mother. It was an interesting morning around here when he put the garden hose in the gas tank of Mother's new sedan."

"Did they send him home?"

"Aurelia had left Philadelphia again. He was sent to boarding school and then to camp during the summer. I was away at college and then in law school and only saw him occasionally. I did visit him at school once and was astonished to see that he was very popular with his schoolmates. Even then he was telling people that his mother was dead."

"Did he ever see her again?"

"She came back to Philadelphia when he was sixteen. This time she stayed. She had finally matured and taken a job in a law office. I understand she tried to see Edwin, but it was too late. He wanted nothing to do with her. The pain was too deep. From time to time over the years she contacted me to ask if I ever heard from Edwin. A friend had sent me a clipping reporting his marriage to your mother. It gave the name and address of his firm. I gave the clipping to Aurelia. From what she told me, she wrote to him around his birthday and at Christmas every year but never heard back. In one of our conversations I told her about the meeting in Scottsdale. Perhaps I had no business sending the obituary notice to him."

"He was a wonderful father to me and a wonderful husband to my mother," Meghan said. She tried to blink back the tears that she felt welling in her eyes. "He traveled a great deal in his job. I can't believe he could have had another life, another woman he may have called his wife, perhaps another daughter he must have loved too. But I'm beginning to think it must be true. How else do you explain Annie and Frances? How can anybody expect my mother and me to forgive that deception?"

It was a question she was asking of herself, not of Cyrus Graham, but he answered it. "Meghan, turn around." He pointed to the prim row of windows behind the couch. "That center window is the one where a little boy stood watch every afternoon, looking for his mother. That kind of abandonment does something to the soul and the psyche."

34

*A*t four o'clock, Mac phoned Catherine at home to see how she was feeling. When he did not get an answer he tried her at the inn. Just as the operator was about to put him through to Catherine's office, the intercom on his desk began to buzz. "No, that's all right," he said hurriedly. "I'll try her later."

The next hour was busy, and he did not get to phone again. He was just at the outskirts of Newtown when he dialed her at the house from the car phone. "I thought if you were home I'd stop by for few minutes, Catherine," he said.

"I'd be glad for the moral support, Mac." Catherine quickly told him about the psychic and that she and the investigator were on their way.

"I'll be there in five minutes." Mac replaced the receiver

and frowned. He didn't believe in psychics. God knows what Meg is hearing about Edwin in Chestnut Hill today, he thought. Catherine's just about at the end of her rope, and they don't need some charlatan creating any more trouble for them.

He pulled into the Collins driveway as a man and a woman were getting out of a car in front of the house. The investigator and the psychic, Mac thought.

He caught up with them on the porch. Bob Marron introduced first himself and then Mrs. Fiona Black, saying only that she was someone who hoped to assist in locating Edwin Collins.

Mac was prepared to see a real display of hocus-pocus and calculated fakery. Instead he found himself in grudging admiration of the contained and poised woman who greeted Catherine with compassion. "You've had a very bad time," she said. "I don't know if I can help you, but I know I have to try."

Catherine's face was drawn, but Mac saw the flicker of hope that came into it. "I believe in my heart that my husband is dead," she told Fiona Black. "I know the police don't believe that. It would be so much easier if there were some way of being certain, some way of proving it, of finding out once and for all."

"Perhaps there is." Fiona Black pressed Catherine's hands in hers. She walked slowly into the living room, her manner observant. Catherine stood next to Mac and Investigator Marron, watching her.

She turned to Catherine. "Mrs. Collins, do you still have your husband's clothes and personal items here?"

"Yes. Come upstairs," she said, leading the way.

Mac felt his heart beating faster as they followed her. There was something about Fiona Black. She was not a fraud.

Catherine brought them to the master bedroom. On the dresser there was a twin frame. One picture was of Meghan. The other of Catherine and Edwin in formal dress. Last New Year's Eve at the inn, Mac thought. It had been a festive night.

Fiona Black studied the picture, then said, "Where is his clothing?"

Catherine opened the door to a walk-in closet. Mac remembered that years ago she and Edwin had broken through the wall to the small adjoining bedroom and made two walk-in closets for themselves. This one was Edwin's. Rows of jackets and slacks and suits. Floor-to-ceiling shelves with sport shirts and sweaters. A shoe rack.

Catherine was looking at the contents of the closet. "Edwin had wonderful taste in clothes. I always had to pick out my father's ties," she said. It was as though she was reminiscing to herself.

Fiona Black walked into the closet, her fingers lightly touching the lapel of one coat, the shoulder of another. "Do you have favorite cuff links or a ring of his?"

Catherine opened a dresser drawer. "This was the wedding ring I gave him. He mislaid it one day. We thought it was lost. He was so upset I replaced it, then found this one where it had slipped behind the dresser. It had gotten a bit tight, so he kept wearing the new one."

Fiona Black took the thin band of gold. "May I take this for a few days? I promise not to lose it."

Catherine hesitated, then said, "If you think it will be useful to you."

THE CAMERAMAN FROM THE PCD PHILADELPHIA AFFILIATE met Meghan at quarter of four outside the Franklin Center. "Sorry this is such a rush job," she apologized.

The lanky cameraman, who introduced himself as Len, shrugged. "We're used to it."

Meghan was glad that it was necessary to concentrate on this interview. The hour she had spent with Cyrus Graham, her father's stepbrother, was so painful that she had to put thoughts of it aside until, bit by bit, she could accept it. She had promised her mother she would hold nothing back from her. It would be difficult, but she would keep that promise. Tonight they would talk it out.

She said, "Len, at the opening, I'd like to get a wide shot of the block. These cobbled streets aren't the way people think about Philadelphia."

"You should have seen this area before the renovation," Len said as he began to roll tape.

Inside the Center they were greeted by the receptionist. Three women sat in the waiting room. All looked well groomed and were carefully made up. Meghan was sure these were the clients whom Dr. Williams had contacted to be interviewed.

She was right. The receptionist introduced her to them. One was pregnant. On-camera she explained that this would be her third child to be born by in vitro fertilization. The other two each had one child and were planning to attempt another pregnancy with their cryopreserved embryos.

"I have eight frozen embryos," one of them said happily as she smiled into the lens. "They'll transfer three of them, hoping one will take. If not, I'll wait a few months, then I'll have others thawed and try again."

"If you succeed immediately in achieving a pregnancy, will you be back next year?" Meghan asked.

"Oh no. My husband and I only want two children."

"But you'll still have cryopreserved embryos stored in the lab here, won't you?"

The woman agreed. "Yes, I will," she said. "We'll pay to have them stored. Who knows? I'm only twenty-eight. I might change my mind. In a few years I may be back, and it's nice to know I have other embryos already available to me."

"Provided any of them survive the thawing process?" Meghan asked.

"Of course."

Next they went into Dr. Williams' office. Meg took a seat opposite him for the interview. "Doctor, again thank you for having us," she said. "What I wish you would do at the outset is explain in vitro fertilization as simply as you did to me earlier. Then, if you'll allow us to have some footage of the lab, and show us how cryopreserved embryos are kept, we won't take up any more of your time."

Dr. Williams was an excellent interview. Admirably succinct, he quickly explained the reasons why women might
have trouble conceiving and the procedure of in vitro fertilization. "The patient is given fertility drugs to stimulate the
production of eggs; the eggs are retrieved from her ovaries;
in the lab they are fertilized, and the desired result is that we
achieve viable embryos. Early embryos are transferred to the
mother's womb, usually two or three at a time, in hopes that
at least one will result in a successful pregnancy. The others
are cryopreserved, or in layman's language, frozen, for even-
tual later use."

"Doctor, in a few days, as soon as it is born, we are going
to see a baby whose identical twin was born three years
ago," Meghan said. "Will you explain to our viewers how
it is possible for identical twins to be born three years
apart?"

"It is possible, but very rare, that the embryo divides into
two identical parts in the Petri dish just as it could in the
womb. In this case, apparently the mother chose to have one
embryo transferred immediately, the other cryopreserved for
transfer later. Fortunately, despite great odds, both procedures were successful."

Before they left Dr. Williams' office, Len panned the camera across the wall with the pictures of children born through
assisted reproduction at the Center. Next they shot footage of
the lab, paying particular attention to the long-term storage
containers where cryopreserved embryos, submerged in liq-
uid nitrogen, were kept.

It was nearly five-thirty when Meghan said, "Okay, it's a
wrap. Thanks everyone. Doctor, I'm so grateful."

"I am too," he assured her. "I can guarantee you that this
kind of publicity will generate many inquiries from childless
couples."

Outside, Len put his camera in the van and walked with
Meghan to her car. "Kind of gets you, doesn't it?" he asked.
"I mean, I have three kids and I'd hate to think they started
life in a freezer like those embryos."

"On the other hand, those embryos represent lives that

wouldn't have come into existence at all without this process," Meghan said.

As she began the long drive back to Connecticut she realized that the smooth, pleasant interview with Dr. Williams had been a respite.

Now her thoughts were back to the moment Cyrus Graham had greeted her as Annie. Every word he said in their time together replayed in her mind.

THAT SAME EVENING, AT 8:15, FIONA BLACK PHONED BOB Marron. "Edwin Collins is dead," she said quietly. "He has been dead for many months. His body is submerged in water."

35

*I*t was nine-thirty when Meghan arrived home on Thursday night, relieved to find that Mac was waiting with her mother. Seeing the question in his eyes, she nodded. It was a gesture not lost on her mother.

"Meg, what is it?"

Meg could catch the lingering aroma of onion soup. "Any of that left?" She waved her hand in the direction of the kitchen.

"You didn't have any dinner? Mac, pour her a glass of wine while I heat something up."

"Just soup, Mom, please."

When Catherine left, Mac came over to her. "How bad was it," he asked, his voice low.

She turned away, not wanting him to see the weary tears that threatened to spill over. "Pretty bad."

"Meg, if you want to talk to your mother alone, I'll get out of here. I just thought she needed company, and Mrs. Dileo was willing to stay with Kyle."

"That was nice of you, Mac, but you shouldn't have left Kyle. He looks forward to you coming home so much. Little kids shouldn't be disappointed. Don't ever let him down."

She felt that she was babbling. Mac's hands were holding her face, turning it to him.

"Meggie, what's the matter?"

Meg pressed her knuckles to her lips. She must not break down. "It's just . . ."

She could not go on. She felt Mac's arms around her. Oh God, to just let go, to be held by him. The letter. Nine years ago he had come to her with the letter she had written, the letter that begged him not to marry Ginger . . .

"I think you'd rather I didn't save this," he'd said then. He'd put his arm around her then as well, she remembered. "Meg, someday you'll fall in love. What you feel for me is something else. Everyone feels that way when a best friend gets married. There's always the fear that everything will be different. It won't be that way between us. We'll always be buddies."

The memory was as sharp as a dash of cold water. Meg straightened up and stepped back. "I'm all right, I'm just tired and hungry." She heard her mother's footsteps and waited until she was back in the room. "I have some pretty disturbing news for you, Mom."

"I think I should leave you two to talk it out," Mac said.

It was Catherine who stopped him. "Mac, you're family. I wish you'd stay."

They sat at the kitchen table. It seemed to Meghan that she could feel her father's presence. He was the one who would fix the late-evening supper if the restaurant had been crowded and her mother too busy to eat. He was a perfect mimic, taking on the mannerisms of one of the captains dealing with a cranky guest. "This table is not satisfactory? The banquette? Of course. A draft? But there is no window open. The inn is sealed shut. Perhaps it is the air flowing between your ears, madame."

Sipping a glass of wine, the steaming soup so appetizing, but untouched until she could tell them about the meeting in Chestnut Hill, Meghan talked about her father. She deliberately told about his childhood first, about Cyrus Graham's belief that the reason he turned his back on his mother was that he could not endure the chance of her abandoning him again.

Meghan watched her mother's face and found the reaction she had hoped for, pity for the little boy who had not been wanted, for the man who could not risk being hurt a third time.

But then it was necessary to tell her about the meeting in Scottsdale between Cyrus Graham and Edwin Collins.

"He introduced another woman as his wife?" There was no expression in her mother's voice.

"Mom, I don't know. Graham knew that Dad was married and had a daughter. He assumed that Dad was with his wife and daughter. Dad said something to him like, 'Frances and Annie, this is Cyrus Graham.' Mom, did Dad have any other relatives you know about? Is it a possibility that we have cousins in Arizona?"

"For God's sake, Meg, if I didn't know that your grandmother was alive all those years, how would I know about cousins?" Catherine Collins bit her lip. "I'm sorry." Her expression changed. "You say your father's stepbrother thought you were Annie. You looked that much like her?"

"Yes." Meg looked imploringly at Mac.

He understood what she was asking. "Meg," he said, "I don't think there's any point in not telling your mother why we went to New York yesterday."

"No, there isn't. Mom, there's something else you have to

know . . ." She looked steadily at her mother as she told her what she had hoped to conceal.

When she finished, her mother sat staring past her as though trying to understand what she had been hearing.

Finally, in a steady voice that was almost a monotone, she said, "A girl was stabbed who looked like you, Meg? She was carrying a piece of paper from Drumdoe Inn with your name and work number in Dad's handwriting? Within hours after she died, you got a fax that said, 'Mistake. Annie was a mistake'?"

Catherine's eyes became bleak and frightened.

"You went to have your DNA checked against hers because you thought you might be related to that girl."

"I did it because I'm trying to find answers."

"I'm glad I saw that Fiona woman tonight," Catherine burst out. "Meg, I don't suppose you'll approve, but Bob Marron of the New Milford police phoned this afternoon . . ."

Meg listened as her mother spoke of Fiona Black's visit. It's bizarre, she thought, but no more bizarre than anything else that's happened these last months.

At ten-thirty, Mac got up to leave. "If I may give advice, I'd suggest that both of you go to bed," he said.

MRS. DILEO, MAC'S HOUSEKEEPER, WAS WATCHING TELEVI-sion when he arrived home. "Kyle was so disappointed when you didn't get home before he fell asleep," she said. "Well, I'll be on my way."

Mac waited until her car pulled out, then turned off the outside lights and locked the door. He went in to look at Kyle. His small son was hunched in the fetal position, the pillow bunched under his head.

Mac tucked the covers around him, bent down and kissed the top of his head. Kyle seemed to be just fine, a pretty normal kid, but now Mac asked himself if he was ignoring any signals that Kyle might be sending out. Most other seven-year-olds grew up with mothers. Mac wasn't sure if the over-whelming surge of tenderness he felt now was for his son, or for the little boy Edwin Collins had been fifty years ago in Philadelphia. Or for Catherine and Meghan, who surely were the victims of the unhappy childhood of their husband and father.

MEGHAN AND CATHERINE SAW STEPHANIE PETROVIC'S IMPAS-sioned interview at the Manning Clinic on the eleven o'clock news. Meg listened as the anchorman reported that Stephanie Petrovic had lived with her aunt in their New Jersey home. "The body is being shipped to Rumania; the memorial mass will be held at noon in St. Dominic's Rumanian Church in Trenton," he finished.

"I'm going to that mass," Meghan told her mother. "I want to talk to that girl."

AT EIGHT O'CLOCK FRIDAY MORNING, BOB MARRON RE-ceived a call at home. An illegally parked car, a dark blue Cadillac sedan, had been ticketed in Battery Park City, Man-hattan, outside Meghan Collins' apartment house. The car was registered to Edwin Collins, and appeared to be the car he was driving the evening he disappeared.

As Marron dialed State Attorney John Dwyer he said to his wife, "The psychic sure dropped the ball on this one."

Fifteen minutes later, Marron was telling Meghan about the discovery of her father's car. He asked if she and Mrs. Collins could come to John Dwyer's office. He would like to see them together as soon as possible.

36

*E*arly Friday morning, Bernie watched again the replay of the interview he had taped at the Manning Clinic. He didn't hold the camera steady enough, he decided. The picture wobbled. He'd be more careful next time.

"Bernard!" His mother was yelling for him at the top of the stairs. Reluctantly he turned off the equipment.

"I'll be right there, Mama."

"Your breakfast is getting cold." His mother was wrapped in her flannel robe. It had been washed so often that the neck and the sleeves and the seat were threadbare. Bernie had told her that she washed it too much, but Mama said she was a clean person, that in her house you could eat off the floors.

This morning Mama was in a bad mood. "I was sneezing a lot last night," she told him as she dished out oatmeal from the pot on the stove. "I think I smelled dust coming from the basement just now. You do mop the floor down there, don't you?"

"Yes, I do, Mama."

"I wish you'd fix those cellar stairs so I can get down there and see for myself."

Bernie knew that his mother would never take a chance on those stairs. One of the steps was broken, and the bannister was wobbly.

"Mama, those stairs are dangerous. Remember what happened to your hip—and now, what with your arthritis, your knees are really bad."

"Don't think I'm taking a chance like that again," she

snapped. "But see that you keep it mopped. I don't know why you spend so much time down there anyhow."

"Yes, you do, Mama. I don't need much sleep, and if I have the television on in the living room, it keeps you awake." Mama had no idea about all the electronic equipment he had and she never would.

"I didn't sleep much last night. My allergies were at me."

"I'm sorry, Mama." Bernie finished the lukewarm oatmeal. "I'll be late." He grabbed his jacket.

She followed him to the door. When he was going down the walk, she called after him, "I'm glad to see you're keeping the car decent for a change."

AFTER THE PHONE CALL FROM BOB MARRON, MEGHAN HURriedly showered, dressed and went down to the kitchen. Her mother was already there, preparing breakfast.

Catherine's attempt at a cheery "Good morning, Meg" froze on her lips as she saw Meg's face. "What is it?" she asked. "I did hear the phone ring when I was in the shower, didn't I?"

Meg took both her mother's hands in hers. "Mom, look at me. I'm going to be absolutely honest with you. I thought for months that Daddy was lost on the bridge that night. With all that's happened this past week I need to make myself think as a lawyer and reporter. Look at all the possibilities, weigh each one carefully. I tried to make myself consider whether he might be alive and in serious trouble. But I know . . . I am sure . . . that what has gone on these last few days was something Dad would never do to us. That call, the flowers . . . and now . . ." She stopped.

"And now, what, Meg?"

"Dad's car was found in the city, illegally parked outside my apartment building."

"Mother of God!" Catherine's face went ashen.

"Mom, someone else put it there. I don't know why, but there's a reason behind all of this. The assistant state attorney wants to see us. He and his investigators are going to try to persuade us that Dad is alive. They didn't know him. We did. Whatever else may have been wrong in his life, he wouldn't send those flowers or leave his car where he'd be sure it would be found. He'd know how frantic we'd be. When we have this meeting, we're going to stick to our guns and defend him."

Neither one of them cared about food. They brought steaming cups of coffee out to the car. As Meghan backed out of the garage, trying to sound matter-of-fact, she said, "It may be illegal to drive one-handed, but coffee does help."

"That's because we're both so cold, inside and out. Look, Meg. The first dusting of snow is on the lawn. It's going to be a long winter. I've always loved winter. Your father hated it. That was one of the reasons he didn't mind traveling so much. Arizona is warm all year, isn't it?"

When they passed the Drumdoe Inn, Meghan said, "Mom, look over there. When we get back I'm going to drop you at the inn. You're going to work, and I'm going to start looking for answers. Promise me you won't say anything about what Cyrus Graham told me yesterday. Remember, he only assumed the woman and girl Dad was with ten years ago were you and me. Dad never introduced them except by their names, Frances and Annie. But until we can do some checking on our own, let's not give the state attorney any more reason to destroy Dad's reputation."

MEGHAN AND CATHERINE WERE ESCORTED IMMEDIATELY TO John Dwyer's office. He was waiting there with investigators Bob Marron and Arlene Weiss. Meghan took the chair next to her mother, her hand protectively covering hers.

It was quickly apparent what was wanted. All three, the attorney and the officers, were convinced that Edwin Collins was alive and about to directly contact his wife and daughter. "The phone call, the flowers, now his car," Dwyer pointed out. "Mrs. Collins, you knew your husband had a gun permit?"

"Yes, I did. He got it about ten years ago"

"Where did he keep the gun?"

"Locked up in his office or at home."

"When did you last see it?"

"I don't remember having seen it in years."

Meghan broke in, "Why are you asking about my father's gun? Was it found in the car?"

"Yes, it was," John Dwyer said quietly.

"That wouldn't be unusual," Catherine said quickly. "He wanted it for the car. He had a terrible experience in Bridgeport ten years ago when he was stopped at a traffic light."

Dwyer turned to Meghan. "You were away all day in Philadelphia, Miss Collins. It's possible your father is aware of your movements and knew you had left Connecticut. He might have assumed that you could be found in your apartment. What I must emphatically request is that if Mr. Collins does contact either one of you, you must insist that he come here and talk with us. It will be much better for him in the long run."

"My husband won't be contacting us," Catherine said firmly. "Mr. Dwyer, didn't some people try to abandon their cars that night on the bridge?"

"Yes. I believe so."

"Wasn't a woman who left her car hit by one of the other vehicles, and didn't she barely escape being dragged over the side of the bridge?"

"Yes."

"Then consider this. My husband might have abandoned his car and gotten caught in that carnage. Someone else might have driven it away."

Meghan saw exasperation mingled with pity in the assistant state attorney's face.

Catherine Collins saw it too. She got up to go. "How long does it usually take Mrs. Black to reach a premise about a missing person?" she asked.

Dwyer exchanged glances with his investigators. "She already has," he said reluctantly. "She believes your husband has been dead a long time, that he is lying in water."

Catherine closed her eyes and swayed. Involuntarily, Meghan grasped her mother's arms, afraid she was about to faint.

Catherine's entire body was trembling. But when she opened her eyes, her voice was firm as she said, "I never thought I would find comfort in a message like that, but in this place, and listening to you, I *do* find comfort in it."

THE CONSENSUS OF THE MEDIA ABOUT STEPHANIE PETROVIC'S impassioned interview was that she was a disappointed potential heir. Her accusation of a possible plot by the Manning Clinic to kill her aunt was dismissed as frivolous. The clinic was owned by a private group of investors and run by Dr. Manning, whose credentials were impeccable. He still refused to speak to the press, but it was clear that in no way did he stand to personally gain by Helene Petrovic's bequest to embryo research at the clinic. After her outburst Stephanie had been taken to the office of a Manning Clinic senior staff member who would not comment on the conversation.

Helene's lawyer, Charles Potters, was appalled when he read about the episode. On Friday morning before the memorial mass, he came to the house and with ill-concealed outrage imparted his feelings to Stephanie. "No matter what her background turns out to be, your aunt was devoted to her work at the clinic. For you to create a scene like that would have been horrifying to her."

When he saw the misery in the young woman's face, he relented. "I know you've been through a great deal," he told her. "After the mass you'll have a chance to rest. I thought some of Helene's friends from St. Dominic's were planning to stay with you."

"I sent them home," Stephanie said. "I hardly know them, and I'm better off by myself."

After the lawyer left, she propped pillows on the couch and lay down. Her unwieldy body made it difficult to get comfortable. Her back hurt all the time now. She felt so alone. But she didn't want those old women around, eyeing her, talking about her.

She was grateful that Helene had left specific instructions that upon her death there was to be no wake, that her body was to be sent to Rumania and buried in her husband's grave.

She dozed off and was awakened by the peal of the telephone. Who now, she wondered wearily. It was a pleasant woman's voice. "Miss Petrovic?"

"Yes."

"I'm Meghan Collins from PCD Channel 3. I wasn't at the Manning Clinic when you were there yesterday, but I saw your statement on the eleven o'clock news."

"I don't want to talk about that. My aunt's lawyer is very upset with me."

"I wish you would talk with me. I might be able to help you."

"How can you help me? How can anyone help me?"

"There are ways. I'm calling from my car phone. I'm on my way to the mass. May I take you out to lunch afterwards?"

She sounds so friendly, Stephanie thought, and I need a friend. "I don't want to be on television again."

"I'm not asking you to be on television. I'm asking you to talk to me."

Stephanie hesitated. When the service is over, she thought, I don't want to be with Mr. Potters and I don't want to be with those old women from the Rumanian Society. They're all gossiping about me. "I'll go to lunch with you," she said.

MEGHAN DROPPED HER MOTHER AT THE INN, THEN DROVE to Trenton as fast as she dared.

On the way she made a second phone call to Tom Weicker's office to tell him that her father's car had been located.

"Does anyone else know about the car being found?" he asked quickly.

"Not yet. They're trying to keep it quiet. But we both know it's going to leak out." She tried to sound offhand. "At least Channel 3 can have the inside track."

"It's turning into a big story, Meg."

"I know it is."

"We'll run it immediately."

"That's why I'm giving it to you."

"Meg, I'm sorry."

"Don't be. There's a rational answer to all this."

"When is Mrs. Anderson's baby due?"

"They're putting her in the hospital on Monday. She's willing to have me go to her home Sunday afternoon and tape her and Jonathan getting the room ready for the baby. She has infant pictures of Jonathan that we can use. When the baby is born, we'll compare the newborn shots."

"Stay with it, at least for the present."

"Thanks, Tom," she said, "and thanks for the support."

PHILLIP CARTER SPENT MUCH OF FRIDAY AFTERNOON BEING questioned about Edwin Collins. With less and less patience, Carter answered questions that grew more and more pointed. "No, we have never had another instance in which there was a question of fraudulent credentials. Our reputation has been impeccable."

Arlene Weiss asked about the car. "When it was found in New York it had twenty-seven thousand miles on the odometer, Mr. Carter. According to the service record booklet, it had been serviced the preceding October, just a little over a year ago. At that time it had twenty-one thousand miles on it. How many miles did Mr. Collins put on the car in an average month?"

"I would say that depended entirely on his schedule. We have company cars and turn them in every three years. It's up to us to have them serviced. I'm fairly meticulous. Edwin tended to be a bit lax."

"Let me put it this way," Bob Marron said, "Mr. Collins

vanished in January. Between October last year and January, was it likely that he put six thousand miles on the car?"

"I don't know. I can give you his appointments for those months and try to figure out through expense accounts to which of those he would have driven."

"We need to try to estimate how much the car has been used since January," Marron said. "We'd also like to see the car phone bill for January."

"I assume you want to check on the time he made the call to Victor Orsini. The insurance company has already looked into that. The call was made less than a minute before the accident on the Tappan Zee Bridge."

They asked about Collins and Carter's financial status. "Our books are in order. They have been thoroughly audited. The last few years, like many businesses, we experienced the cutbacks of the recession. The kind of companies we deal with were letting people go, not hiring them. However, I know of no reason why Edwin would have had to borrow several hundred thousand dollars on his life insurance."

"Your firm would have received a commission from the Manning Clinic for placing Petrovic?"

"Of course."

"Did Collins pocket that commission?"

"No, the auditors found it."

"No one questioned Helene Petrovic's name on the $6,000 payment when it came in?"

"The copy of the Manning client statement in our files had been doctored. It reads 'Second installment due for placing Dr. Henry Williams.' There was no second installment due."

"Then clearly Collins didn't place her so he could swindle the firm out of $6,000."

"I would say that's obvious."

When they finally left, Phillip Carter tried without success to concentrate on the work on his desk. He could hear the phone in the outer office ringing. Jackie buzzed him on the intercom. A reporter from a supermarket tabloid was on the phone. Phillip curtly refused the call, realizing that the only calls that day had come from the media. Collins and Carter had not heard from a single client.

37

Meghan slipped into St. Dominic's church at twelve-thirty, at the midpoint of the sparsely attended mass for Helene Petrovic. In keeping with the wishes of the deceased, it was a simple ceremony without flowers or music.

There was a scattering of neighbors from Lawrenceville in attendance as well as a few older women from the Rumanian Society. Stephanie was seated with her lawyer, and as they left the church, Meghan introduced herself. The young woman seemed glad to see her.

"Let me say goodbye to these people," she said, "and then I'll join you."

Meghan watched as the polite murmurs of sympathy were expressed. She saw no great manifestation of grief from anyone. She walked over to two women who had just come out of church. "Did you know Helene Petrovic well?" she asked.

"As well as anyone," one of them replied pleasantly. "Some of us go to concerts together. Helene joined us occasionally. She was a member of the Rumanian Society and was notified of any of our activities. Sometimes she would show up."

"But not too often."

"No."

"Did she have any very close friends?"

The other woman shook her head. "Helene kept to herself."

"How about men? I met Mrs. Petrovic. She was a very attractive woman."

They both shook their heads. "If she had any special men friends, she never breathed a word about it."

Meghan noted that Stephanie was saying goodbye to the last of the people from church. As she walked over to join her, she heard the lawyer caution, "I wish you would not speak to that reporter. I'd be glad to drive you home or take you to lunch."

"I'll be fine."

Meghan took the young woman's arm as they walked down the rest of the steps. "These are pretty steep."

"And I'm so clumsy now. I keep getting in my own way."

"This is your territory," Meghan said when they were in the car. "Where would you like to eat?"

"Would you mind if we went back to the house? People have left so much food there, and I'm feeling so tired."

"Of course."

When they reached the Petrovic home, Meghan insisted that Stephanie rest while she prepared lunch. "Kick your shoes off and put your feet up on the couch," she said firmly. "We have a family inn, and I was raised in the kitchen there. I'm used to preparing meals."

As she heated soup and laid out a plate of cold chicken and salad, Meghan studied the surroundings. The kitchen had a French country house decor. The tiled walls and terracotta floor were clearly custom made. The appliances were top of the line. The round oak table and chairs were antiques. Obviously a lot of care—and money—had gone into the place.

They ate in the dining room. Here too the upholstered armchairs around the trestle table were obviously expensive. The table shone with the patina of fine old furniture. Where did the money come from? Meghan wondered. Helene had worked as a cosmetician until she got a job as a secretary in the clinic in Trenton, and from there she went to Manning.

Meghan did not have to ask questions. Stephanie was more than willing to discuss her problems. "They are going to sell this house. All the money from the sale and eight hundred thousand dollars is going to the clinic. But it's so unfair. My aunt promised to change her will. I'm her only relative. That's why she sent for me."

"What about the baby's father?" Meghan asked. "He can be made to help you."

"He's moved away."

"He can be traced. In this country there are laws to protect children. What is his name?"

Stephanie hesitated. "I don't want to have anything to do with him."

"You have a right to be taken care of."

"I'm going to give up the baby for adoption. It's the only way."

"It may not be the only way. What is his name and where did you meet him?"

"I . . . I met him at one of the Rumanian affairs in New York. His name is Jan. Helene had a headache that night and left early. He offered to drive me home." She looked down. "I don't like to talk about being so foolish."

"Did you go out with him often?"

"A few times."

"You told him about the baby?"

"He called to say he was going to California. That was when I told him. He said it was my problem."

"When was that?"

"Last March."

"What kind of work does he do?"

"He's a . . . mechanic. Please, Miss Collins, I don't want anything to do with him. Don't lots of people want babies?"

"Yes, they do. But that was what I meant when I said I could help you. If we find Jan, he'll have to support the baby and help you at least until you can get a job."

"Please leave him alone. I'm afraid of him. He was so angry."

"Angry because you told him he was the father of your baby?"

"Don't keep asking me about him!" Stephanie pushed her chair away from the table. "You said you'd help. Then find me people who will take the baby and give me some money."

Meghan said contritely, "I'm sorry, Stephanie. The last thing I came here to do was to upset you. Let's have a cup of tea. I'll clean up later."

In the living room she propped an extra pillow behind Stephanie's back and pulled an ottoman over for her feet.

Stephanie smiled apologetically. "You're very kind. I was rude. It is just that so much has happened so fast."

"Stephanie, what you're going to need is to have someone sponsor you for a green card until you can get a job. Surely your aunt had one good friend who might help you out."

"You mean if one of her friends sponsored me, I might be able to stay."

"Yes. Isn't there someone, maybe someone who owes your aunt a favor?"

Stephanie's expression brightened. "Oh, yes, there may indeed be someone. Thank you, Meghan."

"Who is the friend?" Meghan asked swiftly.

"I may be wrong," Stephanie said, suddenly nervous. "I must think about it."

She would not say anything more.

IT WAS TWO O'CLOCK. BERNIE HAD GOTTEN A COUPLE OF trips out of La Guardia Airport in the morning, then took a fare from Kennedy Airport to Bronxville.

He had had no intention of going to Connecticut that afternoon. But when he left the Cross County he found himself turning north. He had to go back to Newtown.

There was no car in the driveway of Meghan's house. He cruised along the curving road to the cul-de-sac, then turned around. The kid and his dog were nowhere in sight. That was good. He didn't want to be noticed.

He drove past Meghan's house again. He couldn't hang around here.

He drove past the Drumdoe Inn. Wait a minute, he thought. This is the place her mother owns. He'd read that in the paper yesterday. In an instant he'd made a U-turn and driven into the parking lot. There's got to be a bar, he thought. Maybe I can have a beer and even order a sandwich.

Suppose Meghan was there. He'd tell her the same story he told the others, that he was working for a local cable station in Elmira. There was no reason she shouldn't believe him.

The inn's lobby was medium size and had paneled walls and blue-and red checked carpeting. There was no one behind the desk. To the right, he could see a few people in the dining room and busboys clearing tables. Well, lunch hour was pretty well over, he thought. The bar was to the left. He could see that it was empty, except for the bartender. He went to the bar, sat on one of the stools, ordered a beer and asked for the menu.

After he decided on a hamburger he started talking to the bartender. "This is a nice place."

"Sure is," the bartender agreed.

The guy had a name tag that read "Joe"; he looked to be about fifty. The local newspaper was on the back bar. Bernie pointed to it.

"I read yesterday's paper. Looks like the family that owns this place has a lot of problems."

"They sure do," Joe agreed. "Damn shame. Mrs. Collins is the nicest woman you'd ever want to know and her daughter, Meg, is a doll."

Two men came in and sat at the end of the bar. Joe filled their orders, then stayed talking with them. Bernie looked around as he finished his hamburger and beer. The back windows looked out over the parking lot. Beyond that was a wooded area that extended behind the Collins house.

Bernie had an interesting thought. If he drove here at night he could park in the lot with the cars from the dinner crowd and slip into the woods. Maybe from there he could take pictures of Meghan in her house. He had a zoom lens. It should be easy.

Before he left he asked Joe if they had valet parking.

"Just on Friday and Saturday nights," Joe told him.

Bernie nodded. He decided that he'd be back Sunday night.

MEGHAN LEFT STEPHANIE PETROVIC AT TWO O'CLOCK. AT THE door she said, "I'll keep in touch with you and I want to know when you're going to the hospital. It's tough to have your first baby without anyone close to you around."

"I'm getting scared about it," Stephanie admitted. "My mother had a hard time when I was born. I just want it over with."

The image of the troubled young face stayed with Meghan. Why was Stephanie so adamant about not trying to get child support from the father? Of course if she was determined to give the baby up for adoption, it was probably a moot point.

There was another stop Meghan wanted to make before she started home. Trenton was not far from Lawrenceville, and Helene Petrovic had worked there as a secretary in the Dowling Center, an assisted reproduction facility. Maybe somebody there would remember the woman, although she'd left the place for the Manning Clinic six years ago. Meghan was determined to find out more about her.

THE DOWLING ASSISTED REPRODUCTION CENTER WAS IN A small building connected to Valley Memorial Hospital. The reception room held only a desk and one chair. Clearly this place was not on the scale of the Manning Clinic.

Meghan did not show her PCD identification. She was not here as a reporter. When she told the receptionist she wanted to speak to someone about Helene Petrovic, the woman's face changed. "We have nothing more to say on the matter. Mrs. Petrovic worked here as a secretary for three years. She never was involved in any medical procedures."

"I believe that," Meghan said. "But my father is being held responsible for placing her at the Manning Clinic. I need to speak to someone who knew her well. I need to know if my father's firm ever requested a reference for her."

The woman looked hesitant.

"Please," Meghan said quietly.

"I'll see if the director is available."

THE DIRECTOR WAS A HANDSOME GRAY-HAIRED WOMAN OF about fifty. When Meghan was escorted into her office, she introduced herself as Dr. Keating. "I'm a Ph.D., not a physician," she said briskly. "I'm concerned with the business end of the center."

She had Helene Petrovic's file in her drawer. "The state attorney's office in Connecticut requested a copy of this two days ago," she commented.

"Do you mind if I take notes?" Meghan asked.

"Not at all."

The file contained information that had been reported in the papers. On her application form to Dowling, Helene Petrovic had been truthful. She had applied for a secretarial position, giving her work background as a cosmetician and citing her recently acquired certificate from the Woods Secretarial School in New York.

"Her references checked out," Dr. Keating said. "She made a nice appearance and had a pleasant manner. I hired her and was very satisfied with her the three years she was here."

"When she left, did she tell you she was going to the Manning Clinic?"

"No. She said that she planned to take a job as a cosmetician in New York again. She said a friend was opening a salon. That's why we didn't find it surprising that we were never contacted for a reference."

"Then you had no dealings with Collins and Carter Executive Search?"

"None at all."

"Dr. Keating, Mrs. Petrovic managed to pull the wool over the eyes of the medical staff in the Manning Clinic. Where do you think she got the knowledge to handle cryopreserved embryos?"

Keating frowned. "As I told the Connecticut investigators, Helene was fascinated with medicine and particularly the kind that is done here, the process of assisted reproduction. She used to read the medical books when work was slow and often would visit the laboratory and observe what was going on there. I might add that she would never have been allowed to step into the laboratory alone. As a matter of fact, we never allow fewer than two qualified staff people to be present. It's a sort of fail-safe system. I think it should be a law in every facility of this kind."

"Then you think she picked up her medical knowledge through observation and reading?"

"It's hard to believe that someone who had no opportunity to do hands-on work under supervision would be able to fool experts, but it's the only explanation I have."

"Dr. Keating, all I hear is that Helene Petrovic was very nice, well respected but a loner. Was that true here?"

"I would say so. To the best of my knowledge she never socialized with the other secretaries or anyone on this staff."

"No male friends?"

"I don't know for sure, but I always suspected that she was seeing someone from the hospital. Several times when she was away from her desk one of the other girls picked up her phone. They began to tease her about who was her Dr. Kildare. Apparently the message was to call an extension in the hospital."

"You wouldn't know which extension?"

"It was over six years ago."

"Of course." Meghan got up. "Dr. Keating, you've been so kind. May I give you my phone number just in case you remember anything that you think might be of assistance?"

Keating reached out her hand. "I know the circumstances, Miss Collins. I wish I could help."

When she was getting into her car, Meghan studied the impressive structure that was Valley Memorial Hospital. Ten stories high, half the length of a city block, hundreds of windows from which lights were beginning to gleam in the late afternoon.

Was it possible that behind one of those windows there was a doctor who had helped Helene Petrovic to perfect her dangerous deception?

MEGHAN WAS EXITING ONTO ROUTE 7 WHEN THE FIVE o'clock news came on. She listened to the WPCD radio station bulletin: "Assistant State Attorney John Dwyer has confirmed that the car Edwin Collins was driving the night of the Tappan Zee Bridge disaster last January has been located outside the Manhattan apartment of his daughter. Ballistic tests show that Collins' gun, found in the car, was the murder weapon that killed Helene Petrovic, the laboratory worker whose fraudulent credentials he allegedly presented to the Manning Clinic. A warrant has just been issued for Edwin Collins' arrest on suspicion of homicide."

38

*D*r. George Manning left the clinic at five o'clock on Friday afternoon. Three new patients had canceled their appointments, so far only a half dozen or so worried parents had called to inquire about DNA tests to assure themselves that their children were their biological offspring. Dr. Manning knew that it would take only one verified case of a mix-up to cause alarm in every woman who had borne a child through treatment at the clinic. For good and sufficient reasons he dreaded the next few days.

Wearily he drove the eight miles to his home in South Kent. It was such a shame, such a damn shame, he thought. Ten years of hard work and a national reputation ruined, virtually overnight. Less than a week ago he had been celebrating the annual reunion and looking forward to retirement. On his seventieth birthday last January he had announced that he would stay at his post just one more year.

The most galling memory was that Edwin Collins had called when he read an account of the birthday celebration and retirement plans and asked if Collins and Carter could once again serve the Manning Clinic!

ON FRIDAY EVENING, WHEN DINA ANDERSON PUT HER THREE-year-old son to bed, she hugged him fiercely. "Jonathan, I think your twin isn't going to wait till Monday to be born," she told him.

"How's it going, honey?" her husband asked when she went downstairs.

"Five minutes apart."

"I'd better alert the doctor."

"So much for Jonathan and me being on-camera, getting the room ready for Ryan." She winced. "You'd better tell my mother to get right over, and let the doctor know I'm on my way to the hospital."

HALF AN HOUR LATER, IN DANBURY MEDICAL CENTER, DINA Anderson was being examined. "Would you believe the contractions stopped?" she asked in disgust.

"We're going to keep you," the obstetrician told her. "If nothing happens during the night, we'll start an IV to induce labor in the morning. You might as well go home, Don."

Dina pulled her husband's face down for a kiss. "Don't look so worried, Daddy. Oh, and will you phone Meghan Collins and alert her that Ryan will probably be around by tomorrow. She wants to be there to tape him as soon as he's in the nursery. Be sure to bring the pictures of Jonathan as a newborn. She's going to show them with the baby so everyone can see that they're exactly alike. And let Dr. Manning know. He was so sweet. He called today to ask how I was doing."

THE NEXT MORNING, MEGHAN AND HER CAMERAMAN, STEVE, were in the lobby of the hospital, awaiting word of the delivery of Ryan. Donald Anderson had given them Jonathan's newborn infant pictures. When the baby was in the nursery, they would be allowed to videotape him. Jonathan would be brought to the hospital by Dina's mother, and they'd be able to take a brief shot of the family together.

With a reporter's eye, Meghan observed the activity in the lobby. A young mother, her infant in her arms, was being wheeled to the door by a nurse. Her husband followed, struggling with suitcases and flower arrangements. From one of the bouquets floated a pink balloon inscribed, "It's a Girl."

An exhausted-looking couple came out of the elevator holding the hands of a four-year-old with a cast on his arm and a bandage on his head. An expectant mother crossed the lobby and entered the door marked ADMITTANCE.

Seeing these families, Meghan was reminded of Kyle. What kind of mother would walk out on a six-month-old baby?

The cameraman was studying Jonathan's pictures. "I'll get the same angle," he said. "Kind of weird when you think you know exactly what the kid's gonna look like."

"Look," Meghan said. "That's Dr. Manning coming in. I wonder if he's here because of the Andersons."

. . .

UPSTAIRS IN THE DELIVERY ROOM, A LOUD WAIL BROUGHT A smile to the faces of the doctors, the nurses and the Andersons. Pale and exhausted, Dina looked up at her husband and saw the shock on his face. Frantically she pulled herself up on one elbow. "Is he okay?" she cried. "Let me see him."

"He's fine, Dina," the doctor said, holding up the squalling infant with the shock of bright red hair.

"That's not Jonathan's twin!" Dina screamed. "Whose baby have I been carrying?"

39

"*I*t always rains on Saturday," Kyle grumbled as he flipped from channel to channel on the television set. He was sitting cross-legged on the carpet, Jake beside him.

Mac was deep in the morning paper. "Not always," he said absently. He glanced at his watch. It was almost noon. "Turn to Channel 3. I want to catch the news."

"Okay." Kyle clicked the remote. "Look, there's Meg!"

Mac dropped the paper. "Turn up the volume."

"You're always telling me to turn it down."

"Kyle!"

"Okay. Okay."

Meg was standing in the lobby of a hospital. "There is a frightening new development in the Manning Clinic case. Following the murder of Helene Petrovic, and the discovery of her fraudulent credentials, there has been concern that the late Ms. Petrovic may have made serious mistakes in handling the cryopreserved embryos. An hour ago a baby, expected to be the clone of his three-year-old brother, was born here in Danbury Medical Center."

Mac and Kyle watched as the camera angle widened.

"With me is Dr. Allan Neitzer, the obstetrician who just delivered Dina Anderson of a son. Doctor, will you tell us about the baby?"

"The baby is a healthy, beautiful eight-pound boy."

"But it is not the identical twin of the Andersons' three-year-old son?"

"No, it is not."

"Is it Dina Anderson's biological child?"

"Only DNA tests can establish that."

"How long will they take?"

"Four to six weeks."

"How are the Andersons reacting?"

"Very upset. Very worried."

"Dr. Manning was here. He went upstairs before we could speak to him. Has he seen the Andersons?"

"I can't comment on that."

"Thank you, Doctor." Meghan turned to face the camera directly. "We'll be here with this unfolding story. Back to you in the newsroom, Mike."

"Turn it off, Kyle."

Kyle pressed the remote button, and the screen went blank. "What did that mean?"

It means big problems, Mac thought. How many more mistakes had Helene Petrovic made at Manning? Whatever they were, no doubt Edwin Collins would be held equally responsible for them. "It's pretty complicated, Kyle."

"Is anything wrong for Meg? "

Mac looked into his son's face. The sandy hair so like his own that never stayed in place was falling on his forehead. The brown eyes that he'd inherited from Ginger had lost their usual merry twinkle. Except for the color of the eyes, Kyle was a MacIntyre through and through. What would it be

like, Mac wondered, to look in your son's face and realize he
might not belong to you.

He put an arm around Kyle. "Things have been rough for
Meg lately. That's why she looks worried."

"Next to you and Jake, she's my best friend," Kyle said
soberly.

At the mention of his name, Jake thumped his tail.

Mac smiled wryly. "I'm sure Meg will be flattered to hear
it." Not for the first time in these last few days, he wondered
if his blind stupidity in not realizing his feelings for Meg had
forever relegated him in her eyes to the status of friend and
buddy.

MEGHAN AND THE CAMERAMAN SAT IN THE LOBBY OF DAN-
bury Medical Center. Steve seemed to know that she did not
want to talk. Neither Donald Anderson nor Dr. Manning
had come downstairs.

"Look, Meg," Steve said suddenly, "isn't that the other
Anderson kid?"

"Yes, it is. That must be the grandmother with him."

They both jumped up, followed them across the lobby and
caught them at the elevator. Meg turned on the mike. Steve
began to roll tape.

"I wonder if you would speak to us for a moment,"
Meghan asked the woman. "Aren't you Dina Anderson's
mother and Jonathan's grandmother?"

"Yes, I am." The well-bred voice was distressed. Silver hair
framed a troubled face.

By her expression, Meghan knew the woman was aware
of the problem.

"Have you spoken to your daughter or son-in-law since
the baby was born?"

"My son-in-law phoned me. Please. We want to get upstairs. My daughter needs me." She stepped into the elevator,
the little boy's hand grasped tightly in her own.

Meghan did not try to detain her.

Jonathan was wearing a blue jacket that matched the blue of his eyes. His cheeks were rosy accents to his fair complexion. His hood was down, and raindrops had beaded the white-gold hair that was shaped in Buster Brown style. He smiled and waved. "Bye-bye," he called as the elevator doors began to close.

"That's some good-looking kid," Steve observed.

"He's beautiful," Meghan agreed.

They returned to their seats. "Do you think Manning will give a statement?" Steve asked.

"If I were Dr. Manning, I'd be talking to my lawyers." And Collins and Carter Executive Search will need their lawyers too, she thought.

Meghan's beeper sounded. She pulled out her cellular phone, called the news desk and was told that Tom Weicker wanted to talk to her. "If Tom's in on Saturday, something's up," she murmured.

Something was up. Weicker got right to the point. "Meg, Dennis Cimini is on his way to relieve you. He took a helicopter, so he should be there soon."

She was not surprised. The special about identical twins being born three years apart had become a much bigger story. It was now tied into the Manning Clinic scandal and the murder of Helene Petrovic.

"All right, Tom." She sensed there was more.

"Meg, you told the Connecticut authorities about the dead woman who resembles you and the fact that she had a note in her pocket in your father's handwriting."

"I felt I had to tell them. I was sure the New York detectives would contact them at some point about it."

"There's been a leak somewhere. They also learned that you went to the morgue for a DNA test. We've got to carry the story right away. The other stations have it."

"I understand, Tom."

"Meg, as of now you're on leave. Paid leave of course."

"All right."

"I'm sorry, Meg."

"I know you are. Thanks." She broke the connection. Dennis Cimini was coming through the revolving door to the lobby. "I guess that does it. See you around, Steve," she said. She hoped her bitter disappointment wasn't obvious to him.

40

*T*here was an auction coming up on property near the Rhode Island border. Phillip Carter had planned to take a look at it.

He needed a day away from the office and the myriad problems of the past week. The media had been omnipresent. The investigators had been in and out. A talk show host had actually asked him to be on a program about missing persons.

Victor Orsini had not been off the mark when he said that every word uttered or printed about Helene Petrovic's fraudulent credentials was a nail in the coffin of Collins and Carter.

On Saturday just before noon, Carter was at his front door when the phone rang. He debated about answering, then picked up the receiver. It was Orsini.

"Phillip, I had the television on. The fat's in the fire. Helene Petrovic's first known mistake at the Manning Clinic was just born."

"What's that supposed to mean?"

Orsini explained. As Phillip listened, his blood chilled.

"This is just the beginning," Orsini said. "How much insurance does the company have to cover this?"

"There isn't enough insurance in the world to cover it," Carter said quietly as he hung up.

You believe you have everything under control, he thought, but you never do. Panic was not a familiar emotion, but suddenly events were closing in on him.

In the next moment he was thinking of Catherine and Meghan. There was no further consideration of a leisurely drive to the country. He would call Meg and Catherine later. Maybe he could join them for dinner this evening. He wanted to know what they were doing, what they were thinking.

WHEN MEG GOT HOME AT ONE-THIRTY, CATHERINE HAD lunch ready. She'd seen the news brief broadcast from the hospital.

"It was probably my last one for Channel 3," Meg said quietly.

For a little while, both too overwhelmed to speak, the two women ate in silence. Then Meg said, "Mom, as bad as it is for us, can you imagine how the women feel who underwent in vitro fertilization at the Manning Clinic? With the Anderson mix-up there isn't one of them who isn't going to wonder if she received her own embryo. What will happen when errors can be traced and a biological and host mother both claim the same child?"

"I can imagine what it would be like." Catherine Collins reached across the table and grasped Meg's hand. "Meggie, I've lived for nearly nine months on such an emotional see-saw that I'm punch drunk."

"Mom, I know how it's been for you."

"Hear me out. I have no idea how all this will end, but I do know one thing. *I can't lose you.* If somebody killed that poor girl thinking it was you, I can only pity her with all my heart and thank God on my knees that you're the one who's alive."

They both jumped as the door bell rang.

"I'll get it," Meg said.

It was an insured package for Catherine. She ripped it open. Inside was a note and a small box. She read the note aloud: "Dear Mrs. Collins, I am returning your husband's wedding ring. I have rarely felt such certainty as I did when I told investigator Bob Marron that Edwin Collins died many months ago.

"My thoughts and prayers are with you, Fiona Campbell Black."

Meghan realized that she was glad to see tears wash away some of the pain that was etched on her mother's face.

Catherine took the slender gold ring from the box and closed her hand over it.

41

*L*ate Saturday in Danbury Medical Center, a sedated Dina Anderson was dozing in bed, Jonathan asleep beside her. Her husband and mother were sitting silently by the bedside. The obstetrician, Dr. Neitzer, came to the door and beckoned to Don.

He stepped outside. "Any word?"

The doctor nodded. "Good, I hope. On checking your blood type, your wife's, Jonathan's and the baby's, we find that the baby certainly could be your biological child. You are A positive, your wife is O negative, the baby is O positive."

"Jonathan is A positive."

"Which is the other blood type consistent with the child of A positive and O negative parents."

"I don't know what to think," Don said. "Dina's mother swears the baby looks like her own brother when he was born. There's red hair on that side of the family."

"The DNA test will establish absolutely whether or not the baby is biologically yours, but that will take four weeks minimum."

"And what do we do in the meantime?" Don asked, angrily. "Bond to it, love it and maybe find out we have to give it to someone else from the Manning Clinic? Or do we let it lie in a nursery until we know whether or not it's ours?"

"It isn't good for any baby in the early weeks of life to be left in a nursery," Doctor Neitzer replied. "Even our very sick babies are handled as much as possible by the mothers and fathers. And Dr. Manning says—"

"Nothing Dr. Manning says interests me," Don interrupted. "All I've ever heard since the embryo split nearly four years ago was how the embryo of Jonathan's twin was in a specially marked tube."

"Don, where are you?" a weak voice called.

Anderson and Dr. Neitzer went back into the room. Dina and Jonathan were both awake. She said, "Jonathan wants to see his new brother."

"Honey, I don't know . . ."

Dina's mother stood up and looked hopefully at her daughter.

"I do. I agree with Jonathan. I carried that baby for nine months. For the first three I was spotting and terrified I'd lose it. The first moment I felt life I was so happy I cried. I love coffee and couldn't have one sip of it because that kid doesn't like coffee. He's been kicking me so hard I haven't had a decent sleep in three months. Whether or not he's my biological child, by God I've earned him and I want him."

"Honey, Dr. Neitzer says the blood tests show it may be our child."

"That's good. Now, will you please have someone bring my baby to me."

. . .

AT TWO-THIRTY DR. MANNING, ACCOMPANIED BY HIS LAWYER and a hospital official, entered the hospital's auditorium.

The hospital official made a firm announcement. "Dr. Manning will read a prepared statement. He will not take questions. After that I request that all of you leave the premises. The Andersons will not make any statements, nor will they permit any pictures."

Dr. Manning's silver hair was rumpled, and his kindly face was strained as he put on his glasses and in a hoarse voice began to read:

"I can only apologize for the distress the Anderson family is experiencing. I firmly believe Mrs. Anderson gave birth to her own biological child today. She had two cryopreserved embryos in the laboratory at our clinic. One was her son Jonathan's identical twin; the other his sibling.

"Last Monday, Helene Petrovic admitted to me that she had had an accident in the laboratory at the time she was handling the Petri dishes containing those two embryos. She slipped and fell. Her hand hit and overturned one of the lab dishes before the embryos were transferred to the test tubes. She believed the remaining dish contained the identical twin and put it in the specially marked tube. The other embryo was lost."

Dr. Manning took off his glasses and looked up.

"If Helene Petrovic was telling the truth, and I have no reason to doubt it, I repeat, Dina Anderson today gave birth to her biological son."

Questions were shouted at him. "Why didn't Petrovic tell you at that time?"

"Why didn't you warn the Andersons immediately?"

"How many more mistakes do you think she made?"

Dr. Manning ignored them all and walked unsteadily from the room.

. . .

VICTOR ORSINI CALLED PHILLIP CARTER AFTER THE SATUR-day evening news broadcast. "You'd better think of getting lawyers in to represent the firm," he told Carter.

Carter was just ready to leave for dinner at the Drumdoe Inn. "I agree. This is too big for Leiber to handle, but he can probably recommend someone."

Leiber was the lawyer the company kept on retainer.

"Phillip, if you don't have plans for the evening, how about dinner? There's an old saying, misery loves company."

"Then I've got the right plans. I'm meeting Catherine and Meg Collins."

"Give them my best. See you Monday."

Orsini hung up and walked over to the window. Candle-wood Lake was tranquil tonight. The lights from the houses that bordered it were brighter than usual. Dinner parties, Orsini thought. He was sure his name would come up at all of them. Everyone around here knew he worked for Collins and Carter.

His call to Phillip Carter had elicited the information he wanted: Carter was safely tied up for the evening. Victor could go to the office now. He'd be absolutely alone and could spend a couple of hours going through the personal files in Edwin Collins' office. Something had begun to nag at him, and it was vital that he give those files a final check before Meghan moved them out.

MEGHAN, MAC AND PHILLIP MET FOR DINNER AT THE Drumdoe Inn at seven-thirty. Catherine was in the kitchen where she'd been since four o'clock.

"Your mother has guts," Mac said.

"You bet she does," Meg agreed. "Did you catch the evening news? I watched PCD, and the lead story was the combination of the Anderson baby mix-up, the Petrovic murder, my resemblance to the woman in the morgue and the warrant for Dad's arrest. I gather all the stations led with it."

"I know," Mac said quietly.

Phillip raised his hand in a gesture of helplessness. "Meg, I'd do anything to help you and your mother, anything to try to find some explanation for Edwin sending Petrovic to Manning."

"There is an explanation," Meg said. "I believe that and so does Mother, which is what gave her the courage to come down here and put on an apron."

"She's not planning to handle the kitchen herself indefinitely?" Phillip protested.

"No. Tony, the head chef who retired last summer, phoned today and offered to come back and help out for a while. I told him that was wonderful but warned him not to take over. The busier Mother is, the better for her. But he's in there now. She'll be able to join us soon."

Meghan felt Mac's eyes on her and looked down to avoid the compassion she saw in them. She had known that tonight everyone in the dining room would be studying her and her mother to see how they were holding up. She had deliberately chosen to wear red: a calf-length skirt and cowl-neck cashmere sweater with gold jewelry.

She'd made herself up carefully with blusher and lipstick and eyeshadow. I guess I don't look like an unemployed reporter, she decided, glimpsing herself in the mirror as she left the house.

The disconcerting part was that she was sure that Mac could see behind her façade. He'd guess that in addition to everything else, she was worried sick about her job.

Mac had ordered wine. When it was poured, he raised his glass to her. "I have a message from Kyle. When he knew we were having dinner together he said to tell you he's coming to scare you tomorrow night."

Meg smiled. "Of course; tomorrow's Halloween. What's Kyle wearing?"

"Very original. He's a ghost, a really scary ghost, or so he claims. I'm taking him and some other kids trick-or-treating tomorrow afternoon, but he wants to save you for tomorrow night. So if there's a thump on the window after dark, be prepared."

"I'll make sure I'm home. Look, here's Mother."

Catherine kept a smile on her lips as she walked across the dining room. She was constantly stopped by people jumping up from their tables to embrace her. When she joined them, she said, "I'm so glad we came here. It's a heck of a lot better than sitting at home thinking."

"You look *wonderful,*" Phillip said. "You're a real trouper."

The admiration in his eyes was not lost on Meg. She glanced at Mac. He had seen it too.

Be careful, Phillip. Don't crowd Mother, Meghan thought.

She studied her mother's rings. The diamonds and emeralds she was wearing shone brilliantly under the small table lamp. Earlier that evening her mother had told her that on Monday she intended to hock or sell her jewelry. A big tax payment was due on the inn the following week. Catherine had said, "My only regret about giving up the jewelry is that I so wanted it for you."

I don't care about myself, Meg thought now, but . . .

"Meg? Are you ready to order?"

"Oh, sorry." Meghan smiled apologetically and glanced down at the menu in her hand.

"Try the Beef Wellington," Catherine said. "It's terrific. I should know. I made it."

During dinner, Meg was grateful that Mac and Phillip steered the conversation onto safe subjects, everything from the proposed paving of local roads to Kyle's championship soccer team.

Over cappuccino, Phillip asked Meg what her plans were. "I'm so sorry about the job," he said.

Meg shrugged. "I'm certainly not happy about it, but maybe it will turn out all right. You see, I keep thinking that nobody really knows anything about Helene Petrovic. She's the key to all this. I'm determined to turn up something about her that may give us some answers."

"I wish you would," Phillip said. "God knows *I'd* like some answers."

"Something else," Meg added, "I never got to clear out Dad's office. Would you mind if I go in tomorrow?"

"Go in whenever you want, Meg. Can I help you?"

"No thanks. I'll be fine."

"Meg, call me when you're finished," Mac said. "I'll come over and carry things to the car."

"Tomorrow's your day to trick or treat with Kyle," Meg reminded him. "I can handle it." She smiled at the two men. "Many thanks, guys, for being with us tonight. It's good to have friends at a time like this."

IN SCOTTSDALE, ARIZONA, AT NINE O'CLOCK ON SATURDAY night, Frances Grolier sighed as she put down her pearwood-handled knife. She had a commission to do a fifteen-inch bronze of a young Navaho boy and girl as a presentation to the guest of honor at a fund-raising dinner. The deadline was fast approaching and Frances was totally unsatisfied with the clay model she had been working on.

She had not managed to capture the questioning expression she had seen in the sensitive faces of the children. The pictures she had taken of them had caught it, but her hands were simply unable to execute her clear vision of what the sculpture should be.

The trouble was that she simply could not concentrate on her work.

Annie. She had not heard from her daughter for nearly two weeks now. All the messages she'd left on her answering machine had been ignored. In the last few days she'd called Annie's closest friends. No one had seen her.

She could be anywhere, Frances thought. She could have accepted an assignment to do a travel article on some remote, godforsaken place. As a free-lance travel writer, Annie came and went on no set schedule.

I raised her to be independent, Frances told herself. I raised her to be free, to take chances, to take from life what she wanted.

Did I teach her that to justify my own life? she wondered.

It was a thought that had come to her repeatedly in the last few days.

There was no use trying to work any more tonight. She went to the fireplace and added logs from the basket. The day had been warm and bright, but now the desert night was sharply cool.

The house was so quiet. There might never again be the heart-pounding anticipation of knowing that he was coming soon. As a little girl, Annie often asked why Daddy traveled so much.

"He has a very important job with the government," Frances would tell her.

As Annie grew up she became more curious. "What kind of job is it, Dad?"

"Oh, a sort of watchdog, honey."

"Are you in the CIA?"

"If I were, I'd never tell you."

"You are, aren't you?"

"Annie, I work for the government and get a lot of frequent-flyer miles in the process."

Remembering, Frances went into the kitchen, put ice in a glass and poured a generous amount of Scotch over it. Not the best way to solve problems, she told herself.

She put the drink down, went into the bath off the bedroom and showered, scrubbing away the bits of dried clay that were clinging to the crevices in her palms. Putting on gray silk pajamas and a robe, she retrieved the Scotch and settled on the couch in front of the fireplace. Then she picked up the Associated Press item she had torn from page ten of the morning newspaper, a summary of the report issued by the New York State Thruway Authority on the Tappan Zee Bridge disaster.

In part it read: "The number of victims who perished in the accident has been reduced from eight to seven. Exhaustive search has revealed no trace of the body of Edwin R. Collins, nor wreckage from his car."

Now Frances was haunted by the question, is it possible that Edwin is still alive?

He'd been so upset about business the morning he left.

He'd had a growing fear that his double life would be exposed and that both his daughters would despise him.

He'd had chest pains recently, which were diagnosed as being caused by anxiety.

He'd given her a bearer bond for two hundred thousand dollars in December. "In case anything happens to me," he had said. Had he been planning to find a way to drop out of both his lives when he said that?

And where was Annie? Frances agonized, with a growing sense of foreboding.

Edwin had an answering machine in his private office. Over the years, if Frances ever had to reach him, the arrangement was that she would call between midnight and 5 A.M. Eastern time. He always beeped in for messages by six o'clock and then erased them.

Of course that number was disconnected. Or was it?

It was a few minutes past ten in Arizona, past midnight on the East Coast.

She picked up the receiver and dialed. After two rings, Ed's recorded announcement began. "You have reached 203-555-2867. At the beep please leave a brief message."

Frances was so startled at hearing his voice that she almost forgot why she was calling. Could this possibly mean that he is alive? she wondered. And if Ed is alive somewhere, does he ever check this machine?

She had nothing to lose. Hurriedly Frances left the message they'd agreed upon. "Mr. Collins, please call Palomino Leather Goods. If you're still interested in that briefcase, we have it in stock."

. . .

VICTOR ORSINI WAS IN EDWIN COLLINS' OFFICE, STILL GOING through the files, when the private phone rang. He jumped. Who in hell would call an office at this hour?

The answering machine clicked on. Sitting in Collins' chair, Orsini listened to the modulated voice as it left the brief message.

When the call was completed, Orsini sat staring at the machine for long minutes. No business calls about a briefcase are made at this hour, he thought. That's some kind of code. Someone expects Ed Collins to get that message. It was one more confirmation that some mysterious person believed Ed was alive and out there somewhere.

A few minutes later, Victor left. He had not found the object of his search.

42

On Sunday morning, Catherine Collins attended the ten o'clock mass at St. Paul's, but she found it difficult to keep her mind on the sermon. She had been christened in this church, married in it, buried her parents from it. She had always found comfort here. For so long she had prayed at mass that Edwin's body would be found, prayed for resignation to his loss, for the strength to go on without him.

What was she asking of God now? Only that He keep Meg safe. She glanced at Meg, sitting beside her, completely still, seemingly attentive to the homily, but Catherine suspected that her daughter's thoughts were far away as well.

A fragment from the *Dies Irae* came unbidden into Catherine's mind. "Day of wrath and day of mourning. Lo, the world in ashes burning."

I'm angry and I'm hurt and my world is in ashes, Catherine thought. She blinked back sudden tears and felt Meg's hand close over hers.

When they left church they stopped for coffee and sticky buns at the local bakery, which had a half-dozen tables in the rear of the shop. "Feel better?" Meg asked.

"Yes," Catherine said briskly. "These sticky buns will do it every time. I'm going with you to Dad's office."

"I thought we'd agreed I should clear it out. That's why we're in two cars."

"It's no easier for you than it is for me. It will go faster if we're together, and some of that stuff will be heavy to carry."

Her mother's voice held the note of finality that Meghan knew ended further debate.

MEGHAN'S CAR WAS FILLED WITH BOXES FOR PACKING. SHE and her mother lugged them to the building. When they opened the door into the Collins and Carter office suite, they were surprised to find that it was warm and the lights were on.

"Ten to one Phillip came in early to get the place ready," Catherine observed. She looked around the reception room. "It's surprising how seldom I came here," she said. "Your dad traveled so much, and even when he wasn't on the road he was usually out on appointments. And of course I was always tied to the inn."

"I probably was here more than you," Meg agreed. "I used to come here after school sometimes and catch a ride home with him."

She pushed open the door to her father's private office. "It's just as he left it," she told her mother. "Phillip has been awfully generous to keep it undisturbed this long. I know Victor really should have been using it."

For a long moment they both studied the room: his desk,

the long table behind it with their pictures, the wall unit with bookcases and file cabinets in the same cherrywood finish as the desk. The effect was uncluttered and tasteful.

"Edwin bought and refinished that desk," Catherine said. "I'm sure Phillip wouldn't mind if we had it picked up."

"I'm sure he wouldn't."

They began by collecting the pictures and stacking them in a box. Meghan knew they both sensed that the faster the office took on an impersonal look, the easier it would be. Then she suggested, "Mom, why don't you start with the books. I'll go through the desk and files."

It was only when she was seated at the desk that she saw the blinking light on the answering machine, which sat on a low table next to the swivel chair.

"Look at this."

Her mother came over to the desk. "Is anyone still leaving messages on Dad's machine?" she asked incredulously, then leaned down to look at the call display. "There's just one. Let's hear it."

Bewildered, they listened to the message and then the computer voice of the machine saying, "Sunday, October thirty-first, 12:09 A.M. End of final message."

"That message came in only hours ago!" Catherine exclaimed. "Who leaves a business message in the middle of the night? And when would Dad have ordered a brief-case?"

"It could be a mistake," Meghan said. "Whoever called didn't leave a return number or a name."

"Wouldn't most salespeople leave a phone number if they wanted to confirm an order, especially if the order was placed months ago? Meg, that message doesn't make sense. And that woman doesn't sound like an order clerk to me."

Meg slipped the tape out of the machine and put it in her shoulder bag. "It doesn't make sense," she agreed. "We're only wasting time trying to figure it out here. Let's get on with this packing and listen to it again at home."

She looked quickly through the desk drawers and found

the usual assortment of stationery, notepads, paper clips, pens and highlighters. She remembered that when he went over a candidate's curriculum vitae, her father had marked the most favorable aspects of the résumé in yellow, the least favorable in pink. Quickly she transferred the contents of the desk to boxes.

Next she tackled the files. The first one seemed to have copies of her father's expense account reports. Apparently the bookkeeper kept the original and returned a photocopy with Paid stamped across the top.

"I'm going to take these files home," she said. "They're Dad's personal copies of originals already in the company records."

"Is there any point in taking them?"

"Yes, there just might be some reference to Palomino Leather Goods."

They were finishing the last box when they heard the outside door open. "It's me," Phillip called.

He came in, wearing a shirt open at the neck, sleeveless sweater, corduroy jacket and slacks. "Hope it was comfortable when you got here," he said. "I stopped by this morning for a minute. This place gets mighty chilly over a weekend if the thermostat is down."

He surveyed the boxes. "I knew you'd need a hand. Catherine, will you please put down that box of books."

"Dad called her 'Mighty Mouse,' " Meg said. "This is nice of you, Phillip."

He saw the top of an expense file sticking out of one of the boxes. "Are you sure you want all that stuff? It's nuts and bolts, and you and I went all through it, Meg, looking for any insurance policies that might not have been in the safe."

"We might as well take it," Meg said. "You'd only have to dispose of it anyhow."

"Phillip, the answering machine was blinking when we came in here." Meghan took out the tape, snapped it into the machine and played it.

She saw the look of astonishment on his face. "Obviously you don't get it either."

"No. I don't."

It was fortunate that both she and her mother had brought their cars. The trunks and backseats were crammed by the time the last box had been carried down.

They refused Phillip's offer to follow them and help unload. "I'll have a couple of the busboys from the inn take care of it," Catherine said.

As Meghan drove home she knew that every hour she was not tracking down information on Helene Petrovic she would be going through every line of every page of her father's records.

If there was someone else in Dad's life, she thought, and if that woman in the morgue is the Annie that Cyrus Graham met ten years ago, there might be some link in his files that I can trace back to them.

Some instinct told her that Palomino Leather Goods might prove to be that link.

IN KYLE'S EYES, THE TRICK-OR-TREATING HAD BEEN ABSO-lutely great. On Sunday evening he spread his collection of assorted candies, cookies, apples and pennies on the den floor while Mac prepared dinner.

"Don't eat any of that junk now," Mac warned.

"I know, Dad. You told me twice."

"Then maybe it'll start sinking in." Mac tested the hamburgers on the grill.

"Why do we always have hamburgers on Sunday when we're home?" Kyle asked. "They're better at McDonald's."

"Many thanks." Mac flipped them onto toasted buns. "We have hamburgers on Sunday because I cook hamburgers better than anything else. I take you out most Fridays. I make pasta when we're home on Saturdays, and Mrs. Dileo cooks good food the rest of the week. Now eat up if you want to put your costume on again and scare Meg."

Kyle took a couple of bites of his hamburger. "Do you like Meg, Dad?"

"Yes, I do. Very much. Why?"

"I wish she'd come here more. She's fun."

I wish she'd come here more too, Mac thought, but it doesn't look as though that's going to happen. Last night when he'd offered to help her with the packing up of her father's office she'd cut him off so fast his head had been spinning.

Stay away. Don't get too close. We're just friends. She might as well put up a sign.

She'd certainly grown up a lot from the nineteen-year-old kid who had a crush on him and wrote a letter telling him she loved him and please don't marry Ginger.

He wished he had the letter now. He also wished she'd feel that way again. He certainly regretted he hadn't taken her advice about Ginger.

Then Mac looked at his son. No I don't, he thought. I couldn't and wouldn't undo having this kid.

"Dad, what's the matter?" Kyle asked. "You look worried."

"That's what you said about Meg when you saw her on television yesterday."

"Well, she did and so do you."

"I'm just worried that I might have to learn how to cook something else. Finish up and get your costume on."

IT WAS SEVEN-THIRTY WHEN THEY LEFT THE HOUSE. KYLE deemed it satisfactorily dark outside for ghosts. "I bet there really are ghosts out," he said. "On Halloween all the dead people get out of their graves and walk around."

"Who told you that?"

"Danny."

"Tell Danny that's a tall tale everyone tells on Halloween."

They walked around the curve in the road and reached the Collins property. "Now, Dad, you wait here near the hedge where Meg can't see you. I'll go around in back and bang on the window and howl. Okay?"

"Okay. Don't scare her too much."

Swinging his skull-shaped lantern, Kyle raced around the back of the Collins house. The dining room shades were up, and he could see Meg sitting at the table with a bunch of papers in front of her. He had a good idea. He'd go right to the edge of the woods and run from there to the house, yelling "Whoo, whoo," and then he'd bang on the window. That should really scare Meg.

He stepped between two trees, spread his arms and began to wave them about. As his right hand went back, he felt flesh, smooth flesh, then an ear. He heard breathing. Whirling his head around, he saw the form of a man, crouching behind him, the light reflecting off a camera lens. A hand grabbed his neck. Kyle wiggled loose and began to scream. Then he was shoved forward with a violent push. As he fell, he dropped his lantern and began clawing the ground, his hand closing over something. Still screaming, he scrambled to his feet and ran toward the house.

That's some realistic yell, Mac thought, when he first heard Kyle's scream. Then, as the terrified shriek continued, he began to run toward the woods. Something had happened to Kyle. With a burst of speed he raced across the lawn and behind the house.

From inside the dining room, Meg heard the screaming and ran to the back door. She yanked it open and grabbed Kyle as he stumbled through the door and fell into her arms, sobbing in terror.

That was the way Mac found them, their arms around each other, Meg rocking his son back and forth, soothing him. "Kyle, it's okay. It's okay," she kept repeating.

It took minutes before he could tell them what had happened. "Kyle, it's all those stories about the dead walking that makes you think you're seeing things," Mac said. "There was nothing there."

Calmer now, drinking the hot cocoa Meg had made for

him, Kyle was adamant. "There was so a man there, and he had a camera. I know. I fell when he pushed me, but I picked up something. Then I dropped it when I saw Meg. Go see what it is, Dad."

"I'll get a flashlight, Mac," Meg said.

Mac went outside and began moving the beam back and forth over the ground. He did not have to go far. Only a few feet from the back porch he found a gray plastic box, the kind used to carry videotapes.

He picked it up and walked back to the woods, still shining the light before him. He knew it was useless. No intruder stands around waiting to be discovered. The ground was too hard to see footprints, but he found Kyle's lantern directly in line with the dining room windows. From where he was standing he could see Meg and Kyle clearly.

Someone with a camera had been here watching Meg, maybe taping her. Why?

Mac thought of the dead girl in the morgue, then hurried back across the lawn to the house.

THAT STUPID KID! BERNIE THOUGHT AS HE RAN THROUGH the woods to his car. He'd parked it near the end of the Drumdoe Inn parking lot but not so far away that it stood out. There were about forty cars scattered through the lot now, so his Chevy certainly wouldn't have been particularly noticed. He hurriedly tossed his camera in the trunk and drove through town toward Route 7. He was careful to go not more than five miles above the speed limit. But he knew that driving too slow was a red flag to the cops too.

Had that kid gotten a good look at him? He didn't think so. It was dark, and the kid was scared. A few seconds more and he could have moved backwards and the kid wouldn't have known he was there.

Bernie was furious. He'd been enjoying watching Meghan through the camera, and he'd had such a clear view of her. He was sure he had great tapes.

On the other hand he'd never seen anyone so frightened as
that kid had been. He felt tingly and alive and almost ener-
gized just thinking about it. To have such power. To be able
to record someone's expressions and movements and secret
little gestures, like the way Meghan kept tucking her hair
behind her ear when she was concentrating. To scare someone so much that he screamed and cried and ran like that
little kid just now.

To watch Meghan, her hands, her hair . . .

43

Stephanie Petrovic had a fitful night, finally falling into a
heavy sleep. When she awakened at ten-thirty on Sunday
morning, she opened her eyes lazily and smiled. At last things
were working out.

She had been warned never to breathe his name, to forget
she'd ever met him, but that was before Helene was murdered
and before Helene lost the chance to change her will.

On the telephone he was so kind to her. He promised he
would take care of her. He would make arrangements to
have the baby adopted by people who would pay one hundred thousand dollars for it.

"So much?" she had asked, delighted.

He reassured her that there would be no problem.

He would also arrange to get her a green card. "It will be
fake, but no one will ever be able to tell the difference," he
had said. "However, I suggest that you move someplace
where no one knows you. I wouldn't want anyone to recog-

nize you. Even in a big place like New York City people bump into each other, and in your case they'd start asking questions. You might try California."

Stephanie knew she would love California. Maybe she could get a job in a spa there, she thought. With one hundred thousand dollars she'd be able to get the training she'd need. Or maybe she could just get a job right away. She was like Helene. Being a beautician came to her naturally. She loved that kind of work.

He was sending a car for her at seven o'clock tonight. "I don't want the neighbors to see you moving out," he'd told her.

Stephanie wanted to luxuriate in bed, but she was hungry. Only ten days more and the baby will be born and then I can go on a diet, she promised herself.

She showered, then dressed in the maternity clothes she had come to hate. Then she began to pack. Helene had tapestry luggage in the closet. Why shouldn't I have it? Stephanie thought. Who deserves it more?

Because of the pregnancy, she had so few clothes, but once she was back to her normal size she'd fit in Helene's things again. Helene had been a conservative dresser, but all her clothes were expensive and in good taste. Stephanie went through the closet and dresser drawers, rejecting only what she absolutely did not like.

Helene had a small safe on the floor of her closet. Stephanie knew where she kept the combination, so she opened it. It didn't contain much jewelry, but there were a few very good pieces, which she slipped into a cosmetic bag.

It was a shame she couldn't move the furniture out there. On the other hand, she knew from pictures she'd seen that in California they didn't use old-fashioned upholstered furniture and dark woods like mahogany.

She did go through the house and chose some Dresden figurines to take with her. Then she remembered the table silver. The big chest was too heavy to carry, so she put the silver in plastic bags and fastened rubber bands around them to keep it from rattling in the suitcase.

The lawyer, Mr. Potters, called at five o'clock to see how she was feeling. "Perhaps you'd like to join my wife and me for dinner, Stephanie."

"Oh, thank you," she said, "but someone from the Rumanian Society is going to drop in."

"Fine. We just didn't want you to be lonesome. Remember, be sure to call me if you need anything."

"You're so kind, Mr. Potters."

"Well, I only wish I could do more for you. Unfortunately, where the will is concerned, my hands are tied."

I don't need your help, Stephanie thought as she hung up the phone.

Now it was time to write the letter. She composed three versions before she was satisfied. She knew that some of her spelling was bad, and she had to look up some words, but at last it seemed to be all right. It was to Mr. Potters:

Dear Mr. Potters,
    I am happy to say that Jan, the father of my baby, is the one who came to see me. We are going to get maried and he will take care of us. He must get back to his job right awaye so I am leaving with him. He now works in Dallas.
    I love Jan very much and I know you will be pleassed for me.
    Thank you.
                    Stephanie Petrovic

The car came for her promptly at seven. The driver carried her bags out. Stephanie left the note and house key on the dining room table, turned off the lights, closed the door behind her and hurried through the darkness, down the flagstone walk to the waiting vehicle.

ON MONDAY MORNING, MEGHAN TRIED TO PHONE STEPHANIE Petrovic. There was no answer. She settled down at the dining room table, where she had begun to go through her father's business files.

She immediately noticed something. He'd been registered and billed for five days at the Four Seasons Hotel in Beverly Hills, from 23 January to 28 January, the day he flew to Newark and disappeared. After the first two days there were no extra charges on that bill. Even if he ate most of his meals out, Meghan thought, people send for breakfast or make a phone call or open the room bar and have a drink—something.

On the other hand, if he'd been on the concierge floor, it would be very like her father just to go to the courtesy buffet and help himself to juice, coffee and a roll. He was a light-breakfast eater.

The first two days, however, did have extra charges on the bill, like the valet, a bottle of wine, an evening snack, phone calls. She made a note of the dates of the three days when there were no extra expenses.

There might be a pattern, she thought.

At noon she tried Stephanie again, and again the phone was not answered. At two o'clock she began to be alarmed and phoned the lawyer, Charles Potters. He assured her that Stephanie was fine. He'd spoken to her the evening before and she'd said someone from the Rumanian Society was dropping by.

"I'm glad," Meghan said. "She's a very frightened girl."

"Yes, she is," Potters agreed. "Something that isn't generally known is that when someone leaves an entire estate to a charity or a medical facility such as the Manning Clinic, if a close relative is needy and inclined to try to break the will, the charity or facility may quietly offer a settlement. However, after Stephanie went on television literally accusing the clinic of being responsible for her aunt's murder, any such settlement was out of the question. It would seem like hush money."

"I understand," Meghan said. "I'll keep trying Stephanie, but will you ask her to call me if you hear from her? I still think someone should go after the man who got her pregnant. If she gives away her baby, she may someday regret it."

Meghan's mother had gone to the inn for the breakfast and lunch service, and she returned to the house just as Meg was finishing the conversation with Potters. "Let me get busy with you," she said, taking a seat next to her at the dining room table.

"Actually you can take over," Meghan told her. "I really have to drive to my apartment and get clothes and pick up my mail. It's the first of November, and all the little window envelopes will be in."

The evening before, when her mother had returned from the inn, she had told her about the man with the camera who had frightened Kyle. "I asked someone at the station to check it out for me; I haven't heard yet, but I'm sure one of those sleazy programs is putting together a story on us and Dad and the Andersons," she said. "Sending someone to spy on us is the way they work." She had not allowed Mac to call the police.

She showed her mother what she was doing with the files. "Mom, watch the hotel receipts for times when there were no extra expenses for three or four days in a row. I'd like to see if it only happened when Dad was in California." She did not say that Los Angeles was half an hour by plane from Scottsdale.

"And as for Palomino Leather Goods," Catherine said, "I don't know why, but that name has been churning around in my mind. I feel as though I've heard it before, but a long time ago."

Meghan still had not decided if she would stop at PCD on her way to the apartment. She was wearing comfortable old slacks and a favorite sweater. It'll do, she thought. That was one of the aspects she had loved about the job, the behind-the-scenes informality.

She brushed her hair quickly and realized that it was growing too long. She liked it to be collar length. Now it was touching her shoulders. The dead girl's hair had been on her shoulders. Her hands suddenly cold, Meghan reached back, twisted her hair into a French knot and pinned it up.

When she was leaving, her mother said, "Meg, why don't you go out to dinner with some of your friends? It will do you good to get away from all this."

"I'm not much in the mood for social dinners," Meg said, "but I'll call and let you know. You'll be at the inn?"

"Yes."

"Well, when you're here after dark be sure to keep the draperies drawn." She raised her hand, palm upright and outward, fingers spread. "As Kyle would say, 'Give me a high five.' "

Her mother raised her hand and touched her daughter's palm in response. "You've got it."

They looked at each other for a long minute, then Catherine said briskly, "Drive carefully."

It was the standard warning ever since Meg had gotten her driving permit at age sixteen.

Her answer was always in the same vein. Today she said, "Actually I thought I'd tailgate a tractor trailer." Then she wanted to bite her tongue. The accident on the Tappan Zee Bridge had been caused by a fuel truck tailgating a tractor trailer.

She knew her mother was thinking the same thing when she said, "Dear God, Meg, it's like walking through a mine field, isn't it? Even the kind of joking remark that has been part of the fabric of our lives has been tainted and twisted. Will it ever end?"

THAT SAME MONDAY MORNING, DR. GEORGE MANNING WAS again questioned in Assistant State Attorney John Dwyer's office. The questions had become sharper with an edge of sarcasm in them. The two investigators sat quietly as their boss handled the interrogation.

"Doctor," Dwyer asked, "can you explain why you didn't tell us immediately that Helene Petrovic was afraid that she had mixed up the Anderson embryos?"

"Because she wasn't sure." George Manning's shoulders

slumped. His complexion, usually a healthy pink, was ashen. Even the admirable head of silver hair seemed a faded, graying white. Since the Anderson baby's birth he had aged visibly.

"Dr. Manning, you've said repeatedly that founding and running the assisted reproduction clinic has been the great achievement of your lifetime. Were you aware that Helene Petrovic was planning to leave her rather considerable estate to research at your clinic?"

"We had talked about it. You see, the level of success in our field is still not anything like what we would wish. It's very expensive for a woman to have in vitro fertilization, anywhere from ten to twenty thousand dollars. If a pregnancy is not achieved, the process starts all over. While some clinics claim a one out of five success ratio, the honest figure is closer to one out of ten."

"Doctor, you are very anxious to see the ratio of successful pregnancies at your clinic improved?"

"Yes, of course."

"Wasn't it quite a blow to you last Monday when Helene Petrovic not only quit but admitted she might have made a very serious mistake?"

"It was devastating."

"Yet, even when she was found murdered, you withheld the very important reason for quitting that she had given you." Dwyer leaned across his desk. "What else did Ms. Petrovic tell you at that meeting last Monday, Doctor?"

Manning folded his hands together. "She said that she was planning to sell her house in Lawrenceville and move away, that she might go to France to live."

"And what did you think of that plan?"

"I was stunned," he whispered. "I was sure she was running away."

"Running away from what, Doctor?"

George Manning knew it was all over. He could not protect the clinic any longer. "I had the feeling that she was afraid that if the Anderson baby was not Jonathan's twin, it would start an investigation that might reveal many mistakes in the lab."

"The will, Doctor. Did you also think that Helene Petrovic would change her will?"

"She told me she was sorry, but it was necessary. She planned to take a long time off from work and now she had family to consider."

John Dwyer had found the answer he had guessed was there. "Dr. Manning, when was the last time you spoke to Edwin Collins?"

"He called me the day before he disappeared." Dr. George Manning did not like what he saw in Dwyer's eyes. "It was the first contact I had had with him either by phone or letter since he placed Helene Petrovic in my clinic," he said, looking away, unable to cope with the disbelief and mistrust he was reading in the demeanor of the assistant state attorney.

44

Meghan decided to skip going to the office and reached her apartment building at four o'clock. Her mailbox was overflowing. She fished out all the envelopes and ads and throwaways, then took the elevator up to her fourteenth-floor apartment.

She immediately opened the windows to blow away the smell of stale heat, then stood for a moment looking out over the water to the Statue of Liberty. Today the lady seemed remote and formidable in the shadows cast by the late afternoon sun.

Often when she looked at it she thought of her grandfather, Pat Kelly, who had come to this country as a teenager with nothing and worked so hard to make his fortune.

What would her grandfather think if he knew that his daughter Catherine might lose everything he had worked for because her husband had cheated on her for years?

Scottsdale, Arizona. Meg looked over the waters of New York Harbor and realized what had been bothering her. Arizona was in the Southwest. Palomino had the sound of the Southwest.

She went over to the phone, dialed the operator and asked for the area code for Scottsdale, Arizona.

Next she dialed Arizona information.

When she reached that operator, she asked, "Do you have a listing for an Edwin Collins or an E. R. Collins?"

There was none.

Meg asked another question. "Do you have a listing for Palomino Leather Goods?"

There was a pause, then the operator said, "Please hold for the number."

Part
Three

45

On Monday evening when Mac got home from work, Kyle was his usual cheerful self. He informed his father that he had told all the kids at school about the guy in the woods.

"They all said how scared they'd be," he explained with satisfaction. "I told them how I really ran fast and got away from him. Did you tell your friends about it?"

"No, I didn't."

"It's okay if you want to," Kyle said magnanimously.

As Kyle turned away, Mac held his arm. "Kyle, wait a minute."

"What's the matter?"

"Let me take a look at something."

Kyle was wearing an open-necked flannel shirt. Mac pushed it back, revealing yellowish and purple bruises at the base of his son's neck. "Did you get these last night?"

"I told you that guy grabbed me."

"You said he pushed you."

"First he grabbed me, but I got away."

Mac swore under his breath. He had not thought to examine Kyle the night before. He'd been wearing the ghost costume, and under that, a white turtleneck shirt. Mac had thought that Kyle had only been pushed by the intruder with the camera. Instead he had been grabbed around the neck. Strong fingers had caused those bruises.

Mac kept an arm around his son as he dialed the police. Last night he had reluctantly gone along with Meghan when she pleaded with him not to call them.

"Mac, it's bad enough now without giving the media a fresh angle on all this," she had said. "Mark my words, somebody will write that Dad is hanging around the house. The assistant state attorney is sure he's going to contact us."

I've let Meg keep me out of this long enough, Mac thought grimly. She's not going to any longer. That wasn't just some cameraman hanging around out there.

The phone was answered on the first ring. "State Trooper Thorne speaking."

FIFTEEN MINUTES LATER A SQUAD CAR WAS AT THE HOUSE. IT was clear the two policemen were not pleased that they had not been called earlier. "Dr. MacIntyre, last night was Halloween. We're always worried that some nut might be hanging around, hoping to pick up a kid. That guy might have gone somewhere else in town."

"I agree I should have called," Mac said, "but I don't think that man was looking for children. He was directly in line with the dining room windows of the Collins' home, and Meghan Collins was in full view."

He saw the looks the cops exchanged. "I think the state attorney's office should know about this," one of them said.

ALL THE WAY HOME FROM HER APARTMENT, THE BITTER truth had been sinking in. Meghan knew she now had virtual confirmation that her father had a second family in Arizona.

When she'd phoned the Palomino Leather Goods Shop she'd spoken to the owner. The woman was astonished when asked about the message on the answering machine. "That call didn't come from here," she said flatly.

She did confirm that she had a customer named Mrs. E. R. Collins who had a daughter in her twenties. After that she refused to give further information over the phone.

It was seven-thirty when Meg reached Newtown. She turned into the driveway and was surprised to see Mac's red Chrysler and an unfamiliar sedan parked in front of the house. Now what? she thought, alarmed. She pulled up behind them, parked and hurried up the porch steps, realizing that any unexpected occurrence was enough to start her heart pounding with dread.

SPECIAL INVESTIGATOR ARLENE WEISS WAS IN THE LIVING room with Catherine, Mac and Kyle. There was no apology in Mac's voice when he told Meg why he'd called the local police and then the assistant state attorney's office about the intruder. In fact, Meg was sure from the clipped way he spoke to her that he was angry. Kyle had been manhandled and terrified; he might have been strangled by some lunatic, and I wouldn't let Mac notify the police, she thought. She didn't blame him for being furious.

Kyle was sitting between Catherine and Mac on the couch. He slid down and came across the room to her. "Meg, don't look so sad. I'm okay." He put his hands on her cheeks. "Really, I'm okay."

She looked into his serious eyes, then hugged him fiercely. "You bet you are, pal."

Weiss did not stay long. "Miss Collins, believe it or not, we want to help you," she said as Meghan accompanied her to the door. "When you don't report, or allow other people to report, incidents like last night's, you are hindering this investigation. We could have had a police vehicle here in a few minutes if you'd called. According to Kyle, that man was carrying a large camera that would have slowed him down. Please, is there anything else we should know?"

"Nothing," Meg said.

"Mrs. Collins tells me that you were at your apartment. Did you find any more faxed messages?"

"No." She bit her lip, thinking of her call to Palomino Leather Goods.

Weiss stared at her. "I see. Well, if you remember anything that you think will interest us, you know where to reach us."

When Weiss left, Mac said to Kyle, "Go into the den. You can watch television for fifteen minutes. Then we have to go."

"That's okay, Dad. There's nothing good on. I'll stay here."

"It wasn't a suggestion."

Kyle jumped up. "Fine. You don't have to get sore about it."

"Right, Dad," Meghan agreed. "You don't have to get sore about it."

Kyle gave her a high five as he passed her chair.

Mac waited until he heard the click of the den door. "What did you find out while you were at your apartment, Meghan?"

Meg looked at her mother. "The location of the Palomino Leather Goods Shop and that they have a customer named Mrs. E. R. Collins."

Ignoring her mother's gasp, she told them about her call to Scottsdale.

"I'm flying out there tomorrow," she said. "We have to know if their Mrs. Collins is the woman Cyrus Graham saw with Dad. We can't be sure until I meet her."

Catherine Collins hoped the hurt she saw in her daughter's face was not mirrored in her own expression when she said quietly, "Meggie, if you look so much like that dead young woman, and the woman in Scottsdale is that girl's mother, it could be terrible for her to see you."

"Nothing is going to make it easy for whoever turns out to be the mother of that girl."

She was grateful that they did not try to dissuade her.

Instead Mac said, "Meg, don't tell anyone, and I mean *any-one,* where you're going. How long do you expect to stay?"

"Overnight at the most."

"Then for all anyone will know, you're at your apartment. Leave it at that."

When he collected Kyle, he said, "Catherine, if Kyle and I come to the inn tomorrow night, do you think you'd have time to join us for dinner?"

Catherine managed a smile. "I'd love to. What should I have on the menu, Kyle?"

"Chicken McNuggets?" he asked hopefully.

"Are you trying to run me out of business? Come on inside. I brought home some cookies. Take a couple with you." She led him into the kitchen.

"Catherine is very tactful," Mac said. "I think she knew I wanted a minute with you. Meg, I don't like you going out there alone, but I think I understand. Now I want the truth. Is there anything you're holding back?"

"No."

"Meg, I won't let you shut me out anymore. Get used to that idea. How can I help?"

"Call Stephanie Petrovic in the morning, and if she's not there, call her lawyer. I have a funny feeling about Stephanie. I've tried to reach her three or four times, and she's been out all day. I even called her from the car half an hour ago. Her baby is due in ten days and she feels lousy. The other day she was exhausted after her aunt's funeral and couldn't wait to lie down. I can't imagine her being gone so long. Let me give you the numbers."

When Mac and Kyle left a few minutes later, Mac's kiss was not the usual friendly peck on the cheek. Instead, as his son had done earlier, he held Meg's face in his hands.

"Take care of yourself," he ordered, as his lips closed firmly over hers.

46

*M*onday had been a bad day for Bernie. He got up at dawn, settled in the cracked Naugahyde recliner in the basement, and began to watch over and over the video he'd taken of Meghan from his hiding place in the woods. He'd wanted to see it when he got home last night, but his mother had demanded he keep her company.

"I'm alone too much, Bernard," she'd complained. "You never used to go out so much on weekends. You haven't got a girl have you?"

"Of course not, Mama," he'd said.

"You know all the trouble you've gotten into because of girls."

"None of that was my fault, Mama."

"I didn't say it was your fault. I said that girls are poison for you. Stay away from them."

"Yes, Mama."

When Mama got in one of those moods, the best thing Bernie could do was to listen to her. He was still afraid of her. He still shivered thinking of the times when he was growing up and she'd suddenly appear with the strap in her hands. "I saw you looking at that smut on television, Bernard. I can read those filthy thoughts in your head."

Mama would never understand that what he felt for Meghan was pure and beautiful. It was just that he wanted to be around Meghan, wanted to see her, wanted to feel like he could always get her to look up and smile at him. Like last night. If he had tapped at the window and she'd recognized him, she wouldn't have been scared. She'd have run to the door to let him in. She'd have said, "Bernie, what are you doing here?" Maybe she'd have made a cup of tea for him.

Bernie leaned forward. He was getting to the good part again, where Meghan looked so intent on what she was doing as she sat at the head of the dining room table with all those papers in front of her. With the zoom lens he'd managed to get close-ups of her face. There was something about the way she was beginning to moisten her lips that thrilled him. Her blouse was open at the neck. He wasn't sure if he could see the beat of her pulse there or if he only imagined that.

"Bernard! Bernard!"

His mother was at the head of the stairs, shouting down to him. How long had she been calling?

"Yes, Mama. I'm coming."

"It took you long enough," she snapped when he reached the kitchen. "You'll be late for work. What were you doing?"

"Straightening up a little. I know you want me to leave it neat."

Fifteen minutes later he was in the car. He drove down the block, unsure of where to go. He knew he should try to pick up some fares at the airport. With all the equipment he was buying, he needed to make some money. He had to force himself to turn the wheel and head in the direction of La Guardia.

He spent the day driving back and forth to the airport. It went well enough until late afternoon when some guy kept complaining to him about the traffic. "For Pete's sake, get in the left lane. Can't you see this one is blocked?"

Bernie had begun thinking about Meghan again, about whether it would be safe to drive past her house once it got dark.

A minute later the passenger snapped, "Listen, I knew I should have taken a cab. Where'd you learn to drive? Keep up with the traffic, for God's sake."

Bernie was at the last exit on the Grand Central Parkway before the Triborough Bridge. He took a sharp right onto the street parallel to the parkway and pulled the car to the curb.

"What the hell do you think you're doing?" the passenger demanded.

The guy's big suitcase was next to Bernie in the front seat. He leaned over, opened the door and pushed it out. "Get lost," he ordered. "Get yourself a taxi."

He spun his head to look into the passenger's face. Their eyes locked.

The passenger's expression changed to one of panic. "All right, take it easy. Sorry if I got you upset."

He jumped out of the car and yanked his suitcase away just as Bernie floored the accelerator. Bernie cut through side streets. He'd better go home. Otherwise he'd go back and smash that big mouth.

He began to take deliberate deep breaths. That's what the prison psychiatrist told him to do when he felt himself getting mad. "You've got to handle that anger, Bernie," he'd warned him. "Unless you want to spend the rest of your life in here."

Bernie knew he could never go back to prison again. He'd do anything to keep that from happening.

ON TUESDAY MORNING, MEGHAN'S ALARM WENT OFF AT 4 A.M. She had a reservation on America West Flight 9, leaving from Kennedy Airport at 7:25. She had no trouble getting up. Her sleep had been uneasy. She showered, running the water as hot as she could stand it, glad to feel some of the taut muscles in her neck and back loosen.

As she pulled on underwear and stockings she listened to the weather report on the radio. It was below freezing in New York. Arizona, of course, was another matter. Cool in the evenings at this time of year, but she understood it could be fairly warm during the day.

A tan, lightweight wool jacket and slacks with a print blouse seemed to be a good choice. Over it she'd wear her Burberry without the lining. She quickly packed the few things she'd need for an overnight stay.

The smell of coffee greeted her as she started down the

stairs. Her mother was in the kitchen. "You shouldn't have gotten up," Meg protested.

"I wasn't sleeping." Catherine Collins toyed with the belt of her terry-cloth robe. "I didn't offer to go with you, Meg, but now I'm having second thoughts. Maybe I shouldn't let you do this alone. It's just that if there is another Mrs. Edwin Collins in Scottsdale, I don't know what I could say to her. Was she as ignorant as I about what was going on? Or did she knowingly live a lie?"

"I hope by the end of the day I'll have some answers," Meg said, "and I absolutely know that it's better I do this alone." She took a few sips of grapefruit juice and swallowed a little coffee. "I've got to get going. It's a long ride to Kennedy Airport. I don't want to get caught in rush-hour traffic."

Her mother walked her to the door. Meg hugged her briefly. "I get into Phoenix at eleven o'clock, mountain time. I'll call you late this afternoon."

She could feel her mother's eyes on her as she walked to the car.

THE FLIGHT WAS UNEVENTFUL. SHE HAD A WINDOW SEAT AND for long periods of time gazed down at the puffy cushion of white clouds. She thought of her fifth birthday when her mother and father took her to DisneyWorld. It was her first flight. She'd sat at the window, her father beside her, her mother across the aisle.

Over the years her father had teased her about the question she'd asked that day. "Daddy, if we got out of the plane, could we walk on the clouds?"

He'd told her that he was sorry to say the clouds wouldn't hold her up. "But I'll always hold you up, Meggie Anne," he'd promised.

And he had. She thought of the awful day when she'd tripped just before the finish line of a race and had cost her high school track team the state championship. Her father had been waiting when she'd slunk out of the gym, not wanting to hear the consoling words of her teammates or see the disappointment on their faces.

He had offered understanding, not consolation. "There are some events in our lives, Meghan," he'd told her, "that no matter how old we get, the memory still hurts. I'm afraid you've just chalked up one of those events."

A wave of tenderness swept over Meghan and then was gone as she remembered the times when her father's claim of pressing business had kept him away. Sometimes even on holidays like Thanksgiving and Christmas. Was he celebrating them in Scottsdale? With his other family? Holidays were always so busy at the inn. When he wasn't home, she and her mother would have dinner there with friends, but her mother would be up and down greeting guests and checking the kitchen.

She remembered being fourteen and taking jazz dance lessons. When her father came home from one of his trips, she'd shown him the newest steps she'd mastered.

"Meggie," he'd sighed, "jazz is good music and a fine dance form, but the waltz is the dance of the angels." He'd taught her the Viennese waltz.

It was a relief when the pilot announced that they were beginning the descent into Sky Harbor International Airport, where the outside temperature was seventy degrees.

Meghan took her things from the overhead compartment and waited restlessly for the cabin door to open. She wanted to get through this day as quickly as possible.

The car rental agency was in the Barry Goldwater terminal. Meghan stopped to look up the address of the Palomino Leather Goods Shop and when she signed for a car asked the clerk for directions.

"That's in the Bogota section of Scottsdale," the clerk said. "It's a wonderful shopping area that will make you think you're in a medieval town."

On a map she outlined the route for Meghan. "You'll be there in twenty-five minutes," she said.

As she drove, Meghan absorbed the beauty of the mountains in the distance and the cloudless, intensely blue sky. When she had cleared the commercial sections, palms and orange trees and saguaro cactus began to dot the landscape.

She passed the adobe-style Safari Hotel. With its bright oleanders and tall palms, it looked serene and inviting. This was where Cyrus Graham said he had seen his stepbrother, her father, nearly eleven years ago.

The Palomino Leather Goods Shop was a mile farther down on Scottsdale Road. Here the buildings had castlelike towers and crenellated parapet walls. Cobblestone streets contributed to an old-world effect. The boutiques that lined the streets were small, and all of them looked expensive. Meghan turned left into the parking area past Palomino Leather Goods and got out of the car. She found it disconcerting to realize that her knees were trembling.

The pungent scent of fine leather greeted her when she entered the shop. Purses ranging in size from clutches to tote bags were tastefully grouped on shelves and tables. A display case held wallets, key rings and jewelry. Briefcases and luggage were visible in the larger area a few steps down and to the rear of the entry level.

There was only one other person in the shop, a young woman with striking Indian features and thick, dark hair that cascaded down her back. She looked up from her position behind the cash register and smiled. "May I help you?" There was no hint of recognition in her voice or manner.

Meghan thought quickly. "I hope so. I'm only in town for a few hours and I wanted to look up some relatives. I don't have their address and they're not listed in the phone book. I know they shop here and I hoped I might be able to get the address or phone number from you."

The clerk hesitated. "I'm new. Maybe you could come back in about an hour. The owner will be in then."

"Please," Meghan said. "I have so little time."

"What's the name? I can see if they have an account."

"E. R. Collins."

"Oh," the clerk said, "you must have called yesterday."

"That's right."

"I was here. After she spoke to you, the owner, Mrs. Stoges, told me about Mr. Collins' death. Was he a relative?"

Meghan's mouth went dry. "Yes. That's why I'm anxious to stop in on the family."

The clerk turned on the computer. "Here's the address and phone number. I'm afraid I have to phone Mrs. Collins and ask permission to give it to you."

There was nothing to do but nod. Meghan watched the buttons on the phone being rapidly pressed.

A moment later the clerk said into the receiver, "Mrs. Collins? This is the Palomino Leather Goods Shop. There's a young lady here who would like to see you, a relative. Is it all right if I give her your address?"

She listened then looked at Meghan. "May I ask your name?"

"Meghan. Meghan Collins."

The clerk repeated it, listened, then said goodbye and hung up. She smiled at Meg. "Mrs. Collins would like you to come right over. She lives only ten minutes from here."

47

Frances stood, looking out the window at the back of the house. A low stucco wall crowned by a wrought-iron rail enclosed the pool and patio. The property ended at the border of the vast expanse of desert that was the Pima Indian Reservation. In the distance, Camelback Mountain glistened under the midday sun. An incongruously beautiful day for all secrets to be laid open, she thought.

Annie had gone to Connecticut after all, had looked up Meghan and sent her here. Why should Annie have honored her father's wishes, Frances asked herself fiercely. What loyalty does she owe to him or to me?

In the two-and-a-half days since she'd left the message on Edwin's answering machine, she'd waited in an agony of hope and dread. The call she'd just received from Palomino was not the one she'd hoped to get. But at least Meghan Collins might be able to tell her when she had seen Annie, perhaps where Frances could reach her.

The chimes rang through the house, soft, melodious, but chilling. Frances turned and walked to the front door.

WHEN MEGHAN STOPPED IN FRONT OF 1006 DOUBLETREE Ranch Road she found a one-story, cream-colored stucco house with a red tile roof, on the edge of the desert. Vivid red hibiscus and cactus framed the front of the dwelling, complementing the stark beauty of the mountain range in the distance.

On her way to the door she passed the window and caught a glimpse of the woman inside. She couldn't see her face but could tell that the woman was tall and very thin, with hair loosely pinned in a chignon. She seemed to be wearing some sort of smock.

Meghan rang the bell, then the door opened.

The woman gave a startled gasp. Her face went ashen. "Dear God," she whispered. "I knew you looked like Annie, but I had no idea. . . ." Her hand flew up to her mouth, pressing against her lips in a visible effort to silence the flow of words.

This is Annie's mother and she doesn't know that Annie is dead. Horrified, Meghan thought, It's going to be worse for her that I'm here. What would it be like for Mom if Annie had been the one to go to Connecticut and tell her I was dead?

"Come in, Meghan." The woman stood aside, still clutching the handle of the door, as though supporting herself on it. "I'm Frances Grolier."

Meghan did not know what kind of person she had expected to find, but not this woman with her fresh-scrubbed looks, graying hair, sturdy hands and thin, lined face. The eyes she was looking into were shocked and distressed.

"Didn't the clerk at Palomino call you Mrs. Collins when she phoned?" Meghan asked.

"The tradespeople know me as Mrs. Collins."

She was wearing a gold wedding band. Meghan looked at it pointedly.

"Yes," Frances Grolier said. "For appearance sake, your father gave that to me."

Meghan thought of the way her mother had convulsively gripped the wedding band the psychic had returned to her. She looked away from Frances Grolier, suddenly filled with an overwhelming sense of loss. Impressions of the room filtered through the misery of this moment.

The house was divided into living and studio areas extending from the front to the back.

The front section was the living room. A couch in front of the fireplace. Earth-tone tiles on the floor.

The maroon leather chair and matching ottoman to the side of the fireplace, exact replicas of the ones in her father's study, Megan realized with a start. Bookshelves within easy reach of the chair. Dad certainly liked to feel at home wherever he was, Meghan thought bitterly.

Framed photographs prominently displayed on the mantel drew her like a magnet. They were family groups of her father with this woman and a young girl who might easily be her sister, and who was—or rather had been—her half sister.

One picture especially riveted her. It was a Christmas scene. Her father holding a five- or six-year-old on his lap, surrounded by presents. A young Frances Grolier kneeling behind him, arms around his neck. All wearing pajamas and robes. A joyous family.

Was that one of the Christmas Days I spent praying for a miracle, that suddenly Daddy would come through the door? Meghan wondered.

Sickening pain encompassed her. She turned away and saw against the far wall the bust on a pedestal. With feet that now seemed too leaden to move she made her way to it.

A rare talent had shaped this bronze image of her father. Love and understanding had caught the hint of melancholy behind the twinkle in the eyes, the sensitive mouth, the long, expressive fingers folded under the chin, the fine head of hair with the lock that always strayed forward onto his forehead.

She could see that cracks along the neck and forehead had been skillfully repaired.

"Meghan?"

She turned, dreading what she must now tell this woman.

Frances Grolier crossed the room to her. Her voice pleading, she said, "I'm prepared for anything you feel about me, but *please* . . . I must know about Annie. Do you know where she is? And what about your father? Has he been in touch with you?"

KEEPING HIS PROMISE TO MEGHAN, MAC TRIED UNSUCCESS-fully to phone Stephanie Petrovic at nine o'clock on Tuesday morning. Hourly phone calls continued to bring no response.

At twelve-fifteen he called Charles Potters, the lawyer for the estate of Helene Petrovic. When Potters got on the phone, Mac identified himself and stated his reason for phoning and was immediately told that Potters too was concerned.

"I tried Stephanie last night," Potters explained. "I could tell that Miss Collins was disturbed by her absence. I'm going over to the house now. I have a key."

He promised to call back.

An hour and a half later, his voice trembling with indignation, Potters told Mac about Stephanie's note. "That deceitful girl," he cried. "She helped herself to whatever she could carry! The silver. Some lovely Dresden. Practically all of Helene's wardrobe. Her jewelry. Those pieces were insured for over fifty thousand dollars. I'm notifying the police. This is a case of common theft."

"You say she left with the father of her baby?" Mac asked. "From what Meghan told me, I find that very hard to believe. She had the sense that Stephanie was frightened at the suggestion that she go after him for child support."

"Which may have been an act," Potters said. "Stephanie Petrovic is a very cold young woman. I can assure you that the main source of her grief over her aunt's death was the fact that Helene had not changed her will as Stephanie claimed she planned to do."

"Mr. Potters, do you believe Helene Petrovic planned to change her will?"

"I have no way of knowing that. I do know that in the weeks before her death, Helene had put her house on the market and converted her securities to bearer bonds. Fortunately those were not in her safe."

When Mac put down the phone, he leaned back in his chair.

How long could any amateur, no matter how gifted, pull the wool over the eyes of trained experts in the field of reproductive endocrinology and in vitro fertilization? he mused. Yet Helene Petrovic had managed it for years. I couldn't have done it, Mac thought, remembering his intense medical training.

According to Meghan, while Petrovic was working at the Dowling Assisted Reproduction Center she spent a lot of time hanging around the laboratory. She might also have been seeing a doctor from Valley Memorial, the hospital with which the center was affiliated.

Mac made up his mind. He would take tomorrow off. There were some things best handled in person. Tomorrow he was going to drive to Valley Memorial in Trenton and see the director of the facility. He needed to try to get some records.

Mac had met and liked Dr. George Manning but was shocked and concerned that Manning had not immediately warned the Andersons about the potential embryo mix-up. There was no question he'd been hoping for a cover-up.

Now Mac wondered if there was any possibility that Helene Petrovic's abrupt decision to quit the clinic, change her will, sell her house and move to France might have more sinister reasons than her fear of an error in the laboratory. Particularly, he reasoned, since it might still be proven that the Andersons' baby was their biological child, if not the identical twin they'd expected.

Mac wanted to learn if there was any possibility that Dr. George Manning had been connected to Valley Memorial at any point in the several years that Helene Petrovic worked in the adjacent facility.

Manning would not be the first man to throw aside his professional life for a woman, nor would he be the last. Technically, Petrovic had been hired through Collins and Carter Executive Search. Yet only yesterday Manning had admitted that he had spoken to Edwin Collins the day before Collins disappeared. Had they been in collusion over those credentials? Or had someone else on the Manning staff helped her out? The Manning Clinic was only about ten years old. Their annual reports would list the names of the senior staff. He'd get his secretary to copy them for him.

Mac pulled out a pad, and in his neat penmanship, which his colleagues joked was so uncharacteristic of the medical profession, wrote:

1. Edwin Collins believed dead in bridge accident, 28 January; no proof.
2. Woman who resembles Meg (Annie?) fatally stabbed, 21 October.
3. "Annie" may have been seen by Kyle the day before her death.
4. Helene Petrovic fatally shot hours after she quit her job at Manning, 25 October.

(Edwin Collins placed Helene Petrovic at Manning
Clinic, vouching for the accuracy of her false credentials.)

5. Stephanie Petrovic claimed conspiracy by Manning
Clinic to prevent her aunt from changing her will.

6. Stephanie Petrovic vanished sometime between late
afternoon of 31 October and 2 November, leaving a
note claiming she was rejoining the father of her
child, a man she apparently feared.

None of it made sense. But there was one thing he was
convinced was true. Everything that had happened was connected in a logical way. Like genes, he thought. The minute
you understand the structure everything falls into place.

He put aside the pad. He had work to do if he was planning to take tomorrow off for the trip to Dowling. It was
four o'clock. That meant it was two o'clock in Arizona. He
wondered how Meg was doing, how the day, which must be
incredibly difficult for her, was progressing.

MEG STARED AT FRANCES GROLIER. "WHAT DO YOU MEAN
have I heard from my father?"

"Meghan, the last time he was here, I could see that the
world was closing in on him. He was so frightened, so depressed. He said he wished he could just disappear.

"Meghan, you must tell me. *Have you seen Annie?*"

Only a few hours ago, Meg had remembered her father's
warning that some events cause unforgettable pain. Compassion engulfed her as she saw the dawning horror in the eyes
of Annie's mother.

Frances grasped her arms. "Meghan, is Annie sick?"

Meghan could not speak. She answered the note of hope
in the frantic question with a barely perceptible shake of her
head.

"Is she . . . is Annie dead?"

"I'm so sorry."

"No. That can't be." Frances Grolier's eyes searched Meghan's face, pleading. "When I opened the door . . . even though I knew you were coming . . . for that split second, I thought it was Annie. I knew how alike you were. Ed showed me pictures." Grolier's knees buckled.

Meghan grasped her arms, helped her to sit down on the couch. "Isn't there someone I can call, somebody you'd like to have with you now?"

"No one," Grolier whispered. "No one." Her pallor turning a sickly gray, she stared into the fireplace as though suddenly unaware of Meghan's presence.

Meghan watched helplessly as Frances Grolier's pupils became dilated, her expression vacant. She's going into shock, Meghan thought.

Then, in a voice devoid of emotion, Grolier asked, "What happened to my daughter?"

"She was stabbed. I happened to be in the emergency room when she was brought in."

"Who . . . ?"

Grolier did not complete the question.

"Annie may have been a mugging victim," Meghan said quietly. "She had no identification except a slip of paper with my name and phone number on it."

"The Drumdoe Inn notepaper?"

"Yes."

"Where is my daughter now?"

"The . . . the medical examiner's building in Manhattan."

"You mean the morgue."

"Yes."

"How did you find me, Meghan?"

"Through the message you left the other night to call the Palomino Leather Goods Shop."

A ghastly smile tugged at Frances Grolier's lips. "I left that message hoping to reach your father. Annie's father. He always put you first, you know. So afraid that you and your mother would find out about us. Always so afraid."

Meghan could see that shock was being replaced by anger

and grief. "I am so sorry." It was all she could think to say. From where she was sitting, she could see the Christmas picture. I'm so sorry for all of us, she thought.

"Meghan, I have to talk to you, but not now. I need to be alone. Where are you staying?"

"I'll try to get a room at the Safari Hotel."

"I'll call you there later. Please go."

As Meghan closed the door, she heard the steady sobbing, low rhythmic sounds that tore at her heart.

She drove to the hotel, praying that it would not be full, that no one would see her and think she was Annie. But the check-in was fast, and ten minutes later she closed the door of the room and sank down on the bed, her emotions a combination of enormous pity, shared pain and icy fear.

Frances Grolier clearly believed it possible that her lover, Edwin Collins, was alive.

48

On Tuesday morning, Victor Orsini moved into Edwin Collins' private office. The day before, the cleaning service had washed the walls and windows and cleaned the carpet. Now the room was antiseptically clean. Orsini had no interest in even thinking about redecorating it. Not with the way things were going.

He knew that on Sunday Meghan and her mother had cleared the office of Collins' personal effects. He assumed they had heard the message on the answering machine and taken the tape. He could only imagine what they thought of it.

He had hoped they wouldn't bother with Collins' business records, but they'd taken all of them. Sentiment? He doubted it. Meghan was smart. She was looking for something. Was it the same thing he was so anxious to find? Was it somewhere in those papers? Would she find it?

Orsini paused in the unpacking of his books. He'd spread the morning paper on the desk, the desk that belonged to Edwin Collins and soon would be moved to the Drumdoe Inn. A front-page update on the Manning Clinic scandal announced that state medical investigators had been in the clinic on Monday and already rumors were rampant that Helene Petrovic may have made many serious mistakes. Empty vials had been found among the ones containing cryopreserved embryos, suggesting that Petrovic's lack of medical skill may have resulted in embryos being improperly labeled or even destroyed.

An independent source who refused to be identified pointed out that, at the very least, clients who were paying handsomely for maintenance of their embryos were being overcharged. In the worst possible scenario, women who might not be able to again produce eggs for possible fertilization might have lost their chance for biological motherhood.

Featured next to the story was a reproduction of Edwin Collins' letter strongly recommending "Dr." Helene Petrovic to Dr. George Manning.

The letter had been written 21 March, nearly seven years ago, and was stamped received on 22 March.

Orsini frowned, hearing again the accusing, angry voice of Collins, calling him from the car phone that last night. He stared at the newspaper and Edwin's bold signature on the letter of recommendation. Perspiration broke out on his forehead. Somewhere in this office or in the files Meghan Collins had taken home is the incriminating evidence that will bring down this house of cards, he thought. But will anyone find it?

. . .

FOR HOURS, BERNIE WAS UNABLE TO CALM THE RAGE THE sneering passenger had triggered in him. As soon as his mother went to bed Monday night, he'd rushed downstairs to play his videotapes of Meghan. The news tapes had her voice, but the one he'd taken from the woods behind her house was his favorite. It made him wildly restless to be near her again.

He played the tapes through the night, only going to bed as a hint of dawn flickered through the slit in the cardboard he had placed over the narrow basement window. Mama would notice if his bed had not been slept in.

He got into bed fully dressed and pulled up the covers just in time. The creaking of the mattress in the next room warned that his mother was waking up. A few minutes later the door of his room opened. He knew she was looking in at him. He kept his eyes shut. She wouldn't expect him to wake up for another fifteen minutes.

After the door closed again, he hunched up in bed, planning his day.

Meghan had to be in Connecticut. But where? At her house? At the inn? Maybe she gave her mother a hand in running the inn. What about the New York apartment? Maybe she was there.

He got up promptly at seven, took off his sweater and shirt, put on his pajama top in case Mama saw him and went out to the bathroom. There he splashed water on his face and hands, shaved, brushed his teeth and combed his hair. He smiled at his reflection in the mirror on the medicine cabinet. Everyone had always told him he had a warm smile. Trouble was the silver was peeling behind the glass, and the mirror gave back a distorted image like the ones in amusement parks. He didn't look warm and friendly now.

Then, as Mama had taught him to do, he reached down for the can of cleanser, shook a liberal amount of the gritty powder into the sink, rubbed it in vigorously with a sponge, rinsed it away and dried the sink with the rag Mama always left folded over the side of the tub.

Back in the bedroom he made his bed, folded his pajama top, put on a clean shirt and carried the soiled one to the hamper.

Today Mama had bran flakes in his cereal bowl. "You look tired, Bernard," she said sharply. "Are you getting enough rest?"

"Yes, Mama."

"What time did you go to bed?"

"I guess about eleven o'clock."

"I woke up to go to the bathroom at eleven-thirty. You weren't in bed then."

"Maybe it was a little later, Mama."

"I thought I heard your voice. Were you talking to someone?"

"No, Mama. Who would I be talking to?"

"I thought I heard a woman's voice."

"Mama, it was the television." He gulped the cereal and tea. "I have to be at work early."

She watched him from the door. "Be home on time for dinner. I don't want to be fussing in the kitchen all night."

He wanted to tell her that he expected to work overtime but didn't dare. Maybe he'd call her later.

Three blocks away he stopped at a public telephone. It was cold, but the shiver he felt as he dialed Meghan's apartment had more to do with anticipation than chill. The phone rang four times. When the answering machine clicked on, he hung up.

He then dialed the house in Connecticut. A woman answered. It must be Meghan's mother, Bernie thought. He deepened his voice, quickened its pace. He wanted to sound like Tom Weicker.

"Good morning, Mrs. Collins. Is Meghan there?"

"Who is this?"

"Tom Weicker of PCD."

"Oh, Mr. Weicker, Meg will be sorry she missed your call. She's out of town today."

Bernie frowned. He wanted to know where she was. "Can I reach her?"

"I'm afraid not. But I'll be hearing from her late this afternoon. May I have her phone you?"

Bernie thought swiftly. It would sound wrong if he didn't say yes. But he wanted to know when she'd be back. "Yes, have her call. Do you expect her to be home this evening?"

"If not tonight, surely tomorrow."

"Thank you." Bernie hung up, angry that he couldn't reach Meghan, but glad he hadn't wasted a trip to Connecticut. He got back in the car and headed for Kennedy Airport. He might just as well get some fares today, but they'd better not tell him how to drive.

THIS TIME THE SPECIAL INVESTIGATORS OF HELENE PE-trovic's death did not go to Phillip Carter. Instead, late Tuesday morning they phoned and asked if it would be convenient for him to stop in for an informal chat at the assistant state attorney's office in the Danbury courthouse.

"When would you like me to come?" Carter asked.

"As soon as possible," Investigator Arlene Weiss told him.

Phillip glanced at his calendar. There was nothing on it that he couldn't change. "I can make it around one," he suggested.

"That will be fine."

After he replaced the receiver he tried to concentrate on the morning mail. There were a number of references in on candidates whom they were considering offering to two of their major clients. As least so far those clients hadn't pulled back.

Could Collins and Carter Executive Search weather the storm? He hoped so. One thing he would do in the very near future would be to change the name to Phillip Carter Associates.

In the next room he could hear the sounds of Orsini moving into Ed Collins' office. Don't get too settled, Phillip thought. It was too soon to get rid of Orsini. He needed him for now, but Phillip had several replacements in mind.

He wondered if the police had been questioning Catherine and Meghan again.

He dialed Catherine at home. When she answered, he said, cheerfully, "It's me. Just checking to see how it's going."

"That's nice of you, Phillip." Her voice was subdued.

"Anything wrong, Catherine?" he asked quickly. "The police haven't been bothering you, have they?"

"No, not really. I'm going through Edwin's files, the copies of his expense accounts, that sort of thing. You know what Meg pointed out?" She did not wait for an answer. "There are times when even though Edwin was billed for four or five days in a hotel, after the first day or two there were absolutely no additional charges on his bill. Not even for a drink or a bottle of wine at the end of the day. Did you ever notice that?"

"No. I wouldn't be the one to look at Edwin's expense accounts, Catherine."

"All the files I have seem to go back seven years. Is there a reason for that?"

"That would be right. That's as long as you're supposed to retain records for possible audit. Of course the IRS will go back much further if they suspect deliberate fraud."

"What I'm seeing is that whenever Edwin was in California that pattern of noncharges showed up in the hotel bills. He seemed to go to California a great deal."

"California was where it was at, Catherine. We used to make a lot of placements there. It's just changed in the last few years."

"Then you never wondered about his frequent trips to California?"

"Catherine, Edwin was my senior partner. We both always went where we thought we'd find business."

"I'm sorry, Phillip. I don't mean to suggest that you should have seen something that I as Edwin's wife of thirty years never even suspected."

"Another woman?"

"Possibly."

"It's such a rotten time for you," Phillip said vehemently. "How's Meg doing? Is she with you?"

"Meg's fine. She's away today. It would be the one day her boss phoned her."

"Are you free for dinner tonight?"

"No, I'm sorry. I'm meeting Mac and Kyle at the inn." Catherine hesitated. "Do you want to join us?"

"I don't think so, thanks. How about tomorrow night?"

"It depends on when Meg gets back. May I call you?"

"Of course. Take care of yourself. Remember, I'm here for you."

TWO HOURS LATER PHILLIP WAS BEING INTERROGATED IN Assistant State Attorney John Dwyer's office. Special investigators Bob Marron and Arlene Weiss were present with Dwyer, who was asking the questions. Some of them were the same ones Catherine had raised.

"Didn't you at any time suspect your partner might be leading a double life?"

"No."

"Do you think so now?"

"With that dead girl in the morgue in New York who looks like Meghan? With Meghan herself requesting DNA tests? Of course I think so."

"From the pattern of Edwin Collins' travels, can you suggest where he might have been involved in an intimate relationship?"

"No, I can't."

The assistant state attorney looked exasperated. "Mr. Carter, I get the feeling that everyone who was close to Edwin Collins is trying in one way or another to protect him. Let me put it this way. We believe he is alive. If he had another situation, particularly a long-term one, he may be there now. Just off the top of your head, where do you think that could be?"

"I simply don't know," Phillip repeated.

"All right, Mr. Carter," Dwyer said brusquely. "Will you give us permission to go through all the Collins and Carter files if we deem it necessary, or will it be necessary to subpoena them?"

"I wish you *would* go through the files!" Phillip snapped. "Do anything you can to bring this dreadful business to a conclusion and let decent people get on with their lives."

On his way back to the office, Phillip Carter realized he had no desire for a solitary evening. From his car phone he again dialed Catherine's number. When she answered, he said, "Catherine, I've changed my mind. If you and Mac and Kyle can put up with me, I'd very much like to have dinner with you tonight."

AT THREE O'CLOCK, FROM HER HOTEL ROOM, MEGHAN phoned home. It would be five o'clock in Connecticut, and she wanted to be able to talk to her mother before the dinner hour at the inn.

It was a painful conversation. Unable to find words to soften the impact, she told about the grueling meeting with Frances Grolier. "It was pretty awful," she concluded. "She's devastated, of course. Annie was her only child."

"How old was Annie, Meg?" her mother asked quietly.

"I don't know. A little younger than I am, I think."

"I see. That means they were together for many years."

"Yes, it does," Meghan agreed, thinking of the photographs she had just seen. "Mom, there's something else. Frances seems to think that Dad is still alive."

"She *can't* think he's still alive!"

"She does. I don't know more than that. I'm going to stay in this hotel until I hear from her. She said she wants to talk to me."

"What more could she have to say to you, Meg?"

"She still doesn't know very much about Annie's death." Meghan realized she was too emotionally drained to talk any more. "Mom, I'm going to get off the phone now. If you get a chance to tell Mac about this without Kyle hearing, go ahead."

Meghan had been sitting on the edge of the bed. When she said goodbye to her mother, she leaned back against the pillows and closed her eyes.

She was awakened by the ringing of the telephone. She sat up, aware that the room was dark and chilly. The lighted face of the clock radio showed that it was five past eight. She leaned over and picked up the phone. To her own ears, her voice sounded strained and husky when she murmured, "Hello."

"Meghan, this is Frances Grolier. Will you come and see me tomorrow morning as early as possible?"

"Yes." It seemed insulting to ask her how she was. How could any woman in her situation be? Instead, Meghan asked, "Would nine o'clock be all right?"

"Yes, and thank you."

ALTHOUGH GRIEF WAS ETCHED DEEPLY IN HER FACE, FRANCES Grolier seemed composed the next morning when she opened the door for Meghan. "I've made coffee," she said.

They sat on the couch, holding the cups, their bodies angled stiffly toward each other. Grolier did not waste words. "Tell me how Annie died," she commanded. "Tell me everything. I need to know."

Meghan began, "I was on assignment in Roosevelt-St. Luke's Hospital in New York . . ." As in the conversation with her mother, she did not attempt to be gentle. She told about the fax message she had gotten, *Mistake. Annie was a mistake.*

Grolier leaned forward, her eyes blazing. "What do you think that means?"

"I don't know." She continued, omitting nothing, beginning with the note found in Annie's pocket, including Helene Petrovic's false credentials and death and finishing with the warrant issued for her father's arrest. "His car was found. You may or may not know that Dad had a gun permit. His gun was in the car and was the weapon that killed Helene Petrovic. I do not and cannot believe that he could take anyone's life."

"Nor do I."

"Last night you told me you thought my father might be alive."

"I think it's possible." Frances Grolier said, "Meghan, after today I hope we never meet again. It would be too difficult for me and, I suppose, for you as well. But you and your mother are owed an explanation.

"I met your father twenty-seven years ago in the Palomino Leather Shop. He was buying a purse for your mother and debating between two of them. He asked me to help make the choice, then invited me to lunch. That's how it began."

"He'd only been married three years at that time," Meghan said quietly. "I know my father and mother were happy together. I don't understand why he needed a relationship with you." She felt she sounded accusing and pitiless, but she couldn't help it.

"I knew he was married," Grolier said. "He showed me your picture, your mother's picture. On the surface, Edwin had it all: charm, looks, wit, intelligence. Inwardly he was, or is, a desperately insecure man. Meghan, try to understand and forgive him. In so many ways your father was still that hurt child who feared he might be abandoned again. He needed to know he had another place to go, a place where someone would take him in."

Her eyes welled with tears. "It suited us both. I was in love with him but didn't want the responsibility of marriage. I wanted only to be free to become the best sculptor that I was capable of being. For me the relationship worked, open-ended and without demands."

"Wasn't a child a demand, a responsibility?" Meghan asked.

"Annie wasn't part of the plan. When I was expecting her, we bought this place and told people that we were married. After that, your father was desperately torn, always trying to be a good father to both of you, always feeling he was failing both of you."

"Didn't he worry about being discovered?" Meghan asked. "About someone bumping into him here the way his step-brother did?"

"He was haunted by that fear. As she grew up, Annie asked more and more questions about his job. She wasn't buying the story that he had a top-secret government job. She was becoming known as a travel writer. You were being seen on television. When Edwin had terrible chest pains last November he wouldn't let himself be admitted to the hospital for observation. He wanted to get back to Connecticut. He said, 'If I die, you can tell Annie I was on some kind of government assignment.' The next time he came he gave me a bearer bond for two hundred thousand dollars."

The insurance loan, Meghan thought.

"He said that if anything happened to him, you and your mother were well taken care of, but I was not."

Meghan did not contradict Frances Grolier. She knew it had not occurred to Grolier that because his body had not been found a death certificate had not been issued for her father. And she knew with certainty that her mother would lose everything rather than take the money back that her father had given this woman.

"When was the last time you saw my father?" she asked.

"He left here on January twenty-seventh. He was going to San Diego to see Annie, then take a flight home on the morning of the twenty-eighth."

"Why do you believe he's still alive?" Meghan had to ask before she left. More than anything, she wanted to get away from this woman whom she realized she both deeply pitied and bitterly resented.

"Because when he left he was terribly upset. He'd learned something about his assistant that horrified him."

"Victor Orsini?"

"That's the name."

"What did he learn?"

"I don't know. But business had not been good for several years. Then there was a write-up in the local paper about a seventieth birthday party that had been given for Dr. George Manning by his daughter, who lives about thirty miles from here. The article quoted Dr. Manning as saying that he planned to work one more year, then retire. Your father said that the Manning Clinic was a client, and he called Dr. Manning. He wanted to suggest that he be commissioned to start the search for Manning's replacement. That conversation upset him terribly."

"Why?" Meghan asked urgently. "Why?"

"I don't know."

"Try to remember. Please. It's very important."

Grolier shook her head. "When Edwin was leaving, his last words were, 'It's becoming too much for me . . .' All the papers carried the story of the bridge accident. I believed he was dead and told people he had been killed in a light-plane accident abroad. Annie wasn't satisfied with that explanation.

"When he visited her at her apartment that last day, Edwin gave Annie money to buy some clothes. Six one-hundred-dollar bills. He obviously didn't realize that the slip of Drumdoe Inn notepaper with your name and number fell out of his wallet. She found it after he left and kept it."

Frances Grolier's lip quivered. Her voice broke as she said, "Two weeks ago, Annie came here for what you'd call a showdown. She had phoned your number. You'd answered 'Meghan Collins,' and she hung up. She wanted to see her father's death certificate. She called me a liar and demanded to know where he was. I finally told her the truth and begged her not to contact you or your mother. She knocked over that bust I'd sculpted of Ed and stormed out of here. I never saw her again."

Grolier stood up, placed her hand on the mantel and leaned her forehead against it. "I spoke to my lawyer last night. He's going to accompany me to New York tomorrow afternoon to identify Annie's body and arrange to have it brought back here. I'm sorry for the embarrassment this will cause you and your mother."

Meghan had only one more question she needed to ask. "Why did you leave that message for Dad the other night?"

"Because I thought if he were still alive, if that line were still connected, he might check it out of habit. It was my way of contacting him in case of emergency. He used to beep in to that answering machine early every morning." She faced Meghan again.

"Let no one tell you that Edwin Collins is capable of killing anyone, because he isn't." She paused. "But he *is* capable of beginning a new life that does not include you and your mother. Or Annie and me."

Frances Grolier turned away again. There was nothing left to say. Meghan took a last look at the bronze bust of her father and left, closing the door quietly behind her.

49

On Wednesday morning, as soon as Kyle was on the school bus, Mac left for Valley Memorial Hospital in Trenton, New Jersey.

At dinner the night before, when Kyle had left the table for a moment, Catherine had quickly told Mac and Phillip about Meghan's call. "I don't know very much except that this woman has had a long-term relationship with Edwin; she thinks he's still alive, and the dead girl who looks like Meg was her daughter."

"You seem to be taking it very well," Phillip had commented, "or are you still in denial?"

"I don't know what I feel anymore," Catherine had answered, "and I'm worried about Meg. You know how she felt about her father. I never heard anyone sound so hurt as she did when she called earlier." Then Kyle was back and they changed the subject.

Driving south on Route 684 through Westchester, Mac tried to tear his thoughts away from Meghan. She had been crazy about Edwin Collins, a real Daddy's girl. He knew that these past months since she'd thought her father was dead had been hell for her. How many times Mac had wanted to ask her to talk it out with him, not to hold everything inside. Maybe he should have insisted on breaking through her reserve. God, how much time he had wasted nursing his wounded pride over Ginger's dumping him.

At last we're getting honest, he told himself. Everybody knew you were making a mistake tying up with Ginger. You could feel the reaction when the engagement was announced. Meg had the guts to say it straight out, and she was only nineteen. In her letter she'd written that she loved him and that he ought to have the sense to know she was the only girl for him. "Wait for me, Mac," was the way she'd ended it.

He hadn't thought about that letter for a long time. Now he found that he was thinking about it a lot.

It was inevitable that as soon as Annie's body was claimed, it would be public knowledge that Edwin had led a double life. Would Catherine decide she didn't want to live in the same area where everyone had known Ed, that she would rather start fresh somewhere else? It could happen, especially if she lost the inn. That would mean Meg wouldn't be around either. The thought made Mac's blood run cold.

You can't change the past, Mac thought, but you can do something about the future. Finding Edwin Collins if he's still alive, or learning what happened to him if he's not, would release Meg and Catherine from the misery of uncertainty. Finding the doctor Helene Petrovic might have dated when she was a secretary at the Dowling Center in Trenton could be the first step to solving her murder.

Mac normally enjoyed driving. It was a good time for thinking. Today, however, his thoughts were in a jumble, filled with unsettled issues. The trip across Westchester to the Tappan Zee Bridge seemed longer than usual. The Tappan Zee Bridge—where it all began almost ten months ago, he thought.

It was another hour-and-a-half drive from there to Trenton. Mac arrived at Valley Memorial Hospital at ten-thirty and asked for the director. "I called yesterday and was told he could see me."

FREDERICK SCHULLER WAS A COMPACT MAN OF ABOUT forty-five whose thoughtful demeanor was belied by his quick, warm smile. "I've heard of you, Dr. MacIntyre. Your work in human gene therapy is becoming pretty exciting, I gather."

"It is exciting," Mac agreed. "We're on the cutting edge of finding the way to prevent an awful lot of diseases. The hardest job is to have the patience for trial and error when there are so many people waiting for answers."

"I agree. I don't have that kind of patience, which is why I'd never have been a good researcher. Which means that since you're giving up a day to drive down here, you must have a very good reason. My secretary said that it's urgent."

Mac nodded. He was glad to get to the point. "I'm here because of the Manning Clinic scandal."

Schuller frowned. "That really is a terrible situation. I can't believe that any woman who worked in our Dowling facility as a secretary was able to get away with passing herself off as an embryologist. Somebody dropped the ball on that one."

"Or somebody trained a very capable student, although trained her not well enough, obviously. They're finding a lot of problems in that lab, and we're talking about major problems like possibly mislabeling test tubes containing cryopreserved embryos or even deliberately destroying them."

"If any field is calling for national legislation, assisted reproduction is first on the list. The potential for mistakes is enormous. Fertilize an egg with the wrong semen, and if the embryo is successfully transferred, an infant is born whose genetic structure is fifty percent different from what the parents had the right to expect. The child may have genetically inherited medical problems that can't be foreseen. It—" He stopped abruptly. "Sorry, I know I'm preaching to the converted. How can I help?"

"Meghan Collins is the daughter of Edwin Collins, the man who is accused of placing Helene Petrovic at the Manning Clinic with false credentials. Meg's a reporter for PCD Channel 3 in New York. Last week she spoke to the head of the Dowling Center about Helene Petrovic. Apparently, some of Petrovic's coworkers thought she might be seeing a doctor from this hospital, but no one knows who he is. I'm trying to help Meg find him."

"Didn't Petrovic leave Dowling more than six years ago?"

"Nearly seven years ago."

"Do you realize how large our medical staff is here, Doctor?"

"Yes, I do," Mac said. "And I know you have consultants who are not on staff but are called in regularly. It's a shot in the dark, but at this stage, when the investigators are convinced Edwin Collins is Petrovic's murderer, you can imagine how desperately his daughter wants to know if there was someone in her life with a reason to kill her."

"Yes, I can." Schuller began to make notes on a pad. "Have you any idea how long Petrovic might have been seeing this doctor?"

"From what I understand, a year or two before she went up to Connecticut. But that's only a guess."

"It's a start. Let's go back into the records for the three

years she worked at Dowling. You think this person may have been the one who helped her to acquire enough skill to pass herself off as thoroughly trained?"

"Again, a guess."

"All right. I'll see that a list is compiled. We won't leave out people who worked in the fetal research or DNA labs either. Not all the technicians are MDs, but they know their business." He stood up. "What are you going to do with this list? It will be a long one."

"Meg is going to dig into Helene Petrovic's personal life. She's going to collect names of Petrovic's friends and acquaintances from the Rumanian Society. We'll compare names from the personal list with the one you send us."

Mac reached into his pocket. "This is a copy of a roster I compiled of everyone on the medical staff at the Manning Clinic while Helene was there. For what it's worth, I'd like to leave it with you. I'd be glad if you would run these names through your computer first."

He got up to go. "It's a big fishnet, but we do appreciate your help."

"It may take a few days, but I'll get the information you want," Schuller said. "Shall I send it to you?"

"I think directly to Meghan. I'll leave her address and phone number."

Schuller walked him to the door of his office. Mac took the elevator down to the lobby. As he stepped into the corridor, he passed a boy about Kyle's age in a wheelchair. Cerebral palsy, Mac thought. One of the diseases they were starting to get a handle on through gene therapy. The boy gave him a big smile. "Hi. Are you a doctor?"

"The kind who doesn't treat patients."

"My kind."

"Bobby!" his mother protested.

"I have a son your age who'd get along fine with you." Mac tousled the boy's hair.

The clock over the receptionist's desk showed that it was quarter past eleven. Mac decided that if he picked up a sandwich and Coke in the coffee shop off the lobby he could eat it later in the car and drive right through. That way he'd be back in the lab by two o'clock at the latest and get in an afternoon of work.

He reflected that when you passed a kid in a wheelchair, you didn't want to lose any more time than necessary if your job was trying to unlock the secrets of genetic healing.

AT LEAST HE'D MADE A COUPLE HUNDRED BUCKS DRIVING yesterday. That was the only consolation Bernie could find when he awakened Wednesday morning. He'd gone to bed at midnight and slept right through because he was really tired, but now he felt good. This was sure to be a better day; he might even see Meg.

His mother, unfortunately, was in a terrible mood. "Ber-NARD, I was awake half the night with a sinus headache. I was sneezing a lot. I want you to fix those steps and tighten the railing so I can get down to that basement again. I'm sure you're not keeping it clean. I'm sure there's dust filtering up from there."

"Mama, I'm not good at fixing things. That whole staircase is weak. I can feel another step getting loose. You wanna really hurt yourself?"

"I can't afford to hurt myself. Who'd keep this place nice? Who'd cook meals for you? Who'd make sure you don't get in trouble?"

"I need you, Mama."

"People need to eat in the morning. I always fix you a nice breakfast."

"I know you do, Mama."

Today the cereal was lukewarm oatmeal that reminded him of prison food. Nonetheless, Bernie dutifully scraped every spoonful from the bowl and drained his glass of apple juice.

He felt relaxed as he backed out of the driveway and waved goodbye to Mama. He was glad that he'd lied and told her another basement step was loose. One night, ten years ago, she'd said that she was going to inspect the basement the next day to see if he was keeping it nice.

He'd known he couldn't let that happen. He'd just bought his first police scanner radio. Mama would have realized it was expensive. She thought he just had an old television set down there and watched it after she went to bed so she wouldn't be disturbed.

Mama never opened his credit card bill. She said he had to learn to take care of it himself. She handed him the phone bill unopened too, because, she said, "I never call anybody." She had no idea how much he spent on equipment.

That night when he could hear her deep snores and knew she was in a sound sleep, he'd loosened the top steps. She'd had some fall. Her hip really had been smashed. He'd had to wait on her hand and foot for months, but it had been worth it. Mama go downstairs again? Not after that.

Bernie reluctantly decided to work at least for the morning. Meghan's mother had said she would be back today. That could mean *anytime* today. He couldn't phone and say he was Tom Weicker again. Meghan might have already called the station and found out that Tom hadn't tried to get her.

It was not a good day for fares. He stood near the baggage claim area with the other gypsy drivers and those fancy-limousine chauffeurs who were holding cards with the names of the people they were meeting.

He approached arriving passengers as they came down the escalator. "Clean car, cheaper than a cab, great driver." His lips felt stuck in a permanent smile.

The trouble was, the Port Authority had put so many signs around, warning travelers against taking a chance on getting into cars not licensed by the Taxi and Limousine Commission. A number of people started to say yes to him, then changed their minds.

One old woman let him carry her suitcases to the curb, then said she'd wait for him, that he should go for his car. He tried to take the bags with him, but she yelled at him to put them down.

People turned their heads to look at him.

If he had her alone! Trying to get him in trouble when all he wanted to do was be nice. But of course he didn't want to attract attention, so he said, "Sure, ma'am. I'll get the car real quick."

When he drove back five minutes later, she was gone.

That was enough to set him off. He wasn't going to drive any jerks today. Ignoring a couple who called out to him to ask his rate to Manhattan, he pulled away, got on the Grand Central Parkway and, paying the toll on the Triborough Bridge, chose the Bronx exit, the one that led to New England.

By noon he was having lunch, a hamburger and beer, at the bar of the Drumdoe Inn, where Joe the bartender welcomed him back as a regular patron.

50

Catherine went to the inn on Wednesday morning and worked in her office until eleven-thirty. There were twenty reservations for lunch. Even allowing for drop-ins, she knew that Tony could handle the kitchen perfectly well. She would go home and continue to go through Edwin's files.

When she passed the reception area, she glanced into the bar. There were ten or twelve people already seated there, a couple of them with menus. Not bad for a weekday. No question business in general was picking up. The dinner hour especially was almost back to where it had been before the recession.

But that still didn't mean that she could hang onto this place.

She got in her car, reflecting that it was crazy that she didn't make herself walk the short distance between the house and the inn. I'm always in a hurry, she thought, but unfortunately that might not be necessary much longer.

The jewelry she'd hocked on Monday hadn't brought in anything like what she'd expected. A jeweler had offered to take everything on consignment but warned that the market was down. "These are lovely pieces," he'd said, "and the market will be improving. Unless you absolutely need the money now, I urge you not to sell."

She hadn't sold. By pawning them all at Provident Loan, at least she got enough to pay the quarterly tax on the inn. But in three months it would be due again. There was a message from an aggressive commercial real estate agent on her desk. "Would you be interested in selling the inn? We may have a buyer."

A distress sale is what that vulture wants, Catherine told herself as she drove along the macadam to the parking lot exit. And I may have to accept it. For a moment she stopped and looked back at the inn. Her father had fashioned it after a fieldstone manor in Drumdoe, which as a boy he had thought so grand that only the gentry would dare set foot in it.

"I'd welcome the errand that would send me to the place," he'd told Catherine. "And from the kitchen I'd peek in to see the more of it. One day, the family was out and the cook took pity on me. 'Would you like to see the rest?' she asked, taking me by the hand. Catherine, that good woman showed me the entire house. And now we have one just like it."

Catherine felt a lump form in her throat as she studied the graceful Georgian-style mansion with its lovely casement windows and sturdy carved oak door. It always seemed to her that Pop was lurking inside, a benevolent ghost still strutting around, still taking his rest in front of the fire in the sitting room.

He'd really haunt me if I sold it, she thought as she pressed down on the accelerator.

THE PHONE WAS RINGING WHEN SHE UNLOCKED THE DOOR to the house. She rushed to pick it up. It was Meghan.

"Mom, I have to hurry. The plane is starting to board. I saw Annie's mother again this morning. She and her lawyer are flying into New York tonight to identify Annie's body. I'll tell you about it when I get home. That should be around ten o'clock."

"I'll be here. Oh, Meg, I'm sorry. Your boss, Tom Weicker, wanted you to call him. I didn't think to tell you when we talked yesterday."

"It would have been too late to get him at the office anyhow. Why don't you call him now and explain that I'll get back to him tomorrow. I'm sure he isn't offering me an assignment. I'd better rush. Love you."

That job is so important to Meg, Catherine berated herself. How could I have forgotten to tell her about Mr. Weicker's call? She flipped through her memo book, looking for the number of Channel 3.

Funny he didn't give me his direct line, she reflected as she waited for the operator to put her through to Weicker's secretary. Then she reasoned that of course Meg would know it.

"I'm sure he'll want to speak to you, Mrs. Collins," the secretary said when she gave her name.

Catherine had met Weicker about a year ago when Meg had showed her around the station. She'd liked him, although as she'd observed afterwards, "I wouldn't want to have to face Tom Weicker if I'd caused some kind of major foul-up."

"How are you, Mrs. Collins, and how is Meg?" Weicker said as he picked up.

"We're all right, thanks." She explained why she was calling.

"I didn't speak to you yesterday," he said.

My God, Catherine thought, I'm not going crazy as well as everything else, am I? "Mr. Weicker, somebody called and used your name. Did you authorize anyone to phone?"

"No. Specifically, what did this person say to you?"

Catherine's hands went clammy. "He wanted to know where Meg was and when she'd be home." Still holding the receiver, she sank down onto a chair. "Mr. Weicker, somebody was photographing Meg from behind our house the other night."

"Do the police know about that?"

"Yes."

"Then let them know about this call too. And please keep me posted if you get any more of them. Tell Meg we miss her."

He meant it. She knew he did, and he sounded genuinely concerned. Catherine realized that Meg would have given Weicker the exclusive story of what she had learned in Scottsdale about the dead girl who resembled her.

There's no hiding it from the media, Catherine thought. Meg said that Frances Grolier is coming to New York tomorrow to claim her daughter's body.

"Mrs. Collins, are you all right?"

Catherine made up her mind. "Yes, and there's something you should know before anyone else. Meg went to Scottsdale, Arizona, yesterday because . . ."

She told him what she knew, then answered his questions. The final one was the hardest.

"As a newsman, I have to ask you this, Mrs. Collins. How do you feel about your husband now?"

"I don't know how I feel about my husband," Catherine answered. "I do know I'm very, very sorry for Frances Grolier. Her daughter is dead. My daughter is alive and will be with me tonight."

When she was finally able to replace the receiver, Catherine went into the dining room and sat at the table where the files were still spread out as she had left them. With her fingertips, she rubbed her temples. Her head was beginning to ache, a dull, steady pain.

The door chimes pealed softly. Pray God it isn't the state attorney's people or reporters, she thought as she wearily got up.

Through the living room window she could see that a tall man was standing on the porch. Who? She caught a glimpse of his face. Surprised, she hurried to open the door.

"Hello, Mrs. Collins," Victor Orsini said. "I apologize. I should have called but I was nearby and thought I'd take a chance and stop in. I'm hoping that some papers I need might have been put in Edwin's files. Would you mind if I go through them?"

MEGHAN TOOK AMERICA WEST FLIGHT 292 LEAVING PHOENIX at 1:25 and due to arrive in New York at 8:05 P.M. She was grateful she'd been given a window seat. The middle one was not occupied, but the fortyish woman on the aisle seemed to be a talker.

To avoid her, Meg reclined the seat and closed her eyes. In her mind she replayed every detail of her meeting with Frances Grolier. As she reviewed it, her emotions seemed to be on a roller-coaster ride, going from one extreme to another.

Anger at her father. Anger at Frances.

Jealousy that there had been another daughter whom her father loved.

Curiosity about Annie. She was a travel writer. She must have been intelligent. She looked like me. She was my half-sister, Meghan thought. She was still breathing when they put her in the ambulance. I was with her when she died and I'd never known that she existed.

Pity for everyone: for Frances Grolier and Annie, for her mother and herself. And for Dad, Meghan thought. Maybe someday I'll see him the way Frances does. A hurt little boy who couldn't be secure unless he was sure there was a place for him to go, a place where he was wanted.

Still, her father had known two homes where he was loved, she thought. Did he need both of them to make up for the two he'd known as a child, places where he was neither wanted nor loved?

The plane's bar service began. Meghan ordered a glass of red wine and sipped it slowly, glad for the warmth that began to seep through her system. She glanced to one side. Happily, the woman on the aisle was engrossed in a book.

Lunch was served. Meghan wasn't hungry but did have the salad and roll and coffee. Her head began to clear. She took a pad from her shoulder bag and over a second cup of coffee began to jot down notes.

That scrap of paper with her name and phone number had triggered Annie's confrontation with Frances, her demand to know the truth. Frances said that Annie called me and hung up when I answered, Meghan thought. *If only she'd spoken to me then.* She might never have come to New York. She might still be alive.

Kyle had obviously seen Annie when she'd been driving around Newtown. Had anyone else seen her there?

I wonder if Frances told her where Dad worked, Meghan thought, and jotted down the question.

Dr. Manning. According to Frances, Dad was upset after speaking to him the day before Dad disappeared. According to the papers, Dr. Manning said the conversation was cordial. Then what got Dad upset?

Victor Orsini. Was he the key to all this? Frances said that Dad was horrified by something he'd learned about him.

Orsini. Meghan underlined his name three times. He had come to work around the time Helene Petrovic was presented as a candidate to the Manning Clinic. Was there a connection?

The last notation Meghan made consisted of three words. *Is Dad alive?*

The plane landed at eight o'clock, exactly on time. As Meghan unsnapped her seat belt, the woman on the aisle closed her book and turned to her. "I've just figured it out," she said happily. "I'm a travel agent and I understand that when you don't want to talk, you shouldn't be bothered. But I knew I'd met you somewhere. It was at an ASTA meeting in San Francisco last year. You're Annie Collins, the travel writer, aren't you?"

BERNIE WAS AT THE BAR WHEN CATHERINE LOOKED IN AS SHE was leaving the hotel. He watched her reflection in the mirror but immediately averted his eyes and picked up the menu when she looked in his direction.

He didn't want her to notice him. It was never a good idea for people to pay special attention to you. They might start asking questions. Just from that glance in the mirror, he could tell that Meghan's mother looked like a smart lady. You couldn't put too much over on her.

Where was Meghan? Bernie ordered another beer, then wondered if the bartender, Joe, wasn't starting to look at him with the kind of expression the cops had when they'd stop him and ask what he was up to.

All you had to do was say, "I'm just hanging around," and they were all over you with questions. "Why?" "Who do you know around here?" "Do you come here much?"

Those were the questions he didn't want people around here to even start thinking.

The big thing was to have people used to seeing him. When you're used to seeing someone all the time, you never really see him. He and the prison psychiatrist had talked about that.

Something inside him was warning that it would be dangerous to go into the woods behind Meghan's house again. With the way that kid had been screaming, someone had probably called the cops. They might be keeping a watch on the place now.

But if he never ran into Meghan on a job because she was on leave from Channel 3, and he couldn't get near her house, how would he get to see her?

While he sipped his second beer, the answer came to him, so easy, so simple.

This wasn't just a restaurant, it was an *inn.* People stayed here. There was a sign outside that announced VACANCY. From the windows on the south side you should have a clear view of Meghan's house. If he rented a room he could come and go and no one would think anything of it. They'd *expect* his car to be there all night. He could say that his mother was in a hospital but would be getting out in a few days and needed a quiet place where she could take it easy and not have to cook.

"Are these rooms expensive?" he asked the bartender. "I need to find a place for my mother, so she can get her strength back, if you know what I mean. She's not sick anymore, but kind of weak and can't be fussing for herself."

"The guest rooms are great," Tony told him. "They were renovated only two years ago. They're not expensive right now. It's between seasons. In about three weeks, around Thanksgiving, they go up and stay up through the skiing season. Then they get discounted again until April or May."

"My mother likes a lot of sun."

"I know half the rooms are empty. Talk to Virginia Murphy. She's Mrs. Collins' assistant and handles everything."

The room Bernie chose was more than satisfactory. On the south side of the inn, it directly faced the Collins house. Even with all the electronic equipment he'd bought lately he wasn't near the limit on his credit card. He could stay here a long time.

Murphy accepted it with a pleasant smile. "What time will your mother check in, Mr. Heffernan?" she asked.

"She won't be here for a few days," Bernie explained. "I want to be able to use the room till she's out of the hospital. It's too long a trek to drive back and forth from Long Island every day."

"It certainly is and the traffic can be bad too. Do you have luggage?"

"I'll come back with it later."

Bernie went home. After dinner with Mama he told her the boss wanted him to drive a customer's car to Chicago. "I'll be gone three or four days, Mama. It's an expensive new car, and they don't want me to speed. They'll send me back on the bus."

"How much are they paying you?"

Bernie picked a figure out of the air. "Two hundred dollars a day, Mama."

She snorted. "I get sick when I think of the way I worked to support you and got paid next to nothing and you get two hundred dollars a day to drive a fancy car."

"He wants me to start tonight." Bernie went into the bedroom and threw some clothes in the black nylon suitcase that Mama had bought at a garage sale years ago. It didn't look bad. Mama had cleaned it up.

He made sure to bring plenty of tape cassettes for his video camera, all his lenses and his cellular telephone.

He told Mama goodbye, but didn't kiss her. They never kissed. Mama didn't believe in kissing. As usual, she stood at the door to watch him drive away.

Her last words to him were, "Don't get in any trouble, Bernard."

MEGHAN REACHED HOME SHORTLY BEFORE TEN-THIRTY. HER mother had cheese and crackers and grapes on the coffee table in the living room and wine chilling in the decanter. "I thought you might need a little sustenance."

"I need something. I'll be right down. I'm going to get comfortable."

She carried her bag upstairs, changed into pajamas, a robe and slippers, washed her face, brushed her hair and anchored it back with a band.

"That feels better," she said when she returned to the living room. "Do you mind if we don't talk about everything tonight? You know the essentials. Dad and Annie's mother have had a relationship for twenty-seven years. The last time she saw him was when he left to come home to us and never arrived. She and her lawyer are taking the 11:25 red-eye tonight from Phoenix. They'll get to New York around six tomorrow morning."

"Why didn't she wait until tomorrow? Why would anyone want to fly all night?"

"I suspect she wants to be in and out of New York as fast as possible. I warned her that the police would certainly want to see her and there'd probably be extensive media coverage."

"Meg, I hope I did the right thing." Catherine hesitated. "I told Tom Weicker about your trip to Scottsdale. PCD carried the story about Annie on the six o'clock news and I'm sure they'll repeat it at eleven. I think they were as kind to you and me as possible, but it isn't a pretty story. I might add I turned the ringer off on the phone and turned on the answering machine. A couple of reporters have come to the door, but I could see their vans outside and didn't answer. They showed up at the inn, and Virginia said I was out of town."

"I'm glad you gave the story to Tom," Meg said. "I enjoyed working for him. I want him to have the exclusive." She tried to smile at her mother. "You're gutsy."

"We might as well be. And, Meg, he *didn't* call you yesterday. I realize now that whoever did call was trying to find out where you were. I called the police. They're going to keep an eye on the house and check the woods regularly." Catherine's control snapped. "Meg, I'm frightened for you."

Meg thought, who on earth would have known to use Tom Weicker's name?

She said, "Mom, I don't know what's going on. But for now, the alarm is set, isn't it?"

"Yes."

"Then we might as well watch the news. It's time."

IT'S ONE THING TO BE GUTSY, MEG THOUGHT, IT'S ANOTHER to know that a few hundred thousand people are watching a story that makes mincemeat of your private life.

She watched and listened as, with appropriately serious

demeanor, Joel Edison, the PCD eleven o'clock anchor, opened the program. "As reported exclusively on our six o'clock newscast, Edwin Collins, missing since January 28th and a suspect in the Manning Clinic murder case, is the father of the young victim, stabbed to death in mid-Manhattan twelve days ago. Mr. Collins . . .

"Also the father of Meghan Collins of this news team . . . warrant for arrest . . . had two families . . . known in Arizona as husband of the prominent sculptor, Frances Grolier . . ."

"They've obviously been doing their own investigation," Catherine said. "I didn't tell them that."

Finally a commercial came.

Meg pushed the Off button on the remote, and the television went dark. "One thing Annie's mother told me is that the last time he was in Arizona, Dad was horrified by something he'd learned about Victor Orsini."

"Victor Orsini!"

The shock in her mother's voice startled Meg. "Yes. Why? Has something come up about him?"

"He was here today. He asked to go through Edwin's files. He claimed that papers he needed were in them."

"Did he take anything? Did you leave him alone with them?"

"No. Or maybe just for a minute. He was here about an hour. When he left he seemed disappointed. He asked if I was sure that these were all the files we'd brought home. Meg, he begged me for the present not to say anything to Phillip about being here. I promised, but I didn't know what to make of it."

"What I make of it is that there's something in those files that he doesn't want us to find." Meg stood up. "I suggest we both get some sleep. I can assure you that tomorrow the media will be all over the place again, but you and I are spending the day going through those files."

She paused, then added, "I only wish to God we knew what we're looking for."

. . .

BERNIE WAS AT THE WINDOW OF HIS ROOM IN THE DRUMDOE Inn when Meg arrived home. He had his camera with the telescopic lens ready and began taping when she turned on the light in her bedroom. He sighed with pleasure as she took off her jacket and unbuttoned her blouse.

Then she came over and tilted the blinds but didn't completely close them, and he was able to get glimpses of her moving back and forth as she undressed. He waited impatiently when she went downstairs. He couldn't see whatever part of the house she was in.

What he did see made him realize how clever he'd been. A squad car drove slowly past the Collins house every twenty minutes or so. Besides that he saw the beams of flashlights in the woods. The cops had been told about him. They were looking for him.

What would they think if they knew he was right here watching them, laughing at them? But he had to be careful. He wanted a chance to be with Meghan, but he realized now it couldn't be around her house. He'd have to wait until she drove away alone in her car. When he saw her going toward the garage, all he had to do was get downstairs quickly, get into his own car and be ready to pull out behind her when she passed the inn.

He needed to be alone with her, talk to her like a real friend. He wanted to watch the way her lips went up in a curve when she smiled, the way her body moved like just now when she took off her jacket and opened her blouse.

Meghan would understand that he'd never hurt her. He just wanted to be her friend.

Bernie didn't get much sleep that night. It was too interesting to watch the cops driving back and forth.

Back and forth.

Back and forth.

51

Phillip was the first one to call on Thursday morning. "I heard the newscast last night and it's all over the papers this morning. May I come by for a few minutes?"

"Of course," Catherine told him. "If you can pick your way through the press. They're camped outside the house."

"I'll go around to the back."

It was nine o'clock. Meg and Catherine were having breakfast. "I wonder if anything new has developed?" Catherine said. "Phillip sounds upset."

"Remember you promised you wouldn't say anything about Victor Orsini being here yesterday," Meg cautioned. "Anyhow I'd like to do my own checking on him."

When Phillip arrived it was clear that he was very concerned.

"The dam has burst, if that's the proper metaphor," he told them. "The first lawsuit was filed yesterday. A couple who have been paying for storage of ten cryopreserved embryos at the Manning Clinic have been notified there are only seven in the lab. Clearly, Petrovic was making a lot of mistakes along the line and falsifying records to cover them. Collins and Carter have been named as codefendants with the clinic."

"I don't know what to say anymore except that I'm so sorry," Catherine told him.

"I shouldn't have told you. It isn't even the reason I'm here. Did you see Frances Grolier being interviewed when she arrived at Kennedy this morning?"

"Yes, we did." It was Meg who answered.

"Then what do you think of her statement that she believes Edwin is alive and may have started a totally new life?"

"We don't believe that for a minute," Meghan said.

"I have to warn you that John Dwyer is so sure Ed is hiding somewhere that he's going to grill you on that. Meg, when I saw Dwyer Tuesday, he practically accused me of obstructing justice. He asked a hypothetical question: Assuming Ed had a relationship somewhere, where did I think it would be? Clearly you knew where to look for it."

"Phillip," Meghan asked, "you're not suggesting that my father is alive and I know where he is, are you?"

There was no evidence of Carter's usually cheerful and assured manner. "Meg," he said, "I certainly don't believe you know where to reach Edwin. But that Grolier woman knew him so well." He stopped, aware of the impact of his words. "Forgive me."

Meghan knew Phillip Carter was right, that the assistant state attorney would be sure to ask how she knew to go to Scottsdale.

When he left, Catherine said, "This is dragging Phillip down too."

An hour later, Meghan tried calling Stephanie Petrovic. There was still no answer. She called Mac at his office to see if he had managed to reach her.

When Mac told her about the note Stephanie had left, Meghan said flatly, "Mac, that note is a fraud. Stephanie never went with that man willingly. I saw her reaction when I suggested going after him for child support. She's mortally afraid of him. I think Helene Petrovic's lawyer had better report her as a missing person."

Another mysterious disappearance, Meghan thought. It was too late to drive to southern New Jersey today. She would go tomorrow, starting out before daylight. That way she might evade the press.

She wanted to see Charles Potters and ask him to take her through the Petrovic house. She wanted to see the priest who had conducted the service for Helene. He obviously knew the Rumanian women who had attended it.

The terrible possibility was that Stephanie, a young woman about to give birth, might have known something about her aunt that was dangerous to Helene Petrovic's killer.

52

Special investigators Bob Marron and Arlene Weiss requested and received permission from the Manhattan district attorney to question Frances Grolier late Thursday morning.

Martin Fox, her attorney, a silver-haired retired judge in his late sixties, was by her side in a suite in the Doral Hotel, a dozen blocks from the medical examiner's office. Fox was quick to reject questions he felt inappropriate.

Frances had been to the morgue and identified Annie's body. It would be flown to Phoenix and met by a funeral director from Scottsdale. Grief was carved on her face as implacably as it would be in one of her sculptures, but she was composed.

She answered for Marron and Weiss the same questions she had answered for the New York homicide detectives. She knew of no one who might have accompanied Annie to New York. Annie had no enemies. She would not discuss Edwin Collins except to say that, yes, she did think there was a possibility he chose to disappear.

"Did he ever express any desire to be in a rural setting?" Arlene Weiss asked.

The question seemed to penetrate Grolier's lethargy. "Why do you want to know that?"

"Because even though his car had been recently washed

when it was found in front of Meghan Collins' apartment building, there were traces of mud and bits of straw embedded in the tread on the tires. Ms. Grolier, do you think that's the kind of place he might choose to hide?"

"It's possible. Sometimes he interviewed staff members at rural colleges. When he talked about those trips, he always said that life seemed so much less complicated in the country."

WEISS AND MARRON WENT FROM NEW YORK DIRECTLY TO Newtown to talk to Catherine and Meghan again. They asked them the same question.

"The last place in the world I could see my husband is on a farm," Catherine told them.

Meghan agreed. "There's something that keeps bothering me. Doesn't it seem odd that if my father were driving his car, he'd not only leave it where it was sure to be noticed and ticketed but would also leave a murder weapon in it?"

"We haven't closed the door to any possibilities," Marron told her.

"But you're concentrating on *him*. Maybe if you take him out of the picture completely, a different pattern will start to emerge."

"Let's talk about why you made that sudden trip to Arizona, Miss Collins. We had to hear about it on television. Tell us yourself. When did you learn that your father had a residence there?"

When they left an hour later, they took the tape containing the Palomino message with them.

"Do you believe anyone in that office is looking beyond Dad for answers?" Meghan asked her mother.

"No, and they don't intend to," Catherine said bitterly.

They went back into the dining room where they'd been studying the files. Analysis of the California hotel charges pinpointed year by year the times Edwin Collins had probably stayed in Scottsdale.

"But that isn't the kind of information that Victor Orsini would care about," Meg said. "There's got to be something else."

ON THURSDAY AT THE COLLINS AND CARTER OFFICE, JACKIE, the secretary, and Milly, the bookkeeper, conferred in whispers about the tension between Phillip Carter and Victor Orsini. They agreed that it was caused by all the terrible publicity about Mr. Collins and the law suits being filed.

Things had never been right since Mr. Collins died. "Or at least since we thought he died," Jackie said. "It's hard to believe that with a nice, pretty wife like Mrs. Collins, he'd have someone on the side all these years.

"I'm so worried," she went on. "Every penny of my salary is saved for college for the boys. This job is so convenient. I'd hate to lose it."

Milly was sixty-three and wanted to work for two more years until she could collect a bigger social security check. "If they go under, who's going to hire me?" It was a rhetorical question that she frequently asked these days.

"One of them is coming in here at night," Jackie whispered. "You know you can tell when someone's been going through the files."

"Why would anyone do that? They can have us dig for anything they want," Milly protested. "That's what we're paid for."

"The only thing I can figure is that one of them is trying to find the file copy of the letter to the Manning Clinic recommending Helene Petrovic," Jackie said. "I've looked and looked and I can't put my hands on it."

"You'd only been here a few weeks when you typed it. You were just getting used to the filing system," Milly reminded her. "Anyhow, what difference does it make? The police have the original and that's what counts."

"Maybe it makes a lot of difference," Jackie said. "The truth is, I don't remember typing that letter, but then it was seven years ago and I don't remember half the letters that go out of here. And my initials *are* on it."

"So?"

Jackie pulled out her desk drawer, removed her purse and plucked from it a folded newspaper clipping. "Ever since I saw the letter to the Manning Clinic about Petrovic reprinted in the paper, something's been bothering me. Look at this."

She handed the clipping to Milly. "See the way the first line of each paragraph is indented? That's the way I type letters for Mr. Carter and Mr. Orsini. Mr. Collins always had his letters typed in block form, no indentation at all."

"That's right," Milly agreed, "but that certainly looks like Mr. Collins' signature."

"The experts say it's his signature, but I say it's awfully funny a letter he signed went out typed like that."

AT THREE O'CLOCK, TOM WEICKER PHONED. "MEG, I JUST wanted you to know that we're going to run the story you did on the Franklin Clinic in Philadelphia, the one we were going to use with the identical twin special. We'll schedule it on both news broadcasts tonight. It's a good, succinct piece on in vitro fertilization and ties in with what's happened at the Manning Clinic."

"I'm glad you're running it, Tom."

"I wanted to be sure you saw it," he said, his voice surprisingly kind.

"Thanks for letting me know," Meg replied.

MAC PHONED AT FIVE-THIRTY. "HOW ABOUT YOU AND CATHerine coming over here for dinner for a change? I'm sure you won't want to go to the inn tonight."

"No, we don't," Meg agreed. "And we could use the company. Is six-thirty all right? I want to watch the Channel 3 news. A feature I did is being run."

"Come over now and watch it here. Kyle can show off that he's learned to tape."

"All right."

IT WAS A GOOD STORY. A NICE MOMENT WAS THE SEGMENT taped in Dr. Williams' office, when he pointed to the walls filled with pictures of young children. "Can you imagine how much happiness these kids are bringing into people's lives?"

Meg had instructed the cameraman to pan slowly over the photographs as Dr. Williams continued to speak. "These children were born only because of the methods of assisted reproduction available here."

"Plug for the center," Meg commented. "But it wasn't too heavy."

"It was a good feature, Meg," Mac said.

"Yes, I think so. Suppose we skip the rest of the news. We all know what it's going to be."

BERNIE STAYED IN THE ROOM ALL DAY. HE TOLD THE MAID that he wasn't feeling well. He told her that he guessed all the nights he'd spent at the hospital when his mother was so sick were catching up with him.

Virginia Murphy called a few minutes later. "We usually only have continental breakfast room service, but we'll be glad to send up a tray whenever you're ready."

They sent up lunch, then later Bernie ordered dinner. He had the pillows propped up so it looked like he'd been in bed resting. The minute the waiter left, Bernie was back at the window, sitting at an angle so nobody who happened to look up would notice him.

He watched as Meghan and her mother left the house a little before six. It was dark, but the porch light was on. He debated following them, then decided that as long as the mother was along, he would be wasting his time. He was glad he hadn't bothered when the car went right instead of left. He figured they must be going to the house where that kid lived. That was the only one in the cul-de-sac.

The squad cars came regularly through the day, but not every twenty minutes anymore. During the evening, he noticed flashlights in the woods only once. The cops were easing up. That was good.

Meghan and her mother got back home around ten. An hour later, Meghan undressed and got into bed. She sat up for about twenty minutes, writing something in a notebook.

Long after she turned off the light, Bernie stayed at the window thinking about her, imagining being in the room with her.

53

*D*onald Anderson had taken two weeks off from work to help with the new baby. Neither he nor Dina wanted outside assistance. "You relax," he told his wife. "Jonathan and I are in charge."

The doctor had signed the release the night before. He wholeheartedly agreed that it was better if they could avoid the media. "Ten to one some of the photographers will be in the lobby between nine and eleven," he'd predicted. That was the time new mothers and babies usually were discharged.

The phone had been ringing all week with requests for interviews. Don screened them with the answering machine and did not return any of them. On Thursday their lawyer phoned. There was definite proof of malfeasance at the Manning Clinic. He warned them that they'd be urged to join the class action suit that was being proposed.

"Absolutely not," Anderson said. "You can tell that to anyone who calls you."

Dina was propped up on the couch, reading to Jonathan. Stories about Big Bird were his new favorites. She glanced up at her husband. "Why not just turn off that phone?" she suggested. "Bad enough I wouldn't even look at Nicky for hours after he was born. All he'd need to know when he grows up is that I sued someone because he's here instead of another baby."

They'd named him Nicholas after Dina's grandfather, the one her mother swore he resembled. From the nearby bassinet, they heard a stirring, a faint cry, then a wholehearted wail as their infant woke up.

"He heard us talking about him," Jonathan said.

"Maybe he did, love," Dina agreed as she kissed the top of Jonathan's silky blond head.

"He's just plain hungry again," Don announced. He bent down, picked up the squirming bundle and handed it to Dina.

"Are you sure he's not my twin?" Jonathan asked.

"Yes, I'm sure," Dina said. "But he's your brother, and that's every bit as good."

She put the baby to her breast. "You have my olive skin," she said as she gently stroked his cheek to start him nursing. My little paisano."

She smiled at her husband. "You know something, Don. It's really only fair that one of our kids looks like me."

MEGHAN'S EARLY START ON FRIDAY MORNING MEANT THAT she was able to be in the rectory of St. Dominic's church on the outskirts of Trenton at ten-thirty.

She had called the young pastor immediately after dinner the night before and set up the appointment.

The rectory was a narrow, three-story frame house typical of the Victorian era, with a wraparound porch and gingerbread trim. The sitting room was shabby but comfortable with heavy, overstuffed chairs, a carved library table, old-fashioned standing lamps and a faded Oriental carpet. The fireplace glowed with burning logs and breaking embers, dispelling the chill of the minuscule foyer.

Fr. Radzin had opened the door for her, apologized that he was on the phone, ushered her into this room and vanished up the stairs. As Meghan waited, she mused that this was the kind of room where troubled people could unburden themselves without fear of condemnation or reproach.

She wasn't sure exactly what she would ask the priest. She did know from the brief eulogy he'd delivered at the memorial mass that he'd known and liked Helene Petrovic.

She heard his footsteps on the stairs. Then he was in the room, apologizing again for keeping her waiting. He chose a chair opposite hers and asked, "How can I help you, Meghan?"

Not "What can I do for you?" but "How can I help you?" A subtle difference that was oddly consoling. "I have to find out who Helene Petrovic really was. You're aware of the situation at the Manning Clinic?"

"Yes, of course. I've been following the story. I also saw in this morning's paper a picture of you and that poor girl who was stabbed. The resemblance is quite remarkable."

"I haven't seen the paper, but I know what you mean. Actually, that's what started all this." Meghan leaned forward, locking her fingers, pressing her palms together. "The assistant state attorney investigating Helene Petrovic's murder believes that my father is responsible for Helene being hired at Manning and for her death too. I don't. Too many things don't make sense. Why would he want to see the clinic hire someone who wasn't qualified for the job? What did he have to gain by placing Helene in the lab in the first place?"

"There's always a reason, Meghan, sometimes several, for every action any human being makes."

"That's what I mean. I can't find one, never mind several. It just makes no sense. Why would my father have even become involved with Helene if he knew she was a fraud? I know he was conscientious about his job. He took pride in matching the right people to his clients. We used to talk about it often.

"It's reprehensible to put an unqualified person in a sensitive medical situation. The more they investigate the lab at the Manning Clinic, the more errors they're finding. I can't understand why my father would deliberately cause all that. And what about Helene? Didn't she have any conscience in the matter? Didn't she worry about preembryos being damaged or destroyed because of her sloppiness, carelessness or ignorance? At least some stored embryos were intended to be transferred in the hope that they'd be born."

"Transferred and born," Fr. Radzin repeated. "An interesting ethical question. Helene was not a regular churchgoer, but when she did come to mass, it was always the last one on Sunday and she would stay for coffee hour. I had the feeling there was something on her mind that she couldn't bring herself to talk about. But I must tell you that if I were applying adjectives to her, the last three that would come to mind are 'sloppy, careless and ignorant.' "

"What about her friends? Who was she close to?"

"No one I know of. Some of her acquaintances have been in touch with me this week. They've commented on how little they really knew Helene."

"I'm afraid something may have happened to her niece, Stephanie. Did you ever meet the young man who is her baby's father?"

"No. And neither did anyone else from what I understand."

"What did you think of Stephanie?"

"She's nothing like Helene. Of course she's very young and in this country less than a year. Now she's alone. It may just be that the baby's father showed up again and she decided to take a chance on him."

He wrinkled his forehead. Mac does that, Meghan thought. Fr. Radzin looked to be in his late thirties, a little older than Mac. Why was she comparing them? It was because there was something so wholesome and good about them, she decided.

She stood up. "I've taken enough of your time, Fr. Radzin."

"Stay another minute or two, Meghan. Sit down, please. You've raised the question of your father's motivation in placing Helene at the clinic. If you can't get information about Helene, my advice is to keep searching until you find the reason for *his* participation in the situation. Do you think he was romantically involved with her?"

"I very much doubt it." She shrugged. "He seems to have been sufficiently troubled trying to balance his time between my mother and Annie's mother."

"Money?"

"That doesn't make sense either. The Manning Clinic paid the usual fee to Collins and Carter for the placement of Helene and Dr. Williams. My experience in studying law and human nature has taught me that love or money are the reasons most crimes are committed. Yet I can't make either fit here." She stood up. "Now I really must go. I'm meeting Helene's lawyer at her Lawrenceville house."

CHARLES POTTERS WAS WAITING WHEN MEGHAN ARRIVED. She had met him briefly at Helene's memorial service. Now as she had a chance to focus on him, she realized that he looked like the kind of family lawyer portrayed in old movies.

His dark blue suit was ultraconservative, his shirt crisp white, his narrow blue tie subdued, his skin tone pink, his sparse gray hair neatly combed. Rimless glasses enhanced surprisingly vivid hazel eyes.

Whatever items from the house Stephanie had taken with her, the appearance of this room, the first they entered, was unchanged. It looked exactly as Meghan had seen it less than a week ago. Powers of observation, she thought. Concentrate. Then she noticed that the lovely Dresden figures she'd admired were missing from the mantel.

"Your friend Dr. MacIntyre dissuaded me from immediately reporting Stephanie's theft of Helene's property, Miss Collins, but I'm afraid I cannot wait any longer. As trustee I'm responsible for all of Helene's possessions."

"I understand that. I simply wish that some effort could be made to find Stephanie and persuade her to return them. If a warrant is sworn out for her arrest, she might be deported.

"Mr. Potters," she continued, "my concern is much more serious than worrying about the things Stephanie took with her. Do you have the note she left?"

"Yes. Here it is."

Meghan read it through.

"Did you ever meet this Jan?"

"No."

"What did Helene think about her niece's pregnancy?"

"Helene was a kind woman, reserved but kind. Her only comments to me about the pregnancy were quite sympathetic."

"How long have you handled her affairs?"

"For about three years."

"You believed she was a medical doctor?"

"I had no reason not to believe her."

"Didn't she build up a rather considerable estate? She had a very good salary at Manning of course. She was paid there as an embryologist. But she certainly couldn't have made very much money as a medical secretary for the three years before that."

"I understood she'd been a cosmetologist. Cosmetology can be lucrative, and Helene was a shrewd investor. Miss Collins, I don't have much time. I believe you said you would like to walk through the house with me? I want to be sure it's properly secured before I leave."

"Yes, I would."

Meghan went upstairs with him. Here too nothing seemed

to be out of order. Stephanie's packing had clearly not been rushed.

The master bedroom was luxurious. Helene Petrovic had not denied herself creature comforts. The coordinated wall hanging, spread and draperies looked very expensive.

French doors opened into a small sitting room. One wall was covered with pictures of children. "These are duplicates of the ones at the Manning Clinic," she said.

"Helene showed them to me," Potters told her. "She was very proud of the successful births achieved through the clinic."

Meg studied the pictures. "I saw some of these kids at the reunion less than two weeks ago." She picked out Jonathan. "This is the Anderson child whose family you've been reading about. That's the case that started the state investigation of the lab at Manning." She paused, studying the photograph on the top corner. It was of two children, a boy and girl, in matching sweaters with their arms around each other. What was it about them that she should be noticing?

"I really have to lock up now, Miss Collins."

There was an edge in the attorney's voice. She couldn't delay him any longer. Meg took another long look at the picture of the children in matching sweaters, committing it to memory.

BERNIE'S MOTHER WAS NOT FEELING WELL. IT WAS HER AL-lergies. She'd been sneezing a lot, and her eyes were itchy. She thought she felt a draft in the house too. She wondered if Bernard had forgotten and left a window open downstairs.

She knew she shouldn't have let Bernard drive that car to Chicago, even for two hundred dollars a day. Sometimes when he was off by himself too long, he got fanciful. He started to daydream and to want things that could get him in trouble.

Then his temper started. That's when she needed to be there; she could control an outburst when she saw it coming.

She kept him on the straight and narrow. Kept him nice and clean, well fed, saw that he got to his job and then stayed in with her watching television at night.

He'd been doing well for such a long time now. But he'd been acting kind of funny lately.

He was supposed to call. Why didn't he? When he got to Chicago he wouldn't start following a girl and try to touch her, would he? Not that he'd mean to harm her, but there'd been too many times when Bernard got nervous if a girl screamed. A couple of girls he'd hurt real bad.

They said that if it happened again, they wouldn't let him come home. They'd keep him locked up. He knew it too.

THE ONLY THING I HAVE REALLY ESTABLISHED IN ALL THESE hours is the number of times my husband was cheating on me, Catherine thought as she pushed the files away late Friday afternoon. She no longer had any desire to go through them. What good would knowing all this serve her now? It hurts so much, she thought.

She stood up. Outside it was a blustery November afternoon. In three weeks it would be Thanksgiving. That was always a busy time at the inn.

Virginia had phoned. The real estate company was being persistent. Was the inn for sale? They must be serious, she reported. They'd even named the price at which they'd start negotiating. They had another place in mind if Drumdoe wasn't available, or so they said. But it might be true.

Catherine wondered how long she and Meg could twist in the wind like this.

Meg. Would she close in on herself because of her father's betrayal as she had when Mac married Ginger? Catherine had never let on that she knew how heartbroken Meg had been over Mac. Edwin was always the one their daughter had turned to for comfort. Natural enough. Daddy's girl. It ran in the family. I was Daddy's girl too, Catherine thought.

Catherine could see the way Mac looked at Meg these days. She hoped it wasn't too late. Edwin had never forgiven his mother for rejecting him. Meg had built up a wall around herself where Mac was concerned. And great as she was with Kyle in her own way, she chose not to see how hopefully he was always reaching out to her.

Catherine caught a glimpse of a figure in the woods. She froze, then relaxed. It was a policeman. At least they were keeping an eye on the place.

She heard the click of a key in the lock.

Catherine breathed a prayer of gratitude. The daughter who made everything else bearable was safe.

Now maybe for the moment she could stop being haunted by the pictures that had run side by side in the newspapers today, the official publicity head shot of Meg from Channel 3 and the professional head shot Annie had used for her travel articles.

At Catherine's insistence, Virginia had sent over all the papers delivered to the inn, including the tabloids. The *Daily News,* besides using the pictures, had printed a photocopy of the fax Meg had received the night Annie was stabbed.

The headline of their article read: DID THE WRONG SISTER DIE?

"Hi, Mom. I'm home."

For reassurance, Catherine took one more glance at the policeman at the edge of the woods, then turned to greet her daughter.

VIRGINIA MURPHY WAS THE SEMIOFFICIAL SECOND IN COMmand of the Drumdoe Inn. Technically hostess at the restaurant, and reservation clerk as needed, she was in fact Catherine's eyes and ears when Catherine was not around or when she was busy in the kitchen. Ten years younger than Catherine, six inches taller and handsomely rounded, she was a good friend as well as a faithful employee.

Knowing the financial situation at the inn, Virginia worked diligently to cut corners where it wouldn't show. She passionately wanted Catherine to be able to keep the inn. She knew that when all this terrible publicity died down, Catherine's best chance to get on with her life began here.

It galled Virginia that she'd aided and abetted Catherine when that crazy interior designer came in with her violently expensive swatches and tile samples and plumbing-supply books. And that after the expense of the much-needed renovation!

The place looked lovely, Virginia admitted, and it certainly had needed a face-lift, but the irony would be to go through the inconvenience and financial drain of renovating and redecorating only to have someone else come in and buy Drumdoe at a fire-sale price.

The last thing Virginia wanted to do was to cause Catherine any more concern, but now she was getting worried about the man who had checked into room 3A. He'd been in bed since he arrived, claiming he was exhausted from running back and forth from Long Island to New Haven, where his mother was in the hospital.

It wasn't a big deal to send a tray up to his room. They could certainly handle that. The problem was that he might be seriously sick. How would it look if something happened to him while he was here?

Virginia thought, I'm not going to bother Catherine yet. I'm going to let it go at least for another day. If he's still in bed tomorrow night, I'll go up and have a talk with him myself. I'll insist that he allow a doctor to see him.

FREDERICK SCHULLER FROM VALLEY MEMORIAL HOSPITAL IN Trenton called Mac late Friday afternoon. "I've sent the roster of medical staff to Miss Collins by overnight mail. She'll have a lot of reading to do unless she knows what name she's looking for."

"That was very quick," Mac said sincerely. "I'm grateful."

"Let's see if it's helpful. There is one thing that might interest you. I was looking over the Manning Clinic list and saw Dr. Henry Williams' name on it. I'm acquainted with him. He's head of Franklin Clinic in Philadelphia now."

"Yes, I know," Mac said.

"This may not be relevant. Williams was never on staff here, but I remembered that his wife was in our long-term care facility for two of the three years Helene Petrovic worked at Dowling. I used to run into him here occasionally."

"Do you think there's any chance he's the doctor Petrovic may have been seeing when she was at Dowling?" Mac asked quickly.

There was a hesitation, then Schuller said, "This borders on gossip, but I did make a few inquiries in the long-term unit. The head nurse has been there twenty years. She remembers Dr. Williams and his wife very well."

Mac waited. Let this be the connection we're looking for, he prayed.

It was clear that Frederick Schuller was reluctant to continue. After another brief pause he said, "Mrs. Williams had a brain tumor. She had been born and raised in Rumania. As her condition worsened, she lost her ability to communicate in English. Dr. Williams spoke only a few words of Rumanian, and a woman friend came regularly to Mrs. Williams' room to translate for him."

"Was it Helene Petrovic?" Mac asked.

"The nurse never was introduced to her. She described her as a dark-haired, brown-eyed woman in her early to mid-forties, quite attractive." Schuller added, "As you can see, this is very tenuous."

No it isn't, Mac thought. He tried to sound calm when he thanked Frederick Schuller, but when he hung up the phone, he said a silent prayer of gratitude.

This was the first break! Meg had told him that Dr. Williams denied having known Petrovic before she joined the staff of the Manning Clinic. Williams was the expert who could have taught Petrovic the skills she needed to pass herself off as an embryologist.

54

"Kyle, shouldn't you be starting your homework?" Marie Dileo, the sixty-year-old housekeeper gently prodded.

Kyle was watching the tape he'd made of Meg's interview at the Franklin Clinic. He looked up. "In a minute, Mrs. Dileo, honest."

"You know what your Dad says about too much television."

"This is an educational tape. That's different."

Dileo shook her head. "You have an answer for everything." She studied him affectionately. Kyle was such a nice child, smart as a whip, funny and little-boy appealing.

The segment with Meg was ending, and he turned off the set. "Meg is really a good reporter, isn't she?"

"Yes, she is."

Trailed by Jake, Kyle followed Marie into the kitchen. She could tell something was wrong. "Didn't you come home from Danny's a little early?" she asked.

"Uh-huh." He spun the fruit bowl.

"Don't do that. You'll knock it over. Anything happen at Danny's?"

"His mother got a little mad at us."

"Oh?" Marie looked up from the meat loaf she was preparing. "I'm sure there was a reason."

"They put in a new laundry chute in his house. We thought we'd try it out."

"Kyle, you two wouldn't fit in a laundry chute."

"No, but Penny fits."

"You put Penny in the chute!"

"It was Danny's idea. He put her in and I caught her at the bottom and we put a big quilt and pillows down in case I missed, but I didn't, not once. Penny didn't want to stop, but Danny's mother's real mad. We can't play together all week."

"Kyle, if I were you, I'd have my homework done when your father gets home. He is not going to be happy about this."

"I know." With a deep sigh Kyle went for his backpack and dumped his books on the kitchen table. Jake curled up on the floor at his feet.

That desk he got for his birthday was a waste of money, Marie thought. She'd been about to set the table. Well, that could wait. It was only ten past five. The routine was that she prepared dinner and then left when Mac got home around six. He didn't like to eat the minute he walked in, so he always served the meal himself, after Marie had left.

The phone rang. Kyle jumped up. "I'll get it." He answered, listened, then handed the receiver to Marie. "It's for you, Mrs. Dileo."

It was her husband saying that her father had been taken to the hospital from the nursing home.

"Is something the matter?" Kyle asked when she replaced the receiver.

"Yes. My Dad's been sick for a long time. He's very old. I have to get right to the hospital. I'll drop you at Danny's and leave a note for your father."

"Not Danny's," Kyle said, alarmed. "His mother wouldn't like that. Leave me at Meg's. I'll call her." He pressed the automatic dial button on the phone. Meg's number was directly under those of the police and fire departments. A moment later he announced, beaming, "She said come right over."

Mrs. Dileo scribbled a note to Mac. "Take your homework, Kyle."

"Okay." He ran into the living room and grabbed the tape he'd made of Meg's interview. "Maybe she'll want to watch it with me."

THERE WAS A BRISKNESS ABOUT MEG THAT CATHERINE DID not understand. In the two hours since she'd come back from Trenton, Meg had been through Edwin's files, extracted some papers and made several phone calls from the study. Then she sat at Edwin's desk, writing furiously. It reminded Catherine of when Meg was in law school. Whenever she came home for a weekend, she spent most of it at that desk, totally preoccupied with her case studies.

At five o'clock, Catherine looked in on her. "I thought I'd fix chicken and mushrooms for dinner. How does that grab you?"

"Fine. Sit down for a minute, Mom."

Catherine chose the small armchair near the desk. Her eyes slid past Edwin's maroon leather chair and ottoman. Meg had told her that they were duplicated in Arizona. Once an endearing reminder of her husband, they were now a mockery.

Meg put her elbows on the desk, clasped her hands and rested her chin on them. "I had a nice talk with Fr. Radzin this morning. He offered the memorial mass for Helene Petrovic. I told him I couldn't find any reason why Dad would have placed Petrovic at the Manning Clinic. He said words to the effect that there was always a reason for someone's actions, and if I couldn't find it, maybe I should reexamine the whole premise."

"What do you mean?"

"Mom, I mean that several traumatic things happened to us at once. I saw Annie's body when she was brought to the hospital. We learned that Dad almost certainly had not died in the bridge accident and we began to suspect that he had been leading a double life. On the heels of that, Dad was blamed for Helene Petrovic's false credentials and now for her murder."

Meg leaned forward. "Mom, if it hadn't been for the shock of the double life and Petrovic's death, when the insurers refused to pay, we would have taken a much longer look at the reason we thought Dad was on that bridge when the accident happened. Think about it."

"What do you mean?" Catherine was bewildered. "Victor Orsini was talking to Dad just as he was driving onto the ramp. Someone on the bridge saw his car go over the edge."

"That someone on the bridge obviously was mistaken. And Mom, we only have Victor Orsini's word that Dad was calling him from that spot. Suppose, just suppose, Dad had already crossed the bridge when he called Victor. He might have seen the accident happening behind him. Frances Grolier remembered that Dad had been angry about something Victor had done, and that when Dad called Dr. Manning from Scottsdale, he had seemed really distraught. I was in New York. You were away overnight. It would be just like Dad to tell Victor he wanted to see him immediately, instead of next morning, as Victor said. Dad may have been insecure in his personal life, but I don't think he ever had any doubts professionally."

"You're saying that Victor's a liar?" Catherine looked astounded.

"It would be a safe lie, wouldn't it? The time of the call from Dad's car phone was exactly right and could be verified. Mom, Victor had been at the office a month or so when the recommendation for Petrovic went to Manning. He could have sent it. He was working directly under Dad."

"Phillip never has liked him," Catherine murmured. "But, Meg, there's no way to prove this. And you come up with the same question: Why? Why would Victor, any more than Dad, put Petrovic in that lab? What would he have to gain?"

"I don't know yet. But don't you see that as long as the police think Dad is alive, they're not going to seriously examine any alternative answers in Helene Petrovic's murder?"

The phone rang. "Ten to one it's Phillip for you," Meg said as she picked it up. It was Kyle.

"We've got company for dinner," she told Catherine when she replaced the receiver. "Hope you can stretch the chicken and mushrooms."

"Mac and Kyle?"

"Yes."

"Good." Catherine got up. "Meg, I wish I could be as enthusiastic as you about all these possibilities. You have a theory and it's a good defense argument for your father. But maybe it's just that."

Meg held up a sheet of paper. "This is the January bill for Dad's car phone. Look at how much that last call cost. He and Victor were on for eight minutes. It doesn't take eight minutes to set up a meeting, does it?"

"Meg, Dad's signature was on the letter to the Manning Clinic. That's been verified by experts."

AFTER DINNER, MAC SUGGESTED THAT KYLE HELP CATHERINE with clearing the table. Alone with Meghan in the living room he told her about Dr. Williams' connection to Dowling and possibly to Helene.

"Dr. Williams!" Meghan stared at him. "Mac, he absolutely denied knowing Petrovic before Manning Clinic. The receptionist at Manning saw them having dinner together. When I asked Dr. Williams about it, he claimed that he always took a new staff member out for dinner as a friendly gesture."

"Meg, I think we're onto something, but we still can't be *sure* it was Helene Petrovic who accompanied Williams when he visited his wife," Mac cautioned.

"Mac, it fits. Williams and Helene must have been involved with each other. We know she had a tremendous interest in lab work. He's the perfect one to have helped her falsify her curriculum vitae and to have guided her when she arrived at Manning."

"But Williams left Manning Clinic six months after Petrovic started to work there. Why would he do that if he was involved with her?"

"Her home is in New Jersey, not far from Philadelphia. Her niece said that she was often away for hours on Saturday and Sunday. Much of that time may have been spent with him."

"Then where does your father's letter of recommendation come in? He placed Williams at Manning, but why would he have helped Petrovic get her job there?"

"I have a theory about that, and it involves Victor Orsini. It's starting to fit, all of it."

She smiled up at him, the closest he'd seen to a genuine smile on her lips for a long time.

They were standing in front of the fireplace. Mac put his arms around her. Meghan immediately stiffened and shifted to move out of his embrace, but he would have none of it. He turned her to face him.

"Get it straight, Meghan," Mac said. "You were right nine years ago. I only wish I had seen it then." He paused. "You're the only one for me. I know it now, and you do too. We can't keep wasting time."

He kissed her fiercely, then released her, stepping back. "I won't let you keep pushing me away. Once your life settles down again, we're going to have a long talk about *us.*"

KYLE BEGGED TO SHOW THE TAPE OF MEG'S INTERVIEW. "IT'S only three minutes, Dad. I want to show Meg how I can tape programs now."

"I think you're stalling," Mac told him. "Incidentally, Danny's mother caught me at home when I was reading Mrs. Dileo's note. You're grounded. Show Meg the tape, but then don't even *think* television for a week."

"What'd you do?" Meg asked in a whisper when Kyle sat beside her.

"I'll tell you in a minute. See, here you are."

The tape ran. "You did a good job with that," Meg assured him.

THAT NIGHT MEGHAN LAY IN BED FOR A LONG TIME, UNABLE to sleep. Her mind was in turmoil, going over all the new developments, the connection of Dr. Williams to Petrovic, her suspicions about Victor Orsini. Mac. I told the police if they'd stop concentrating on Dad they'd find the real answers, she thought. But Mac? She wouldn't let herself think about him now.

All this, yet there was something else, she realized, something that was eluding her, something terribly, terribly important. What was it? It had something to do with the tape of her interview at the Franklin Center. I'll ask Kyle to bring it over tomorrow, she thought. I have to see it again.

FRIDAY WAS A LONG DAY FOR BERNIE. HE HAD SLEPT UNTIL seven-thirty, real late for him. He suspected right away that he had missed Meghan, that she'd left very early. Her blinds were up, and he could see her bed was made.

He knew he should call Mama. She'd told him to call, but he was afraid. If she had any idea he wasn't in Chicago, she'd be angry. She'd make him come home.

He sat by the window all day, watching Meghan's house, waiting for Meghan to return. He pulled the phone as far as the cord would stretch so he didn't lose sight of the house when he phoned for breakfast and lunch.

He'd unlock the door, then when the waiter knocked, Bernie would leap into bed and call, "Come in." It drove him crazy that he might miss Meghan again while the waiter was fussing with the tray.

When the maid knocked and tried to open the door with her master key she was stopped by the chain. He knew she couldn't see in.

"May I just change the towels?" she asked.

He figured he'd better let her do that at least. Didn't want her to get suspicious.

Yet as she passed him, he noticed that she looked at him funny, the way people do when they're sizing you up. Bernie tried hard to smile at her, tried to sound sincere when he thanked her.

It was late afternoon when Meghan's white Mustang turned into her driveway. Bernie pressed his nose against the window, straining to catch a glimpse of her walking up the path to the house. Seeing her made him happy again.

Around five-thirty, he saw the kid dropped off at Meghan's house. If it wasn't for the kid, Bernie could be hiding in the woods. He could be closer to Meg. He'd be taping her so that he could keep her. Could watch her and be with her whenever he wanted. Except for that stupid kid. He hated that kid.

He didn't think to order dinner. He wasn't hungry. Finally at ten-thirty his wait was over. Meghan turned on the light in her bedroom and undressed.

She was so beautiful!

AT FOUR O'CLOCK FRIDAY AFTERNOON, PHILLIP ASKED Jackie, "Where's Orsini?"

"He had an appointment outside the office, Mr. Carter. He said he'd be back around four-thirty."

Jackie stood in Phillip Carter's office, trying to decide what to do. When Mr. Carter was upset he was a little scary. Mr. Collins never used to get upset.

But Mr. Carter was the boss now, and last night her husband, Bob, told her that she owed it to him to tell him that Victor Orsini was going through all the files at night.

"But maybe it's Mr. Carter doing it," she had suggested.

"If it is Carter, he'll appreciate your concern. Don't forget, if there's any trouble between them, Orsini is the one who'll leave, not Carter."

Bob was right. Now Jackie said firmly, "Mr. Carter, it may

be none of my business, but I'm pretty sure Mr. Orsini is coming in here at night and going through all the files."

Phillip Carter was very quiet for a long minute, then his face hardened and he said, "Thank you, Jackie. Have Mr. Orsini see me when he comes in."

I wouldn't want to be in Mr. Orsini's boots, she thought.

Twenty minutes later she and Milly dropped all pretense of not listening as through the closed door of Phillip Carter's office, they could hear his raised voice castigating Victor Orsini.

"For a long time I have suspected you of working hand-in-glove with Downes and Rosen," he told him. "This place is in trouble now, and you're preparing to land on your feet by going with them. But you seem to forget that you have a contract that specifically prohibits you from soliciting our accounts. Now get out and don't bother to pack. You've probably taken plenty of our files already. We'll send your personal items on to you."

"So that's what he was doing," Jackie whispered. "That is really bad." Neither she nor Milly looked up at Orsini when he passed their desks on his way out.

If they had, they would have seen that his face was white with fury.

ON SATURDAY MORNING, CATHERINE WENT TO THE INN FOR the breakfast hour. She checked her mail and phone calls, then had a long talk with Virginia. Deciding not to stay for the lunch serving, she returned to the house at eleven o'clock. She found that Meg had been taking the files to her father's study and analyzing them, one by one.

"The dining room is such a mess that I can't concentrate," Meg explained. "Victor was looking for something important, and we're not seeing the forest for the trees."

Catherine studied her daughter. Meg was wearing a plaid silk shirt and chinos. Her chestnut hair was almost shoulder length now, and brushed back. That's what it is, Catherine thought. Her hair is just that little bit longer. The picture of Annie Collins in yesterday's newspapers came to mind.

"Meg, I've thought it through. I'm going to accept that offer on Drumdoe."

"You're *what?*"

"Virginia agrees with me. The overhead is simply too high. I don't want the inn to end up on the auction block."

"Mom, Dad founded Collins and Carter, and even under these circumstances, there must be some way you can take some money out of it."

"Meg, if there were a death certificate, there would be partnership insurance. With lawsuits pending there won't be a business before long."

"What does Phillip say? By the way, he's been around a lot lately," Meg said, "more than in all the years he worked with Dad."

"He's trying to be kind, and I appreciate that."

"Is it more than kindness?"

"I hope not. He'd be making a mistake. I have too much to deal with before I even think in that direction with any-one." She added quietly, "But you don't."

"What's that supposed to mean?"

"It means that Kyle isn't the greatest busboy. He was keep-ing an eye on you two and reported with great satisfaction that Mac was kissing you."

"I am not interested—"

"Stop it, Meg," Catherine commanded. She stepped around the desk, yanked open the bottom drawer, pulled out a half-dozen letters and threw them on the desk. "Don't be like your father, an emotional cripple because he couldn't forgive rejection."

"He had every reason not to forgive his mother!"

"As a child, yes. As an adult with a family who deeply loved him, no. Maybe he wouldn't have needed Scottsdale if he'd gone to Philadelphia and made peace with her."

Meg raised her eyebrows. "You can play rough, can't you?"

"You bet I can, Meg, you love Mac. You always have. Kyle needs you. Now for God's sake, put yourself on the line and quit being afraid that Mac would be imbecile enough to want Ginger if she ever showed up in his life again."

"Dad always called you Mighty Mouse." Meg felt tears burning behind her eyes.

"Yes, he did. When I go back to the inn, I'm going to call the real estate people. One thing I can promise. I'll raise their ante till they beg for mercy."

AT ONE-THIRTY, JUST BEFORE SHE RETURNED TO THE INN, Catherine poked her head into the study. "Meg, remember I said Palomino Leather Goods sounded familiar? I think Annie's mother may have left the same message on our home phone for Dad. It would have been mid-March seven years ago. The reason I can pinpoint it is that I was so furious when Dad missed your twenty-first birthday party that when he finally got home with a leather purse for you, I told him I'd like to hit him over the head with it."

ON SATURDAY, BERNIE'S MOTHER COULD NOT STOP SNEEZING. Her sinuses were beginning to ache, her throat was scratchy. She had to do something about it.

Bernard had let dust pile up in the basement, she just knew it. No question about it, that had to be it. Now the dust was filtering through the house.

She became angrier and more agitated by the minute. Finally, at two o'clock, she couldn't stand it anymore. She had to get down there and clean.

First she heaved the broom and shovel and mop into the basement. Then she filled a plastic bag with rags and cleanser and threw it down the stairs. It landed on the mop.

Finally Mama tied on her apron. She felt the bannister. It wasn't that loose. It would hold her. She'd go slowly, a step at a time, and test each stair before she put her weight on it.

She still didn't know how she'd managed to fall so hard ten years ago. One minute she'd been starting down the stairs, the next she was in an ambulance.

Step by step, with infinite care, she descended. Well, I did it, she thought as she stepped on the basement floor. The toe of her shoe caught in the bag of rags and she fell heavily to the side, her left foot bending beneath her.

The sound of Mama's ankle bone breaking resounded through the clammy basement.

55

*A*fter her mother went back to the inn, Meghan phoned Phillip at home. When he answered, she said, "I'm glad to get you. I thought you might be in New York or at one of your auctions today."

"It's been a rough week. I had to fire Victor yesterday afternoon."

"Why?" Meg asked, distressed at this sudden twist of events. She needed Victor available while she was trying to tie him to the Petrovic recommendation. Suppose he left town? So far she didn't have any proof, couldn't go to the police with her suspicions about him. That would take time.

"He's a slippery one, Meg. Been stealing our clients. Frankly, from one or two remarks your dad made just before he disappeared, I think he suspected that Victor was up to something."

"So do I," Meg said. "That's why I'm calling. I think he might have sent out the Petrovic letter when Dad was away.

Phillip, we don't have any of Dad's Daily Reminders with his business appointments. Are they in the office?"

"They should have been with the files you took home."

"I would think so, but they're not. Phillip, I'm trying to reach Annie's mother. Like a fool I didn't get her private number when I was out there. The Palomino Leather Goods Shop contacted her and then gave me directions to her house. I have an idea that Dad may not have been in the office when that letter about Petrovic went to Manning. It's dated March 21st, isn't it?"

"I believe so."

"Then I'm onto something. Annie's mother can verify it. I did reach the lawyer who came out here with her. He wouldn't give me the number but said he'd contact her for me."

She paused, then said, "Phillip, there's something else. I think Dr. Williams and Helene Petrovic were involved, certainly while they worked together and maybe even before then. And if so, it's possible he's the man Petrovic's neighbor saw visiting her apartment."

"Meg, that's incredible. Do you have any proof?"

"Not yet, but I don't think it will be hard to get."

"Just be careful," Phillip Carter warned her. "Williams is very well respected in medical circles. Don't even mention his name until you can back up what you say."

FRANCES GROLIER PHONED AT QUARTER TO THREE. "YOU wanted to talk to me, Meghan."

"Yes. You told me the other day that you only used the Palomino code a couple of other times in all those years. Did you ever phone our house with that message?"

Grolier did not ask why Meg wanted to know. "Yes, I did. It was nearly seven years ago, on March 10th. Annie had been in a head-on collision and wasn't expected to live. I'd tried the machine in the office, but as it turned out, it had been accidentally unplugged. I knew Edwin was in Connecticut and I *had* to reach him. He flew out that night and was here two weeks until Annie was out of danger."

Meg thought of March 18th seven years ago, her twenty-first birthday. A black-tie dinner dance at Drumdoe. Her father's phone call that afternoon. He had a virus and was too sick to get on the plane. Two hundred guests. Mac with Ginger, showing pictures of Kyle.

She'd spent the night trying to smile, trying not to show how bitterly disappointed she was that her father was not with her on this special night.

"Meghan?" Frances Grolier's controlled voice at the other end of the phone was questioning.

"I'm sorry. Sorry about everything. What you've just told me is terribly important. It's tied to so much of what's happened."

Meghan returned the receiver to its cradle, but held onto it for several minutes. Then she dialed Phillip. "Confirmation." Quickly she explained what Frances Grolier had just told her.

"Meg, you're a whiz," Phillip told her.

"Phillip, there's the bell. It must be Kyle. Mac is dropping him off. I asked him to bring something over for me."

"Go ahead. And Meg, don't talk about this until we get a complete picture to present to Dwyer's office."

"I won't. Our assistant state attorney and his people don't trust me anyhow. I'll talk to you."

KYLE CAME IN SMILING BROADLY.

Meghan bent down to kiss him.

"Never do that in front of my friends," he warned.

"Why not?"

"Jimmy's mother waits at the road and kisses him when he gets off the bus. Isn't that disgusting?"

"Why did you let me kiss you?"

"It's okay in private. Nobody saw us. You were kissing Dad last night."

"He kissed me."

"Did you like it?"

Meg considered. "Let's just say that it wasn't disgusting. Want some cookies and milk?"

"Yes, please. I brought the tape for you to watch. Why do you want to see it again?"

"I'm not sure."

"Okay. Dad said he'll be about an hour. He had to pick up some stuff at the store."

Meghan brought the plate of cookies and the glasses of milk into the den. Kyle sat on the floor at her feet; using the remote control, he once again started the tape of the Franklin Center interview. Meg's heart started to pound. She asked herself, What is it I saw in this tape?

In the last scene in Dr. Williams' office, when the camera panned over the pictures of the children born through in vitro fertilization, she found what she was looking for. She grabbed the remote from Kyle and snapped the Pause button.

"Meg, it's almost over," Kyle protested.

Meg stared at the picture of the little boy and girl with identical sweaters. She had seen the same picture on the wall of Helene Petrovic's sitting room in Lawrenceville. "It *is* over, Kyle. I know the reason."

The phone rang. "I'll be right back," she told him.

"I'll rewind. I know how."

It was Phillip Carter. "Meg, are you alone?" he asked quickly.

"Phillip! I just found confirmation that Helene Petrovic knew Dr. Williams. I think I know what she was doing at the Manning Clinic."

It was as though he hadn't heard her. "Are you alone?" he repeated.

"Kyle is in the den."

"Can you drop him off at his house?" His voice was low, agitated.

"Mac's out. I can leave him at the inn. Mother's there. Phillip, what is it?"

Now Carter sounded unbelieving, near hysteria. "I just heard from Edwin! He wants to see both of us. He's trying to decide if he should turn himself in. Meg, he's desperate. Don't let anyone know about this until we have a chance to see him."

"Dad? Phoned you?" Meg gasped. Stunned, she grasped the corner of the desk for support. In a voice so shocked it was barely a whisper, she demanded, "Where is he? I've got to go to him."

56

*W*hen Bernie's mother regained consciousness, she tried to shout for help, but she knew none of the neighbors could hear her. She'd never make it up the stairs. She'd have to drag herself into Bernard's TV area where there was a phone. It was all his fault for not keeping the place clean. Her ankle hurt so much. The pains were shooting up her leg. She opened her mouth and took big gulps of air. It was agony to drag herself along the dirty, rough concrete floor.

Finally she made her way into the alcove her son had fashioned for himself. Even with all the pain she was in, Mama's eyes widened in amazed fury. That big television! Those radios! Those machines! What was Bernard doing, throwing away money on all these things?

The phone was on the old kitchen table that he'd carried in when one of their neighbors put it at the curb. She couldn't reach it, so she pulled it down by the cord. It clattered on the floor.

Hoping she hadn't broken it, Bernie's mother dialed 911. At the welcome sound of a dispatcher's voice, she said, "Send an ambulance."

She was able to give her name and address and tell what had happened before she fainted again.

"KYLE," MEG SAID HURRIEDLY, "I'M GOING TO HAVE TO leave you at the inn. I'll put a note on the door for your dad. Just tell my mother that something came up, that I had to leave right away. You stay with her. No going outside, okay?"

"Why are you so worried, Meg?"

"I'm not. It's a big story. I have to cover it."

"Oh, that's great."

At the inn, Meg watched until Kyle had reached the front door. He waved and she waved back, forcing a smile. Then she put her foot on the accelerator.

She was meeting Phillip at a crossroads in West Redding, about twenty miles from Newtown. "You can follow me from there," he had hurriedly told her. "It's not far after that, but it would be impossible for you to find it alone."

Meg did not know what to think. Her mind was a jumble of confused thoughts and confused emotions. Her mouth was so dry. Her throat simply would not swallow. *Dad was alive and he was desperate!* Why? Surely not because he was Helene Petrovic's murderer. Please, dear God, anything but that.

When Meg found the intersection of the narrow country roads, Phillip's black Cadillac was waiting. It was easy to spot him. There was no other car in sight.

He did not take the time to speak to her but held up his hand and motioned for her to follow him. Half a mile later he turned sharply onto a narrow hard-packed dirt road. Fifty yards after that the road twisted through a wooded area and Meghan's car vanished from the view of anyone driving past.

. . .

VICTOR ORSINI HAD NOT BEEN SURPRISED BY THE SHOW-
down with Phillip Carter Friday afternoon. It had never been
a question of *if* it would happen. The question for months
had been *when.*

At least he had found what he needed before he lost access
to the office. When he left Carter, he had driven directly to
his house at Candlewood Lake, fixed himself a martini and
sat where he could look over the water and consider what he
ought to do.

The evidence he had was not enough alone and without
corroboration, would not stand up in court. And in addition,
how much could he tell them and still not reveal things that
could hurt him?

He'd been with Collins and Carter nearly seven years, yet
suddenly all that mattered was that first month. It was the
linchpin connecting everything that had happened recently.

Victor had spent Friday evening weighing the pros and
cons of going to the assistant state attorney and laying out
what he thought had happened.

The next morning he jogged along the lake for an hour, a
long healthy run that cleared his head and strengthened his
resolve.

Finally, at two-thirty Saturday afternoon, he dialed the
number Special Investigator Marron had given him. He half-
expected that Marron might not be in his office on Saturday,
but he answered on the first ring.

Victor identified himself. In the calm, reasoned voice that
inspired confidence in clients and job candidates, he asked,
"Would it be convenient if I stopped by in half an hour? I
think I know who murdered Helene Petrovic . . ."

FROM THE FRONT DOOR OF THE DRUMDOE INN, KYLE
looked back and watched Meghan drive away. She was on a
story. Cool. He wished he was going with her. He used to

think he'd be a doctor like Dad when he grew up but had decided being a reporter was more fun.

A moment later a car zoomed out of the parking lot, a green Chevy. That's the guy who didn't run over Jake, Kyle thought. He was sorry he didn't get a chance to talk to him and thank him. He watched as the Chevy turned down the road in the direction Meg had gone.

Kyle went into the lobby and spotted Meg's mother and Mrs. Murphy at the desk. They both looked serious. He went over to them. "Hi."

"Kyle, what are you doing here?" That's a heck of a way to greet a kid, Catherine thought. She ruffled his hair. "I mean, did you and Meg come over for some ice cream or something?"

"Meg dropped me off. She said to stay with you. She's working on a story."

"Oh, did she get a call from her boss?"

"Somebody called her and she said she had to leave right away."

"Wouldn't that be great if she's being reinstated?" Catherine said to Virginia. "It would be such a morale booster for her."

"It sure would," Murphy agreed. "Now what do you think we should do about that guy in 3A? Frankly, Catherine, I think there's something a little wrong with him."

"Just what we need."

"How many people would stay in a room for nearly three days and then go charging out so fast he almost knocked people down? You just missed him, but I can tell you there appeared to be nothing sick about Mr. Heffernan. He tore down the stairs and ran through the lobby, carrying a video camera."

"Let's take a look at the room," Catherine said. "Come with us, Kyle."

The air in 3A was stale. "Has this room been cleaned since he checked in?" Catherine asked.

"No," Murphy said. "Betty said he would let her in just to

change the towels, that he just about threw her out when she tried to clean up."

"He must have been out of bed sometime. Look at the way that chair is pulled up to the window," Catherine commented. "Wait a minute!" She crossed the room, sat in the chair and looked out. "Dear God," she breathed.

"What is it?" Virginia asked.

"From here you can look directly into Meg's bedroom windows." Catherine rushed to the phone, glanced at the emergency numbers listed on the receiver and dialed.

"State police. Officer Thorne speaking."

"This is Catherine Collins at the Drumdoe Inn in Newtown," she snapped. "I think a man staying at the inn has been spying on our house. He's been locked in his room for days, and just now he drove away in a mad hurry." Her hand flew to her mouth. "Kyle, when Meg dropped you off did you see if a car followed her?"

Kyle sensed that something was very wrong, but surely it couldn't be because of the nice guy who was such a good driver. "Don't worry. The guy in the green Chevy is okay. He saved Jake's life when he drove past our house last week."

In near despair, Catherine cried, "Officer, he's following my daughter now. She's driving a white Mustang. He's in a green Chevy. *Find her! You've got to find her!*"

57

The squad car pulled into the driveway of the shabby one-story frame house in Jackson Heights, and two policemen jumped out. The shrill ee-aww of an approaching EMS

ambulance sounded over the screech of a braking elevated
train at the station less than a block away.

The cops ran around the house to the back door, forced it
open and pounded down the stairs to the basement. A loose
step gave way under the weight of the rookie, but he grabbed
the railing and managed to keep from falling. The sergeant
stumbled over the mop at the foot of the stairs.

"No wonder she got hurt," he muttered. "This place is
booby-trapped."

Low moans from a crudely enclosed area drew them to
Bernie's alcove. The police officers found the elderly woman
sprawled on the floor, the telephone beside her. She was lying
near an unsteady table with an enameled-steel top heaped
with phone books. A worn Naugahyde recliner was directly
in front of a forty-inch television set. A shortwave radio,
police scanner, typewriter and fax machine crowded the top
of an old dresser.

The younger cop dropped down on one knee beside the
injured woman. "Police Officer David Guzman, Mrs. Heffernan," he said soothingly. "They're bringing a stretcher to
take you to the hospital."

Bernie's mother tried to speak. "My son doesn't mean any
harm." She could barely get the words out. She closed her
eyes, unable to continue.

"Dave, look at this!"

Guzman jumped up. "What is it, Sarge?"

The Queens telephone directory was spread open. On
those pages nine or ten names were circled. The sergeant
pointed to them. "They look familiar? In the last few weeks
all of these people reported threatening phone calls."

They could hear the EMS team. Guzman ran to the foot of
the stairs. "Watch out or you'll break your necks coming
down here," he warned.

In less than five minutes, Bernie's semiconscious mother
had been secured to a stretcher and carried to the ambulance.

The police officers did not leave. "We've got enough prob-
able cause to take a look around," the sergeant commented.

He picked up papers next to the fax machine and began to thumb through them.

Officer Guzman pulled open the knobless drawer of the table and spotted a handsome wallet. "Looks as though Bernie might do a little mugging on the side," he commented.

As Guzman stared at Annie Collins' picture on her driver's license, the sergeant found the original of the fax message. He read it aloud. " 'Mistake. Annie was a mistake.' "

Guzman grabbed the phone from the floor. "Sarge," he said, "you'd better let the chief know we found ourselves a murderer."

EVEN FOR BERNIE IT WAS HARD TO KEEP FAR ENOUGH BEHIND Meghan's car to avoid being seen. From the distance he watched her begin to follow the dark sedan. He almost lost both cars after the intersection, when they suddenly seemed to vanish. He knew they must have turned off somewhere, so he backed up. The dirt road through the woods was the only place they could have gone. He turned onto it cautiously.

Now he was coming to a clearing. Meghan's white car and the dark sedan were shaking up and down as they covered the uneven, rutted ground. Bernie waited until they were past the clearing and into another wooded area, then drove the Chevy through the clearing.

The second clump of woods wasn't nearly as deep as the first. Bernie had to jam on his brakes to avoid being seen when the narrow track abruptly turned into open fields again. Now the road led directly to a distant house and barn. The cars were heading there.

Bernie grabbed his camera. With his zoom lens it was possible to track them, until they drove behind the barn.

He sat quietly, considering what he should do. There was a cluster of evergreens near the house. Maybe he could hide the Chevy there. He had to try.

.   .   .

IT WAS PAST FOUR, AND THE FADING SUNLIGHT WAS OB-
scured by thickening clouds. Meg drove behind Phillip along
the winding, bumpy road. They came out of the wooded
area, crossed a field, went through another stretch of woods.
The road straightened out. In the distance she saw buildings,
a farmhouse and barn.

Is Dad here in this godforsaken place? Meg wondered. She
prayed that when she came face to face with him, she would
find the right words to say.

I love you, Daddy, the child in her wanted to cry.

Dad, what happened to you? Dad, why? the hurt adult
wanted to scream.

Dad, I've missed you. How can I help you? Was that the
best way to start?

She followed Phillip's car around the dilapidated buildings.
He parked, got out of his sedan, walked over and opened the
door of Meg's car.

Meg looked up at him. "Where's Dad?" she asked. She
moistened lips that now felt cracked and dry.

"He's nearby." Phillip's eyes locked with hers.

It was the abrupt way he answered that caught her attention. He's as nervous about this as I am, she thought as she
got out of the car.

58

*O*ictor Orsini had agreed to be at John Dwyer's office
in the Danbury courthouse at three o'clock. Special investigators Weiss and Marron were there when he arrived. An hour

later, from their impassive faces, he still did not know if they were putting any stock in what he was telling them.

"Let's go through this again," Dwyer said.

"I've gone through it a dozen times," Victor snapped.

"I want to hear it again," Dwyer said.

"All right, all right. Edwin Collins called me on his car phone the night of January 28th. We spoke for about eight minutes until he disconnected because he was on the ramp of the Tappan Zee Bridge and the driving was very slippery."

"When do you tell us everything you talked about?" Weiss demanded. "What took eight minutes to say?"

This part of the story was what Victor had hoped to gloss over, but he knew unless he told the complete truth he would not be believed. Reluctantly, he admitted, "Ed had learned a day or two before that I'd been tipping off one of our competitors to positions our major clients would be looking to fill. He was outraged and ordered me to be in his office the next morning."

"And that was your last contact with him?"

"On January 29th I was waiting in his office at eight o'clock. I knew Ed was going to fire me, but I didn't want him to think I'd cheated the firm out of money. He'd told me that if he found proof that I'd been pocketing commissions, he'd prosecute. At the time I thought he meant kickbacks. Now I think he was referring to Helene Petrovic. I don't think he knew anything about her, then must have found out and thought I was trying to pull a fast one."

"We know the commission for placing her at the Manning Clinic went into the office account," Marron said.

"He wouldn't have known that. I've checked and found that it was deliberately buried in the fee received for placing Dr. Williams there. Obviously Edwin was never supposed to find out anything about Petrovic."

"Then who recommended Petrovic to Manning?" Dwyer asked.

"Phillip Carter. It had to be. When the letter endorsing her credentials was sent to Manning on March 21st almost seven years ago, I'd only been at Collins and Carter a short time. I'd never even heard that woman's name until she was murdered less than two weeks ago. And I'd bet my life Ed didn't either. He was away from the office the end of March that year, including March 21st."

He paused. "As I've told you, when I saw the newspaper with the reprint of the letter supposedly signed by him, I knew it was a phony."

Orsini pointed to the sheet of paper he had given to Dwyer. "With his old secretary, who was a gem, Ed had gotten in the habit of leaving a stack of signed letterheads she could use if he wanted to dictate over the phone. He trusted her completely. Then she'd retired, and Ed wasn't that impressed with her replacement, Jackie. I can remember him ripping up those signed letterheads and telling me that from then on he wanted to see everything that went out over his signature. On the blank letterheads he always signed in the same place, where his longtime secretary had left a light pencil mark: thirty-five lines down and beginning on the fiftieth character. You've got one in your hands now.

"I've been going through Ed's files, hoping that there might be other signed letterheads that he'd missed. I found the one you're holding in Phillip Carter's desk. A locksmith made a key for me. I imagine Carter was saving this in case he needed to produce something else signed by Edwin Collins.

"You can believe me or not," Orsini continued, "but thinking back to that morning of January 29th, when I waited in Ed's office, I had the distinct feeling he'd been there recently. The *H* through *O* drawer in the filing cabinet was open. I'd swear he had been looking at the Manning file for any record of Helene Petrovic.

"While I was waiting for him, Catherine Collins phoned, worried that Ed wasn't home. She'd been at a reunion in Hartford the night before and found the house empty when she returned. She tried the office, to see if we'd heard from him. I told her about speaking to him the night before when he was on the ramp of the Tappan Zee Bridge. At that time I didn't know anything about the accident. She was the one who suggested that Ed might have been one of the victims.

"I realized it was possible, of course," Victor said. "Ed's last words to me were about how slippery the ramp was, and we know the accident took place less than a minute later. After talking to Catherine, I tried to call Phillip. His phone was busy, and since he lives only ten minutes from the office, I drove to his house. I had some idea we might want to drive down to the bridge and see if they were pulling victims out of the water.

"When I arrived, Phillip was in the garage, just getting in his car. His jeep was there as well. I remember he made a point of telling me he'd brought it down from the country to have it serviced. I knew he had a jeep that he used to get around his farm property. He'd drive the sedan up and then switch.

"At the time I thought nothing of it. But in this last week I reasoned that if Ed wasn't involved in that accident, went to the office and found something that sent him to Carter's home, whatever happened to him took place there. Carter could have driven Ed away in his own car and hidden it somewhere. Ed always said Phillip had a lot of rural property."

Orsini looked at the inscrutable faces of his interrogators. I've done what I had to do, he thought. If they don't believe me, at least I tried.

Dwyer said in a noncommittal tone, "This may be helpful. Thank you, Mr. Orsini. You'll hear from us."

When Orsini left, the assistant state attorney said to Weiss and Marron, "It fits. And it explains the findings of the forensic lab." They had just received word that analysis of Edwin Collins' car revealed traces of blood in the trunk.

59

$\mathcal{I}$t was nearly four o'clock when Mac completed his last errand and started home. The butcher, the baker, the candlestick maker, he thought. He'd gone to the barber, picked up the dry cleaning and stopped at the supermarket. Mrs. Dileo might not be back from taking care of her father to do the usual shopping on Monday.

Mac felt good. Kyle had been thrilled to be visiting with Meg. There'd certainly be no problem for Kyle if Mac succeeded in rekindling the feelings Meg had once had for him. Meggie, you don't have a chance, Mac vowed. You're not getting away from me again.

It was a cold, overcast day, but Mac had no thought of weather as he turned onto Bayberry Road. He thought of the hope in Meg's face when they'd talked about Petrovic's connection to Dr. Williams and the possibility that Victor Orsini had forged Edwin's name to Petrovic's letter of recommendation. She'd realized then that her father might be proven innocent of any connection to the Petrovic case and the Manning Clinic scandal.

Nothing can change the fact that Ed had a double life all those years, Mac thought. But if his name is cleared of murder and fraud, it will be a hell of a lot easier for Meg and Catherine.

The first warning that something was wrong came as Mac neared the inn. There were police cars in the driveway, and the parking lot was blocked. A police helicopter was landing. He could see another one with the logo of a New Haven television station already on the ground.

He pulled his car onto the lawn and ran toward the inn.

The door of the inn was flung open, and Kyle rushed out. "Dad, Meg's boss didn't call her to cover a story," he sobbed. "The man who didn't run over Jake is the guy who's been watching Meg. He's following her in his car."

Meg! For a split second Mac's vision blurred. He was in the morgue looking down at the dead face of Annie Collins, Meg's half sister.

Kyle grabbed his father's arm. "The cops are here. They're sending helicopters to look for Meg's car and the guy's green car. Mrs. Collins is crying." Kyle's voice broke. "Dad, don't let anything happen to Meg."

TAILING MEGHAN AS SHE FOLLOWED THE CADILLAC DEEPER into the countryside, Bernie felt slow, burning anger. He'd wanted to be alone with her with no one else around. Then she'd met up with that other car. Suppose the guy Meg was with tried to give him trouble? Bernie patted his pocket. It was there. He never could remember if he had it with him. He wasn't supposed to carry it, and he'd even tried to leave it in the basement. But when he met somebody he liked and started to think about her all the time, he got nervous and a lot of things started to be different.

Bernie left the car behind the clump of evergreens, took his camera and carefully approached the cluster of ramshackle buildings. Now that he was up close he could see that the farmhouse was smaller than it seemed from a distance. What he'd thought was an enclosed porch was actually a storage shed. Next to that was the barn. There was just enough space for him to slide in sideways between the house and the storage shed.

The passageway was dark and musty, but he knew it was a good hiding place. From behind the buildings he could hear their voices clearly. He knew that, like the window in the inn, this was a good place for him to watch and not be seen.

Reaching the end of the passageway, he peeked out just enough to see what was going on.

Meghan was with a man Bernie had never seen before, and they were standing near what appeared to be an old well, about twenty feet away. They were facing each other, talking. The sedan was parked between them and where Bernie was hiding, so he crouched down and crept forward, hidden from sight by the car. Then he stopped, lifted his camera and began to videotape them.

60

"*P*hillip, before Dad gets here, I think I know the reason for Helene Petrovic being at Manning."

"What is it, Meg?"

She ignored the oddly detached tone in Phillip's voice. "When I was in Helene Petrovic's house yesterday, I saw pictures of young children in her study. Some of them are the same pictures I'd seen on the walls of Dr. Williams' office at the Franklin Center in Philadelphia.

"Phillip, those kids weren't born through the Manning Clinic, and I'm sure I understand Helene's connection to them. She wasn't losing embryos at Manning through carelessness. I believe she was stealing those embryos and giving them to Dr. Williams for use in his donor program at Franklin."

Why was Phillip looking at her like that? she wondered suddenly. Didn't he believe her? "Think about it, Phillip," she urged. "Helene worked under Dr. Williams for six months at Manning. For three years before that, when she was a secretary at Dowling, she used to haunt the laboratory. Now we can connect her to Williams at that time as well."

Now Phillip seemed at ease. "Meg, it fits. And you think that Victor, not your father, sent the letter recommending Petrovic to Manning?"

"Absolutely. Dad was in Scottsdale. Annie had been in an accident and was close to death. We can prove Dad wasn't in the office when that letter was sent."

"I'm sure you can."

THE CALL FROM PHILLIP CARTER TO DR. HENRY WILLIAMS had come in at 3:15 Saturday afternoon. Carter had demanded that Williams be summoned from examining a client. The conversation had been brief but chilling.

"Meghan Collins has tied you to Petrovic," Carter told him, "although she thinks Orsini sent the letter of recommendation. And I know that Orsini's been up to something, and may even suspect what happened. We could still be all right, but no matter what, keep your mouth shut. Refuse to answer questions."

Somehow Henry Williams managed to get through the rest of his appointments. The last one was completed at four-thirty. That was when the Franklin Assisted Reproduction Center closed on Saturdays.

His secretary looked in on him. "Dr. Williams, is there anything else I can do for you?"

Nobody can do anything for me, he thought. He managed a smile. "No, nothing, thank you, Eva."

"Doctor, are you all right? You don't look well."

"I'm fine. Just a bit weary."

By 4:45 everyone on the staff had left and he was alone. Williams reached for the picture of his deceased wife, leaned back in his chair and studied it. "Marie," he said softly, "I didn't know what I was getting into. I honestly thought that I was accomplishing some good. Helene believed that too."

He replaced the picture, folded his hands under his chin and stared ahead. He did not notice that the shadows outside were deepening.

Carter had gone mad. He had to be stopped.

Williams thought of his son and daughter. Henry Jr. was an obstetrician in Seattle. Barbara was an endocrinologist in San Francisco. What would this scandal do to them, especially if there was a long trial?

The truth was going to come out. It was inevitable. He knew that now.

He thought of Meghan Collins, the questions she had asked him. Had she suspected that he was lying to her?

And her father. Appalling enough to know without having to ask that Carter had murdered Helene to silence her. Had he anything to do with Edwin Collins' disappearance as well? And should Edwin Collins be blamed for what others had done?

Should Helene be blamed for mistakes she hadn't made?

Dr. Henry Williams took a pad from his desk and began to write. He had to explain, to make it very clear, to try to undo the harm he had done.

When he was finished, he put the pages he had written in an envelope. Meghan Collins was the one who deserved to present this to the authorities. He had done her and her family a grave disservice.

Meghan had left her card. Williams found it, addressed the envelope to her at Channel 3 and carefully stamped it.

He stopped for a long minute to study the pictures of the children who had been born because their mothers had come to his clinic. For an instant the bleakness in his heart was relieved at the sight of their young faces.

Dr. Henry Williams turned out the light as he left his office for the last time.

He carried the envelope to his car, stopped at a nearby mailbox and dropped it in. Meghan Collins would receive it by Tuesday.

By then it wouldn't matter to him anymore.

. . .

THE SUN WAS GETTING LOWER. A WIND WAS FLATTENING THE short blades of yellowed grass. Meghan shivered. She'd grabbed her Burberry when she'd rushed out of the house, forgetting she'd removed the lining for her trip to Scottsdale.

Phillip Carter was wearing jeans and a boxy winter jacket. His hands were in its roomy pockets. He was leaning against the open fieldstone well.

"Do you think Victor killed Helene Petrovic because she decided to quit?" he asked.

"Victor or Dr. Williams. Williams might have panicked. Petrovic knew so much. She could have sent both of them to prison for years if she ever talked. Her parish priest told me he felt she had something on her mind that troubled her terribly."

Meg began to tremble. Was it just nerves and the cold? "I'm going to sit in the car till Dad gets here, Phillip. How far does he have to come?"

"Not far, Meg. In fact he's amazingly nearby." Phillip took his hands out of his pockets. The right hand held a gun. He gestured toward the well. "Your psychic was right, Meg. Your dad's under water. And he's been dead a long time."

DON'T LET ANYTHING HAPPEN TO MEG! IT WAS THE PRAYERful plea Mac whispered as he and Kyle entered the inn. Inside, the reception area was teeming with police and media. Employees and guests watched from doorways. In the adjacent sitting room, Catherine was perched at the edge of the small sofa, Virginia Murphy beside her. Catherine's face was ashen.

When Mac approached her, she reached up and clasped his hands. "Mac, Victor Orsini's talked to the police. Phillip was behind all this. Can you believe it? I trusted him so completely. We think he's the one who called Meg, pretending to be Edwin. And there's a man who's following her, a dangerous man with a history of obsessive attachments to unsuspecting women. He's probably the one who scared Kyle on Halloween. The New York police phoned John Dwyer about him. And now Meghan is gone, and we don't know why she left or where she is. I'm so afraid I don't know what to do. I can't lose her, Mac. I couldn't stand that."

Arlene Weiss rushed into the sitting room. Mac recognized her. "Mrs. Collins, a traffic helicopter crew thinks they spotted the green car on an old farm near West Redding. We told them to stay out of the area. We'll be there in less than ten minutes."

Mac gave Catherine what he hoped was a reassuring embrace. "I'll find Meg," he promised. "She'll be all right."

Then he ran outside. The reporter and cameraman from New Haven were rushing toward their helicopter. Mac followed them, scrambling behind them into the chopper. "Hey, you can't get on here," the burly reporter shouted over the roar of the engine revving up for takeoff.

"Yes, I can," Mac said. "I'm a doctor. I may be needed."

"Shut the door," the reporter yelled to the pilot. "Get this thing in the air."

MEGHAN STARED IN CONFUSION. "PHILLIP, I . . . I DON'T UN-derstand," she stammered. "My father's body is in that well?" Meg stepped forward, placing her hands on the rough, rounded surface. Her fingertips curled over the edge, feeling the clammy dampness of the stone. She was no longer aware of Phillip or the gun he was pointing at her or the barren fields behind him or the cold, biting wind.

She stared down into the yawning hole with numbing horror, imagining her father's body lying at the bottom.

"You won't be able to see him, Meg. There isn't much water down there, hasn't been for years, but enough to cover him. He was dead when I pushed him in, if that's any consolation. I shot him the night of the bridge accident."

Meg whirled on him. "How could you have done that to

him? He was your friend, your partner. How could you have done that to Helene and Annie?"

"You give me too much credit. I had nothing to do with Annie's death."

"You meant to kill me. You sent me the fax saying Annie's death was a mistake." Meg's eyes darted around. Was there any way she could get to her car? No, he'd shoot her before she'd taken a step.

"Meghan, *you* told me about the fax. It was like a gift. I needed people to believe that Ed was still alive, and you delivered the way I could do it."

"What did you do to my father?"

"Ed called me from the office the night of the accident. He was in shock. Talked about how close he'd come to being caught in the bridge explosion. Told me he knew Orsini was cheating on us. Told me that Manning had talked about us placing an embryologist named Petrovic Ed had never heard of. He'd gone directly to the office and had been through the Manning file and couldn't find any reference to her. Blamed it on Orsini.

"Meghan, try to understand. It would have been all over. I told him to come to my house, that we'd figure it out, confront Orsini together in the morning. By the time he walked in my door he was ready to accuse me. He'd pieced it all together. Your father was very smart. He left me no choice. I knew what I had to do."

I'm so cold, Meghan thought, so cold.

"Everything was fine for a while," Phillip continued. "Then Petrovic quit, telling Manning she'd made a mistake that was going to cause a lot of trouble. I couldn't take a chance that she'd give everything away, could I? The day you came to the office and talked about the girl who'd been stabbed, how much she looked like you, that was when you told me about the fax. I knew your father had something going out West somewhere. It wasn't hard to figure he might have had a daughter there. This seemed the perfect time to bring him back to life."

"You may not have sent the fax, but you made the phone call that sent Mother to the hospital. You ordered those roses and sat next to her when they were delivered. How could you have done that to her?"

Only yesterday, Meghan thought, Fr. Radzin told me to look for the reason.

"Meghan, I lost a lot of money in my divorce. I spent top dollar for property I'm trying to hold on to. I had a miserable childhood. I was one of ten kids living in a three-bedroom house. I'm not going back to being poor again. Williams and I found a way to make money with nobody hurt. And Petrovic cashed in, too."

"Stealing embryos for the Franklin Center donor program?"

"You're not as smart as I thought, Meghan. There's so much more to it than that. Donor embryos are small time."

He raised the pistol. She could see the muzzle aimed at her heart. She watched his finger tighten on the trigger, heard him say, "I kept Edwin's car in the barn till last week. I'll keep yours in its place. And you can join him."

In a reflex action, Meghan threw herself to the side.

His first bullet went over her head. His second hit her shoulder.

Before he could fire again, a figure came hurtling from nowhere. A heavy figure with a rigid outstretched arm. The fingers that grasped the knife and the shimmering blade itself were one, an avenging sword that sought out Phillip and found his throat.

Meghan felt blinding pain in her left shoulder. Blackness enveloped her.

61

*W*hen Meghan regained consciousness she was lying on the ground, her head in someone's lap. She forced her eyes open, looked up and saw Bernie Heffernan's cherubic smile, then felt his moist kisses on her face and lips and neck.

From somewhere in the distance she heard a whirring sound. A plane? A helicopter. Then it faded and was gone.

"I'm glad I saved you, Meghan. It's all right to use a knife to save someone, isn't it?" Bernie asked. "I never want to hurt anybody. I didn't want to hurt Annie that night. It was a mistake." He repeated it softly, like a child. "Annie was a mistake."

MAC LISTENED TO THE RADIO EXCHANGE BETWEEN THE PO-lice helicopter and the squad cars that were rushing to the area. They were coordinating strategy.

Meg is with two killers, he realized suddenly—that nut who was in the woods Sunday night and Phillip Carter.

Phillip Carter, who betrayed and murdered his partner, then posed as protector to Catherine and Meghan, privy to every step of Meg's search for truth.

Meghan. Meghan.

They were in a rural area. The helicopters were beginning to descend. Vainly Mac searched the ground below. It was going to be dark in fifteen minutes. How could they pick out a car when it was dark?

"We're at the outskirts of West Redding," the pilot said, pointing ahead. "We're a couple of minutes from where they spotted the green Chevy."

. . .

HE'S CRAZY, MEG THOUGHT. THIS WAS BERNIE, THE CHEER-ful parking attendant who often told her about his mother. How did he get here? Why was he following her? And he said he had killed Annie. Dear God, he killed Annie!

She tried to sit up.

"Don't you want me to hold you, Meg? I'd never hurt you."

"Of course you wouldn't." She knew she had to soothe him, keep him calm. "It's just that the ground is so cold."

"I'm sorry. I should have known that. I'll help you." He kept his arm around her, hugging her as they awkwardly struggled together to their feet.

The pressure of his arm around her shoulder intensified the pain from the bullet wound. She mustn't antagonize him. "Bernie, would you try not to . . ." She was going to pass out again. "Bernie," she pleaded, "my shoulder hurts so much."

She could see the knife he had used to kill Phillip lying on the ground. Was this the knife that had taken Annie's life?

Phillip's gun was still clutched in his hand.

"Oh, I'm sorry. If you want I'll carry you." His lips were on her hair. "But, stand here for just a minute. I want to take your picture. See my camera?"

His camera. Of course. He must have been the cameraman in the woods who had almost strangled Kyle. She leaned against the well as he videotaped her and watched as he walked around Phillip's body, taping him.

Then Bernie laid the camera down and came over to her. "Meghan, I'm a hero," he bragged. His eyes were like shiny blue buttons.

"Yes, you are."

"I saved your life."

"Yes you did."

"But I'm not allowed to carry a weapon. A knife is a weapon. They'll put me away again, in the prison hospital. I hate it there."

"I'll talk to them."

"No, Meghan. That's why I had to kill Annie. She started to scream. All I did when I saw her that night was to walk up behind her and say, 'This is a dangerous block. I'll take care of you.' "

"You said that?"

"I thought it was you, Meghan. You'd have been glad to have me take care of you, wouldn't you?"

"Yes, of course I would."

"I didn't have time to explain. There was a police car coming. I didn't mean to hurt her. I didn't even know I was carrying the knife that night. Sometimes I don't remember I have it."

"I'm glad you were carrying it now." The car, Meg thought. My keys are in it. It's my only chance. "But Bernie, I don't think you should leave your knife here for the police to find." She pointed to it.

He looked back over his shoulder. "Oh, thank you, Meghan."

"And don't forget your camera."

If she wasn't fast enough, he'd know that she was trying to get away. And he'd have the knife in his hand. But when he turned and started to walk the half-dozen steps to Phillip's body, Meghan whirled, stumbling in her weakness and haste, yanked open her car door and slid behind the wheel.

"Meghan, what are you doing?" Bernie shrieked.

His hands grabbed the handle of the car door as she clicked the lock. He hung onto the handle as she threw the car into gear and plunged her foot down on the gas pedal.

The car leaped forward. Bernie kept his grip on the handle for ten feet, shouting at her, then let go and fell. She careened around the buildings. He was emerging from the passageway between the house and shed when she headed down the dirt road through the open fields.

She had not reached the wooded area when in the rearview mirror she saw his car lurch forward in pursuit.

. . .

THEY WERE PASSING OVER A WOODED AREA. THE POLICE helicopter was in front of them. The photographer and cameraman were straining their eyes.

"Look!" the pilot shouted. "There's the farmhouse."

Mac never knew what made him look back. "Turn around," he shouted. "Turn around."

Meg's white Mustang shot out of the woods, a green car inches behind it, repeatedly smashing into it. As Mac watched, the Chevy pulled alongside the Mustang and began sideswiping it, trying to run it off the road.

"Go down," Mac shouted to the pilot. "That's Meghan in the white car. Can't you see he's trying to kill her."

MEGHAN'S CAR WAS FASTER, BUT BERNIE WAS A BETTER driver. She had managed to stay ahead of him for a short time, but now could not escape him. He was slamming into the driver's side door. Meghan's body whipped back and forth as the air bag ballooned from the center of the wheel. For an instant she could not see, but she kept her foot on the accelerator, and the car zigzagged wildly through the field as Bernie kept attacking it.

The driver's side door smashed into her shoulder as the Mustang teetered and flipped over on its side. An instant later flames burst through the hood of the engine.

BERNIE WANTED TO WATCH MEGHAN'S CAR BURN, BUT THE police were coming. He could hear the scream of approaching sirens. Overhead he heard the din of a helicopter coming closer. He had to get away.

Someday you'll hurt someone, Bernie. That's what worries us. That's what the psychiatrist had told him. But if he got home to Mama, she'd take care of him. He'd get another job parking cars where he could be home every night with her. From now on he'd only make phone calls to women. Nobody would find out about that.

Meghan's face was fading from his mind. He'd forget her the way he forgot all the others he had liked. I never really hurt anyone before and I didn't mean to hurt Annie, he reminded himself as he drove through the hastening darkness. Maybe they'll believe me if they find me.

He drove through the second patch of woods and reached the intersection where they'd turned off onto the dirt road. Headlights snapped on. A loudspeaker said, "Police, Bernie. You know what to do. Get out of the car with your hands in the air."

Bernie began to cry. "Mama, Mama," he sobbed as he opened the door and lifted his arms.

THE CAR WAS ON ITS SIDE. THE DRIVER'S DOOR WAS PRESSING against her. Meghan felt for the button to release the seat belt but could not find it. She was disoriented.

She smelled smoke. It began pouring through the vent. Oh God, Meghan thought. I'm trapped. The car was resting on the passenger door.

Waves of heat began to attack her. Smoke filled her lungs. She tried to scream but no sound came.

MAC LED THE FRANTIC RACE FROM THE HELICOPTER TO Meg's car. Flames from the engine shot up higher just as they reached it. He could see Meg inside, struggling to free herself, her body illuminated by the flames that were spreading across the hood. "We've got to get her out through the passenger door," he shouted.

As one, he, the pilot, the reporter and cameraman put their hands on the superheated roof of the Mustang. As one they pushed, rocked, pushed again.

"Now," Mac shouted. With a groan they threw their weight against the car, held while tortured palms blistered.

And then the car began to move, slowly, resistantly, then finally in rapid surrender it slammed onto its tires, once more upright.

The heat was becoming unbearable. As in a dream, Meghan saw Mac's face and somehow managed to reach over and release the door lock before she passed out.

62

The helicopter landed at the Danbury Medical Center. Dazed and blinded with pain, Meghan was aware of being taken from Mac's arms, lifted onto a stretcher.

Another stretcher. Annie being rushed into Emergency. No, she thought, no. "Mac."

"I'm here, Meggie."

Blinding lights. An operating room. A mask over her face. *The mask being removed from Annie's face in Roosevelt Hospital.* "Mac."

A hand over hers. "I'm here, Meggie."

SHE AWOKE IN THE RECOVERY ROOM, AWARE OF A THICK bandage on her shoulder, a nurse looking down at her. "You're fine."

Later they wheeled her to a room. Her mother. Mac. Kyle. Waiting for her.

Her mother's face, miraculously peaceful when their eyes met. Seeming to read her thoughts. "Meg, they recovered Dad's body."

Mac's arm around her mother. His bandaged hands. Mac, her tower of strength. Mac, her love.

Kyle's tearstained face next to hers. "It's all right if you want to kiss me in front of people, Meg."

. . .

ON SUNDAY NIGHT, THE BODY OF DR. HENRY WILLIAMS WAS
found in his car on the outskirts of Pittsburgh, Pennsylvania,
in the quiet neighborhood where he and his wife had grown
up and met as teenagers. He had taken a lethal dose of sleeping pills. Letters to his son and daughter contained messages
of love and pleas for forgiveness.

MEGHAN WAS ABLE TO LEAVE THE HOSPITAL ON MONDAY
morning. Her arm was in a sling, her shoulder a vague,
constant ache. Otherwise she was recovering rapidly.

When she arrived home, she went upstairs to her room to
change to a comfortable robe. As she started to undress, she
hesitated, then went to the windows and closed the blinds
firmly. I hope I get over doing that, she thought. She knew it
would be a long time before she would be able to banish the
image of Bernie shadowing her.

Catherine was getting off the phone. "I've just cancelled
the sale of the inn," she said. "The death certificate has been
issued, and that means all the joint assets Dad and I held are
unfrozen. The insurance adjustors are processing payment of
all Dad's personal policies as well as the one from the business. It's a lot of money, Meg. Remember, the personal policies have a double indemnity clause."

Meg kissed her mother. "I'm so glad about the inn. You'd
be lost without Drumdoe." Over coffee and juice she scanned
the morning papers. In the hospital, she'd seen the early
morning television news reports about the Williams suicide.
"They're combing the Franklin Center records to try to find
out who received the embryos Petrovic stole from Manning."

"Meg, what a terrible thing it must be for people who had
cryopreserved embryos there to wonder if their biological
child was born to a stranger," Catherine Collins said. "Is
there enough money in the world for anyone to do something
like that?"

"Apparently there is. Phillip Carter told me he needed money. But Mom, when I asked him if that was what Petrovic was doing, stealing embryos for the donor program, he told me I wasn't as smart as he'd thought. There was more to it. I only hope they find out what in the records at the center."

Meghan sipped the coffee. "What could he have meant by that? And what happened to Stephanie Petrovic? Did Phillip kill that poor girl? Mom, her baby was due around this time."

THAT NIGHT WHEN MAC CAME, SHE SAID, "DAD WILL BE BUR-ied day after tomorrow. Frances Grolier should be notified about that and told the circumstances of Dad's death, but I dread calling her."

Mac's arms around her. All the years she'd waited for them.

"Why not let me take care of it, Meggie?" Mac asked.

And then they'd talked. "Mac, we don't know everything yet. Dr. Williams was the last hope for understanding what Phillip meant."

ON TUESDAY MORNING, AT NINE O'CLOCK, TOM WEICKER phoned. This time he did not ask the teasing-but-serious question he'd asked yesterday: "Ready to come back to work, Meg?"

Nor did he ask how she was feeling. Even before he said, "Meg, we've got a breaking story," she sensed the difference in his tone.

"What is it, Tom?"

"There's an envelope marked 'Personal and Confidential' for you from Dr. Williams."

"Dr. Williams! Open it. Read it to me."

"You're sure?"

"Tom, open it."

There was a pause. She visualized him slitting the envelope, pulling out the contents.

"Tom?"

"Meg, this is Williams' confession."

"Read it to me."

"No. You have the fax machine you took home from the office?"

"Yes."

"Give me the number again. I'll fax it to you. We'll read it together."

Meghan gave the number to him and rushed downstairs. She got to the study in time to hear the high-pitched squeal of the fax. The first page of the statement from Dr. Henry Williams slowly began to emerge on the thin, slick paper.

It was five pages long. Meghan read and reread it. Finally the reporter in her began to pick out specific paragraphs and isolated sentences.

The phone rang. She knew it was Tom Weicker. "What do you think, Meghan?"

"It's all there. He needed money because of the bills from his wife's long illness. Petrovic was a naturally gifted person who should have been a doctor. She hated seeing cryopreserved embryos destroyed. She saw them as children who could fill the lives of childless couples. Williams saw them as children people would pay a fortune to adopt. He sounded out Carter, who was more than willing to place Petrovic at Manning, using my father's signature."

"They had everything covered," Weicker said, "a secluded house where they brought illegal aliens willing to be host mothers in exchange for ten thousand dollars and a bogus green card. Not a high price when you think Williams and Carter were selling the babies for a minimum of one hundred thousand dollars each.

"In the past six years," Weicker went on, "they've placed more than two hundred babies and were planning to open other facilities."

"And then Helene quit," Meghan said, "claiming she'd made a mistake that was going to become public.

"The first thing Dr. Manning did after Petrovic quit was to call Dr. Williams and tell him about it. Manning trusted Williams and needed to talk to someone. He was horrified at the prospect of the clinic losing its reputation. He told Williams how upset Petrovic was and that she thought she'd lost the Anderson baby's identical twin when she slipped in the lab.

"Williams called Carter, who immediately panicked. Carter had a key to Helene's apartment in Connecticut. They weren't romantically involved. Sometimes he'd need to transport embryos she'd brought from the clinic immediately after they were fertilized and before they were cryopreserved. He'd rushed them to Pennsylvania to be transferred to a host womb."

"Carter panicked and killed her," Weicker agreed. "Meg, Dr. Williams gave you the address of the place where he and Carter kept those pregnant girls. We're obliged to give that information to the authorities, but we want to be there when they arrive. Are you up to it?"

"You bet I am. Tom, can you send a helicopter for me? Make it one of the big ones. You're missing something important in the Williams statement. He was the person Stephanie Petrovic contacted when she needed help. He was the one who had transferred an embryo into her womb. She's due to give birth now. If there's one redeeming feature about Henry Williams, it's that he didn't tell Phillip Carter that he'd hidden Stephanie Petrovic. If he had, her life wouldn't have been worth a plugged nickel."

TOM PROMISED TO HAVE A HELICOPTER AT THE DRUMDOE Inn within the hour. Meghan made two phone calls. One to Mac. "Can you get away, Mac? I want you with me for this." The second call was to a new mother. "Can you and your husband meet me in an hour?"

. . .

THE RESIDENCE DR. WILLIAMS DESCRIBED IN HIS CONFESSION was forty miles from Philadelphia. Tom Weicker and the crew from Channel 3 were waiting when the helicopter carrying Meghan, Mac and the Andersons touched down in a nearby field.

A half-dozen official cars were parked nearby.

"I struck a deal that we'll go in with the authorities," Tom told them.

"Why are we here, Meghan?" Dina Anderson asked as they got into a waiting Channel 3 car.

"If I was sure, I would tell you," Meghan said. Every instinct told her she was right. In his confession, Williams had written, "I had no idea when Helene brought Stephanie to me and asked me to transfer an embryo into her womb that if a pregnancy resulted, Helene intended to raise the baby as her own."

THE YOUNG WOMEN IN THE OLD HOUSE WERE IN VARIOUS stages of pregnancy. Meghan saw the heartsick fear on their faces when they were confronted by the authorities. "You will not send me home, please?" a teenager begged. "I did just what I promised. When the baby is born, you will pay me, please?"

"Host mothers," Mac whispered to Meghan. "Did Williams indicate if they kept any records of whose babies these girls are carrying?"

"His confession said they're all the babies of women who have embryos cryopreserved at Manning," Meghan said. "Helene Petrovic came here regularly to be sure these girls were well cared for. She wanted all the cryopreserved embryos to have a chance to be born."

Stephanie Petrovic was not there. A weeping practical nurse said, "She's at the local hospital. That's where all our girls give birth. She's in labor."

. . .

"WHY ARE WE HERE?" DINA ANDERSON ASKED AGAIN AN hour later, when Meghan returned to the hospital lobby.

Meghan had been allowed to be with Stephanie in the last moments of her labor.

"We're going to see Stephanie's baby in a few minutes," she said. "She had it for Helene. That was their bargain."

Mac pulled Meghan aside. "Is it what I think?"

She did not answer. Twenty minutes later the obstetrician who had delivered Stephanie's baby stepped off the elevator and beckoned to them. "You can come up now," he said.

Dina Anderson reached for her husband's hand. Too overwhelmed to speak, she wondered, Is it possible?

Tom Weicker and the cameraman accompanied them and began taping as a smiling nurse brought the blanket-wrapped infant to the window of the nursery and held it up.

"It's Ryan!" Dina Anderson shrieked. "It's Ryan!"

THE NEXT DAY, AT A PRIVATE FUNERAL MASS AT ST. PAUL'S, the mortal remains of Edwin Richard Collins were consigned to the earth. Mac was at the grave with Catherine and Meg.

I've shed so many tears for you, Dad, Meg thought. I don't think I have any left in me. And then she whispered so silently that no one could hear, "I love you, Daddy."

Catherine thought of the day when her door bell had rung and there stood Edwin Collins, handsome, with the quick smile she'd so loved, a dozen roses in his hands. *I'm courting you, Catherine.*

After a while I'll remember only the good times, she promised herself.

Hand in hand the three walked to the waiting car.